MAIDEN VOYAGE

"Fee?"

Jayne tried to sound innocent, [but knew exac]tly what MacGregor referred to. [   ] [cap]tain's thick black brow[   ] whatever you charge t[   ] that is where I plan to [   ]

"A barrel, you say." A[sur]vey of her. "You've got more than t[c]ertain, but you haven't the girth. I couldna[   ]half so much."

Jayne narrowed her eyes, not at all complimented. "How honest of you."

"If, I was going to add, it was money to be bartered. You know, lass, something far more valuable is at stake."

He was standing very close now, all dark and rock hard and immovable, and Jayne couldn't draw a breath that wasn't filled with the scent of him. He was teasing her—they both knew it—so why did she let him set her insides to churning?

"We've had this conversation before, Captain MacGregor," she said, her line of sight trained just past his broad left shoulder and the coarse black hair that brushed against his shirt. "Surely you remember my answer."

"You had more options then. 'Tis possible you might have changed your mind."

"You'd take advantage of a woman on a shore far from home?"

His eyes glinted dangerously. "Aye."

"You're a cad, captain."

"And since when is a woman not beguiled by such?"

"When the woman is me."

EVELYN ROGERS

DESERT HEAT

ZEBRA BOOKS
KENSINGTON PUBLISHING CORP.

ZEBRA BOOKS are published by

Kensington Publishing Corp.
475 Park Avenue South
New York, NY 10016

First Printing: July, 1993

Printed in the United States of America

To Mother
With love

Chapter One

Jayne studied the President of the United States and decided she should not have worn the feathered hat.

Unlike the other women in her family, she didn't wear feathers well. How could she hope to get serious consideration from the stern-faced head of state sitting behind his wide mahogany desk when a blue satin bonnet waved like a signal flag every time she moved her head?

Sweat trickled between her breasts, a sure sign of nervousness.

"Mr. President," she began with an unfortunate break in her voice. She cleared her throat, sat on the edge of her chair, and with hands wrapped firmly around the reticule in her lap, began again. "I'm very grateful you consented to see me."

James Madison nodded solemnly, determined to get quickly to the business at hand. He wasn't good at small talk; that was the First Lady's forte. Dolley was the reason he'd agreed to this interview; she'd been most persuasive after coming across the petition. All nonsense as far as he was concerned, over a matter long ago put to rest.

Serious looking young thing, this Miss Jayne Worthington, despite the frivolous bonnet. Intelligent, wide set eyes, black as her hair and lit with the same evangelical spark he'd seen on many a campaign trail. She was tall, too, a damned sight taller than he, but no bigger in girth than the saplings Dolley had ordered for the White House lawn.

"You claim that your brother is alive," he said.

"I *know* he is," said Jayne with a nod, the white feather bobbing. "I ask only that you instruct our consul in Tripoli to approach the bashaw for news of his whereabouts."

"That's all?"

"If you prefer, I could deal with the consul general in Tangier. Whatever you think best."

Stifling a smile, Madison glanced at the petition she'd sent weeks ago. Jayne could do nothing but watch his bald pate as he glanced through the dozen pages outlining her efforts in Josh's behalf. Letters . . . petitions . . . pleas made to the few governmental officials who consented to an interview. And after years of effort, the highest official in the land.

In his high ruffled shirt and black vested suit, the President made a formidable appearance, despite his five-foot-four frame and slight build. And he was smart, too. Even his political enemies said so, including Jayne's hypercritical stepfather, a lawyer in both Washington and New York.

The President ought to see how she'd poured her heart into every word he was reading. Josh had been gone thirteen years now, more than half of her life. For her, his absence and his silence signified not that he had died, but that he was in terrible trouble. Somewhere in a rat-infested Tripolitan prison, or in a remote corner of the Sahara, beneath a relentless sun, he waited for someone to rescue him.

With the whole world accepting his demise, Jayne was the only one left who could be that someone.

At last Madison set aside the parchment pages and met her gaze, his piercing blue eyes seemingly reading her thoughts. So be it. She had nothing to hide. If only her own government and the government of Tripoli could say the same.

The President liked the steadiness of Miss Worthington's returning stare. Too many shifty eyes in Washington. Too many glib tongues whose words rang false in the halls of government, too many oratorical lies that went down like honey and came back like tainted pork.

Have to remember that, he thought. Honey . . . pork. Dolley would get a laugh.

Madison forced his concentration to the unpleasant matter at hand. "You realize, of course, that when your brother's ship—"

"The *Philadelphia*," said Jayne.

"—of course, the *Philadelphia*. When it went down in Tripoli harbor—"

"In 1803, Mr. President. A long time ago."

"I'm aware of the facts, Miss Worthington," the President said in mild rebuke, "since at the time I was Mr. Jefferson's Secretary of State. I also remember that there was no mention of a Joshua Worthington among the crew taken hostage. And none, eighteen months later, when the bashaw released the men."

"Three hundred and one officers and crew," said Jayne, unabashed. "Freed after payment of tribute. There should have been three hundred and two."

"You seem so certain." Madison fingered Jayne's petition. "Yet you have no corroborating testimony that he actually set foot in Tripoli."

"I have his letters that say he was aboard the ship." She snapped open her reticule.

"No need to show them. I trust your word, and besides, you've quoted them liberally in your petition. The problem is the intervening time. After thirteen years you still believe, without any written proof or oral testimony, that he was taken prisoner along with the other brave officers and men. Men, I might add, who have sworn they last saw a young boy thrashing about in the waters of the harbor as the bashaw's guards swept down upon them. They did not report seeing him ashore."

Madison wished he could put a cloak of kindness over what seemed to him a logical conclusion, but he saw no recourse to bluntness. "You must accept the probability, Miss Worthington, that your brother never got out of the water alive."

Jayne held herself still. She'd heard the edict before, and she wasn't about to flinch at the harsh words, even though they came from her President. "My brother is a fine swimmer."

"He could have been injured when the ship went aground and thus rendered unable to save himself."

Jayne's chin tilted upwards. "He wasn't."

Elbows propped on the desk, Madison steepled his fingers and regarded his fervent quest. "Are you possessed of powers that allow you to see into the past?"

"Josh and I were very close, Mr. President. I'd know in my heart if he were dead, but my heart tells me he lives. I have no choice but to listen."

Jayne felt a rush of love for the spindly youth who

remained in her mind fourteen years of age, frightfully clever and, except when Millicent was nearby, always quick to laugh. She could not believe that laughter had been stilled.

"Do you have any siblings, Mr. President?"

"Three brothers and three sisters, and, for good measure, more than a score of nieces and nephews. We share a strong family bond, but I would not begin to lay claim to special knowledge of them other than what they include in our correspondence. It is thus, I believe, with most families."

But not with mine.

Sighing, Jayne kept the words to herself. This was going badly. All the anguish and devotion of her being, when put into words, made her sound at best like a determined know-everything, and at worst, like an addled and somewhat hysterical female.

She caught the President's glance at the mantel clock on a side wall of his study, and a chill settled in her heart. Determined she might be, and addled when it came to her guest, but she was smart enough to see the inevitable.

"Am I to assume, Mr. President, that you will not write the bashaw of Tripoli in my name requesting information about one Joshua Worthington, cabin boy aboard the *Philadelphia?*"

"Yusuf Karamanli is a proud and forceful ruler—"

"A tyrant, you mean."

"Not a term used in diplomatic circles"—Madison's eyes twinkled for a moment—"but not entirely inaccurate."

"He owned the pirate ship that the *Philadelphia* was chasing when it ran aground."

"Not quite true. He protected that ship and

others. While we have no definite proof, it is likely that he profited from their activities along the Barbary Coast. As your petition indicates, you have been in correspondence with him."

"I've written but I've not received a reply."

"His silence is, perhaps, a form of answer." Madison eyed her solemnly, the burden of his office weighing heavily in his heart. "I will pay you the courtesy of a more tangible response, but not, I fear, one you will welcome. The matter of the hostages taken from the United States vessel *Philadelphia* in the year 1803 was settled once and forever in 1805 when all were accounted for, either through release or official notification of death. Six, I believe, did not survive the ordeal, but they have all been identified and their families notified. At no place or time does the name of Joshua Worthington appear, either in the prison records which our own consul has studied, or in audiences with Bashaw Karamanli."

Madison stood. "Therefore you must, for your own peace of mind, accept the truth. Your brother was last seen alive the afternoon of October 31, 1803, splashing through the waters of Tripoli harbor. In this year of our Lord, 1816, you must accept the verities I lay before you. Mourn him and put his spirit to rest, and then, pray God, you can get on with your life."

Jayne soon found herself outside the Pennsylvania Avenue townhouse that was the President's abode during repairs to the White House. Straightening her bonnet for the hundredth time since she'd donned it in early afternoon, she wondered if in insisting upon this meeting she hadn't done more harm than good.

"Shall you be needing a carriage?" asked the doorman.

Jayne nodded absently. A gust of wind whistled down the avenue, and she buttoned her caped pelisse tight at her throat. Washington was cool, even in late spring; the trees lining the sidewalk had scarcely begun to bud, and the low-hanging clouds possessed a leaden color, as though they were burdened with snow.

The doorman signaled a passing carriage. She climbed inside, barely aware of his assistance, gave directions for her stepfather's Washington townhouse, and settled back to stare out the window at the passing scene. She saw few details.

She'd been so sure of her cause for so many years. Her faith had held strong, despite her mother's skepticism, and that of her half sister, and the series of stepfathers who, each in turn, had assured her that Josh lived only in her memory. Randolph Forbes, the latest of Millicent's husbands, was the worst.

"Got what he deserved, running off like that and leaving your poor mother," he'd told her soon after the wedding three years ago.

Poor mother? Millicent Catherine Shannon Taylor Worthington Hogan Kindred Forbes hadn't been poor since her first marriage when she was twenty and, Jayne had figured out from birth and wedding records, already expecting Marybeth. Darling Marybeth, Mama's favorite—only she was never Mama or Mother. Millicent, she was to be called. Jayne—and Josh, too, when he'd been around—had complied.

And, of course, Marybeth. But Marybeth, four years Jayne's senior and two years older than Josh, found compliance easy, since she and Millicent thought so much alike.

"Oh, Josh," Jayne whispered into the close air of the carriage, "should I give up? Are you really gone?"

She waited for an answer but heard only the horse's hooves on the cobblestones, the creak of springs, and the slow, sad beating of her heart.

Tears sprang to her eyes — rare tears — as she remembered Josh from their years on the Worthington Virginia farm. Years spent more with their father than Millicent, who preferred living in town, and then later, after his death, with his aging mother, their beloved Granny Worth.

She'd told the President that she and Josh had been close, but she knew he hadn't understood, not really, just how dependent on each other they had been. For love, for loyalty, for fun. Except when she was riding about what remained of Worthington Farm — the portion Millicent reluctantly agreed not to sell — Jayne hadn't had fun in years.

Not since the death of their grandmother, when they'd gone to Millicent's New York home, to sister Marybeth, to the latest stepfather. She and Josh had sworn eternal fealty to one another. Avid readers, they'd used all the flowery phrases their young minds could imagine, but in essence they'd sworn to help the other in times of need.

After the forced move from the country, Josh had been the one to leave, running off to sea when life around Millicent grew difficult, but Jayne continued to take the covenant seriously. She took everything seriously. Which was why, according to her exasperated mother, she had never been able to deal with men very well—not any of her stepfathers, nor the few beaux who had come calling. Nor, it seemed, the President of the United States.

All that night in the Forbes townhouse, empty except for a skeleton staff of servants, and throughout the next few days in a posting chariot on the journey to New York, Jayne considered President Madison's words, and she wondered what she should do. Write more letters? That's all she'd done for years. At school in New York she'd found an Arab student, daughter of a visiting potentate, to teach her the language of Tripoli, and she'd sent countless unanswered missiles across the sea.

In January, on reaching her twenty-fifth year, she'd come into the inheritance left her by Granny Worth. And she'd inherited Josh's portion, too. A formidable estate, it turned out, bonds and certificates worth far more than she imagined, and she'd been emboldened to quicken her quest for information, going so far as to seek an audience with the highest officeholder in the land. What use was money if one didn't put it to good use?

She asked the question just as the chariot pulled up in front of Forbes' Vandam Street mansion. Despite the midnight hour, lights sparkled like jewels at every window on the first two floors, and she could hear the laughter and music over the noise of a passing coach and four. She should have known there would be a party in progress when she returned—and little concern for how she had fared. Millicent had only one use for money, and that was pursuing pleasure. Randolph Forbes, stiffly formal in most respects, did not seem to object. Marybeth, husband William Browne docilely in tow, helped her think up

15

ways for that pursuit.

Jayne was the odd one. Serious in the midst of laughter, dreaming while others schemed, she even looked different. Too tall, too thin, too dark, not short and fair-skinned and rounded, like Millicent and Marybeth.

The catalog of her shortcomings was endless — long neck, long legs, and, according to Millicent, far too long of face. It was true she didn't smile very often, not where anyone could see her, but she'd had very little cause.

Jayne sighed, wishing she had returned to her Virginia home instead of New York. But Millicent had wanted to know what the President said. Or so she had claimed.

Exiting the carriage, Jayne paid the driver and, with her single piece of luggage in hand, walked wearily up the front stoop and into the brilliantly lit foyer. The glare caused her to blink.

"Don't squint, Jayne. It will only cause wrinkles."

Rebellious in her tired state, Jayne squinted all the more as she glanced toward her mother. Millicent stood in the open double doorway to the right, red hair carefully coiffed into a cascade of curls more suitable to a woman half her age, one hand resting dramatically high on the door frame. Her short, voluptuous body was clad in emerald green satin; at her back caroused a ballroom of jovial guests dressed in equal brilliance.

Good evening, Jayne, my darling daughter. Did you meet with success? Will the President help you prove my darling son is alive?

They were not words Jayne expected to hear. *Don't squint.* Millicent was nothing if not consistent.

"I'm exhausted from the journey," said Jayne. "If you have no objection, I'd like to go to my room."

Millicent freed herself from the stance she'd taken and hurried forward to wrap plump, beringed fingers around her daughter's arm. "Oh, but I do object." She nodded toward the closed parlor door opposite the ballroom. "We must talk."

Jayne didn't bother to protest. Once Millicent got something in her mind, she was like a windstorm, blowing and going until her energies were spent.

Millicent snapped her fingers for the aged butler to take Jayne's valise. Really, she thought, the girl shouldn't have been carrying it; such chores were for servants and carriage drivers. Jayne certainly had the money to hire sufficient help.

The remembrance of Jayne's money brought her sharply to the matter at hand. Closing the parlor door behind her, she watched as her younger daughter unbuttoned her pelisse and removed the bonnet she'd received as a gift from Marybeth on her twenty-fifth birthday. The feather drooped abominably; Jayne would never learn how to take care of her things.

Including her future, which was why Millicent was taking charge.

She studied her daughter with great care. A private child, docile usually but with moments of prickly stubbornness. Got it from her father, along with that terrible coloring. Simply refused to go out with a parasol as protection against the sun.

And that thick black hair and those dreadful dark eyes. Made her look as though she were perpetually in mourning.

"The President was not sympathetic to your cause,

17

was he?" she asked outright.

"No, he wasn't."

"Your Uncle Randolph warned you."

"My 'uncle,' as you call him—" Jayne broke off. She'd never broken Millicent of calling her husbands 'uncle' to her children, and she wasn't likely to do so tonight.

"I had to talk to the President."

"And so you did." Millicent eyed her daughter shrewdly. She did not miss the shadows beneath her eyes and the unusual slump to her shoulders, both encouraging signs. "Surely now you will admit that Joshua is dead."

Jayne winced. Somehow the words on her mother's lips sounded far worse than they had coming from Madison. She'd heard them many times before, but tonight, for the first time, she wondered if perhaps her mother hadn't been right all along.

"Jayne, it's time to face facts. You need to wed."

The same old subject, Jayne thought wearily. Her thick lashes rested on her cheeks, and she called on the last of her energy simply to remain upright. "Please, let's not talk about this tonight."

"We must."

"There's no one I have the least interest in marrying."

"Which is why I've seen fit to take care of the selection myself. In fact we're making the announcement Saturday night."

A moment passed before Jayne realized what Millicent had said. Her eyes flew open, and exhaustion fled. "What are you talking about?"

"I'm talking about a second son-in-law. Your sister married a man of my choosing. William Browne has

18

proven a good and faithful provider, even though the marriage has been barren. I have picked equally well for you."

Jayne's mind raced through the list of possible choices, all vapid pleasure-seekers of various ages and girths, none of whom had ever uttered a sensible word in her hearing. With none could she carry on a conversation, much less join in a conjugal bed.

A knock sounded at the door.

"There he is now. A bit soon, I regret, but still and all, it's past time we got the details of the merger over and done."

Panic fluttered in the pit of Jayne's stomach as her mother bade the newcomer to enter. She blinked once, twice, then stared in open astonishment at Leander Forbes, Uncle Randolph's nephew. Leander had not been on the quickly considered husband list.

"Do come in," said Millicent with a wave of her hand. "Jayne and I were just discussing the marriage."

"Millicent," Jayne managed, ignoring her would-be betrothed, "this isn't fair—"

"Of course it isn't," Millicent tittered. "I should leave the room and let you two lovebirds work out your own arrangements. But I know you too well. It will be postpone and postpone, and I absolutely refuse to have a spinster daughter living in this house one day longer than necessary."

She uttered the last words with a little laugh, but Jayne wasn't fooled. Windstorm Millicent was in action, and she wouldn't slow down until she'd blown everything and everyone into the places of her choice.

Jayne looked at Leander. Forty, shorter than she

19

with a tendency to portliness, pale blue eyes set in a pasty face — she doubted he ever went into the sun. His dress, unlike that of his businesslike uncle, tended toward foppishness, as evidenced by his yellow satin breeches and matching high-collared coat. The son of Randolph's deceased and only brother, a New York merchant, Leander was possessed of a law degree but as far as she knew, he'd never developed much of a career.

Not once had Jayne considered the kind of a man she might one day marry, but she knew that he would not, in any way, resemble the bridegroom her mother had named.

Nor was Jayne anything resembling Leander's ideal mate. Too scrawny, he thought, although he'd bet she had long legs beneath that drab gray gown. He looked forward to having them wrapped around him. And her features weren't bad — high cheekbones, full lips. Too much shrewdness in the eyes, but he didn't intend to gaze at her overmuch. Turn out the bedside lantern, that was his rule, and get down to business. All women were alike in the dark.

Jayne didn't miss the lustful glint in Leander's eyes. Her gaze flew to Millicent, who was smiling triumphantly. She saw with sudden clarity her mother's intent. Formerly dependent, Jayne now had money of her own. Millicent wanted to keep that money close at hand; as wife of Randolph Forbes's only blood kin, Jayne would never be far away. And Leander, always governed by his strong-willed uncle, would have control of her funds.

A lifetime of Millicent and Marybeth, of Randolph and Leander . . .

Bile rose in her throat. "Please excuse me," she

said, heading for the door. "I think I'm going to be sick."

Clutching her middle with one hand, the other clamped across her mouth, she rushed from the room, past sister Marybeth and Uncle Randolph standing in the foyer, and dashed up the stairs. Ignoring their cries, she did not pause until she was safely in the third-floor bedroom Millicent reserved for her visits.

Jayne slammed the bolt into place, then splashed water on her face from a bowl atop the dressing table and pressed a linen cloth to her temples. In the dim light from a lantern beside the bowl, with the nausea receding, she stared into the looking glass. A hollow-eyed stranger stared back.

Numbness beyond despair settled upon her. Was this to be her life, a gaunt, dreamless woman wed to a lascivious, spineless fop?

No, Worthless, it's not for you.

Jayne cried out as she heard the whispered words. Only her brother had ever called her Worthless, and then always in jest. Wild eyes cast about the room. Flickering shadows mocked her from every corner.

"Josh?" she asked in a small voice. "Are you there?"

All was silent. But she'd heard the proclamation clear enough. It *couldn't* have come from her own troubled mind. And what if it had? From half a world away, Josh might be trying to communicate through her own thoughts.

Stranger things had happened, she told herself in desperation, although she didn't try to name them. At the end of a day filled with doubts, she wanted above all else to believe in something again . . . to believe that Josh was close by.

Arms wrapped about her middle, she turned back to the mirror. "No, Josh," she said, "it's not for me."

What to do? Except where Josh was concerned, Jayne had always made concessions to others . . . to her father and grandmother, albeit willingly, and later to Millicent, who demanded she and Josh leave Virginia for New York.

Worst of all, she'd assented to Josh's running away.

Preferring to ride about the countryside, she'd meekly enrolled in a private boarding school; with her mother's proclivity for widowhood, she'd even accepted three stepfathers. But not Leander Forbes. Enough was enough.

Besides, Josh had spoken. She'd heard it. It could not be the result of panic and exhaustion, nor her imagination, nor even her own voice. He'd spoken, just as her quest was about to die —

Somewhere he lived. The quest must continue. Despite the rejection in Washington and the unanswered letters to Tripoli.

Tripoli. How many descriptions she had read and how much more she had envisioned — the narrow city streets, the robed men and veiled women, the mosques and towering minarets, and on beyond the outer gates, a blinding sun falling on endless rock and sand. Jayne's heart pounded as she considered what had always been an impossible idea. But then she'd never had the funds. Now she did.

Tripoli. Surely it wouldn't be too difficult to book passage to the Mediterranean port. And once there, she would force Bashaw Yusuf Karamanli to see her. A tyrant he might be, but if she took a page or two

22

from her mother's book, maybe she could become something of a tyrant on her own.

Besides, she reasoned, as she turned toward the bed, she'd already alienated one head of state. Why not two?

Chapter Two

CYRUS BYRD, LTD.
IMPORTER OF FINE GOODS

"Fine goods, is it?" Andrew MacGregor muttered as he read the scrolled letters on the streetfront door. "You've got that right, you son of a cur."

Behind him a mule-drawn wagon loaded with squealing pigs rolled noisily along the cobblestoned New York street, encouraged by the barking hound at the right rear wheel. The afternoon cacophony blended with a hundred city sounds of mounted riders and carriages, of shopkeepers at their storefronts, of pedestrians scurrying along the wooden walk, their nimble feet avoiding the impediments of refuse and sewage that came with civilization.

Give me a storm at sea any day, thought Andrew, letting himself inside the Byrd establishment. *And,* he added, *a Barbary pirate over a Yankee merchantman.*

In one glance his eyes absorbed the dimly lit interior scene — a single musty room of bare oak panels, separated by shuttered six-foot cabinets, two suited clerks at cluttered desks behind a waist-high counter that ran the width of the room, and at the rear a bannistered stairway.

One of the clerks stood. "Can I help you?"

"Aye, that you can. Where's Cyrus Byrd?"

The clerk adjusted a pair of wireframed glasses resting on the bridge of a narrow nose, muttering to himself, "My, my." The newcomer was trouble, he could see right away. It showed in the size of him, filling the doorway as he did, and in the jut of his square jaw and set of his shoulders, their width and power undisguised by the fit of his black seaman's coat, and it showed in the grip of his large weathered fists resting at his sides.

Most of all, trouble glared like a beacon light out of the scowling eyes. When they settled on him from beneath a line of thick black brows and the low brim of a visored cap, the clerk couldn't contain a nervous flutter. A glance at his companion, who kept his attention screwed to a set of figures on the paper before him, gave evidence he could expect little help from that particular quarter.

The clerk cast a nervous glance at the stairway. "Mr. Byrd is occupied, I'm afraid. Can I help you?"

"Has an upstairs perch, does he?"

Andrew didn't wait for the man's reply. Flipping open a hinged section of the countertop, he made fast for the stairway. With a protesting "You can't go up there!" echoing behind him, he took the steps two at a time and emerged onto a narrow hallway, unlit except for the natural light from double windows at the far ends to right and to left. Directly in front of the stairway was an ornately carved door; a brass plaque hung in the center, its message a single word: PRIVATE.

A twisted grin broke Andrew's grim, dark visage. "Only the virtuous deserve privacy, Cyrus, m'boy. And that sure as hell isna you."

Andrew flung open the door. A wide oak desk faced him, and behind it a corpulent, red-faced man with graying hair circling a bald pate like a crown. Pasty hands flattened on the oak surface as the lone occupant of the room stared up at the intruder.

"See here," Cyrus Byrd snapped, "what's the meaning of this?"

"There's much meaning, Mr. Byrd," Andrew said without a trace of a smile, "and you'd be wise to note, a touch of madness t' boot." He pulled back a heavy, matching oak chair, letting the legs scrape across the uncarpeted floor, settled his muscular frame in its hard, unwelcoming embrace, and leaned back, his eyes pinning Byrd in place.

"Captain Andrew MacGregor of the *Trossachs,* come to discuss a matter of a thousand pounds."

The words rolled out of the broad chest like thunder cracking over the Scottish hills for which Andrew's frigate was named. Tossing the cap onto the desk, he ran blunt fingers through a shock of thick black hair and continued to stare at his most recent and unexpected adversary, a man who until a week ago he would have labeled business associate.

A momentary fear, sharp as cats' claws, caught at Byrd. What the devil was MacGregor doing here in his office? It was bad enough the import trade forced him to deal with such riffraff, even through intermediaries. Direct confrontation was beyond consideration.

Especially when the brute's muscled frame barely fit into a chair. Byrd forcefully stilled an inclination to fidget. MacGregor might have hands to crush the cornerstone of the Byrd Import Building, and a stare that could punch holes in its walls, but nothing in his

26

size or strength gave evidence he was smart.

"You've heard from my attorney, I assume," said Byrd, purposefully officious. "I also assume you can read, captain, and thus know my stand on this matter. Six months ago we signed a mutual contract for deliverance of a certain cargo from the ports of Liverpool and Tripoli. Thursday last I paid what I consider that same cargo to be worth. You have no more money coming. Now I request that you leave immediately; otherwise I shall have to summon the authorities. In truth, my clerks have probably already done so."

Andrew allowed himself a slight smile. Cyrus Byrd was no more or less than he'd expected—an avaricious and foolishly loquacious termite trying to eat his way through an honest man's profits, and a termite most likely with an equally avaricious ant of a New York barrister urging him on.

Having dealt with such insects before, Andrew saw need of reminding the termite just how fine the cargo had been. "Woolens from England, embroidered silks from the Mediterranean, almonds and dried figs—"

"The figs were rotten."

"If so, and I've no reason to believe you speak the truth, they took on the rot in your warehouses."

"Don't be ridiculous. I've already had to clear them out so that the stench would not become a permanent fixture."

"Destroyed the evidence, did you? I'd bet the sails on my frigate that you got a fine sum for a ton of fine figs."

Byrd cleared his throat and drummed fat fingers against the desk. "Conjecture on your part, and nothing more. Worse, they were delivered late. Supposed to be for the Christmas market, not spring."

Andrew snorted in disgust. "You're a dishonest man, Cyrus Byrd. There was nothing wrong with the goods, nor with the time of arrival. I want the money"—need it, too, he could have added—"and I want it now."

Byrd cleared his throat. "Look over the correspondence from my lawyer more carefully. I have no intention of paying for goods I cannot turn around for profit."

Scorn bit like bile at Andrew's innards as he watched the merchant's arrogant red face. When he reached inside his coat pocket, he saw with pleasure the flare of alarm in Byrd's pale eyes and the twitch of nervousness in the plump lips.

Expects a weapon, does he? Would that he could wave under the importer's nose a curved desert dagger still hot from the Sahara sun. Instead, Andrew pulled out the document that had been delivered earlier in the day to the *Trossachs* as it lay at anchor in the East River harbor. He'd read every legally-couched word carefully. The initial payment, made before the cargo had been offloaded, would be all that was forthcoming, according to the importer's hired minion, one Randolph Forbes, Esquire, Attorney at Law.

The document went on to quote statutes from the sovereign state of New York and from international maritime law. Andrew crushed the papers in one hand and tossed them onto the desk. "Before I leave port next week, I'll have what's coming to me."

Byrd straightened the lapels of his black wool morning coat and fluffed the ruffled collar at his throat, then gave a cursory, critical glance at the seaman's coat and open-necked shirt, the thick shoulder-length hair and the storm-blue eyes of the captain.

He did not look long at the eyes.

"Empty words, Captain MacGregor. You are in the United States of America now, not out on some lonely stretch of ocean where you might consider yourself final authority. And even on the oceans, may I remind you that my country defeated yours rather soundly in our recent hostilities."

Andrew admitted to a flare of patriotism, and a matching anger at the smug American. He also saw the irony of his ire. In the Highlands village he once called home he'd met with naught but stone walls and stone hearts, yet here he was ready to defend his country against an insignificant slight.

Andrew did not claim to be a totally rational man.

"English ships, Mr. Byrd," he said. "You defeated English ships, not Scottish. 'Tis a common mistake Yanks make. Comes from ignorance."

Byrd flushed. "One and the same. You fly under the same flag."

"You'd know they're not the same," Andrew snapped back, "if you ever heard the bagpipes blasting loud across the field of battle. They're enough to turn a thief to honesty. Perhaps I should have played the pipes today instead of trying reason."

"See here, MacGregor, enough of this nonsense. You Scots are a stubborn lot, and unruly, too. You've got all you're getting. Try to collect more, you'll get what's coming to you, all right, but it won't be anything you'll enjoy."

"Are you threatening me, Cyrus? If so, I'd call it a

29

puny effort. I'll show you how 'tis done."

With effortless grace and an ominous intensity, Andrew's tight-muscled body eased from the chair. In three strides his long, strong legs took him to the fireplace at the side of the room; in one steady sweep he gripped the handle of the poker and stalked the tight-lipped merchant to his lair behind the desk, holding the heavy rod of iron in the air as his ancestors might once have wielded a halberd.

Byrd cowered in his chair while Andrew gripped the poker at both ends, lowered the makeshift weapon to the back of the merchant's shoulders, and proceeded to bend it to the shape of a horseshoe, not stopping until he had rested the metal like a shawl around his adversary's short, thick neck. He leaned close; the importer's breath had a sour smell, as though something inside him had gone bad.

"What are you doing?" squeaked Byrd.

"You think we Scots an unruly lot, do you? Keep to your thieving ways, Cyrus, m' boy, and you'll wish that's all we were."

Andrew backed away, the glare from his eyes pinning the importer to the chair. "I'll be at Washington Tavern when you decide 'tis best to be an honest man."

Byrd held his breath until the captain was out the door. Alone, he grabbed for a handkerchief from an inside coat pocket and mopped sweat from his brow. A God-damned bully, he thought. Just because he hadn't inflicted any actual harm—

The door burst open; Byrd started, then gave a scornful glance at the two clerks who hurried into the office. The arrival of his underlings gave rebirth to his courage and to his sharp tongue.

"Can no one read the word 'private' anymore?" he growled.

"We thought—" the first clerk began, then stopped when he saw the poker, adjusting his glasses to get a better look.

"Are you all right?" asked the second. "We debated summoning the watch, and when we didn't hear any shouting—"

"All troubles do not arise with a roar, you fools." Byrd lifted the poker from around his neck and placed it carefully on the desk. Eyes on the twisted iron, he muttered, "Get out. I have to think this through."

The clerks scurried from the room as rapidly as they'd entered, and Byrd shifted to stare out the window at his back, his attention turning to the thousand masts that rose above the East River harbor two blocks away. Andrew MacGregor dared defy him, did he? Who was this uncouth sailor to insist on payment when he'd already received more than Byrd had wanted to give? And what would he demand if he knew how much those sugary figs had actually brought?

His lawyer had talked him into a far-too-healthy settlement; for such advice, Randolph Forbes would be rewarded with a proportionate reduction in his own inflated fee. Serve him right. Thought himself high and mighty, him and that silly wife of his. Cyrus wouldn't attend one of their balls even if they asked him.

And as for MacGregor, he needed a lesson in how to do business with a Yankee. Byrd smiled. Not for nothing had he clawed his way out of the waterfront street of his birth to become one of the wealthiest

31

importers in town. MacGregor needed a lesson; Cyrus Byrd knew just what that lesson would be.

An hour later, ensconced in a dark, dank corner of Washington Tavern a block away from the *Trossachs'* berth, Andrew accepted a tankard of ale from a buxom serving girl. She leaned close, pressed her body against his shirt sleeve, and smiled into his eyes. Breath as sour as Cyrus's, Andrew thought, coming through a set of mottled teeth.

He laughed at himself. Must be far gone to notice such details with a pair of ripe breasts stroking him like a friendly hound. He contented himself with rubbing a hand across the girl's wide posterior, ending the exploration with a friendly pat. "Be gone with you, Kate. I'd not be much good to you tonight."

"You not much good?" Her laugh came sharp and quick, filled with suggestion. "That's not what I hear. I'd as soon believe the river out there was runnin' dry."

"Then you'd best go check the docks. Must be a hundred ships mired in the mud."

She roared lustily, giving the comment more response than it deserved, and shifted her attention to a nearby trio of drunken sailors who showed promise of providing a more profitable, if less enjoyable, night.

Andrew downed half the tankard, far from his first of the evening. "Yankee merchants are a sorry lot," he growled, then stared into the ale as though he expected the brew to argue.

" 'Tis a verity, Cap'n Mac," agreed his companion,

a bearded and braided old salt who went by the name Oakum.

"Had me acting like a circus bear," Andrew continued, "showing off what a big and powerful brute I am, strutting around as though I had more muscle than sense."

"Ye was provoked, as any man o' sense would be," Oakum said. "Inferior goods indeed! The scoundrel's a liar and a thief. Wouldn't know quality if it bit him in the arse."

Privately Oakum observed what a rare fret the captain was in, as cantankerous as he'd seen him in the three years he'd served as first mate aboard the *Trossachs*.

Andrew downed the rest of the ale without taking breath, then shoved the tankard aside with a callous-hardened palm. He sat back in the chair, long legs stretched in front of him under the table beside his discarded coat, boots crossed at the ankle. He rubbed at the open throat of his shirt.

"Too late smart, that's what I am. Shouldna have allowed the unloading until the agreed upon sum was tucked away in my quarters. Took half." Blunt fingers ran through a shock of thick black hair. " 'Tis not enough."

Oakum kept his reaction to a nod. More than any of the others in the crew, he knew the captain's plans for the money. No, not just plans. Dreams, more like. Cap'n Mac needed cash, or at least he thought he did. Oakum was not one to argue, even though for himself he'd come to wish no more out of life than a berth aboard a seaworthy ship like the *Trossachs* and service under the best captain ever to unfurl sails to the wind.

The two sat at the splintered table, silent in the midst of laughter and occasional angry voices that came like the blare of ships' horns out of the stale, smoky air. Andrew summoned the serving girl for another ale, again ignoring the pair of charms she used to smooth his shirt sleeve and the wide, swaying hips that marked her departure. All he could see was a red-faced scoundrel with a supercilious glint in his eye.

Andrew didn't care for supercilious glints—hadn't since he was a lad. They drove a man of his temperament to intemperate acts, the case in point this afternoon's demonstration with the poker. Trouble was, he had no answers to the current dilemma, other than to stalk back to Cyrus Byrd, Ltd., Importer of Fine Goods, and beat the devil out of the thief.

Which would only bring the authorities down on him, and a New York barrister crawling from under a rock to write up another paper legally robbing a hard-working seaman of his due.

What he needed was to get riproaring drunk—he was more than halfway there now—and take the serving wench to bed. Maybe a couple of 'em. See to some of his needs, and maybe his mind would be cleared enough to manage the rest.

If only he didn't have such important plans for the thousand pounds, he'd content himself with dismantling a certain importer's office and go on his way. Maybe dismantle the importer himself. Andrew sighed. God, what a surly beast he was this evening. Oakum deserved better. He was a good man, a good first mate, and more, a friend who knew when to talk and when to keep quiet.

"Cap'n Mac, we got ourselves company."

34

Andrew followed Oakum's gesture. Through the smoke he could make out, standing just inside the tavern door, the slender figure of his youngest crewman, an eighteen-year-old who went by the name of Boxer. The lad claimed with little justification to have made his living with his fists before going to sea. An unlikely past for one so spindly of frame and delicate of features, but no one questioned the word of a seaman when a ship was far from land — especially when he performed his duties with cheerful alacrity as was the case with Boxer.

His long, fair hair caught by a band at his neck, Boxer waved toward the captain, then turned as though he were speaking to someone behind him.

"Ain't alone, looks like," said Oakum.

"So it does. Better be something important. The lad's on afternoon watch."

The figure to whom Boxer spoke was hidden in the folds of a hooded and caped black cloak, tall as the young seaman, but as near as Andrew could tell, more slight of build.

Oakum caught on first. "Now why did the lad do something like that? Might's well pump water down t' the sea."

His brain fuzzied by the ale, Andrew said, "Make your meaning clear, mate. No riddles tonight."

"Oh, me meaning will be clear right enough. If I'm not mistaken, 'tis a little surprise our Boxer has brought, Cap'n Mac. Like a pup laying a bone afore its master, the lad has seen fit t' ease your troubles on this fretful day. He's giftin' ye wi' a woman."

Chapter Three

It was the smell of the place that got to Jayne, more than the dimness, more than the noise from what sounded like a thousand burly men . . . more, even, than the knowledge she must be demented to be here.

Forcing the fetid air into her lungs, she stepped deeper into the tavern's gloomy depths. Used to the late afternoon light outside, her eyes adjusted until she could make out the crowd of men. A few dozen, she decided, not a thousand, but they all seemed to be leering in her direction.

Impossible. Men did not leer at Jayne Worthington, for which she was grateful. She, in turn, did not leer at them.

Heart pounding and palms damp, she held the cloak close to her body. Though they were a roughly clad and ill-groomed lot, as different as possible from an assembly at the Forbes abode, she found no particular reason to fear since in truth they paid her little more attention than the smoke in the air.

They couldn't even *see* her, for mercy's sake, not in her protective garb. Her nerves were on edge, that was all. This was the East River waterfront, a nest for criminals too horrible to describe—according to Uncle Randolph.

But her stepfather *always* looked on the bleak side of everything. Surely not every man in the place was a thief or a murderer or a defiler of women and children.

She took a deep breath and lectured herself on the need for pluck. How could she hope, singlehandedly, to make arrangements for sailing halfway round the world, actually make the probably storm-tossed voyage, and then find her uninvited way into the palace of the bashaw of Tripoli if she couldn't summon the nerve to walk into a New York tavern?

Josh deserved a more courageous liberator. With images of her freckle-faced brother sharp in her mind, she stiffened her spine and followed Boxer, the crewman she'd met on the deck of the *Trossachs,* as he hurried through the crowded tavern in the direction of the table farthest from the door. The pair of them drew more than a few glances, most aimed at the fair young man with the fragile good looks, and not the hooded figure who might just as well be a monk.

Boxer came to halt at the table and tugged her beside him. "Had a caller, Cap'n Mac, with a business proposition. Came with cash in hand." He grinned broadly. "Thought ye'd want t' know."

"Now there's a switch, the woman offering t' pay," said the man to Jayne's left. A weathered fellow of some fifty years, bearded, she noticed, his gray hair plaited into a pair of thick braids, coarse-featured but with a kindly look to his eye that took the offense from his words.

In an establishment like this she should expect

some rough talk, she reminded herself, and some skepticism as to her motives — at least until she'd had a chance to state her case.

"Though with the cap'n here," the man went on, "I shouldna be surprised."

"Pig's whiskers," Boxer exclaimed. "Ye know she's a woman, do ye? Hoped my bringing 'er here would be a surprise."

"Oh, it was, lad, it was," said the second man at the table, "especially since you've got the afternoon watch."

As Boxer attempted to explain away the abandonment of his post, Jayne shifted her gaze toward the deep, rumbling voice and took her first look at the seaman she'd heard lauded along the waterfront, Captain Andrew MacGregor of the frigate *Trossachs,* a Scottish mariner who plied the waters between Glasgow, Tripoli, and New York, as fine a man who ever sailed the seas, according to all she'd been told, and a savior to his crew, if she could believe half of what Boxer had said.

One look at the captain and she forgot the smoke and the noise and the rowdy men. One look and she could consider nothing else but the particulars of Boxer's saintly Captain Mac . . . the hooded, seablue eyes that were trained on the boy . . . the physical power of him so evident in the half-buttoned shirt, the musculature of his chest and biceps outlined by the stretch of white linen, the dark hairs curling in the hollow of his throat, the squared jaw and strong, straight nose, the raven-black hair falling loose to his shoulders, the strong lips curved ever so slightly in disdain.

She especially noticed the lips. They did not, in

any way, belong to a saint.

Standing three feet from him in the protection of a hooded pelisse and able to see no lower than the wide leather belt at his waist, she could feel his masculinity; it emanated from him like heat from a roaring blaze. She couldn't have been more affected by the total picture if he'd jumped up and hit her in the stomach with his fist.

Jayne Worthington, spinster from Virginia, lately of Washington and New York, was looking at a man — *really* looking at an incredibly manly man — for the first time in her twenty-five years, picking up details and nuances of face and form as if she'd done so from the time she reached twelve.

She fought to draw a single breath, forgetful of the tavern's stench, forgetful of her purpose, forgetful of everything but Captain MacGregor and what the simple act of gazing upon him was doing to her interior workings. The experience was a revelation, hinting as it did of facets to herself she had not heretofore imagined. For some absurd, unknown reason, she could not look away.

He shifted his gaze to the shadowed opening of her hood. Even though he could not possibly read her expression or her interest or the reason behind her stunned silence, she felt as though his eyes were locked with hers, and it was fist-in-the-stomach time again.

" 'Tis a foolish thing to come cash in hand to the docks," he said. "If Boxer can be believed."

"He can." Jayne blushed at the squeak she made; it contrasted far too sharply with the rich thickness of his words. She cleared her throat and told herself to be as forthright and tenacious as she had been with the President.

"The boy speaks figuratively, of course." Stronger, better, she thought. "The money he refers to is hidden on my person."

It was Andrew's turn to be alerted. He hadn't expected such a well-spoken voice, but rather something more in the line of Kate's coarseness. Which reminded him, he was out of ale, and he signaled for another round.

Jayne caught the broad wink of the girl, who was leaning over a nearby table, her blouse gaping low across a pair of ample and, Jayne blushed to notice, brown-tipped breasts. A quick glance at the captain's grin proved he noticed, too, and rationality returned. What madness had possessed her to follow the youth to such an unsavory place? She hadn't known their destination, she reminded herself, not until they had halted outside. By then, it had seemed foolishly timid of her to balk at following through on her afternoon's quest.

But she hadn't expected to confront anyone quite like Captain Andrew MacGregor. Except for the momentary ogling of a half-naked woman, he sat like a dark and brooding deity in this sheltered corner of the room, black hair falling loose and uncombed to his wide shoulders, dark eyes staring out like coals at the edge of a banked fire.

He *sat*. That was part of the problem, she told herself. She'd always thought captains more gentlemanly, at least when addressing a lady. This . . . this boor was the man she hoped would take her across the ocean to the foreign ports of the Mediterranean. The thought made her shiver, though she didn't know quite why since she'd never been one to worry about social niceties before.

"Miss Worthington," said Boxer with a sweeping gesture, jostling her mind from its musings, "this be the captain I told you about, and Oakum here is first mate. The best two seafarers ever to tred a deck, though I'm bound to admit they're the only two I've served under."

"Good evening, gentlemen," said Jayne. If either caught the irony in her voice, neither gave a sign.

"Lad, ye've not got the sense God gave a gull," said Oakum with a shake of his head. "Sounds like a lady ye've brought, and this ain't no place fer such."

Jayne rewarded the comment with a wry and unseen twitch of her lips. Oakum, at least, was not a total social dolt. He gave further proof by offering her the chair beside him, which she promptly accepted, and her youthful guide took the remaining place separating her and the captain.

The serving girl arrived with the ale, stared in open curiosity at the cloak, winked at the still grinning Boxer, and with a twist of her posterior in the captain's direction, took her leave.

"I do believe you were a pugilist after all," said Andrew. "Suffered a few too many blows to the head. Oakum's right. You shouldna 've brought a woman here. Not unless the business you spoke of draws her to the docks on a regular basis."

"Oh, she's a lady, all right. Speaks right proper and polite."

Andrew took a swallow of ale, the alcohol blending with the drinks that had gone before. Miss Worthington's hidden figure was beginning to irritate him mightily. For some reason he was reminded of Cyrus Byrd, sitting smugly behind his wide desk.

Dealing with Yanks, no matter the gender, was difficult enough when an honest seaman could see the cut of their jib.

For all any of them knew, the woman had eyes the color of blood and fangs as long as her chin. Or—a more tantalizing thought—a hungry cast to her glance and full red lips that could wander over a man like a ketch feathering the waves.

It was the latter image that caught in his ale-dulled brain. "Don't be deceived by fine words," he said by way of tutelage to the boy. "There's all kinds o' whores."

"Captain MacGregor!"

Jayne tossed the hood of her cloak against her shoulders and smoothed a dark curl back from her face, anchoring it firmly in the twist of hair at her nape. The captain might be ruggedly handsome and in a fine physical state, but he was also rude and crude and, she suspected, more than a little drunk. Thank goodness the momentary spell he had cast over her was gone.

"I am not suffering from deafness, Captain MacGregor, nor am I a habitué of the city's riverfront taverns. If your shoretime is limited to such environs, it's quite possible you've never met anyone like me."

Andrew looked in vain for a hunger in her glance and a ripeness to her lips. What he saw was a raised chin, prim mouth, and black eyes that flashed only anger, and all of it set in a slender face that might have been pretty if her hair weren't pulled back so tightly it stretched the skin against her bones.

He also saw the curious glances thrown her way by the trio of revelers at the nearest table. In displaying her gender and her spirit, his visitor had proven herself not so much a woman of courage as one who lacked good sense.

" 'Tis beyond possible, Miss Worthington, that you are unique in my experience. Gone all the way to certainty."

Jayne twisted her hands in her lap. Should she go on with her business, or should she bolt for the door? Why couldn't Josh send her some kind of message, as he'd done in her room? The sad truth was that the *Trossachs* was her best chance at leaving soon for a direct sailing to the Mediterranean. And according to all she'd been told, MacGregor was her best chance at arriving safely.

There was nothing to it but to stiffen her spine once again, a procedure that was beginning to pain her lower back. "Shall we get to the business which brought me here?"

Andrew looked at the proud tilt of her chin, then down to the high neck of the gray gown just visible above the open throat of her cloak. Too skinny for his tastes, best he could tell, and she wrapped herself in enough cloth to carpet the *Trossachs* deck. But still there was something about her . . . something that kept his attention far longer than had the buxom serving girl.

"By all means, let's get t' business."

"I wish to purchase passage to the Mediterranean. Tripoli if possible, but anywhere along the Barbary Coast will do."

"And who might be wantin' such a thing?"

"Why, I do, of course."

Andrew shook his head. Must be the ale.

"You seem to have difficulty understanding, captain. I'll speak slowly if that will be of any help. I, Jayne Worthington, being of sound mind and possessing sufficient resources, and having reached an age of maturity"—she ignored the captain's snort—"find myself in great need of confronting the bashaw of Tripoli on a personal matter that is no one's concern but mine. To do so, I must find passage aboard a seaworthy vessel."

She took a deep breath, proud that her voice had not betrayed her nervousness, and watched as the captain substituted his empty tankard for her untouched serving of ale.

"Throughout my consultations along the dock," she continued, her confidence growing, "I have heard your name mentioned repeatedly as one who sails directly from New York to Tangier and subsequent ports of call along the North African coast. You also came highly recommended as a capable mariner and navigator, which put my mind at rest as I've never set foot on anything larger than a Potomac skiff."

Andrew let his eyes roam around the tavern before he settled them on the surprising woman seated across from him. Eyes still remarkably frank, if anything her chin tilted a fraction upward, she might have been sitting in a London tearoom discussing the time of day. Truly surprising, she was, and Andrew wasn't often taken aback by the opposite sex.

"Let me get this straight," he said.

"By all means," said Jayne, who was beginning to wonder if the highly lauded Captain Andrew MacGregor deserved his reputation for intelligence. Perhaps a man's physical development was in inverse ratio to the development of his more cerebral faculties. It was a theory she'd never considered until now. No, she thought, impossible, because under such conditions, her ersatz betrothed, Leander Forbes, would be a genius.

"Your mind seems to be wandering, Miss Worthington."

"Sorry," she said guiltily. "Please go on."

"I want to be sure I'm hearing you correctly. You, a Christian woman of maturity, wish to travel as a single female aboard an all-male merchant ship to an Islamic country where you can confront, for reasons you choose to keep private, one of the most notorious despots in the world."

Jayne sat straighter in her chair. "That is correct."

"You must have a hell of a reason for going."

"I do."

Across the table, Andrew shook his head. Maybe the stiff-backed Miss Worthington really was a woman of courage, but she still came up several slips short in berthing at the dock of good sense. Thinking once again of Cyrus Byrd and of his mealy-mouthed clerks, and now this black-eyed, undernourished harridan, he could come to only one conclusion. As a nation, the United States of America was not overburdened with a brilliant populace.

"The bashaw." Again he shook his head. "Never been much of a friend to Yanks. Of course, maybe you haven't heard about the *Philadelphia,* and the men he took hostage. 'Twas a long time ago."

"I've heard," she shot back.

"Brought your President to his knees, as I recall, afore he let 'em go."

"President Jefferson chose to negotiate for the release of the Americans."

45

"Paid thousands of pounds in tribute, after he swore he wouldn't. Some say as much as half a million."

Sixty thousand dollars, she could have said, and added that the captain's own government had been paying tribute to the bashaw for decades just to keep his pirates away from British ships. And to the sultan of Morocco, the dey of Algiers, and the bey of Tunis, who likewise supported a fleet of robber ships. But to throw such facts at him might lead to further arguments and worse, hints of her purpose. She didn't want to hear how foolish she was. She would get all the lectures she could handle when Millicent and Uncle Randolph found out what was going on.

"All that was a long time ago, Captain MacGregor," she said.

As if, Andrew thought bitterly, one could forget the past. Gesturing for Boxer to move aside, he took the chair next to Miss Worthington, leaned close, and got a better look at her proud features. Eyes wide and overlarge, owing to the thin lines of her face, nose straight and leading down to full pink lips — surprisingly sensuous lips, he saw now, if she didn't hold them so tight. A smooth complexion, tawny as a wind-sprung spar on a summer's eve when the sun caught in its fibers, the skin marred only by a sliver of a scar at her right temple. He speculated as to the cause of the cut. If he knew her better, he'd ask.

Hell, he'd ask anyway. "How'd you get the scar?"

Hurt flashed in the depths of her eyes, then was gone with the return of scorn. "None of your business."

Sweet breath, good teeth. He decided to goad her

46

further. "So it's passage you want. There's only one cabin with room to spare, and that's mine." He placed a hand on her shoulder; even through the thickness of cape and cloak and gown, she felt no more substantial than a cloud. "And one bunk."

He gave her credit—she didn't flinch, not from the hand nor the suggestion of his words.

"The bunk is yours, too, of course," she said, resisting the urge to jerk free of his warmth.

"It could be an interesting journey, Miss Worthington." He moved close, purposefully letting his ale-thick breath brush across her cheek. She smelled surprisingly of gardenias, a scent he'd always been partial to, and he felt an unexpected jolt deep in his loins.

She looked at him out of the corner of her eye, a courtesan's glance although he doubted she realized it. Miss Worthington knew little of women's wiles, and Andrew found himself looking upon her in a less critical light.

"Interesting for you, perhaps, Captain MacGregor, but rather tedious for me."

She'd meant her glance to be brief, to register scorn and rejection, but when their eyes met, she found looking away impossible. For just an instant his eyes softened a shade away from stormy blue; for just an instant, he was looking at her as though she were not his adversary but rather, someone he could like.

"Tell me, Miss Worthington, do you never laugh?" Like his eyes, his voice had softened, and she caught more than ever the exotic Scottish burr. "Do you never take the pins from your hair where the breeze can catch it? Do you once in a while let the joy of

47

living bring a smile to your lips?"

Powerless to do otherwise, Jayne let his voice and his words cast a spell over her. She closed her eyes, and for a moment she was riding over a sun-kissed Virginia hill, hair unbound just as the captain had described, and oh yes, the laughter bubbling unbidden from deep inside as she forgot her past and her present and the uncertainties of her future, all her energies devoted to the moment of freedom.

Oh yes. I know how to laugh, she could have said. But Jayne was a very private person and she recognized even in her muddled state that the captain's sympathy was at best temporary, and at worst, illusory. He could never become her confidant.

She reached up to wrap her slender fingers around his hand. Removing the offending appendage from her shoulder, she set it firmly on the table. Her expression remained steady, but in truth the warmth and strength she'd felt in the captain's hand had been startling, the touching of her skin to his surprisingly intimate. Staring into his eyes, she thought she saw the same surprised reaction. What wonderfully expressive eyes, she thought, with their fine lines at the corners. He must look often into the sun.

He winked, and at last she admitted the futility of her request. Captain MacGregor wanted far more for the passage than she was willing to pay. She was not and never had been a younger version of Millicent Forbes, nor was she a sympathetic sister to Marybeth, both of whom would have flirted openly with the captain and just possibly have followed through with a great deal more. Jayne might not be practiced in dealing with men, but she understood what she did *not* want to do.

"Tell me, Captain MacGregor, are you married?"

Andrew shuddered. " 'Tis a trap I've avoided. Why?"

"I was wondering if in addition to being a boor, you were an adulterer as well."

Oakum choked on a swallow of ale.

She stood. "I'm certain there are many women who would find the invitation to share your quarters positively exhilarating. I, however, am not one of them. It has become apparent that I was in error to seek out passage aboard the *Trossachs,* and out of my mind to have approached you here. I would rather swim the Atlantic Ocean than spend one night upon your ship."

Andrew had expected the rejection—had even fostered it with his insulting words—but he hadn't expected the tight-lipped spinster to be quite so forceful in the deliverance. Leaning back in his seat, he growled in Boxer's direction, "Get the lady out o' here. Our business is at an end."

The wide-eyed youth nodded solemnly, all trace of his former good humor gone. "Yes, sir, Cap'n Mac."

Jayne gave him a final nod to let him know she was in complete agreement with the leave taking, her eyes lingering a fraction longer than she'd intended. He sat there in the corner like a storm cloud rising out of an ocean swell—or at least the way she imagined such a cloud would look. And all she had done was make a perfectly straightforward business proposition.

She whirled away. With hood once again firmly in place, she ignored the drunken jibes from the neighboring table and began her journey toward the door.

"I'll go along," said Oakum, "to see no harm comes to 'er."

Andrew managed a grin. He'd forgotten all about his first mate, sitting quietly to the side.

"I've a feeling Miss Worthington can take care o' herself."

"Do ye, Captain Mac? To me she was a surprising miss, for all her sharp tongue and crazy ideas. Makes a man want to protect her. Keep her from treading in water over her head."

Andrew barked out a laugh. "Helpless, is she? You don't know much about women, mate. Not much substance and character to 'em, and what's there is dedicated to selfish pursuits. Need a man, but once they've got him, there's not a one won't try to twist him to do as they bid."

"And do they bring ye no comfort?" Oakum ventured.

"You know me too well for denial. We trade in silks and figs, mate. A woman trades in sex. Not, I'll grant you, Miss Worthington. 'Tis a skill she doesn't yet ken."

Oakum retreated to silence. He did indeed know the captain, well enough to understand his bitterness. But he knew enough of the world to know his captain was wrong.

Especially about Miss Worthington. He watched as she wended her way toward the tavern door. In the depths of her eyes and the set of her mouth, he'd caught signs of sadness, even despair, signs Captain Mac had missed. Something was dreadful wrong in the woman's life, something forcing her to a journey that even she, if she was to be honest, would have to call insane.

She was halfway to the door when a shaft of sunlight fell through the opened door of the tavern, heralding the arrival of a pair of uniformed New York officers of the law, their painted leathern hats pulled low over grim visages, sticks held firmly at their sides. Silence descended on the tables like fog.

"There he is," shouted the short, black-suited man who'd come in with them. "In the corner," he added as he adjusted a pair of wireframed glasses on the bridge of his nose.

Jayne stepped aside as the officers stomped past. Andrew stood to face them.

When they came to the table, one of the officers bellowed into the stillness, "Captain Andrew Mac-Gregor, you are under arrest for assault and battery on the person of one Cyrus Byrd, citizen of New York, and for threatening same with further bodily harm."

Chapter Four

"You tole your mama what you're up to?"

It was a good and logical question, Jayne thought as she sat at the dressing table in her Vandam Street bedroom, and one very much in keeping with the woman who asked it.

She glanced from her own reflection in the looking glass and on to that of Alva Turner, who stood at her back. Tall and thin, the shine of her ebony skin broken by the wrinkles of fifty years and her black hair streaked with gray, Alva had lost none of the spark in her dark, all-seeing eyes.

"Don't worry," said Jayne. "I plan to tell her as much as she needs to know."

Alva shook her head. "Mercy!"

"I will," repeated Jayne, shifting once again to the task of pinning her hair into some semblance of order at the nape of her neck. "It's just that I'd hoped to have all the arrangements set before speaking. I know as well as you what a row it's going to cause."

"Row don't quite cover what'll happen around here. If the good Lord will forgive my sayin' so, Miz Forbes gonna raise Holy Hell."

Jayne knew all too well Alva was right. She'd been

with the Worthington family since before even Josh was born, at first working in the fields, then moving to the more exalted position of house servant, and after Granny Worth's death and Josh's departure, to the care of Jayne. Never as a slave—the Worthingtons didn't own slaves—but as a trusted servant and oftentimes the closest friend Jayne had in the world.

For years Millicent had wanted to get rid of her—"Doesn't know her place and she certainly doesn't understand even the rudiments of turning you out in proper fashion"—but in this one area Jayne had always been adamant. Alva remained.

Jayne smiled at the two images in the ornate three-foot-high looking glass. Scrolled gilt border with carved rosettes at the corners, its high panel inset flaunting the painted form of a half-clad Venus, the glass seemed all wrong for holding the women's likenesses.

She and Alva were far too gaunt, too practical, too *unadorned*. It was the best description she could come up with, Jayne in a simple white wrapper and Alva in her black servant's dress. The frame had been selected by Millicent; about the only thing that could be said in its favor was that it went with the rest of the room, from the flounced satin draperies at the double windows to the bright floral carpet to the mahogany bed with its carved Cupid's quiver and torch ornamenting the front of the pink-draped tester.

Millicent had selected *everything*. Jayne had never rested comfortably in the room, had always felt as though she were only passing through, like some boarder who was using the facilities for a temporary stay. Which, indeed, she often was, preferring as she did to spend most of her days in the country.

Jayne stood.

"That the best you gonna do with your hair?" asked Alva.

"What's wrong with it? I wear it like this all the time."

"That's what I'm gettin' at. Pulled back so tight you can't hardly keep your eyes open nor your mouth closed."

Jayne ignored the criticism, which she knew was given with all the best intentions in Alva's heart.

"My Miz Jayne be a far sight prettier than Miz Marybeth any day of the week," Alva was wont to say. All Jayne needed was "a little fixin', kinda the way you has to add salt to the stew if all the flavors gonna come out."

Slipping into the dress her mother had bought for the evening, she stared into the mirror while Alva fastened the buttons down the back. It suited her little better than did the room — little puff sleeves that seemed to stretch her already long arms to a simian length, low sheered bodice that called attention to her small bosom, high waistline that made her look six feet tall, and the whole thing in a pale yellow that took all the vibrancy from her skin. Jayne did indeed look like a tasteless stew.

But she'd promised Millicent she would wear the gown, in much the same way she promised most everything, the primary purpose being to avoid disagreement.

Too bad her appearance wasn't quite disastrous enough to make Leander Forbes forget her inheritance. He was waiting downstairs, along with a hundred other guests, anticipating the announcement of their engagement, even though since her return he'd communicated only through written correspondence.

"Business," he'd claimed in a feathery scrawl, "keeps me away until Saturday night." Until, he could have added, the public acknowledgment of their betrothal, arranged without a single private encounter between bride and groom. The coward.

Millicent had turned a deaf ear to Jayne's protestations, and Jayne had gone quietly about making her own plans.

Or at least she'd tried. Too well she recalled her first attempt at securing ocean passage. She could barely remember the details of her interview with Captain Andrew MacGregor without blushing. And for some reason she remembered those details so often. Sometimes she wondered what had happened in the intervening three days since she'd rushed from the tavern and left the captain to his fate with the New York police.

The assault charges seemed perfectly in keeping with the character — or lack of same — he had revealed to her. Jayne shuddered each time she remembered the hulking brute who'd sat in the smokey corner and raked her over with his eyes, swilling ale and offering indecent proposals while she presented a perfectly legitimate business request.

What if she had never met him personally but, going by his reputation as the best skipper on the Atlantic, had booked passage through an intermediary and then found herself aboard his frigate? Would he have then expected her to share his bed?

Did he think a skinny, swarthy spinster exhibiting all the signs of running away would be so desperate or so eager she would willingly acquiesce to all his crude demands? After all, sea voyages were long and men had their needs. And with the *Trossachs* being primarily a cargo ship, she might very well have been the only woman passenger on board.

Jayne had never been kissed, except for a peck on the cheek from a neighbor farm lad back in Virginia ten years before, but she knew what went on between men and women. Granny Worth had been the first to reveal the curious facts, in such quaint terms that Jayne had barely got the message about the two genders having actually to touch. Then had come Millicent, for once seeing to her parental responsibilities, green eyes gleaming throughout a more descriptive telling. Lastly, after a return from her one-week wedding trip with bridegroom William Browne, there had been Marybeth.

"A woman has her duties," the older sister had said when she invaded Jayne's bedroom. Despite Jayne's attempts to evict her, Marybeth had gone on to add a few intimate details, not sparing the tidings that "a lot of pain goes part and parcel" with the duties.

"William won't be the kind to insist too often," she ended. "Thank goodness for that."

Jayne had caught a hint of regret, or maybe it was disappointment, in her sister's voice. The conclusion had been clear: Millicent liked the mating process; Marybeth didn't . . . at least she didn't like it with the man she'd wed, although both before the wedding and afterwards, she never passed up a chance to flirt with every man who came within a radius of three feet.

Their mother had selected William Browne; she'd

also selected Leander Forbes. Sharing a bed with Leander was just as unthinkable as sharing a frigate bunk with Andrew MacGregor, but not, Jayne had to admit, at all for the same reasons.

"I'm going to Tripoli," she said louder than she intended as she pulled away from Alva and began to pace the room. "I'm going to find a nice safe passage aboard a passenger ship, and when I get there, I'll talk to everybody I can who might have some news of Josh. And don't give me that look, Alva. I've got the money to do it and the determination."

"Never said one word about you lacking either one. Maybe some common sense, truth to tell."

Jayne took a long, slow look around the room. "Even you must admit there's nothing to keep me here. My friends are married, and most of them have already started their families. The Virginia land is down to only a few hundred acres, and you can watch over that for me while I'm gone."

"Miz Jayne, you makes it sound like a trip down to Georgia. You talkin' about a place you gotta drop off the end of the earth t' get to."

Jayne stopped at the door, and her eyes, round and dark, took on a faraway expression, as though she could see through the walls of her room, through the restrictions of wood and brick and outside trees, as though she could see into eternity.

"It's the end of the earth I need, Alva. It's the only place I can find what I'm looking for."

She stepped into the hall, and Alva listened to her footsteps growing fainter as she headed for the stairs. In her mind, the servant could still see the wide, sad eyes and proud set of the mouth of her beloved child.

Jayne *was* her child, even if another woman was the mama and the color of her skin was all wrong. It was Alva who'd been there when she was a crying baby, ready with a sugar tit and a gentle hug, and it was Alva who'd patched her scraped knees when she'd fallen off that mean ole horse she loved to ride, and it was Alva who'd dried her tears when the first Miz Worthington passed on.

Thinking of that poor baby sailing out on the water and going to a Godless country with nothing but heathen savages roaming the wilds almost broke Alva's heart. She wouldn't say much, though, only a little the way she'd already done to let the baby know she cared.

What she suspected was that maybe Miz Jayne was right. Maybe she really needed to go to the end of the earth to find what she was lookin' for. Funny thing, as much as Alva remembered the love between those two chillins, she had a strong suspicion that whether Miz Jayne knew it or not, she was looking for something more than brother Josh.

A string quartet was playing a lively minuet when Jayne stepped into the ballroom that opened off the front foyer. A thousand candles glittered from the overhead chandeliers and from the sconces that lined the brocaded walls, and in the center of the room more than two dozen couples stepped in stately splendor to the pervasive rhythm.

The usual crush of well-dressed humanity skirted the dance floor, reminding Jayne of the gilt border on her bedroom looking glass. Most of the women were in brilliant rainbow hues, and, with the exception of a scattering of dandies, most of the men wore black.

Leander Forbes, standing on the far side of the room, was one of the exceptions. His legs were a bit thin to wear the calf-length lavender breeches and white stockings he sported, and his shoulders too narrow for the wide lapels of his lavender coat. Had Millicent, Jayne wondered, been picking out his wardrobe, too?

"Oh, dear," said Millicent in Jayne's right ear, as though to think of her was to summon her presence. "I had so thought that dress would do."

Usually when her mother came out with one of her *oh, dear* comments, Jayne responded with silence; tonight she was in a more reckless mood.

"At least my pallid appearance serves as contrast to Leander," she said, casting a glance down at her mother, who was resplendently clad in a low-cut, clinging sapphire blue sarcenet gown, a white, jeweled feather rising out of a mass of artificially enhanced red hair.

Millicent searched past the dancers for her husband's nephew; when her thick-lashed green eyes found him, they flashed with humor, but only for a moment. Lavender on a man? Her husband's nephew was not, unfortunately, without his flaws.

She shifted attention to Jayne, to her angular body and her unfortunately sallow skin. The yellow silk really was a poor choice, but she'd never figured out just how to compensate for the girl's dusky coloring. Inherited her complexion from her father. A farmer, of all things. Millicent never should have married a man of the soil.

"Well, Jayne," she said dourly, "after the wedding

I expect you to show your husband how to dress more somberly. You do it so well."

"There's not going to be a wedding," said Jayne, ignoring the cut. She spoke by rote, knowing full well her mother was going to make the announcement anyway. Millicent was certain her private nature rendered her incapable of causing a public scene; once the news was abroad, that same nature would keep her from canceling the nuptials and bringing down public scandal on one and all.

Millicent didn't know her quite so well as she thought. Her mother could make all the announcements she wanted; this time Jayne would go about making her own arrangements for her life and when everything was set—possibly when she was on her way to the dock—then the final, legitimate announcement concerning her intentions would be made. By the one person who ought to make it, Jayne Catherine Worthington herself.

"Ah, dearest Millicent, fetching as usual. You make me proud."

Both women turned toward Randolph Forbes, who was emerging from the crowd to join them just inside the ballroom doorway. A tall and portly man of fifty-five, balding, his complexion ruddy, Forbes had always struck Jayne as a man of great vigor. The appreciative look he gave to the low cut of his wife's gown confirmed her opinion.

Dressed far more handsomely than his nephew, and slightly more subdued, Forbes was clad in a dress coat of light blue silk, white ruffled shirt, and black breeches, tightly fitted and extending over his highly polished black boots. Despite his portliness, he wore the ensemble well. A successful man in all endeavors was Uncle Randolph and apparently healthy as well, since he'd already survived longer than any of Millicent's husbands save Jonathan Worthington.

Philanderer or no, Jayne didn't like him. Too often she'd heard him gloating over a business arrangement that enriched his coffers while it destituted some poor unfortunate who'd been represented by an attorney of lesser accomplishments. Or, she'd suspected more than once, by an attorney who accepted clandestine remuneration from one Randolph Forbes for allowing the latter to have his way.

Ruthless and cold, that was Uncle Randolph. Not once had he encouraged her in her search for news of Josh. More often than not he had little knowledge and less concern about anything having to do with his younger stepdaughter; it was the older offspring who drew his eye. Marybeth flirted with him with only slightly less enthusiasm than she did the rest of upper class New York. Millicent never seemed to mind, and neither did Marybeth's spouse.

"Dearest Jayne, you're looking fetching this evening."

It took Jayne a moment to realize her stepfather was addressing her.

"I am?" she asked.

"How droll you are. Leander will so enjoy your wit."

As much as my wealth? Jayne almost said the words aloud but her mother was right. She did hate a public scene.

The minuet ended, and as the music faded the dancers scattered away from the center of the floor, their chatter filling the ballroom. But not loudly enough to drown out sister Marybeth's high-pitched laugh coming from somewhere in the crowd.

The laughter increased in volume and Jayne thought she saw a tightening of her mother's lips. The tightening gave way almost immediately to a smile as Marybeth joined the family gathering.

"I do so wish William were here and not taking care of that boring old business in Boston," Marybeth said, pouting prettily.

It seemed to Jayne her brother-in-law was frequently called out of town.

Leander, resplendent in lavender and moving in a mist of cloying cologne, sidled up and before she could stop him, planted a wet kiss on the back of her hand.

"Dear Miss Worthington," he said, stroking her fingers as he held them close to a lavender lapel. Despite her fervent tugging, he managed to kiss her hand once again. "Dear Jayne."

Jayne hadn't been *deared* so much since before Granny Worth passed away. Nothing like a little money in the bank, she thought wryly, to bring out a woman's charms.

"Ah, all of us together," said Millicent with a sigh. "With the exception of William, of course. What a wonderful family we are."

Jayne managed to keep from rolling her eyes.

"We're drawing quite a lot of attention," Millicent went on, casting a bright-eyed look around the ballroom. "Randolph, I really think there's no reason to postpone the announcement. Jayne is of course naturally shy. Please, my darling, don't launch into a tedious speech. Not that you ever could, of course, but we don't want to frighten my dear daughter with too many words of praise."

Jayne bit the inside of her cheek to keep from bursting into laughter. Or perhaps she was trying to stave off tears. Everyone within hearing distance would know the truth behind the betrothal—that financial considerations, not love, was the motivating force.

What was it to her anyway since the whole thing was a sham? She held herself stiffly, at last managing to free her hand, and watched as her stepfather made his way to the music stand at the side of the room. With one gesture he roused the relaxing musicians to a modest fanfare. The crowd quietened.

"Friends, please get yourselves the libation of your choice, for we have a toast to make on this happy night."

The crowd tittered as the servants passed among them with trays of wine and ale for the gentlemen and for the ladies a fruit concoction that Jayne had always suspected was laced with whiskey, one of her mother's methods for keeping her soirées lively.

"Mrs. Forbes and I—" Forbes paused until he had complete silence. "Mrs. Forbes and I," he repeated, "take great pleasure in announcing the upcoming nuptials of her daughter Jayne and my nephew Leander."

The news was met with more than a few gasps and knowing nods. "Hear, hear," someone in the crowd remarked. "To Leander and Jayne."

The would-be bride stared into her cup of punch, hoped silently that she was right about the whiskey, and downed the drink in one swallow, gesturing right away for another.

With whisperings about the hall and shouts of congratulation, she was just about to begin on her second toast when a commotion in the foyer behind her stilled the progress of the cup halfway to her lips.

"A wedding is it t' be, and not an ocean voyage?"

She turned in amazement to the booming Scottish voice. Captain Andrew MacGregor, unshaven and his mane of black hair in disarray, his powerful body clad in a white linen shirt and tight brown breeches tucked into a pair of calf-high boots, stood not six feet away, a glint of mocking scorn lighting his sea-blue eyes.

Chapter Five

For a moment, no one spoke, and the intruder's words hung in the air, backed by a chorus of rustling as the ballroom guests shifted to get a better view of the proceedings.

They could have broken into a welcoming song and Jayne would not have known since she could hear nothing but the pounding of her heart . . . could see nothing but Andrew MacGregor, who stood in the foyer like a colossus, legs spread, arms at his sides, the Forbes' frail and ancient butler tugging like a tenacious moth at the sleeve of his shirt.

One step took her from the edge of the ballroom into the entryway, drawing her nearer to the captain the way a compass needle edged to north. Andrew's eyes boldly locked with hers, and a familiar, unseen fist pounded into her abdomen.

His lips twitched into the hint of a smile, and his stare retained the hint of mockery. "I dinna expect to see you here, Miss Worthington."

Jayne found her voice, if not the power to draw a deep breath. "Nor I you, captain." A sudden anger prompted her to add, "I thought our acquaintance was ended clearly enough the other night. Or so I hoped."

Dizzy from his efforts to serve as sentinel, the butler released the intruder's shirtsleeve. "I couldn't stop him, Mrs. Forbes," he said, whining. "Like a beast he was, throwing open the door and demanding to see Mr. Forbes."

Millicent flicked her eyes to the butler, then returned immediately to the "beast." The magnificent beast, she amended, all six feet and more of him, and she wondered how long it would take to count the hairs in the opening at his throat. He looked deliciously wrong standing on the polished marble floor of her pink-walled foyer, a high and brilliant chandelier casting flickering light on the unruly mass of midnight black hair that fell to his broad shoulders and on the bronzed and bristled planes of his face.

And something else was wrong . . . he seemed to be an acquaintance of her mousy younger daughter. She glanced at Jayne with puzzlement and, she admitted grudgingly as she stepped beside her, a touch of rare respect.

"You know this man?"

Jayne was uncertain how to respond. She could identify him, yes, but know him? No more than she knew the sun, though she could call it by name. What she could *not* give a name to was the tumult he had started within her simply by charging like a bull into her home. He was nothing to her. She had disliked him intensely and she had thought never to see him again.

"See here," boomed the forgotten Randolph Forbes, who had made his way through the ballroom crowd to stand behind Jayne's left ear. She jumped at the unexpected roar, but he continued in the same thunderous tone. "What's this commotion about?"

"It would seem we have a late arriving guest," said Millicent.

It was Randolph's turn to stare at the imposing, roughly clad figure that filled the foyer. He tugged at the front of his blue silk coat and held himself tall. "This is a private gathering, sir. You've come to the wrong address."

Andrew's eyes slowly left Jayne and focused on the portly figure behind her. The hint of a smile on his lips turned to open scorn.

"If you're Randolph Forbes, there's no mistake. I'm Andrew MacGregor, captain of the *Trossachs,* and we've business to discuss." His voice rolled out of his broad chest, deeper and richer in pitch than the attorney's, and what it lacked in volume it more than made up in steely strength.

Forbes was exactly as Andrew had imagined he would be—fine clothes and a proud lift to his head, but, despite the erectness of his bearing, unmistakable evidence of muscles turned to paunch. His hands would be clean and soft, without a doubt, and his cunning eyes adept at hiding an equally cunning soul.

Andrew scanned the small gathering in the doorway—the older woman with the pile of red curls and the lowcut gown and the glint in her eye, and the younger woman with the paler red hair but an equally challenging dress and an equally interested eye. Then there was the fop in lavender, who stood well behind Jayne Worthington, a protective—or was it nervous?—hand on her shoulder.

Could this be the fiancé he'd heard announced just

as he was coming through the door? The woman who'd braved a tavern full of drunken sailors, who'd boldly laid out a plan for sailing the ocean all the way to Bashaw Yusuf Karamanli's door, who'd taken his insults without a flinch and thrown back a few of her own — that woman would surely never settle for a peacock who looked like a bowl of fruited cream.

Andrew caught himself. There was little telling what any woman would do.

"Cyrus Byrd warned me about you," said Randolph. "I thought you were safely locked away in jail."

"Jail!" said Millicent, outwardly shocked but inwardly calculating whether the excitement that the man's presence aroused was worth a possible scandal.

"Jail," whispered Marybeth, licking her lips and calculating only what it would feel like to get her hands in that unruly head of hair.

"You'll be back there soon enough if you don't clear out," added Randolph.

It was the watchful Jayne whose silence seemed to speak louder than the bombastic attorney. Curious creature she was, Andrew thought, standing tall and straight, her neck long as a swan's, her slender body scarcely filling out her ugly gown. Somehow she held his attention over the prettier pigeons fluttering nearby.

"The jail's not made that'll hold Andrew MacGregor for long," he said to her.

Nor the woman created to stay him from his course, he reminded himself as he looked once again at Forbes. "As to your client's warning, 'tis I who should have been warned about him. A peril to honest working men, he is. And," he added with a menacing edge to his voice, "so are those who advise him."

The mutterings of the crowd in the ballroom grew louder, and more than one man offered the suggestion that Forbes throw the man out on his ear. No one, however, offered to help.

Jayne wasn't surprised. Her eyes drifted down from the captain's unkempt mane of hair, to the bristle-shadowed face, to the wide shoulders and expanse of hirsute chest visible in the opening of his shirt, to the narrow waist and flat abdomen, to the fit of his tight breeches around his manhood, to the powerful thighs and the long, strong calves that disappeared into a pair of tall black boots.

He'd been imposing enough seated behind a table in the tavern; standing a few feet away in the supposed sanctity of her home, he was overwhelming.

She'd thought Randolph Forbes handsomely and, despite his unpleasant nature, gentlemanly attired, but compared to Captain MacGregor, who was in no way a gentleman, he looked as effeminate as a girl.

As did every other man in the house. Her inclination ought to be revulsion at the sight of him, or at least a retention of the momentary anger she'd felt when he first walked in. He'd insulted and scoffed her, hadn't he? So why did she find herself fascinated by the sound of his voice and the feral aura of his presence?

"I'll not leave," said Andrew, his watchful eyes still on Randolph, "until I've seen justice done."

Randolph believed him, assuring himself at the same time not to be overly concerned. He'd dealt before with brutes like MacGregor—well, maybe not

69

exactly like MacGregor, but close enough. Cyrus Byrd was a greedy bastard. Randolph had counseled against paying such a paltry sum for the captain's quality cargo, and he'd told him it was a mistake to have thrown him in jail on what might easily prove to be foundless charges.

"You've seen the ruined poker. He's nothing but a Scottish savage," Byrd had replied in his office only this morning. "And I've no doubt he's a fool, too, taking partial payment the way he did."

Savage, yes, Randolph thought as he took the man's measure. But something about the look in his eye said he was little like a fool. It ought to be Cyrus facing the heat of Scottish ire. Mentally raising the fee he'd charge the importer, Randolph waved toward the parlor door. "We can talk in there."

"Perhaps I should join you," said Millicent, her eyes trained on the captain.

"Me, too," said Marybeth.

Jayne kept silent, as did Leander, whose hand she had removed from her shoulder.

"I won't be long," snapped Randolph. "See to your guests, Millicent. Start the dancing again."

Andrew followed him into the dimly lit room that opened off the foyer. His eyes quickly picked out the scattering of furniture, the Duncan Phyfe sofa and matching chairs, the carved chest, the tall case clock, the Persian carpet, the shell-shaped cabinet in a side corner . . . all expensive, he knew, since he'd been importing and exporting such goods over the years.

Randolph faced him in the center of the parlor. "How did you get out of jail?"

Andrew scratched at the growth of beard on his unshaven cheek. "I'd like to say 'twas American justice at its finest that recognized a false charge and a false imprisonment. In truth, I knew the sergeant on duty. When we were both no more than lads, we sailed together in the Orient."

"He let you go?" asked Randolph sharply.

"Aye. After confining me these past three days and after I paid a substantial fee for the rent of a cell, which I must tell you is greatly overpriced. It'll take three weeks of ocean air to cleanse the stench from my nostrils."

"How did you find me?" asked Randolph, then waved an impatient hand. "Oh, never mind. My residence is no secret, I suppose."

"No more than is the reason I'm here," countered Andrew. "A matter of justice, as I said, and of a payment overdue."

"Or so you claim."

Randolph studied the mariner for a moment, weighing the wisdom of scoffing at his demands. The lawyer preferred his confrontations in a court of law, not in his home before a roomful of friends, and absolutely never with someone like MacGregor, whose size and strength were exceeded only by his boldness. Damn that Cyrus Byrd. Tonight's intrusion would be the talk of New York by morning.

Accepting the inevitable, he strode to a drop-leaf desk on the wall behind the sofa and scribbled a sum of money on a piece of paper.

"Here," he said, thrusting the paper in Andrew's direction. "This ought to satisfy you."

Andrew eased around the sofa and read the amount. "Double it, and 'tis settled."

"Impossible."

Andrew named another New York barrister.

71

"You've heard of him, I'll be bound. I'm thinking of using Cyrus Byrd's example and hiring my own personal minion."

"See here, MacGregor, are you threatening me with court action?"

" 'Tis not a threat, Mr. Forbes, but a strategy. A little sauce for the goose, as they say."

The two men eyed one another for a moment.

Randolph let out a long, slow breath. "With Cyrus it was the poker, with me a bothersome court suit. You tailor your strategy, as you put it, to your opponent, I see. Cyrus was most certainly wrong, Captain MacGregor. You are not a fool. I'll see that the money is delivered from my client's account first thing in the morning."

"I'm glad you're a man of reason, Mr. Forbes."

Andrew waited for the attorney to extend a hand as a seal to the agreement, but Randolph's arms stayed close to his sides. Just as well, Andrew thought. He'd have to count his fingers after a handshake with a Yankee lawyer.

"First thing in the morning," he said with a nod, backing away. "I'll be waiting aboard ship." He was already gripping the doorknob when a thought occurred to him.

"The lass. Miss Worthington. What's she to you?"

"My stepdaughter," answered Randolph, a wary look in his eye as he belatedly remembered that the mariner and she had seemed to know one another.

"And the woman in blue, would that by any chance be the lass's mother?"

At Randolph's nod, he added, "And the other—" He caught himself; he'd almost said the other hungry one.

"You must mean Marybeth. She's Jayne's sister. Half sister, actually. But they are no concern of yours."

Andrew persisted. "And the purple peacock?"

"I assume you are referring to my nephew."

"Miss Worthington's betrothed, I've no doubt." Andrew shook his head. "Seems a waste."

"See here," Randolph puffed, "that's no concern of yours." His eyes narrowed. "At least I assume it isn't. The girl's a strange one. She's not been up to mischief, has she?"

What a slimy son of a cur, thought Andrew, and he goaded him with a suggestive grin. "Depends on the kind of mischief you had in mind."

Andrew would have bet the morrow's money that the attorney was thinking naught of an ocean voyage to Tripoli.

"I'll not have the girl—"

And neither will I, thought Andrew as he dismissed the balance of Forbes' diatribe against his stepdaughter. The thought disturbed, although Andrew had no idea why he would want to possess a scrawny, purse-lipped lass with a tongue ready to take a man to task instead of paradise.

Like most of the Yanks he'd been meeting on this stop in port, Forbes was a fool, worrying as he did about the wrong female. 'Twas the other one, the half sister, and even the mother who would more willingly join a seaman in his bunk.

By the time Forbes had finished his unheeded lecture, Andrew was out the door. He came upon Jayne standing in the middle of the foyer, her half sister and mother a half step behind. Jayne's cheeks were stained a pink he'd not noticed even in the tavern

73

when he'd proved himself a boor, the blush brought on, he suspected, by a maternal harangue.

From the ballroom came the strains of violins, but few of the guests had pulled themselves away from the ballroom door.

"See here, captain," said Millicent, stepping close. "Jayne refuses to divulge where or how she knows you. As her mother, I must insist you do so." She ignored the scowl on her husband's face. "We can talk in private if you think it wise."

Implying, regardless of who might hear, that Jayne had been up to no good.

The mother and the captain stared at one another, Millicent's green eyes lit with both a challenge and an offer, despite the difference in their years and the nearness of her spouse, and Andrew's blue eyes holding an acknowledgement of the message and a trace of icy scorn.

Millicent read his meaning, and for a moment her regard was laced with a malice that took even the hardened Andrew aback.

"Randolph, darling," she said faintly, bringing a lace handkerchief to her temple, "please give me your arm. There's been too much excitement this evening. Surely you can make this man go away."

"Millicent," said daughter Marybeth, who stepped up to take her mother's place, "you need to rest. I'll see that the captain is escorted to the street."

Like her mother, the woman's eyes held both challenge and suggestion, but she was not bright enough to read the captain's response.

A nest of vipers, that's what he had stumbled into. Except for Miss Jayne Worthington, who seemed to fit in little, either by looks or by temperament. No matter the purpose for her curious, proposed journey, she'd get fair training here for handling the bashaw's court.

He shifted his glance to her. She had a steady look to her, he gave her credit for that, and she did have truly fine eyes. Oakum had claimed to see something helpless in her, a need to be protected, although from what, his first mate had not been prepared to say.

But Andrew could, a bitter recognition knifing through him. The lass needed protection from the family that should have been ready to love and defend. They'd turn on her like a pack of animals if she got in their way—a ravenous hound in the case of the stepfather, and as for the women, they were no more than bitches in heat.

He'd never seen much value or comfort in families; he saw nothing tonight to make him change his mind.

"I'd offer you my bunk again, lass," he said, "but it's doubtful I'd get a different answer. This one"—he nodded in the sister's direction—"would be eager enough to share a captain's quarters. She'd offer comfort, I'll be bound, but not so much a challenge as yourself. And you might have noted, I'm not a man to turn away from challenge."

"Randolph," Millicent shrilled, "get this man out of my house."

The lawyer started forward.

"Another step, Mr. Forbes," said Andrew calmly, "and I'll break you in two."

Randolph hesitated.

"Really!" said Millicent, and a rush of whispers rustled over the attendant audience in the ballroom.

Marybeth edged backwards toward the sound, her expression a combination of fright and puzzlement, as though she wasn't sure whether she'd just been insulted but even if she hadn't, the captain was more man than she was ready to take on.

It was Jayne who rallied with a response that held neither threat nor fear. Head tilted high, eyes steady, she was once again the woman who'd accosted him in the riverfront tavern. If she was fearful or embarrassed, she didn't let it show.

"Captain MacGregor, you've insulted us all quite enough for one evening. Please leave."

Andrew nodded solemnly. " 'Tis the 'please' that works, Miss Worthington, although I meant you no insult. Before I go, I'll offer a word of advice, whether wanted or no. Find yourself another ship, lass, if you're determined to leave, but take care in Tripoli. 'Tis not a place you'll understand. And for God's sake, get yourself some different clothes. A dress in claret 'twould be nice."

He grinned, stepped close, and ran a rough finger along her cheek and down the slope of her throat. He felt her tremble beneath his touch, and he felt the pounding of her pulse, but he did not feel even a hint that she was about to draw away.

"Nothin' pale, you understand. Pale is for children and cowards, and you're neither one. Aye, claret, or another rich hue. 'Twould bring out the bonnie color of your skin."

A month later Jayne stood on the deck of a United States passenger ship, the hood of her wine-red cloak thrown back, her hair loose and damply flowing in the wind that came off the rolling Atlantic waves.

Overhead the full panoply of sails snapped lustily, and beneath her feet the salty wooden deck pitched and fell. With hands firmly grasping the rail, she held her position with all the grace and ability of a sailor born to the sea, a skill she credited to her years spent riding half-tamed horses over the Virginia countryside. While the rough weather and the gathering storm clouds had driven all but the crew below deck, she had joyously kept to the place she staked out her first day on board.

"Worthington's Watch," the captain had called it. The kindly, gray-haired, gently spoken captain who knew only that she was sailing to England to visit a brother. He had little knowledge of just how far she would have to go after disembarking at Liverpool.

"You'll be seasick," her mother had warned. "You'll turn your stomach inside out and pray you were back on shore."

Mother was wrong. Blood singing in her veins, Jayne had never felt better in her life.

Looking into the black clouds rising against the horizon, she could still remember another storm, the one that had erupted after Andrew MacGregor's leavetaking a few busy weeks ago . . . the accusations and questions thrown at her by her family, the speculative looks of the guests, the edginess of her ersatz betrothed.

It all seemed so long ago, and yet it could have happened yesterday, the details were so clearly etched in her mind. Andrew MacGregor had taunted and embarrassed her in front of a host of family and what he would assume were friends. But she'd held her own against him when everyone else had by turns flirted and argued and quavered with righteous indignation.

And she'd held her own, too, after he'd gone and she'd been forced to explain how they met. It had taken days of discussion, but at last Millicent had agreed to her journey—more, Jayne knew, to get her surprisingly stubborn and enterprising daughter away from New York's punctilious gossips than to encourage a genuine search for her son.

"You'll find he's dead," she had said.

"At least," Jayne had countered, "I'll know the truth."

Even Randolph had acquiesced, going so far as to provide her with a letter of introduction to the consul general in Tangier. He, too, must have been eager to get her out of town.

Neither believed she would get within a mile of the bashaw of Tripoli, and they'd sent her off with warnings to that effect.

Only Alva had shed a tear; only Alva would be missed.

In a brief, stiff scene of good-bye, Leander had said he would be waiting for her return, both to New York and to sensibility. It was threat enough to send her round the world.

The tie of Jayne's cloak pulled loose in the wind and snapped against her cheek. She bound it tight. She liked the garment, one of several she'd purchased for the journey. And it wasn't actually claret, although even the salesclerk had called it such.

Cranberry, she thought. Good old American cranberry. And it did, as someone had once suggested, bring out the color of her skin. So did the rich blue of the gown it covered—a blue that matched the ocean's hue at dawn, a blue that matched a Scottish captain's eyes.

The similarity was just a coincidence, however, and not a purposeful tribute to the man. The most she could say in Andrew MacGregor's favor was that his intervention—she gave it the kindest name she could think of—had forced her into a public and immediate implementation of her plans. The cost had been a lingering of memories and the sacrifice of a concentrated mind.

Josh ought to be all she was considering, the center of her thoughts, but for a long time after MacGregor had gone she felt the abrasive stroke of his finger on her cheek and throat; for a long time she recalled the twist of his lips and the way he'd called her a challenge.

I'm not a man to turn away from challenge.

He'd been teasing her . . . Jayne Worthington, skinny spinster with the backbone to hold her ground when all around her were stepping away from his glare. He had not glared at her, choosing instead a far more destructive weapon—his brief, intimate touch. He'd known what the effect would be, and now, so did Jayne. When his hand had been close to her lips, she'd felt a sudden urge to kiss his palm.

What would he taste like? Salty, no doubt, like the sea. A sudden hollow feeling gripped her stomach; she would have liked to blame the sensation on the rolling deck, but it was the cursed memories that were at fault.

The Mediterranean, the Barbary Coast, Tripoli were all vast places. Surely their paths would not cross.

And what if they did? a nagging voice asked.

If they did, she answered right back, she would be forced to challenge him again.

Chapter Six

"What do I do now?"

Jayne's softly spoken question was meant for none but her own ears as she stood in the arched outer doorway of the United States consul general's office. Too bad, she thought, that she couldn't come up with the answer as well, but for the moment her mind was occupied with only disappointment.

What a contrast the feeling was to her hopefulness earlier in the afternoon when the ship she'd boarded in Liverpool at last reached Tangier. From the deck she'd looked down on a thousand mingling people, sailors and robed Arabs for the most part; if there was a woman in sight, she couldn't have identified her.

And the sounds drifting up from the wharf, discordant voices speaking a hundred different tongues. She'd tried to pick out the Arabic words, to reassure herself that she'd prepared herself well for the ordeal that faced her. Except for scattered phrases, she'd failed but she hadn't lost her hope.

She'd kept the feeling while the captain arranged for her transportation to the Kasbah, the ancient walled fortress in the heart of Tangier where the consulate was located. She'd even kept it during the harrowing ride in an awkward donkey cart through the narrow, twisting streets that led to her destination, which was also the highest point in the city. And after her arrival, not once had it flagged during the three-hour wait for entry to the consul general's inner sanctum on the building's second floor.

Despite all that optimism, she'd met with no greater success in a Moorish government building in Morocco than she had in the Washington brownstone where she'd confronted her President.

"You have come a great distance on a fruitless mission, Miss Worthington," the consul general had said immediately after listening to her opening remarks.

Jayne had not been disheartened by his bluntness.

"Your stepfather was most indulgent in writing this letter of introduction," he had added after she thrust Uncle Randolph's message on his desk.

Indulgent? Uncle Randolph? Jayne's lips had curved into a stiff smile.

"An audience with Bashaw Yusuf Karamanli is out of the question," the official had barked when she refused to show any sign of defeat. Jayne could have sworn he bounced a time or two in his Moroccan leather chair.

And last:

"Your brother is dead, Miss Worthington. The government of the United States of America, the entire Barbary Coast, and I am certain the rest of your family, at least those having an acquaintance with sensibility, know nothing that would contradict this fact."

He'd spoken in stentorian tones, for an instant resembling both Randolph and Leander Forbes, whereupon Jayne, refusing to present him with a chastened attitude, had risen to her feet, thanked him for his time, and whirled from his desk to make a proud, dramatic exit, her claret cloak billowing in her wake.

The pride and drama had lasted through the adjoining cubicle provided for the consul general's adjutant, and on to the outer archway where she now stood.

"What do I do now?" she asked herself again. It was a question worthy of repetition.

"Miss Worthington," a voice whispered.

She looked up and down the empty hallway of the government building, but no one appeared in any of the arched doorways that lined the walls.

"Miss Worthington."

The whisper came from the rear. She turned and saw the adjutant regarding her with great seriousness from behind his small, cluttered desk. She'd forgotten all about him as she'd come sweeping through his office. He was a brown-haired, brown-eyed man of forty, slight of build, his narrow face a slick-smooth red as though he'd lost the thin top layer of skin. Sensitive to the Moroccan sun, Jayne diagnosed, doubting he very much enjoyed his Mediterranean post.

She sought to remember his name. "Mr. Kennamer, isn't it?"

He nodded. "Ralph Kennamer, Miss Worthington. I couldn't help overhearing your conversation with the consul. Not everything, you understand," he added with a twitch of his lips and a pull at the lapels of his coat, "but the door wasn't closed completely, you see, and—"

"It's all right, Mr. Kennamer," Jayne assured him. "I understand." She hesitated, but he remained silent. "Did you want something?"

"Want something?"

"You called my name."

"Oh." His brow furrowed, then smoothed. "Why, yes I did. So much on my mind, you know. As I said, I couldn't help overhearing what you said, and then what he said . . . and I couldn't help wondering if perhaps, since the consul saw fit to turn down your request—quite rightly, I'm certain, from his point of view, you understand—well, please don't think me forward, but would you be in need of a place to stay tonight?"

A nervous man was Ralph Kennamer, Jayne thought, but not unkind. Or was he?

"Where did you have in mind, Mr. Kennamer?"

His blush performed the extraordinary feat of making a red face redder. "There are quarters here in the consulate. For visitors. I'm sure the consul general would have offered them to you had you not left . . . well, you must admit, a bit precipitously."

Doubts of the adjutant's intentions brought a flush of embarrassment to Jayne's cheeks. Unlike his superior, Ralph Kennamer was trying to be helpful. In her defense, she remembered that the last man who offered her sleeping arrangements had not planned for her to sleep alone.

More realistically, she admitted that the first offer had been nothing more than a crude taunt.

"They're not quarters, exactly," Kennamer said, "just one room on the floor above, small, really, and I'm sure not at all what you're used to."

She smiled to show her thanks. "I've been aboard one ship or another for almost three months, Mr. Kennamer, grateful for accommodations that wouldn't serve a large dog. I loved the sea, I truly did, but the thought of lying in a bed that doesn't swoop and sway—" A thought struck her. "This room *does* have a bed, doesn't it? I mean, Moroccans don't use hammocks, or any such thing, do they?"

"Oh, it's got a bed all right. Not so grand as you're used to back in New York. Forgive me, I couldn't help overhearing that's where your stepfather lives."

Jayne decided there was nothing the adjutant had not overheard, but she didn't mind. Her quest hadn't been a private matter since the moment Andrew MacGregor invaded the Forbes' New York home.

Learning that she had left her one piece of baggage downstairs with the Naval officer who served as sentry, Kennamer assured her—in at least a thousand words—that he would have her belongings brought upstairs, then escorted her up a stairway as narrow and winding as the streets of the Kasbah.

She thanked him profusely, closed the door, and welcomed the silence and privacy as she would a cool drink of water. Quickly she removed her cloak and tossed it on the bed. The woolen garment was too heavy for the September weather in Tangier, but it was the only thing she owned that came close to resembling the robes of Moroccan women. The hood had substituted as a veil.

The first thing that caught her eye was an open doorway leading to a small balcony, large enough for two people to stand. She hurried to the open air, leaned against the waist-high barrier, and was gifted with one of the most beautiful sights she had ever seen: to the right the tile-roofed, terraced buildings of Tangier, leading down from the highly situated Kasbah and crowded together so that nothing of the narrow streets, nor of the refuse that cluttered them, was visible; to the left the ornate minaret of an old mosque rising from another expanse of flat, tiled roofs; and over it all mystical shapes of shadow that were right out of a child's fairy tale.

Straight ahead lay a curved strip of white sandy beach ending in an expanse of water part Atlantic Ocean, part Mediterranean Sea, and all of it glistening with the reflection of the setting sun.

No one—not even Uncle Randolph—could be dour or downhearted in the midst of such exotic beauty. She soaked in the radiance, letting the ocean breeze play with a few unbound tendrils of hair that danced about her face, closing her eyes to listen to the rhythmic beat and mournful melody of a song being played on a lute somewhere down below. The cadence matched the flow of her life's blood, and a smile found its tentative way to her face.

A knock at the door brought her reluctantly indoors. It was a servant of the consulate, a Moroccan in loose-fitting shirt and trousers, who brought her the lone valise she had allowed herself for her journey. If he was surprised at the sight of a Christian woman in Western garb thanking him in Arabic for his efforts, he did not let it show.

Setting the valise aside, Jayne turned her attention to her quarters. The room was small, just as the adjutant had warned, but it was large enough for a small bed with a carved-wood head and foot, a companion leather-bottom chair, and a two-drawer dresser, above which hung a looking glass framed in scrolled brass. Like the doorways, the frame was arched; like the rest of the consulate, the walls were chiseled stone; like all of Tangier, the air was perfumed with unfamiliar spices and incense and the comfortably familiar tang of the nearby sea.

Her eye fell to the thick wool carpet that covered most of the tile floor. Impulse drove her to kneel and bury her fingers in the multi-colored pile. A work of art, she thought, studying the intricate patterns of wool loops. As she looked around the room she realized that she felt far more comfortable in its environs than she ever had in Vandam Street.

Maybe it was because everything had a unity and a purpose. Just like Jayne herself . . . now. No matter what happened tonight or tomorrow or the day after, she would be actively pursuing a cause that for years had weighed heavily upon her heart. If she met with rejection — a highly likely event since she'd already done just that her first day on the Barbary Coast — she would not have to listen to a chorus of "I told you so" from the people who should be most supportive of that cause.

Unbuttoning the collar of her blue gown, and then another button, and another, much as she had unfastened the shackles of a faultfinding family, she sat and gave in to another impulse. Quickly she pulled off stockings and shoes. With skirt and petticoat pulled to her bent knees, she planted her feet apart and wiggled her toes in the rug, weight braced against her elbows, eyes closed, her head lolled backwards against her shoulders so that the top of her head almost touched the floor.

A silly thought struck her. With both back and neck arched in imitation of the doors and looking glass frame, she truly did match the unity of the room. The sweet-smelling room. The salty-air room.

Jayne sniffed. The *very* salty-air room, with definite overtones of . . .

Slowly she raised her head and forced her eyes open, telling herself she was imagining something that absolutely could not be. A shadow fell across the carpet. She looked toward the balcony. The doorway was blocked by the silhouette of a man, his features hidden but not his height nor width. Recognition froze her in place.

"Well, lass, I see you took the ocean voyage instead o' the husband. The choice suits you well."

The deep voice with its trace of a Scottish burr stirred her from shock, and she saw herself as the captain must see her—ankles and calves exposed, dress unbuttoned halfway to her waist, her body lounging in sensual enjoyment against a Moroccan rug . . . as though she were offering herself to whoever might stroll in a third-floor balcony door.

Swallowing hard, she scrambled to her feet, nervous fingers working at her hair, then shifting to the opening in her gown.

A hurried and inept attempt to refasten the buttons brought a laugh—a sobering sound—from the doorway, and she curled her hands into fists at her side.

"Captain MacGregor, do you ever wait to be asked into someone's home? And how in the world did you get up here?"

"One question at a time, Miss Worthington. I wait when there's a possibility of an invitation. And I scaled the wall. No special feat. I've clambered through storm-tossed rigging many a time, and there are footholds in the broken stone."

He sounded so reasonable, as though by exhibiting distress she were the one behaving in an extraordinary manner. Jayne sighed in exasperation. "Which doesn't explain *why* you're here."

Why, indeed. This time Andrew had no ready comeback. He'd taken care of his business at the consulate—delivery of a box of Scottish snuff for the consul general—had chanced to glance up when he was out the door, and had seen a sight that shook him: Miss Jayne Worthington, Yankee spinster and, for all her spirit, tight-lipped prude, standing high above the Kasbah, an ocean breeze ruffling her hair, a smile of pleasure playing at her parted mouth.

When she'd retreated inside, he'd been enticed to follow, thinking there was, perhaps, more to Miss Jayne than he had supposed.

"Captain MacGregor!" Her voice snapped him from his musing. "I must ask you to leave."

And then again, he reconsidered, mayhap not so much. But he couldn't forget the image of her standing on the balcony, or, more surprising, the picture she'd presented as she lay upon the rug. She might be too thin for his tastes, but she had a trim ankle and a nicely curved calf, and the open throat of her gown had revealed a gentle rise of breast he would not have expected.

He stepped farther into the room and came to halt in front of her. Fine eyes she had, wide and deep and dark; at least he'd remembered those right. And there was that tiny scar at the edge of her temple, an unusual beauty mark for a woman. In Jayne Worthington's case, it didn't make her exactly beautiful but it did add a note of mystery to her face.

"If you're concerned about the proprieties, don't worry," he said, leaning close enough to pick up the scent of gardenias on her tawny skin. "I stayed in the shadows on the journey up the wall. No one knows I'm here."

His blue eyes glinted, and Jayne's stomach twisted.

"That does not reassure me in the least," she snapped. "You could have your way with me and then scamper down the wall, like the lizard you're beginning to resemble, and who would be the wiser?"

Andrew grinned. "The two of us, wouldna you say, since we'd have the knowledge of each other."

Jayne swallowed, for a moment imagining just what a knowledge of the captain's powerful body would include. She knew much of it anyway, just from a quick glance at the open shirt and tight

90

breeches that he wore. His grin broadened, and she looked away.

"This is most improper." Her cheeks burned.

" 'Tis an argument that sinks of its own weighty inconsistencies, lass. Most improper it is for a single woman of your situation and background to be here in an Islamic country unescorted and on a mission of some mystery."

"It's not a mystery. Not since you barreled your way into my home."

"And it was afore that?" Andrew pondered her words for only a moment. "Ah, I ken wha' you say. The loving family did not know of your traveling plans until I made mention of them."

"I was going to tell them in my own good time."

"And do they know why you're here?"

"Of course they know. I have their blessing." Well, sort of, she thought, as much blessing as her actions ever got.

She said no more, and Andrew waited patiently for her to continue, his dark gaze resting on her slender face.

Stirring nervously, Jayne took a step backwards. "If you absolutely must know, I'm looking for my brother."

"Has someone misplaced the lad?"

"You speak in jest, captain, but as a matter of fact, I believe that someone has. Specifically, the bashaw of Tripoli."

Andrew scratched his head. "Must be the spar that caught me just above the ear last week. I can't be hearing right."

"I should imagine your head is hard enough to bear most any blow."

Andrew nodded admiringly. "I'll give you this much, lass. You're not one to simper or run from a fight."

"I'm not afraid of you, if that's what you mean."

"E'en though you know I could, as you said, have my way with you. From thigh to boot, one leg o' mine would match your weight."

"Your thighs are the farthest thing from my mind, Captain MacGregor," said Jayne.

"Pity," said Andrew. "I've been considering yours. Especially since you displayed such an interesting curve of calf."

"Oh! I thought we were having a serious conversation."

"I'm always serious about a woman's legs, Miss Worthington."

"And little else, save your own predicaments. You were serious enough in your threats to Uncle Randolph, as I recall."

She turned from him, and Andrew observed the stiffness of her shoulders, the proud tilt of her head. He didn't much care for the thick knot of hair that rested above the collar of her gown, but he did like the smooth expanse of neck it revealed.

He shook his head. There he went again, thinking of the woman's physical traits when she shouldn't be offering any interest to him at all. He wasn't interested in particular women, even the voluptuous ones, just the particular pleasures they offered to share.

Miss Worthington was neither voluptuous nor sharing, but then that was her right. Andrew was strong on an individual's rights. And she did have a point; he'd grown used to considering only himself.

"I apologize," he said. " 'Tis your brother we should be discussing and not . . ." He caught himself. No need to bring up body parts again. " 'Tis just that you keep catching me by surprise, and there's few in the world can manage that feat."

Jayne waited a minute to speak, waited for another insult or another innuendo to be thrown at her back, but when she was met with only silence, she found herself wanting to talk. Captain MacGregor really did sound contrite. Perhaps . . . just perhaps . . . he would understand. After all, he and Josh had one thing in common — they both had been drawn to the sea.

And they both, she added wryly, liked to tease her unmercifully. She knew full well the captain wasn't interested in her as a woman. She was a curiosity, nothing more, and for that reason he might find her situation of more than passing interest. Besides, she had no one else to talk to, and for all her independent pride, she knew she couldn't *always* handle matters alone.

She made the telling brief, omitting the early years, dwelling on Josh's departure and disappearance, on her letters and their inadequate answers, even her disappointing interviews in Washington and Tangier.

"I admit all the evidence points to his drowning. All except a body washed ashore. I've read about the Tripoli harbor. It's shallow in places and the tides are tricky, but eventually Josh would have been found."

Andrew had difficulty keeping a sympathetic expression on his face. The lass was daft if she believed that after all these years her precious brother would be found alive.

"And there's one other thing," she said. "I don't know if you have a family or not, captain—"

"There's naught but myself."

The sharpness in his words took her aback.

"I'm sorry."

" 'Tis nothing I regret."

"Our experiences have been different. Josh and I were very close. I'd know if he had died."

Andrew lost his patience. "A fanciful idea," he snapped.

"Not at all," Jayne snapped right back. "There are some things in this world, Captain MacGregor, that are more real than what we can touch."

"Touching's all I ask. A woman . . . a ship." A fleet of ships, he could have said, for he, too, had a dream. But his was for something more substantial than a brother who, if he *were* alive, had not bothered to reach his sister the way she had tried to reach him.

Jayne twisted her hands at her waist. "I should have known you wouldn't understand."

"And what do you plan to do now?" he asked. He shouldn't have cared since he had no plans nor desires to involve himself in her absurd predicament. And yet, he wanted to know.

Jayne suddenly saw the answer to the same question she'd been asking herself. "What I should have done in the first place. Instead of bothering with the consul general, asking him to write the consul in Tripoli, who would in turn get me an audience with the bashaw, I should have gone directly to the bashaw himself."

The skeptical light in his eye drove her on. "You can make yourself useful, instead of badgering me all the time. If your route takes you along the African coast, then you can provide my passage."

Miss Worthington was as spirited as she was demented, Andrew thought. And a little slow to learn her lessons. Had she so completely forgotten his offer in Washington Tavern? If so, he'd have to remind her in a way she wouldn't forget.

Purposefully he let his gaze roam over her face, the slope of her neck, the smooth, tawny skin beneath the hollow of her throat. The dress, a handsome blue, fitted nicely against her slender frame—still too thin, he had to remind himself—and he liked the pink toes peeking out from beneath the hem. They gave her an unexpectedly wanton look.

Once again his eyes met hers. "It's possible arrangements can be made, Miss Worthington, although it's time I called you Jayne, is it not? Since we're about to negotiate the fee."

Chapter Seven

"Fee?"

Jayne tried to sound innocent, but she knew exactly what MacGregor referred to. Ignoring the slight lift of the captain's thick black brows, she persevered. "I'll pay whatever you charge to store a barrel on the deck, since that's where I plan to stay. Plus, of course, whatever meals are required."

"A barrel, you say." Andrew took another slow survey of her. "You've got more than the height, 'tis certain, but you haven't the girth. I couldna charge half so much."

Jayne narrowed her eyes, not at all complimented. "How honest of you."

"If, I was going to add, it was money to be bartered. You know, lass, something far more valuable is at stake."

He was standing very close now, all dark and rock hard and immovable, and Jayne couldn't draw a breath that wasn't filled with the scent of him. He was teasing her—they both knew it—so why did she let him set her insides to churning? What she ought to do was tease him right back, call his hand the way a card player called a bluff, force him to admit he hadn't the least desire for intimacy with her.

As bold as she was, she hadn't quite that much nerve. Besides, she didn't know how to flirt.

"We've had this conversation before, Captain MacGregor," she said, her line of sight trained just past his broad left shoulder and the coarse black hair that brushed against his shirt. "Surely you remember my answer."

"You had more options then. 'Tis possible you might have changed your mind."

"You'd take advantage of a woman on a shore far from home?"

His eyes glinted dangerously. "Aye."

"You're a cad, captain."

"And since when is a woman not beguiled by such?"

"When the woman is me." *I'm not my mother, nor my sister,* she could have added, but she decided he had figured that out back in New York.

"Proud words, Jayne." He edged even nearer, until their breaths mingled, and his gaze was pinned to her parted lips. "I'm thinking a sampling would be a good thing. To make sure, you ken, we'd not be making a mistake."

"I don't know what you mean," Jayne managed, wondering if maybe she shouldn't take hold of his shoulders to help bolster her wavery knees. He was just so big . . . so overpowering . . . and his lips were so very close.

"Have you never been kissed, lass?"

She swallowed. "Of course." Once, long ago, by a neighboring boy . . . on the cheek.

"And did you not like it? If you're thinking it

was enough, you need to try it again."

His lips softly touched hers. Jayne felt as though she'd been struck by a lightning bolt. She couldn't move, couldn't breathe, her entire being concentrated on their fragile joining. Fragile, perhaps, but strong enough, it seemed, to withstand the fiercest storm . . . or the passing of eternity. She couldn't imagine moving away, for to do so would end the rush of warmth and light that had overtaken all her senses.

To kiss her lightly, briefly, was all Andrew had meant to do . . . to tease her, to take the defiant glint out of her eye. But she had a soft feel to her, and a sweetness he hadn't expected. He repeated the touch, this time with his hands resting on her shoulders. He slanted the kiss, moving his mouth seductively against her unresisting lips, feeling the tension in her body where his fingers touched, and then the hint of release, the slight movement forward that in a more wanton woman would have been equal to tearing off her clothes.

His hands moved upward until he was cradling her face, his fingers tickled by loose tendrils of fine black hair, his loins tingling with the message he was getting from her mouth.

As his kiss deepened, Jayne found herself curling against him, like a fresh-picked flower brought too close to a flame. When his tongue found hers, its rough tip tantalizing her with suggestions she didn't understand, she had to grasp the folds of his shirt to remain upright. Through the linen she could feel his heat, and she wondered just how hot his skin would be, how slick, how hard, how different from hers.

His hands, large and strong enough to crush her, were gentle against her face; it was his mouth that seared . . . his tongue that tormented. She was trapped by his heat and by his power, and the worst thing was, she was absolutely thrilled.

The madness of desire took hold of Andrew, as intense as it was unexpected. He grasped at sanity and thrust her away, but he could not bring himself to break their bond completely by loosening his hold on her shoulders. She stood still as a porcelain figurine, raised eyes both bright and bewildered, full lips made fuller by his assault. Her fingers clutched tighter at his shirt, and the delicate scar seemed to throb at her temple.

Andrew's desire became disgust. Did she realize how close she came to being taken with brutal thoroughness on a Moroccan rug? God help her, it was only her first day in port. If this was the way she was going to behave, she would never survive.

And damned if he knew why he cared. Climbing onto her balcony had been an impulsive act, initiated more from surprise at spying her in the middle of the Kasbah than from an urge to see to her welfare.

And, too, Andrew was not above a little showing off.

"You've little protection against the world, have you?" he asked, his arms dropping away from her. "Or maybe you're not so innocent as you seem."

He spoke harshly. She needed harshness now, the fool.

The strategy worked. The brightness and the bewilderment died, replaced by glinty rage.

She slapped him, and she enjoyed the sting of

her hand against his face as much as she'd welcomed the touch of his lips.

"You bastard," she hissed.

Unexpectedly, he felt a surge of rage that matched her own. "Aye," he said, curling the word out as he might a whip. He rubbed at his face. "A bastard who prefers a pliable woman. One who knows how to please a man and how to take some pleasure for her own."

Jayne shouldn't have been hurt, no more than she should have weakened the moment he touched her, but his words cut her like a knife.

And she shouldn't goad him further, but she could no more be silent than she could have swum the ocean just as she once threatened to do.

"I thought you wanted a challenge. That's what you told me in New York."

"A challenge, aye, but only when the lass possesses that which I'd call a reward."

Jayne gasped. She knew she was not what men wanted in a woman, but she had never heard it expressed so overtly, and by a man who had just tasted the sweetness she had to give.

She didn't understand his anger nor his insults. She'd done nothing but return his kiss. Her first taste of desire, so sweet only moments ago, turned bitter on her lips.

"Please leave," she managed. "I can protect myself far better than you think. Especially from a bastard like you."

A savage light lit his hooded eyes. " 'Tis a word you've grown fond of." Coming from his tight lips, the observation sounded menacing.

"Only because I've been inspired. The first time

we met I knew you were not a gentleman, but I didn't know just how low you were. All I ask is that in the future you leave me alone. If you see me drowning, pass me by."

His coldness sucked all the warmth from the room.

"My pleasure, Miss Worthington. If I do indeed see you drowning, I promise to sail right on by as you sink beneath the waves."

"Damn, damn, damn!"

Andrew slammed shut the drawer of his cabin desk.

"Oakum!" he shouted.

The door creaked open to admit his first mate. Oakum shuffled into the room, hitched his breeches, and took a thoughtful look at the master of his ship, who was standing hunched over his desk, the light from the brass lamp at his elbow casting devilish shadows on his bristled face.

It didn't take a man of special cleverness to tell that trouble was afoot.

"No need t' shout, Cap'n Mac." Oakum frequently found it best to bark right back when the captain was riled, but only when the two were alone. "In case you've forgotten, me own quarters is right next door."

Andrew scowled as he rifled through the papers on the desk. "Watch your tongue, mate. I'll have no back talk from the crew." He growled the words, but they were issued more by rote than by intent to chastise.

"Aye, aye, cap'n."

Oakum's response sprang from the respect he

held for MacGregor, as well as from the knowledge it was best not to push him too far, especially when he was in one of his rare moods. Oakum hadn't seen him like this in months, as best he could recall not since that trouble back in New York.

"Someone's taken the manifest," Andrew snapped.

Oakum scratched at his beard. Cap'n Mac knew the cargo as if he'd loaded it himself, every last barrel and bale and box, so why was he needing the manifest? But it was not Oakum's duty to question Andrew MacGregor, nor his inclination to sail into the wind of the captain's stormy vexation.

"Boxer took it to the second mate," said Oakum. "I'll fetch it right away."

"Nae, don't bother." Andrew sat down heavily in his chair and ran a hand through his hair. "Can't remember now what I wanted with the blasted thing."

He glanced about the cabin—at the bunk and brassbound fitted drawers underneath and at the small box at its base, at the oil lamps suspended from the teak-paneled walls, at the wide window opened outward to the dark Tangier harbor, and last at the Moroccan rug covering much of the plank floor.

For a moment he pictured a woman sitting at his feet, a swath of blue gown pulled up to reveal curvaceous legs, her throat exposed, as well as a tempting portion of her breasts, and a look of utter contentment gracing her smiling face.

Until she'd spied him in the door. With most women, he brought out a smile; with Miss Jayne Worthington, he drove it away.

Bastard. She must have said it a dozen times. The name had rankled more than she knew, not because it was inappropriate, but because that's exactly what he was.

Oakum made for the door.

"Stay, Master Oakum," said Andrew, subdued. "I feel the need of a drink, and I'd like not to drink alone."

"I'll do me part," said Oakum with a grin, "if it's companionship ye need."

Andrew filled a pair of glasses from a decanter of claret on the desk. "I'd offer a toast, but there's nary a thing to drink to . . . except to the drink itself. Here's to wine."

"T' wine," echoed Oakum, who took his customary upright place by the window, his back braced against the wall. He was a rum and ale man, himself, but Andrew MacGregor preferred a more genteel libation. 'Twas a sign of his heritage, to the first mate's way of thinking.

They drank in silence for a moment, and Oakum watched the scowl return to the captain's face.

"I've no aim to interrupt your thoughts, Cap'n Mac, but have ye by any chance been dealin' with Yanks?"

Andrew shot him a sideways glance. "What makes you ask?"

"Because they can rile ye faster than a poorly lashed sail."

A smirk eased Andrew's scowl, but the look in his eyes remained hard. "Do you recall the lass who tried to buy passage aboard the *Trossachs?* Back in New York, it was."

"Aye," said Oakum, puzzled.

"You said she was helpless, or words to that effect."

" 'Twas how she seemed t' me."

"You misjudged Miss Worthington. She's made it all the way to Tangier. Right now she's in her country's consulate dreaming up who knows what mischief."

"Hell's fire."

"I've said a few oaths myself, mate, since I left her. Wants passage to Tripoli, still, just as she did before, so she might have an audience with Karamanli. Naturally I turned her down."

"Naturally." Oakum studied his captain carefully. MacGregor wasn't a man to let a woman disturb his peace of mind, or even linger in his thoughts once she was out of sight—or out of his bed. Oakum wasn't laying blame for the trait. Since his wife and child had died of the fever a score of years before, he'd been pretty much the same.

But Cap'n Mac was a young man. At least he was to Oakum, who at fifty had fifteen years on him. He should be thinking of marriage, of planting the seed for an heir. A son, much like Oakum's beloved Jamie—now that was a reason for owning a fleet o' ships.

Cap'n Mac saw no value in begetting heirs. Which was, to Oakum, a few compass points off from the way he ought to be headed.

"Did she say this time why she's so all powerful determined to see the bashaw?" asked Oakum.

Andrew shrugged. "That she did, though I'd as soon not know. The reason's stupid, even for a Yank." He summarized the woman's story, punctuating it regularly with shakes of his head.

104

"She must love 'er brother very much," said Oakum.

"She hasn't seen him in thirteen years."

"Hell's fire."

A silence descended between them, broken at last by Oakum. "I had a brother once. We was right close afore he went off t' some battle or other. Can't remember for the life o' me what the fightin' was about. But the lad dinna come home."

Andrew swirled the claret in the bottom of his glass and watched the lamplight catch on its blood-red surface.

"I had a brother once, too. At least my father had another son. As you can well imagine, we were not close. You know my feeling about families. They're more trouble than they're worth."

It was an observation that did not invite rebuttal.

Andrew downed the wine, then poured them each a second glass and the men drank in silence. They were halfway through their third when he spoke.

" 'Tis true, you know, Oakum."

"What's true, Cap'n Mac?"

"What she called me."

No need to ask who did the callin'. And no need to tell the captain he'd had all the wine he needed, seeing as how they'd be leaving at dawn for Algiers and he'd have a head as heavy as a barrel of lead. MacGregor could hold his liquor as well as any sailor, and that was saying a great deal, considering the success of the grogshops in every port. But a whit too much alcohol, a rare practice but not totally unknown, and he got to brooding. 'Twas no more healthy than the sickness he'd suffer on the following morn.

"Called me a bastard," said Andrew, staring into the dregs at the bottom of his glass.

"Ye've been called that afore."

"Aye, by men. And they said it only once. She saw fit to repeat the charge."

"Ye dinna hit the lass, did ye?"

"I kissed her."

Oh, ho, thought Oakum, but he spoke without so much as a hitch in his brow. "Not much in the way of punishment. Not with the way wenches take t' ye."

Andrew laughed sharply. "Miss Worthington's an exceptional woman. She resisted my charms. Told me if I ever saw her drowning, to sail right on by."

"No offense intended, cap'n," said Oakum, thinking he might take a likin' to the lass, "but were ye bothered by the name callin' or by the resistance?"

Andrew glanced up from his glass in time to see a twinkle in his first mate's eyes. He was tempted to tell the full truth—that she didn't resist right away, and it was only when he was backing away like a carp from a fisherman's hook that she came to her senses and slapped his face.

And labeled him with deadly accuracy. Andrew had grown up with the *bastard* stamp of shame. When he was no more than a lad, he'd left his Highlands village with it ringing in his ears. Which wouldn't have been so bad, except that the charge had finally been thrown at him by the one man he'd hoped would love him and would understand. The laird of the land whose word was the law throughout the county. The man who refused to acknowledge the fruit of his youthful indiscretion. Andrew's father.

He'd made his way in the world, scrambled and fought and toiled for his right to a captain's quarters. He'd earned his stature, by God, and no skinny, narrow-minded old maid was going to push him back into that shame.

But you treated her badly, a voice whispered, *and besides, she's not so skinny.*

"Did ye say somethin', Cap'n Mac?" asked Oakum.

Andrew shook off his melancholy. "Did I? Maybe so. Another drink?"

"I've too many years on these old bones to carouse half the night." Oakum rested his empty glass beside the decanter. "Ye'll pardon me, cap'n, but I've duties to tend if we're t' set sail on the morrow. Trouble is, ye see, dawn seems to come earlier wi' each passin' morn."

As the door closed behind the first mate, there was a stirring in the small box at the foot of the captain's bunk. A shadow drifted across the rug, barely noticed by Andrew. Nor did he pay much mind to the long, hairy arm, thin as a rope, that wound itself around his neck. What did draw his attention, however, were the four-inch fingers that yanked the hair at his nape.

"All right, Atlas, come aboard."

The creature scrambled into Andrew's lap, long arms lying atop long legs, frail body resting against his chest, a fifth appendage wrapped around the arm of the chair. Andrew glanced down into the small, pensive face of the spider monkey that had taken over the ship a year ago after being rescued from his abusive Arab owner in the Kasbah of Tangier. After a quick, futile check for vermin in a triangle of chest hairs close to Andrew's throat, Atlas picked at a loose hair that had fallen on his master's shirtfront, tested it with his mouth, and stared right back, the pale, triangular patch of hair on his forehead twitching over a pair of very human eyes.

Tonight Andrew had no smile for the animal, but he drew comfort from the warmth of the diminutive body as he stared into the dark outside the open window. The wail of a lonesome fog horn drifted in on a chill breeze. Atlas held to his position as Andrew poured himself another drink to toast the sound. Tonight was a night for toasting anything that spoke of the present, or even the future; he was far better off forgetting about the past.

But he couldn't get Miss Jayne Worthington out of his mind. She was, indeed, as she'd pointed out to him once, like no one he'd ever met. Except not as stand-offish as she'd like him to think. She'd been all woman in his arms, if only for a moment. And, he thought, remembering the cloak tossed carelessly on her bed, she'd taken his advice and chosen a color as rich as the wine he drank.

Ralph Kennamer, adjutant to the U.S. consul general, hefted Jayne's valise in his hand and cast a worried eye around the milling throng on the Tangier dock.

"I'm not certain this is a wise thing to do, Miss Worthington."

"Nonsense," she said from the depths of her deep hood. "I could have taken care of this myself."

Except that she was, in truth, glad he'd volunteered to accompany her on her quest. Under the best of conditions, women didn't have much standing in a Muslim country; in the midst of a hundred sailors, the only standing they had depended upon how soon they could be positioned on their back.

Had she been more her natural self, she might have handled the difficulties of the morning's task. But she'd found little sleep in her consulate bed, and for some reason her nerves were on edge in a way she'd never experienced before.

"There's a captain down this way I'm told will take passengers," Kennamer said with a wave of his hand toward a distant row of sailing ships.

Jayne's stomach knotted as she followed his gesture. Not one of the ships, she noted with a rush of relief, resembled the *Trossachs* as it had appeared in its East River berth.

"I haven't met him personally, you understand," the adjutant went on, "nor been able to get references as to his character and reliability, but the gentleman I asked on the last wharf—well, you wouldn't actually call him a gentleman, but he was able to keep a fairly civil tongue in his head—anyway, he said this captain, the one I just mentioned—"

Jayne fought against screaming. "Please, Mr. Kennamer. Did you get a name?"

"Rashid, is what the man said. Captain Something-or-Other Rashid. He's supposed to speak English, although I know you said that wasn't a requirement, since you've learned Arabic. A most unusual accomplishment, I must say."

As they wended their way through the crowd, Jayne devoted her poor store of energy to ignoring both the adjutant's ramblings and the curious stares cast toward her protective cloak and hood. Around her she heard mostly the chatter of Arabic and what sounded to her inexpert ear like Spanish and perhaps Italian. The occasional French was more easily identifiable, and of course the English she heard from time to time.

At last Kennamer halted, Jayne close beside him.

"How unfortunate," he said. "This can't possibly be the dhow the gentleman referred to. Why, it's hardly seaworthy. . . ."

He droned on about the shortcomings of the small ship and as Jayne's reluctant eyes roamed over the flaking paint on the hull, the half-rotted gangplank, the suspicious sway of the main mast in the morning wind, she had to admit he was right in his assessment.

Nor was she encouraged by the sharp-eyed, smiling man in a loose-fitting stained-white robe and trousers who came down the gangplank to greet them. A thin mustache lined his equally thin upper lip, and his head was covered with a swath of white wool no cleaner than his robe.

"I am Captain Aziz Rashid," he said in a sing-song voice. "May I be of service on this Allah-blessed morning?"

His smile broadened when Kennamer explained what he wanted, and a gold incisor flashed between a row of mottled, jagged teeth.

"Missy Lady," he said with a nod to Jayne, "you

would honor us with your presence aboard my un-worthy ship."

"I don't know —" Kennamer began.

Before he could launch into the thousand things he didn't know, Jayne cut him off with a sharp, "Mr. Kennamer!"

"Yes?" he asked, apparently unabashed, as though he was used to being interrupted.

"Let me talk to the captain, please." Jayne's head throbbed with each word she spoke. "It is, after all, my journey we are trying to arrange."

Whereupon she proceeded to ascertain — in halting Arabic as much to shut out further advice as to practice her use of the language — what kind of quarters would be available, what would be the exact charge, would she be assured of privacy, would the captain be able to advise her on how to get to the palace of the bashaw once they arrived in Tripoli, and on and on until she feared she was sounding as windy as the adjutant.

She stopped once when she became aware of a bystander, a robed and hooded Arab who seemed much too interested in what she had to say. The most she could make out of his features were a puckered scar slashing across his swarthy cheek and a pair of narrow, shifty eyes. She shuddered involuntarily when the eyes rested on her. At last he moved on, and she continued until she was satisfied that the dhow would suffice.

It wasn't a hundredth as good as either of the ships she'd sailed on thus far in her journey, but it was here and it was available, and for Jayne that's all that mattered. Especially since its captain was neither Scottish nor absurdly muscled, and he showed not the least interest in either her person or her purpose, his eagerness aroused by only the money her passage would bring.

As if to justify his presence, Ralph Kennamer launched into a series of questions that were very much like the ones she had just asked. Jayne ceased to listen and for the first time since she'd arisen from her restless bed shortly after dawn, she lost control of her thoughts. Like a tidal wave, the shame of the previous afternoon washed over her . . . the kiss . . . the explosion of yearning . . . the readiness to experience whatever Andrew MacGregor had in mind.

He'd taken her by surprise, that was the trouble, suddenly looming in her doorway and then assaulting her when she'd demonstrated the spirit to stand up to his rudeness.

You didn't think his kiss was rude yesterday, a small voice inside her whispered. Overhead a circling gull cawed as if in agreement, an opinion echoed by the creak of the shifting dhow.

Of course I did, she whispered back, and in a moment of honesty added, *after he backed away.*

Jayne knew too well the heart of her disgrace—she hadn't fought him; rather, he had been the one to break the kiss. Worse, during the hours after he left she'd relived again and again the brush of his lips against hers, and the touch of his tongue. As though she hadn't had enough. As though she wanted more.

The result the morning after was an edginess that marred her concentration and a strange emptiness inside, like a hunger that no food or drink could sate. She credited the feeling to the way Captain

112

MacGregor had, once again, mocked her inadequate womanliness, letting her know in unmistakable terms he preferred women who could both give and receive pleasure. Which, she had obviously demonstrated, she could never do.

The memory of his words were like a cold fist around her heart.

"Missy Lady, do we make the deal?" Captain Rashid asked in English.

The impatience in his voice gave proof Rashid had asked the question more than once, and she forced aside her brooding thoughts. What was done, was done. She must take care of today.

"We make the deal." Somehow she couldn't bring herself to shake the man's dirty hand, but then she wasn't sure if that was the proper procedure anyway. "When do we leave?"

"As soon as Missy Lady is aboard."

"Good," she said, and told herself she spoke the truth. The sooner she got under way, the sooner she would be facing the bashaw. And the sooner she would learn the truth about Josh. *That* was the only consideration she could allow. No more maundering on about rude men with dark and hungry eyes and lips that mocked as easily as they aroused.

Josh. The name became a litany in her mind.

She felt a tremor of anticipation as she thanked Ralph Kennamer for his help and took hold of the valise, glad to have it back in her possession since it contained everything of value she'd brought on her quest.

Awkwardly she made her way up the gangplank. Not even the stare of the eavesdropping Arab, who

113

stood in the shadows a dozen yards away from the dhow, could make her question what she was about.

Later, after a quick, discouraging inspection of the airless hole Captain Rashid called a stateroom, and after making certain her valise was securely locked, she took up her post at the port rail of the dhow. With the waters of the Mediterranean slipping by, she watched as the huge rock marking the Strait of Gibraltar grew small, then smaller, and at last faded from view.

Only a few days ahead lay Tripoli. A few days of discomfort were nothing compared to her years of worry. She knew in her heart that somehow she would hear the news of her brother's fate.

Chapter Eight

Two weeks after the *Trossachs* sailed from Tangier, a voyage slowed by a stop in Algiers and by a gale sweeping out of the northeast, Andrew set course along the African coastline for the final day's journey to Tripoli.

Two miles west of his destination, the afternoon sun heating the shirt on his back, he saw from the starboard rail the city's minarets rising like Scotch pines above the flat landscape. With Oakum at the wheel and Atlas crouched close by his elbow, he spied in the distance to port a pair of British merchant ships steered on an opposite track. The ships were soon out of sight; except for an occasional white gull or sooty black storm petrel swooping and soaring overhead, the frigate was alone on the sea.

The birds flew against a clear and brilliant sky, colored a still, deep blue that gave proof of a limitless universe, but in the aftermath of the storm the wind continued to blow lustily across the ruffled ocean swells, snapping the frigate's sails and rigging, provoking a groan of protest from her wooden hull.

And a chatter of chastisement from the spider monkey, whose hands and tail gripped a topsail halyard as easily as they might once have grasped a Venezuelan tree.

The prow plowed through the white-tipped waves, angled skyward for one tremulous moment as though the ship would search the heavens for lost clouds, and the next, burying the bare-breasted figurehead and half the forecastle into the boundless deep.

Blood singing in his veins, Andrew rode the repetitions of soar-and-plunge as a man of a different calling might ride an untamed stallion, booted feet planted firmly on the salt-speckled deck, head bare to the breeze, the full sleeves of his white linen shirt snapping lustily like the overhead sails. The air, perfumed by the sea over which it raced, held traces of a cooler clime as it held off the heat pulsing from the desert just beyond land's end. The unusual briskness brought a smile to Andrew's lips, a sudden slash of white breaking the sun-browned cragginess of his face.

Oakum, observing from his post at the wheel, called out, " 'Tis a fine afternoon for a sail, Cap'n Mac."

Still smiling, Andrew waved in agreement.

About time, the first mate thought. The captain had been out of sorts since Tangier, pushing the men as well as himself, taking little pleasure from what was ordinarily a pleasurable way of life. Oakum credited the change to the American woman Captain Mac had seen briefly one Moroccan afternoon. A switch in the captain's outlook wasn't necessarily a bad thing, that was for sure, although he'd just as soon it took a more temperate turn.

Without analyzing the cause, Andrew knew as well as Oakum that he'd not been himself, that the usual joys of shipboard routine had not been his.

And true joys they were. He'd not boarded a ship until he ran away from his Highlands village at the age of twelve, but from the moment he felt the pitch of a deck beneath his feet, he'd realized the ocean was his home.

As the years went by, his visits on land became nothing more than economic necessity and, pragmatic and lustful man that he was, occasions for womanly companionship. On his most recent forays ashore he'd taken care of the economics, but the urges of the flesh had gone unsatisfied. Worse, they'd been piqued almost beyond his control.

He gave thought to the woman who had wanted to be here beside him at this moment, but not for the purpose of sating any hungers she'd aroused. Jayne Worthington's quest was mad and he wasn't sure she had the strength to persevere against the troubles she'd clearly underestimated—both reasons for relegating her to the status of forgotten memories.

But she had one trait that kept bringing her to mind: her devotion to her cause. He'd never met anyone of apparently sound mind so willing to sacrifice money and safety in such a hopeless pursuit. Even if it weren't so hopeless, she would never succeed; she was far too imprudent and she didn't know the first thing about handling men.

He suspected she was very much aware of the second and probably of the first, but that didn't seem to slow her down. Nae, when she discussed her situation, her high, tawny cheeks had been flushed with a tinge of pink and her black eyes had flashed with zealous light. When they'd kissed, that same zeal had transferred itself into a heated response.

He'd expected to embrace an unyielding termagant . . . to kiss a pair of cold lips. Damned if after one brief touch she hadn't melted like tallow under a flame. Again, she'd underestimated what she was up against, for Andrew had been ready and willing to rest her against the carpet and trouble himself between her shapely legs.

The fool was bound for disaster. If she somehow managed to get back to her home safely—without her brother, of course, who had to be long dead—he'd bet a keg of rum she'd be damaged in some way. And she'd get damned little comfort from Randolph Forbes and the rest of the clan of barracudas awaiting her return.

Andrew felt a wave of disgust at the thought, then reminded himself, not for the first time, that she wasn't his concern. She was part of that clan. Maybe her innocence wasn't all that sincere. And maybe he ought to forget they'd ever met.

If you see me drowning, pass me by.

Aye, he most certainly would.

He glanced down at Atlas, whose round brown eyes peered accusingly out of a small face, the fur blown smooth against an equally small head.

"Don't look at me that way, Atlas. I'll pitch you overboard."

Atlas showed no sign of distress or chagrin, and

Andrew shifted his gaze to the more soothing sight of the rolling sea.

At last the crescent-shaped town of Tripoli came into view, along with the shapes of a half-dozen ships at anchor between the *Trossachs* and the quay. Tripoli Harbor was misnamed, being little more than a small concavity, open to the pounding seas from the northeast, its choppy waters hiding a perilous web of rocks and reefs. Many a deep-draft vessel had foundered on its shoals.

Adding to the natural protection was a long, rocky mole that had been erected by slaves, their labor urged on by the whip of the bashaw's janissaries. Over the course of years he'd been sailing, Andrew had counted at least a dozen ships run aground on the narrow strip.

"Eight fathoms, Cap'n Mac," one of his men called from his post close to the prow. The words echoed over the roar of the wind.

An ample depth for the draw of the *Trossachs,* but it would not last long. "Cut speed to six knots," he instructed Oakum over his shoulder.

"Aye, aye, cap'n." The first mate began to bark orders to the sailors on deck to trim sail.

Confident in the abilities of his crew, Andrew turned his attention back to the harbor. For no reason in particular he wondered just where Joshua Worthington had met his final reward. The lad had drowned; from the little his sister had related, Andrew was certain of it. The *Philadelphia* had wedged herself tightly on a long, shallow sandbank known to the Tripolitans as Kaliusa Reef, one of many that didn't show up on any chart. Experienced mariners knew the treachery that lay beneath the water; not so the American captain, who'd gone down in disgrace a few hundred yards off shore.

His men had been ferried close to land, then shoved into the water to fight their way through the crashing surf. Thirteen years later Andrew still heard Tripolitans, squatting outside the coffee houses, talk about how they had assisted in the capture, describing with wide gestures and narrow smiles how they'd forced the prisoners to struggle toward the beach just below the bashaw's fortress.

If all who bragged had actually taken part in the disaster, by Andrew's estimate the Americans must have been outnumbered a hundred to one.

"Pretty sight, ain't it, Cap'n Mac?" asked the seaman Boxer, who'd sidled up to the rail without Andrew's notice and begun to stroke the monkey's furry back.

Andrew glanced at the lad, whose fair head came not quite to his shoulders. The seaman's youthful brown eyes were alight with enjoyment, and a grin stretched across his hairless face.

"Aye," Andrew said, returning to his study of the harbor, "a pretty sight it is."

He spoke the truth. From this distance, the crescent-shaped Tripoli presented a fine view with its white, flat-roofed buildings clustered along the waterfront, the bashaw's fortress castle looming protectively to the east, and scattered amongst the manmade structures contrasting patches of greenery, date palms, mulberry and olive trees, oleanders and jasmines, all suggestive of a garden paradise. From the ship they could even see portions of the crenelated town walls, the cupolas of bathhouses, and of course, the minarets.

A paradise, indeed, a land of antelopes and ostriches, a tropical wonder as far as the eye could see.

Andrew knew better. Decay would be obvious as they neared quayside, the buildings cracked from roof to base, the trees and shrubs scraggly along the ten-mile strip of town. Even the fortress walls that protected the bashaw were crumbling, and the crowded streets filled with fetid refuse. Three miles inland, where the streets and buildings ended, the sands of the Sahara dusted the edges of civilization. Here no ocean breezes cooled, and a layer of heat sat low on the land like the lid on a pot.

But for now it was beautiful, and Andrew could enjoy such a sight as well as any man.

"Looks like the harbor's taken another ship, Cap'n Mac." Boxer gestured toward Kaliusa Reef, and Andrew saw what had drawn the lad's attention. A thirty-foot dhow, its main mast snapped in half, lay canted in the shallows, the port rail brushing against choppy waves, the starboard slanted toward the sky.

Andrew's practiced eye picked out the shabby condition of the craft, and, too, the crewmen scurrying on the awkward deck amongst the fallen rigging and sail.

"Must not have happened long ago," he said.

" 'Tis that rascal Aziz Rashid's craft," yelled Oakum over the blustery wind.

"Should we offer assistance?" asked Boxer.

Andrew's powerful shoulders lifted in a shrug. " 'Tis unlikely this is Rashid's first experience in running aground." He nodded toward the bow of the *Trossachs*. "Already the sight has distracted the crew from their tasks, and we've difficulties enough getting ourselves to the quay."

Picking up the excitement, Atlas bounced up and down on the port rail.

"I'll be willin' to take one o' the smaller craft—" Boxer began.

Andrew clamped a hand on the sailor's arm. " 'Tis a noble thought, lad, but I doubt if the men on the dhow are in any danger. Not unless you count the shortchanging that's sure to come when they're paid. Now get Atlas below deck and see to your duties. There's work t' be done."

Andrew directed his attention to the tricky business of navigating the *Trossachs* into position for an easy docking. The frigate was no more than fifty yards from the waiting berth, well past the reef which had claimed the dhow, all hands aboard working in unison like the well-matched team they were, when Boxer once again came running back to Andrew, gesturing wildly toward the wrecked ship.

"They've got troubles, Cap'n Mac."

"Boxer—" Andrew began impatiently.

From the corner of his eye he caught sight of a sixteen-foot launch fighting its way through the surf away from the canted dhow. He counted a half dozen sailors in the boat, dark swarthy figures in sailor's garb. And one in a billowing cloak the color of claret wine.

"Damn," he said. It was impossible. Couldn't be her. But he knew, of course, that it was.

All except the cloaked figure were bailing fiercely, but even from a distance he could tell the small vessel was taking on water fast. At this rate, they would sink beneath the waves long before they reached the sandy shore. The sailors could swim, but what about a slender woman wrapped in a water-soaked cloak?

If you see me drowning, pass me by.

He'd readily agreed.

"God damn!" he said.

Ordinarily Andrew was a man of his word. He'd have to watch any future promises he made concerning Miss Jayne Worthington.

Already a small crowd was gathering on the beach, but he saw no indication that any of the other ships in the harbor were planning a rescue.

He glanced toward Oakum, who remained behind the wheel. "Can you handle the docking?"

"Aye, Cap'n Mac. Ye've taught me well enough."

"Good. I'll take the longboat." He shook his head in disgust. "To rescue our Yankee damsel in distress."

"Yer sure 'tis she?"

"Aye, I'm sure."

The grizzled old tar knew enough not to grin, but in his heart he couldn't be sorry that the woman had come back into his captain's life, e'en if she did make him a grouch. Not once did he doubt Cap'n Mac's ability to save her life.

In the midst of creaking ropes and shouting men, the longboat was lowered. Andrew, Boxer, and two of the *Trossachs'* younger sailors, brothers from Peking named Chang and Chin, manned the oars through the light harbor traffic, fighting the tide that carried them into shore and away from the dhow's launch.

Andrew put his powerful muscles into play, his

123

mariners fighting to match his lead as they sped through the water, but the launch had taken on two feet of water by the time the bow of the longboat pulled within a half dozen yards.

Oblivious to the fast-approaching rescue, one of the dhow's crewmen dived headfirst into the surf; his fellow sailors, abandoning their futile bailing, followed suit.

"What are you doing?" The woman's scream echoed over the wind and waves as she struggled to stand in the small craft. Already her cloak was sodden, denying her the mobility to bail water or to swim. The hood flapped against her back, and her black hair streamed wildly in the wind as the water rose above her knees.

"Miss Worthington!" Andrew shouted. "Jayne!"

Frenzied black eyes searched him out, but he saw no recognition in their depths. She clutched a bulky valise to her breast, as though it were a life preserver, and tried to move toward him, but the weight of wet wool trapped her within the confines of the fast-sinking launch.

Without thinking, Andrew dived overboard and came up at the side of the boat. The water lapped at his shoulders. Jayne saw only a dark head rising beside the leaky craft and strong hands reaching out, but they were enough to give her a rush of strength. She catapulted herself toward her unknown rescuer, her valise striking him full in the face as she fell into the water at his side.

Andrew cursed profusely, certain his nose was broken, but when he tried to remove the offending luggage from her grasp, Jayne held on with a vigor that surprised him.

"No," she yelled above the roar of wind and water, "it's mine."

Her cloak acted like both an anchor and a vise, wrapping around the two of them, threatening to take them both beneath the surf. Andrew might have accepted death in a stormy sea, but to drown in the shoals of Tripoli Harbor was a fate he couldn't tolerate. Powerful hands ripped the valise from Jayne's hands and tossed it into the longboat, then set to rending the offensive cloak.

"Watch out, Cap'n Mac," yelled Boxer from the longboat, backed by the excited chatter of Chang and Chin.

The warning came too late as a sudden wave swamped the pair. Both swallowed brine. When Jayne came up coughing, panic took the last of her reason, and in the band of water between the two boats she struggled in Andrew's arms, fighting for air, desperate to propel herself in the direction her property had taken.

Andrew lost his hold on her. Freed of his support, she fell victim to another crashing wave. The force of the water carried her backward toward the sinking launch. Her head struck a metal oarlock just below the water's surface and without a sound, she ceased her struggles. Before Andrew could react, her body grew lax, as though boneless, and she slipped silently beneath the waves. In the murky water, not even the tatters of her cloak were visible.

Chapter Nine

Slowly, painfully, Jayne returned to consciousness. She kept her eyes closed, aware of only two things: she was lying in a bed, blanket tucked close to her chin, and her pillow-cushioned head was pounding fiercely.

In the painful jumble that was her mind, she fought for a coherent thought, but she came up with only the frightening conclusion that something was terribly wrong.

Disjointed images rushed at her—scenes of a shipwreck, of booted feet pounding against the slanted deck, and then a scramble overboard, the water rising, the sense of desertion. . . . A despondent cry caught in her throat, and the tears burned behind her closed lids.

Stop it, she warned herself. These crazy imaginings—if that's what they were—only made things worse. She held herself very still, willing away both the pain in her head and this new-found tendency to panic. From somewhere close by she heard the pounding of rain, and beneath her the bed rocked, a motion that had become comfortably familiar over the last few months. She added another fact to her small store of information. She was on a ship.

But not Captain Aziz Rashid's dhow. For one thing, she didn't have to keep her knees tucked against her chin to fit on the mattress, and for another, the air wasn't stagnant with rot.

It was the dhow that had gone down . . . of course, now she remembered . . . and next, the small boat that was to take her to safety. She had been so afraid, remembering the stories about Josh floundering in the water, wondering if she was to meet the fate that had been ascribed to him. And then . . .

She simply couldn't remember what happened next. She had no idea how she had been transported from a small, sinking launch just off the Tripoli coast to here . . . wherever *here* was.

Something—or someone—shifted somewhere in the room. She was not alone. The thought was not comforting. Her eyelashes fluttered open for a moment and she caught a glimpse of paneled walls, a square window that opened onto blackness, and a brass lamp flickering in the dimly lit space. Everything else lurked in shadows thick as the shadows in her mind.

"Hallelujah," someone whispered before a door opened and closed, and she heard the fading footsteps of whoever had been watching her.

Before she could react, she heard another stirring. Breathing deeply, she caught traces of a new scent added to the salty dampness that blew in through the open window . . . something entirely unfamiliar . . . something exotic, even in this exotic

127

land, and not entirely pleasant. Wet fur came to mind.

Ridiculous, she thought. The pain in her head had somehow affected her sense of smell as well as her reason.

The scent grew stronger, and she felt a hard tug at her hair splayed across the pillow. She turned her head, forced her sore eyes open . . . and stared at the gaping jaws of a hairy ape!

Jayne shrieked and came off the bunk, covers forgotten, just as the door to the cabin opened. Behind her, the creature from the wild screamed, and together the two of them filled the cabin with a piercing cacophony.

A tall, human figure loomed before her; to her terrified and dizzy mind, it spelled RESCUE and she threw herself into its strength, holding on tight, eyes squeezed closed, her heart pounding in her throat.

Strong arms enfolded her, and as her cries became a dying whimper, she became dimly aware of the warmth of broad hands spread against the bare skin of her back.

"Hush, Atlas," a deep voice ordered. Instantly the creature ceased to scream, and Jayne could hear nothing more than her own ragged breath and the thundering of her heart.

"Boxer said you'd awakened, but he neglected to mention the liveliness of the occasion. I'll give you this much, lass. You know how to thank a man, although I'd prefer a mite less noise."

She knew that deep, resonant voice. As the fog of fear lifted from her brain, she also knew that her body was feeling far too easily the rough fibers

128

of a seaman's woolen coat, and the chill wind against her neck . . . her back . . . her behind.

It couldn't be. None of it.

Easing her hold, she glanced at herself and saw nothing but skin all the way to her toes. In a small room that was far more adequately illuminated than she'd first thought, she was standing without a stitch of clothes.

Not so the man against whom she leaned. Black boots and trousers, a wide leather belt — why hadn't she felt the metal buckle against her ribs? — an open woolen coat sparkling with droplets of seawater trapped in its inky fibers, a brown throat and neck . . .

You know how to thank a man.

Jayne felt shivery both inside and out as she forced herself to look up at the visage of Captain Andrew MacGregor, solemn except for the glint in his eyes, his shoulder-length hair disheveled, his strong face shadowed by bristles so close she could isolate them one by one.

She yelped and leapt away, hands fighting to cover the more personal places on her unclothed body. But there were too many places and too few hands, and her face burned with embarrassment.

Drowning, she thought, would have been a better fate.

Andrew watched her efforts with the studied interest of a man who liked to look at naked women. Not that he hadn't got a good look a few hours ago, when he'd taken the damp clothes from her body and laid her in his bed. Her skin, smooth as silk, was tawny all over, a rich, smooth color, like the underside of a silk-moth's wing.

129

She was slender, too, not really thin the way he'd supposed, but then he was used to wide-hipped wenches in taverns and voluptuous coquettes in the occasional homes he visited as part of his trade.

The promise that came from his one glance at Miss Jayne Worthington's ankles and calves had been more than aptly kept when he saw the rest of her. Graceful thighs and gently rounded hips, a narrow waist, and breasts that had made his palms itch to test the way they would feel in his hands.

And all of her the color of golden satin — except for the thick patch of black pubic hair between her thighs and the brown tips of her breasts. He'd felt like the bastard she called him when he looked upon her naked, helpless form. But it would have taken a saint not to notice the way she was together. And Andrew had never considered himself a saint.

What a devil, Jayne thought as she watched the warmth in his eyes heighten to a scorching blaze. She could feel the heat of his stare, and worse, she could imagine what he must be thinking . . . not that she was incredibly desirable, but that she was certainly available, and to a man like Captain MacGregor, that would be enough.

"A gentleman would look the other way," she said with all the scorn she could muster.

Andrew's lips twitched. "And how would you be knowing that, Miss Worthington? Been caught naked a time or two, is that it?"

"I most certainly have not!"

A high-pitched chatter came from beneath the tangle of covers at the bed. Jayne glanced sideways and saw what appeared to be the tip of a thin and hairy tail curling out from beneath the blanket.

Her head renewed its vicious throb. This was a nightmare. It had to be.

"You frightened him," said Andrew as he slipped the coat from his shoulders and handed it to Jayne.

She welcomed the scratchiness as she slipped it on, and she tried to ignore the scent of the captain caught in its threads.

"I frightened *him?*"

Wondering just what kind of *him* they were discussing, she wrapped the coat as tightly as she could manage around her body, but it still hung in thick folds from the slope of her shoulders, extending to her knees, the sleeves drooping well past the tips of her fingers. She was tempted to crouch on the rug and cover the rest of her legs, but Captain MacGregor might take her altered position as some kind of capitulation . . . or even a supplication, the way he'd made assumptions at the Moroccan consulate.

To her everlasting chagrin, she was learning the boundless ego of the man.

Grinning wolfishly, Andrew said, "Aye, you frightened him, which was why he screamed. You've a way about you, lass, that brings out the beast in us all."

"I thought you were always a beast, captain," Jayne threw right back, refusing to be daunted by his smile or his words. But she couldn't refuse an inner urge to give him a more thorough perusal. He was wearing a shirt identical to the one she'd seen in her stepfather's foyer . . . white against the brown of his skin, full-sleeved, and unfastened far

131

below the hollow of his throat, revealing a dusting of black chest hairs and more expanse of muscle than she cared to see just now. The black breeches stretched across a flat abdomen and around strong thighs, as well as cupping—

She refused to give the portion of his anatomy a name, although a foolish question occurred. Did all his breeches fit him as well?

"When you're done, I'll take care of Atlas."

Jayne's cheeks burned. Maybe she should have flipped out something concerning turn about being fair play, but for the life of her the words wouldn't form on her lips.

"You keep an ape named Atlas?"

"Not actually an ape. Nothing so grand. A spider monkey, in fact."

Andrew reached beneath the blanket, and she watched in awe and trepidation as his hand emerged, gripped by four black, wrinkled and very long fingers. Next came a spindly arm, a small and rounded head, and at last the rest of the scrawny beast that had sent her flying from the bed, naked as the day she was born.

She saw now that he was no more than two feet high, with disproportionately long arms, legs and tail. Most of his slender body was covered by silky nut-brown fur, except for the lighter underparts and a triangle just above his eyes and around his mouth, which didn't at all gape with two-inch incisors the way she'd imagined earlier. In truth, the mouth was rather small and pulled most definitely into a pout as the monkey gazed up at her with round, accusing eyes.

As if she had been the one to startle him.

132

The eyes stayed on her as Andrew led him to the door. "Find Boxer," he instructed, thrusting the animal into the passageway, then for good measure let out a whistle that sometimes brought the young seaman on the run.

He turned to face her, and in the isolation of the cabin she found herself missing the presence of the monkey. She also found herself suddenly dizzy from the steady pounding in her head. She swayed and Andrew grabbed her before she could fall. Thrusting fingers into the thick, tangled hair on the back of her head, she felt a knot the size of a hen's egg. No wonder she was in pain.

He led her to the bunk, and she sat gingerly, letting her bare legs dangle over the side. She caught him eyeing her exposed flesh, and she felt a fluttery tension in the pit of her stomach. Andrew MacGregor had a way of looking at a woman that made her think he was stroking her with his hand. Or made her wish that he were.

Jayne sighed in disgust of herself, and in disgust of him she lay back and pulled the blanket up over the awkwardly oversized coat. The position was most uncomfortable—she could barely rest her head on the pillow for the thickness of the woolen collar—but she wasn't about to complain.

"Got a chill, have you?" said Andrew. "There's extra blankets in the hold."

Jayne ignored the sarcasm. "Please tell me where I am."

"Why, lass, you're where I've been trying to get you for months. In my bunk."

"I know *that*," she said in irritation, and then a fluster set in. "I mean I know it's your bunk, not

133

that you've been trying to get me here."

His low laugh brought a burning flush to her cheeks.

"I mean," she went on, "where is this ship?"

Something about the foolish way she was lying there, looking like a frightened kitten in the oversized coat, shielding herself with a flimsy cover as though he were some kind of animal with uncontrollable lust, brought an end to Andrew's good humor. The teasing had gone on long enough. From the beginning its purpose had been to drive a little sense into her head. Her presence was ample evidence that from the beginning, the idea hadn't worked.

Women on board ship were always trouble. Especially one as obsessive and muddleheaded as Miss Jayne Worthington. She shouldn't be here. He'd never wanted her here. Hell, he was even sorry she wasn't as skinny as he'd believed. And she could bat those fine black eyes all she wanted; she was going ashore as soon as she could stand upright for more than five minutes.

Andrew leaned back against the edge of his desk. "You're in Tripoli Harbor," he said. "You should be happy instead of huddling in fear, although how in hell you expected to get here aboard that leaky craft of Rashid's, I can't figure."

His brusqueness stung. "We almost made it," she said, and wished she could appear more dignified in the face of his scorn. "If the storm hadn't damaged the mast, we'd have been safe enough."

"Are you Rashid's champion now?" asked Andrew, thinking the lass seemed strangely attracted to lost causes.

"I'm not that stupid. He was the first to make his way for shore. I thought captains went down with their ships."

"Not if they can help it, although 'tis considered better form if they're the last to leave."

As much as he maddened her, Jayne couldn't imagine Andrew MacGregor abandoning his crew.

Before he could respond, another thought struck her.

"You saved me, didn't you?"

"Aye." He sounded as though he were confessing to a crime. "I recognized the color of your cloak."

Too well, she remembered her specific instructions in Morocco to let her drown.

You know how to thank a man.

The trouble was, she didn't . . . or at least she hadn't. That's not at all what her nude embrace had meant. He knew it, too, the teasing scoundrel.

"Please accept my gratitude," she said stiffly. She wanted to mean the words . . . with all her heart, she did . . . but he looked so cold and mocking, sitting at the edge of his desk, arms folded across a half-unbuttoned shirt, waiting for her to say or do something foolish, or at least admit he was justified in his ridicule. She knew she didn't sound sincere.

"You could have walked to shore," he said with a shrug, "but I wasn't sure you'd figured that out."

Jayne was suddenly elated that she'd hadn't sounded sincere. Of course she hadn't known the depth of the water. All she'd been thinking of was Josh and how he'd supposedly met his death . . . and the horrible irony of having a second Worthington follow in his course.

135

But the captain wouldn't understand. And she'd be damned if she would leave herself open to his ridicule again.

She shifted in the bed, trying for comfort, but the scratchy bulk of the wool coat reminded her all too quickly of her naked state. "Who undressed me?" she asked, knowing the answer even as she asked.

"The men tossed coins for the honor."

The truth was Andrew had refused to let anyone near her. Not because he wanted her for himself; far from it. But he wasn't a complete rascal, despite the woman's opinion of him.

Jayne suffered a flash of humiliation. "Are you sure it wasn't the loser who got the task?"

" 'Twas a jest, Miss Worthington," he said, puzzled by her response. She might not know much about handling men, but she couldn't be totally oblivious to the effect her nakedness would have on a crew of sailors long at sea.

"Since you were in no condition to take care of yourself," he added, "I put you to bed."

If he'd meant to console her, he'd done a very poor job, for Jayne's humiliation increased tenfold. Captain MacGregor's strong, work-roughened hands had taken the clothes from her body . . . the cloak and the dress . . . the petticoat, the chemise, and stockings. And, she thought with a burning blush, even her underdrawers.

She didn't try for assurance that he'd undressed her in the dark or that he'd kept his eyes away from her intimate parts. A man like Andrew MacGregor would look at everything. Her stomach twisted and she felt a quickening of her pulse. Had he liked what he saw?

Not that she cared.

They looked at one another. From the glint in the captain's eyes, she wondered if he could have read her mind, and then the longer and the deeper she looked into the incredible sea-blue depths, she found herself not much caring if he had.

Her gaze dropped to his lips. They parted slightly, and Jayne felt a strange stirring inside, as though a part of her long closed was beginning to open. The feeling, small though it was, struck her as both exciting and frightening. Willing herself to remain calm, she tried to sit, but the coat kept her pinned to the bunk.

"I'll not attack you, Jayne, if that's a worry."

She swallowed hard. Dealing with MacGregor was far easier if he called her lass or Miss Worthington. Jayne was such an ordinary name, despite the fancy spelling her mother had put to it, but on the lips of a man like him, it didn't sound ordinary at all.

The coat seemed suddenly warm beyond endurance, and far too redolent of a Scottish sea captain. A desperate need for her own clothes took hold of her, but a hurried look around the cabin failed to reveal them.

Andrew didn't miss the desperation. "If you're looking for your belongings, they're safe enough." He rubbed his nose, which was still sore from the rescue. "You fought hard for the valise. What are you carrying, the crown jewels?"

Jayne welcomed the edge of sarcasm. "You mean you haven't checked?" The question came readily. Too well, she remembered how she'd caught Cap-

137

tain Rashid attempting to break the lock. Since the valise contained all the money she'd brought with her, she ended up keeping it by her side.

Andrew didn't bother with a denial. He'd had enough with the woman's sharp tongue and suspicions. "I'll have it brought in directly. Along with your clothes that have been drying in the wind."

Two strides took him to the bed, and he pulled back the blanket. "And I'll thank you for the return of my coat. Since we're so concerned about the protection of property."

The set of his mouth did not encourage Jayne to argue, but neither would she behave as he expected and cower on the bed in maidenly alarm. "Turn your back and it's yours."

"So is the room and the blanket and the bunk. I'll take no more than the coat, but I want it now."

He held out a hand.

Anger propelled Jayne to a sitting position. "Bastard," she hissed.

"Aye," he said, no more than a twitch of a brow indicating emotion. "I still want the coat. Take it off or I'll do it for you."

Chapter Ten

Jayne thought of her nakedness beneath the black wool.

"The coat," Andrew repeated.

"I heard you," she snapped.

As if he wasn't speaking clearly enough. As if she didn't see his broad, callused hand ready to take what he wanted.

Slowly she looked up to meet his determined glare. A chill shivered through her. He had a hard, cold look about him that made her miss the heat of a few minutes ago. Whatever had been opening inside her closed tightly, and she felt the same tense coldness that she read in his eyes.

He wanted his coat so badly, he could have it. Awkwardly, she pulled herself to her knees and turned her back to him, dropping the garment from her shoulders and letting it pool on the bed across her bare calves. She wasn't sure how much of a rear view he'd gotten when he undressed her, but she didn't much worry if he was getting one now.

He wouldn't care for what he saw, anyway.

And the night air felt wonderful on her skin. *Wonderful,* after the heavy wool coat, which was scratchy and hot and reeking of Andrew. How she ever could have found the sea-and-man scent of him appealing, she couldn't imagine.

Andrew had expected an argument, or even an awkward disrobing beneath the covers, and he stared in wonder at the gentle curves of her body, at the smooth, womanly fullness of her buttocks that she shamelessly offered for inspection. Damned if he knew from one minute to the next what the woman was going to do, and he found himself inexplicably angered by that fact.

Didn't she understand the vulnerability of her situation?

He tossed the jacket to the floor and clamped his hands on her shoulders, pulling her backwards against him, wrapping his fingers around her throat. His head was close to hers as he whispered into a mass of tangled black hair.

"You're a fool, Jayne Worthington, an American woman in a world that is foreign to you. And you've come on a fool's mission."

She held herself stiffly, and he could see from her profile that her lips were set in rigid rage. Still, he could feel the curve of her buttocks against his thighs, and even after the dunking he caught the scent of gardenias that she always carried on her warm, smooth skin. Forever spring, he thought, then wondered whether he was as big a fool as she.

His hand drifted lower, to the slope of her breasts, the spread fingers widely spaced enough to touch both dark tips if he was of a mind. She felt warm under his palm, and soft, and while he had meant to warn her and to frighten her, and even to punish her for all her insulting words, a sudden urge to do far more took hold of him.

As if burned, he lifted his hand, but not before he felt the thundering of her heart, not from passion, he knew, but from panic. Here he was getting all hot and hard over a deranged American virgin whose intimate parts must be as dry as the desert. He was tempted to test between her legs to see if he was right.

Andrew crushed the urge. He wasn't a rutting animal, for God's sake, and he didn't have to take his pleasure by force. He'd get himself a woman—a real woman—the first chance he got.

Taking up the coat, he backed away from the bed.

"Cover yourself, lass," he said, as much in disgust of himself as of her. "Try to get some rest. Your belongings will be brought in. I'll not warn you again of the dangers you face, and the certain failure of your search."

Jayne grabbed for the blanket. By the time she turned around, her nakedness protected, the door to the captain's cabin was closing, but her body continued to tingle where he had touched. She fought for righteous indignation, but as she listened to the echo of his footsteps, a strange sense of desertion washed over her, worse even than the feeling she'd experienced when the dhow's crewmen had jumped from the launch.

In the most personal of ways, he had rejected her once again.

She sought refuge beneath the covers, but nothing could save her from the lingering warmth of his hand on her chest. And nothing could save her from the memory of how he'd almost caressed her breasts, and of how her skin had heated and her nipples had tightened and of how she'd wanted him to caress her

141

more than she'd ever wanted anything in her life.

Lord help her, she'd even felt a strange tingle in her most intimate parts. As if she was waiting for him to do more than he'd already done. As if she *yearned* for him to do more. How she ever could have exposed herself to him in such a stupid way, she could not imagine. But he'd been so arrogant and demanding and she'd known he wanted to intimidate her into some sort of acquiescence . . . to force her into a cowering simper.

Jayne had left all her cowering simpers behind in New York. And in their place, she'd found . . .

What had she found? The ready answer was a tendency to wantonness that shook her to her soul. Here and in the Tangier consulate, she'd practically invited him to take liberties. If she were a more desirable woman, that is exactly what he would have done. Thank goodness for her lack of charms.

Huddled beneath the covers, Jayne let out a sigh that she felt down to her toes. Just as he'd said, she was on a fool's mission, but only if she started to want something that would only bring her great unhappiness.

Wanton pleasures were for Millicent and Marybeth. Jayne had been cut from a different cloth. They were slippery chiffon in all the shades of the rainbow, insubstantial, transparent, designed for beauty and not endurance.

Jayne was bombazine. Gray and black. Nothing decorative about her. But she was tough, and she knew how to persevere.

Tomorrow, summoning her tattered dignity, she would offer thanks for Andrew's rescue—somehow, in private, she'd begun to call him by his given name.

She'd apologize for taking over his cabin, and assure him that anything she had said or done that could in the least way be taken as licentious was the result of her anxiety about her brother, or the near drowning, or the blow to the head.

Or anything else she could come up with that kept him from the simple truth: he stirred to wakefulness dark, drowsing forces within her, powerful forces her mother had tried to describe and that she had scorned, personal forces she could no longer pretend did not exist.

"Chang and Chin are saying she's your responsibility."

"Damned if she is!"

Andrew shifted his gaze from the flickering lights along the Tripoli shore onto the grizzled countenance of his first mate. The clouds had cleared, but dawn was still an hour away. Both men had been unable to sleep, and they'd met on the starboard deck where Andrew had gone for a smoke.

" 'Tis an old Chinese custom," Oakum insisted. "Since ye saved her from a watery grave."

Andrew drew on his pipe; the Turkish tobacco tasted sharp on his tongue, and the smoke curled like a snake into the stillness of the moonlit early morn.

"Then I suggest our Oriental friends see to her safety. They'll soon be begging to go back to that blackguard pirate we rescued them from."

Forestalling further argument, he turned the conversation to the tentative plans for a quick journey to Derna, eastward along the North African coast. He needed to take care of business in the busy port town before returning to take on a cargo of Tripolitan goods for the English markets at Glasgow and Liverpool.

The talk grew desultory, neither man having much interest in a discourse on work on such a starry night, with the wind holding still after the earlier rain and the moon casting a ghostly light across the masts.

At last silence fell between them, and Andrew listened to the lap of water against the frigate's hull and remembered, against his will, the vision of Jayne Worthington kneeling in his bunk. The picture made the palms of his hands itch.

She was still there, sleeping the sleep of the pure and innocent, he had no doubt, leaving him to pace the deck with a kind of frustration he hadn't experienced since he was an adolescent nearing his first port after months at sea.

"About the lass, Cap'n Mac—"

Oakum's words brought him to the present with a start. "I told you we'll put her ashore and be on our way."

"Ye ken Karamanli is a right terrible tyrant."

"He'll have to be to get his message across. She's not one to listen with care."

"She's just a lass—"

"That's like saying the Atlantic is just water. Lasses like Miss Worthington can shake the foundations of civilization itself. You've a soft heart, Oakum. Unlike me. I want no more t'do with her. She's already cost me a fine longboat."

"It wasna the lass's fault. One of the bashaw's own ships was poorly navigated just as you tried to bring her on board—"

144

"No need to remind me. But we wouldn't have been in the water if not for her. Believe me, mate. Miss Jayne Worthington is nothing but trouble and I've got enough to worry about without taking on her woes."

"She's a comely lass. Ye dinna think —"

"No, I don't." Andrew tapped the pipe against the starboard rail and ruthlessly shoved aside all pictures of the naked Jayne. "And she's not comely in the least. Skin and bone and a tongue that lashes like loose rope in a storm."

No need to let Oakum know what she was really like. No need to admit that memories of her had him pacing the deck when he ought to be getting a wink of sleep before the dawn.

"The longboat was in need of repair," said Oakum.

"But not a major overhaul. Believe me, mate, the woman is just not worth the trouble she's caused."

A small cry from down the deck snapped Andrew to attention, and he realized he and Oakum had been standing dangerously close to the window of his cabin. A head of tangled dark hair appeared in the opening, and in a shaft of moonglow he caught sight of a delicate and very angry face turned in his direction. The silvery light did little to soften the fire in the pair of dark, long-lashed eyes.

"Let me know in the morning how much the long-boat was worth, Captain MacGregor." Jayne Worthington's voice sliced sarcastically into the still, cool air. "I'll pay for the damn thing, and then rest assured, I'll be off this cursed boat before you can say 'comely' three times."

145

Chapter Eleven

Jayne tapped her foot impatiently against the tile floor of the corridor. She was somewhere deep in the fortress palace of the bashaw of Tripoli, and she was angry.

For two hours she'd been kept buried in this labyrinth of hallways and closed-off rooms, waiting for an audience with Yusuf Karamanli. Long gone were the self-directed reminders that she had waited thirteen years for this moment, and she could very well handle a slightly longer wait.

Two hours! And what a gloomy place to wait, not at all gloriously lavish and wickedly decadent as she'd imagined. Even the lone courtyard she'd passed was covered with a rooflike grate of heavy iron.

Jayne renewed the pacing that had intermittently occupied her time, but the exercise did little to ease the anxiety that had been building within her like steam in a lidded pot. It didn't help that she could feel watchful eyes upon her every second of the time.

And it also didn't help that before arriving at the palace she'd met with coldness from the American consul in the small, dingy consulate off one of the town's ill-paved and refuse-cluttered streets. It was an attitude he'd probably picked up from correspondence with his superior, the consul general in Tangier.

Worst of all, it didn't help that every time she tried to settle an image of Josh in her mind, all she could see was the profile of a very tall and very arrogant Scottish sea captain standing on the pre-dawn deck of his ship and discussing her as though she were a stray pup he should have let drown.

Not comely. As if she didn't know.

Despite the closeness of the air, she secured the hood of her salt-stiffened cloak tightly in place — the tatters had been mended by the sailmaker aboard the *Trossachs,* the young sailor Boxer had told her as he escorted her to the consulate in early morning — and silently enumerated the special tortures that would be most appropriate for a man like Andrew MacGregor.

Everything she settled on involved violence to various parts of his anatomy, beginning with a close clipping of his black mane and descending somewhat farther south. She was a farm girl; she knew how bulls and stallions were castrated, and she figured it wasn't much different for a man.

A thought occurred. Eunuchs were very much a part of the bashaw's world. She was certain one had escorted her to the bowels of his master's palace. Maybe she could ask Karamanli details on the procedure. She did like to be specific in her plan for torture; it made the contemplation so much more satisfying.

Not comely. As if she cared what the captain thought. The small, sharp pain she'd felt somewhere around her heart when she'd heard the words had been nothing more than surprise, and if she carried the discomfort still, it was only because she had worries on her mind. She simply hadn't bothered to reason the memory away.

A shadow fell across her path. She glanced up to see a towering, robed figure filling one end of the corridor. Bearded, swarthy, his eyes dark and cold, he ordered in Arabic that she was to follow him, and with a hundred tiny mice scrambling around in her stomach she followed the ripples of his black robe through another series of corridors, at last pausing before an ornately carved wooden door, which opened silently as if by magic.

Her guide stepped aside, and she entered. The large room, with its high, curved portals opened to the sunlight and the breeze from the sea, was everything she'd expected.

According to her extensive readings, Yusuf Karamanli liked opulence; here at last was proof. The walls of the room were pristine porcelain, and a dozen brilliantly colored rugs covered the marble floors. Pillows, some as large as carts and shot with threads of precious metal, lay scattered over the rugs, and to one side she saw a tile-lined pool of water surrounded by potted palms, like a desert oasis transported by magic carpet to the ruler's private room.

Karamanli also demanded security, and she counted at least twenty janissaries uniformed in scarlet and another twenty robed figures she took to be aides scattered about the room as randomly as the pillows. *Cologhlis.* Mercenaries, some of them, hired along with the janissaries to keep order. A small and violent army, reputed to be highly skilled in their work, no matter the mutilation and mayhem required.

The uniformed guards wore golden sabres strapped

to their sides, and she suspected that under the robes, so did the aides. Along with an assortment of muskets, daggers, and tomahawks.

It seemed an overabundance of protection when the lone visitor was an unarmed female of rather slight build. Did they believe she'd steal the treasure chests which reportedly never left the bashaw's presence? Her eyes did not search for the chests; instead, they settled on the chamber's primary decoration— Bashaw Yusuf Karamanli himself.

He sat on a four-foot dais at the far end of the room, his chair a high-backed throne inlaid with mosaic and trimmed with gold-fringed, jewel-encrusted velvet. The bashaw matched the chair's splendor. A large man, he was made to appear larger by the fullness of his robe—emerald green silk striated with golden threads, its crimson velvet collar rolled loosely against his bull-like neck. A beribboned turban topped his massive head, and around his waist was strapped a diamond-encrusted belt.

Rather an overabundance of splendor, Jayne decided as she remembered the gloom of the rest of the palace, to go along with the overabundance of protection. Bordering on the garish, if she were to be hypercritical.

A majestic black beard masked much of Karamanli's face, but from fifty feet away she could see he was a handsome man. And his dark steady eyes told her he was completely in control. She felt his power as though he had crushed her in one of the large, brown hands resting on the throne's velvet-covered arms.

Jayne dared a few tentative steps, then stopped to curtsy. "Your Highness," she said in Arabic.

"Come forward," he answered in kind.

Beneath the mended cloak her legs trembled, and she felt her heart beating fast. Worse, the mice scrambling about her stomach seemed to have multiplied, and a trickle of sweat tickled the valley between her breasts. As much as she could, she withdrew into her hood.

You faced the President of the United States with a steadfast heart.

The reminder did little to ease Jayne's anxiety. James Madison didn't go about ordering the lashing of those who crossed him. And he didn't, as she'd read in one account of the bashaw, sentence a miscreant to go riding through the streets backward on a jackass with a sheep's entrails hung around his neck and then subject him to five hundred *bastinadoes,* beatings on the bare soles of his feet.

Madison had simply explained with great civility that she didn't know what she was talking about.

She knew full well that Karamanli was likely to do the same. What she didn't know was the level of his civility.

With at least forty pairs of eyes watching her every move, she made her way across the room, reminding herself that she must not trip on one of the hundred pillows or else she would surely lose what little credibility she had.

The closer she got to the dais, the more she felt the dominance of the bashaw's will; it radiated from him like heat from the sun. It was the eyes, she decided. She wouldn't get anywhere unless she could look him straight in the eyes. Eventually, when she had settled the terrible turmoil that had taken over much of her insides, she would. Until then, she was content to hide in the confines of her hood.

"Miss Jayne Worthington, is it not?" He spoke in heavily accented English, his voice thick and dark as pitch.

It was her turn to answer in kind. "Yes, Your Highness." A little soft, but not too bad, considering the circumstances. "I trust you have received the letters I wrote over the past few years."

He snapped his massive, beringed fingers. "Remove it."

Confused, Jayne felt as though the carpet were being tugged from beneath her feet. "Remove what?"

"You are American, is this not so? An infidel. There is no need to cover your head."

Clumsily, she untied the hood and let it fall against her back, exposing the black hair she'd twisted into a bun at her nape, exposing the fright in her eyes.

Everything mattered so much. Josh mattered. The idea that he might be under the dominance of this tyrant was enough to turn blood to ice. Laughing, carefree Josh, who'd so loved his freedom.

She edged close to despair . . . and then a wonderful thing happened. Love for her brother washed over her and gave her the strength she'd been needing. Why should she cower before a despot who terrorized his own people, who beat and enslaved them, who demanded tribute to keep himself in opulence while their own homes fell into disrepair?

Besides, cowering had never got her anywhere. Back straight and chin high, she at last managed to meet his steady gaze. "I've come a long way, Your Highness, to find a lost American boy. A man, now, but he was a boy when he came ashore thirteen years ago."

The bashaw gave no sign that he'd heard a word she

151

said, but neither did he order her to silence.

"He was aboard the *Philadelphia* when it ran aground, but he was not among the released prisoners. In the spirit of cooperation that now exists between our countries, I ask that you help me find out where he is."

Jayne wasn't able to see exactly how Karamanli managed the feat, but somehow he summoned one of his aides, who knelt obsequiously by the chair and listened in rapt silence while the bashaw whispered in his ear.

She held herself quiet and still, a thousand reasons for the hurried conference racing through her mind. Someone who knew of Josh was being summoned . . . the bashaw wished to send for the consul as witness when he revealed the missing American's whereabouts . . . he needed a jackass and garland of entrails for the parading of an audacious female infidel through the streets.

Anything was possible. Especially anything bad, she thought, as her brief rush of optimism faded back into despair. What did Karamanli care for the love that a stranger—a worthless female—bore her brother? Hadn't he killed his own brother to take over the Tripolitan throne? It was in all the reports she had read, but she hadn't let herself dwell on the tragedy before.

Not until now.

While Jayne's mind was working and her heart was growing heavier with each unwelcome thought, the door opened behind her. She turned to watch the veiled figure of a woman enter the bashaw's chamber, a brass platter of peeled fruit in her hands. Bare feet pattered past Jayne, and the woman placed the platter on a small, cushioned stool beside the throne. She sat beside the stool, her silken robe swirled gracefully across the dais, and lifted heavily lashed eyes to the bashaw.

A beauty, Jayne thought. The bashaw might turn from thoughts of brotherly love, but he was widely known as a participant in love of another kind. His harem was reputed to be the envy of the sultan of Morocco, the bey of Tunis, and the dey of Algiers.

Karamanli stroked the woman's cheek, but he kept his eyes on Jayne. "I find myself with only two wives to comfort my waning years." He sighed, as though he were all alone in the world, as though he hadn't a hundred other women at his disposal any time of the day or night.

What about Joshua Worthington, she wanted to ask. Josh would be twenty-nine. Had he taken a wife? Or a mistress? Was he celibate? Or a eunuch? It was a consideration that had never before occurred to her, and she thrust it from her mind.

Shifting his hand from the woman to the platter, the bashaw fingered the fruit, then sat back to munch on a fig.

Summoning her courage, Jayne persevered in her quest, describing Josh as he'd looked when last she saw him, informing the bashaw of all that she'd learned about how he left the ship, and ending with her theory that perhaps he was separated from the other prisoners in the confusion ashore.

"He could have found refuge anywhere in the town," she said, "and eventually made his home here in Tripoli. Or perhaps he's been taken as a slave." She attempted an encouraging smile. "I know the bashaw is all powerful. One word from him, and the whereabouts of my brother will be made public."

Karamanli licked the juice from his fingers and without a glance at her, selected another section of fruit, this time a plump black grape.

Two more grapes disappeared into the midst of the heavy, gray-streaked beard, and suddenly Karamanli stood. Jayne felt more than heard the snapping to attention of the men in the room. The woman at his feet knelt. Jayne held to her proud stance at the base of the dais. Little else was left to her.

In a swirl of emerald and gold, the bashaw turned toward a curtain of silk behind the chair.

"Bashaw Karamanli!" Jayne spoke without thinking, and dared to take the first step that would raise her to his level. "My brother Josh. Can you not help me? I've waited so long."

A heavy hand clamped on her arm, and she glanced sideways into the steely eyes of one of the guards. She quavered under his stare, but she could not back down, not now, not after all the trouble she'd been through to get here, and so she held her ground.

"Please," she said, directing her regrettably shaky voice toward the bashaw. "You're my last hope." The guard's hand was like an anchor on her arm, but she held her place and she did not look away.

Karamanli half-turned in her direction. One glance at the guard and the offending hand was removed.

"Your President Jefferson learned to his regret that I am a difficult man with whom to deal. He threatened Tripolitan shores with his Navy, and in the end he paid the tribute that was required as an apology for the insult."

Karamanli allowed a smile of smugness to play on his face, and a bath of sunlight sparkled against the diamonds at his waist. "Today you invade my country and my solitude with claims that I lied. That I have not released all those for whom the ransom was paid. It would seem you have not learned from your President's example."

Jayne swallowed a half dozen sharp retorts. "I meant no insult, Your Highness," she managed, disgusted at the obsequious tone she heard in her own voice.

"And yet you say this brother of yours lives," said Karamanli. "In a dungeon, perhaps, beneath the fortress? Have you come to offer money for his release?"

The callousness of the man halted her attempts at prudence. "If it would free him, that is exactly what I would do," she snapped. "But any tribute I might pay would not buy one jewel on your belt."

His eyes flashed dangerously, and for a minute Jayne feared she had gone too far.

"And I would not take it if the money were offered. Go home, Miss Worthington. I know nothing of this brother you speak of, and in Tripoli, I know everything."

Again the emerald robe swirled, and he disappeared behind the curtain of silk, leaving Jayne to stare after him in stunned silence. He'd told her the very thing that had been the stuff of her nightmares. Worse than the words had been the flat certainty in his eyes when he'd looked down at her. Josh's fate was unknown, and would remain so. She wanted to cry.

She ventured a quick glance around the room; the guards and aides stared back in cool disdain, a final insult to her efforts. Even the woman, to whom she looked for a hint of sympathy, regarded her as though she were no more important than a fly invading the chamber on an ocean breeze to buzz around the fruit.

This final affront gave her the strength she needed. Tilting her chin a notch toward the high ceiling, she spoke in Arabic. "I'll need an escort from the palace. Someone please see that I am provided one."

At last she got what she asked for. As though she'd summoned him with a djinn, the same robed giant who had escorted her to the bashaw's chamber appeared before her, and within minutes she was standing outside the main gate of the fortress walls, traffic rumbling loudly along the street.

The crumbling fortress walls, she noted, although the thought brought little satisfaction. They still supported battlements across the high stone ridge.

With the hood of her cloak firmly back in place, she decided to summon one of the donkey carts that served as public transportation. She stepped away from the gate, painfully aware of the attention she was attracting from the crowd of robed men milling outside the fortress.

Some instinct, a sense of foreboding, made her glance over her shoulder at the crowd. One man stood out. A man whose swarthy cheek was marred by a puckered scar, and whose narrow, shifty eyes were pinned to her like the sight on a gun. It was the man from the Tangier quay lurking only a half dozen feet away. It couldn't be, and yet she was certain that it was.

She gasped in surprise, dimly aware of rapidly approaching horse's hooves and of heavy wooden wheels rumbling down the stone street. The Arab came at her, shouldering aside the men around him. Instinct made her turn in flight. Firm hands shoved against her back, and she stumbled into the street.

A black horse, large as a mountain, thundered into her path. She felt a tug on her cloak, heard a youthful cry, felt herself pulled to the ground just as the mighty hooves struck the stones not two feet from her head, at once followed by the massive wooden wheels of an ancient cart rolling crookedly past, throwing dust and debris in its wake.

She choked and grabbed for her middle, huddling at the side of the street, the terror of the moment overtaking her senses. Excited chatter rose around her; she could pick out only isolated words, something about a boy pulling her back in time to avoid disaster. Nothing about the man who had attempted to kill her. For such was the situation. She knew it beyond all doubt, even though she had not the slightest idea why.

Jayne caught her breath, in her confusion realizing she couldn't sit by the side of the road until she figured things out, and so she accepted help in standing, brushed at her cloak, and assured the concerned assemblage that she was all right, her use of Arabic surprising them as much as did her presence.

The hood had loosened in the fall, as well as the bun at her nape, and the Arabs stared at her exposed face and hair. Only prostitutes and Jewesses were allowed to go through the city without headdressings, and they couldn't figure out which she might be.

Then someone whispered something about *Amerikahyim,* and that seemed to settle the issue.

Choosing a nearby Arab with a concerned look to his eye, she asked about the boy who had saved her.

"You stumble," he said with a shrug. "The boy bravely risked his life to pull you to the ground."

"Where is he? I'd like to thank him."

Again the Arab shrugged, this time in silence.

Jayne hurriedly studied the crowd, but she saw no likely candidates for the position of hero. Then she looked across the street. Standing at the entryway to a narrow alley, just outside a shaft of sunlight, was a small robed figure, his head and face hidden beneath folds of white wool.

As she stared at him, he pulled the hood of his robe aside, and she could have sworn he flashed her a quick smile.

The figure turned and disappeared down the alley. Jayne pulled away from the crowd, and with a quick glance to make sure the street was clear, hurried after. If this were indeed the boy who had saved her life, he was the one person she'd met along the Barbary Coast who had done something to help her without insult or demands for reward.

For such, he deserved her thanks.

Chapter Twelve

Catching up with the boy was not so easy as Jayne had hoped. She ran up one crowded street and down the next, past enormous piles of refuse with their attendant packs of dogs, past half-clothed children crouched against cracked and crumbling walls, jumping aside to avoid the camels and donkeys led through the dust-choked passageways.

Always she kept sight of the youth's robe; it was a beacon leading her through an exotic, chaotic world.

Once her path was barred by a gaunt, wraithlike figure, his body looped in burlap, his head and face covered with dung, his arms outspread as if he would embrace her.

Heart pounding in her throat, she came to a quick halt. He ranted in a gibberish she could not understand, and when she saw the wild light of insanity in his eyes, she knew him as one of the idiots allowed to run the streets. Allah's blessed people, they were considered. Gasping for breath, fearing she had lost her quarry, she ducked beneath one of the arms and picked up the pace of pursuit.

The boy appeared suddenly at a distant corner, and she had the distinct impression that he was waiting for her . . . that he was leading her on. For what purpose she couldn't imagine, but then she had quit ascribing reasons for actions the moment Andrew MacGregor appeared in her room in Tangier.

She certainly couldn't attribute any rationality to what she was currently about. In the beginning of this mad dash, she'd wanted to thank the boy. But now, something else seemed to be driving her on. It was as though some special spirit, a heretofore unknown indomitable force, was guiding her, giving her no choice but to continue.

Like her quest for Josh, this run through the Tripolitan streets must have a successful end.

He was gone as suddenly as he had appeared, and she made her way to the corner, rounded onto the intersecting street, and ran into the young Arab. Backing up a step, he met her surprised stare with a friendly nod.

The robe she'd been following hung loosely on his lanky frame, and a pair of sandaled, dirty feet edged out from beneath the hem. The head covering had fallen back enough to allow her a good look at his face. Brown skin, bright brown eyes, white teeth that flashed a brilliant smile.

"Oh," she said, feeling foolish because she could think of nothing else to say, and concentrated a moment on catching her breath and easing the stitch in her side.

The boy just stared and continued to smile.

They stood beside one of the city's numerous coffee houses. Farther along, a pair of Arabs sat crosslegged on a marble bench outside an open door, their curious eyes turned to Jayne's exposed features. The mingled scents of coffee, cinnamon, and cloves wafted through the immediate air, a welcome change from the pervasive stench of the streets.

She looked back at the boy. Fourteen, she estimated, the age of Josh when he ran away to sea. Her heart took a little twist. More than ever, she felt the inevitability of their meeting.

The youth bowed from the waist. "The lady was not injured in the fall. This pleases me."

"You speak English."

"Not so good. But I make the difficult endeavor."

Jayne returned his smile. "I want to thank you for saving my life."

"Allah guided me."

"No one else was so guided. You alone were quick-witted enough to pull me to safety." Remembering the malevolence in the shifty eyes of her would-be assassin, Jayne hugged herself. "I can't imagine why I was shoved in the first place."

"Tripoli is a place most dangerous, Miss Worthington." He drew the name out as though it were the words to a chant.

Jayne started. "You know my name?"

"A servant at the palace. Friend to a donkey driver. He spoke of the American woman who dared to visit the bashaw. The tale was quick to spread."

"Dared to visit? I came in friendship and sought the bashaw's help. Nothing more."

"No other one—"

He stumbled, searching for the right word, hoping not to offend the American lady. "Please to understand what I say. No one of your sex has made such an attempt."

What a polite young man, Jayne thought, so different from the Tripolitans she'd met thus far. So concerned for her well being and the delicacy of his speech. Her heart filled with gratitude.

"Does your bashaw carve up foreign ladies for breakfast?" she asked, smiling.

"This was something unknown." His dark eyes glinted. "Until Miss Worthington."

"You're teasing me."

"Only a small teasing."

How right she had been to follow the boy, Jayne decided, and she let go completely the tensions that had gripped her since she felt those hard hands on her back. Beyond rational explanation, the boy made her feel that all was right with the world . . . and if it wasn't all right, then soon it would be made so.

They fell silent as a cart rumbled along the narrow street close beside them, followed by an ungainly camel, decorated in fringe and bearing a linen-draped palanquin on its towering back. Body pressed to the wall of the coffee house, Jayne stared up at the high enclosure. Inside was the shadowy figure of a woman, obviously wealthy since a large retinue of black female slaves and guards flanked the camel as it lumbered past.

Jayne was almost overcome with the thick clouds emitting from the vases of burning perfume carried by the attendants.

Coughing, she turned back to the boy and was surprised to see he had wrapped his head in cloth and shifted to face the wall. Strange, she thought, then decided he'd been trying to get away from the sickly sweet scent.

She took up the conversation where they had left off. "As you can see, I survived the terrible journey into the bashaw's fortress. It was on the street that I ran into danger."

The boy peeked out from his headdress, a visible eye searching his immediate surroundings. The danger was past, he saw with relief, and once again he gave her the full view of his face.

"The man with the scar," he said, for a change scowling.

"You saw him? He did push me, didn't he? I knew it. But why? I haven't the vaguest idea who he is, but I saw him in Tangier on my first stop."

"This is strange."

"I agree. More than strange. It's frightening," she said, admitting to a return of worry, "and I was determined not to let anything frighten me on my quest."

"You must let Mohammed help you."

"But I'm a Christian—"

The boy grinned. "Not *that* Mohammed. Allow me to present my most humble self. Mohammed, child of the streets, at your service."

Jayne felt comforted by the smile, if not the offer. "I don't see how you can help."

"It is within my most humble power to provide shelter for the storm that threatens the city."

Jayne glanced up at the clear blue sky. "A storm?"

"Before the day is done. In this you must trust me."

Mohammed gave her his most innocent smile, the one he used to charm the women of his family. A practiced expression, yes, but he discovered it was easy to be pleasant to the American lady with the too-worried eyes. She had been brave to follow him, and she spoke to him as though he were a man, not a child to be ignored.

She truly was in danger, though he knew not why.

Even as he used her for his purposes, he must see to her care.

Jayne considered her options. Unfortunately, she couldn't come up with any. Except to put her faith in an Arab boy named Mohammed, a confessed child of the streets, the only person among a host of older, stronger men who had possessed the quickness of body and mind to save her from harm. If their meeting really *were* inevitable, why consider ending their relationship so soon?

All right, so he'd led her on a merry chase through the Tripolitan streets, deliberately teasing her to follow. Perhaps he was as lonely as she, although she couldn't imagine anyone with such a charming smile and manner without friends.

The important thing was not to give in to despair. So what if the bashaw had disappointed her, and she had picked up a menacing enemy, and everyone she'd turned to had called her fool?

Or at least they'd hinted. Only Captain MacGregor had outrightly stated his opinion, and why she kept remembering that and all the other things he had said and done when she had far more important things to consider, Jayne couldn't imagine.

"Could you please call me Jayne?" she asked. "Miss Worthington is such a mouthful."

"You do me great honor with this request. In my heart, Miss Jayne, I know we will be friends."

"I feel the same way. And of course I trust you, Mohammed. Lead me to your shelter from the storm."

Which he proceeded to do, again up and down streets, hurrying just ahead while she followed, hood in place, her eyes casting about for a squinty man with a scar on his cheek.

Mohammed made certain she did not fall too far behind. She was of great interest to him, this woman from a faraway land, and his eager mind was ready to learn what she could teach him. He didn't plan to remain in Tripoli forever. There was nothing to keep him here.

He took her to a house on the edge of town, close to where the sands of the Sahara brushed against Tripolitan buildings and the vegetation became little more than scattered wild grasses growing valiantly in the shifting dunes.

Already the wind from the sea had grown cool and damp, and the dark clouds turned the afternoon sky to the dimness of night. They entered through a back door opening onto an alleyway. The interior was dark, and Jayne stumbled against an unyielding piece of furniture her searching hands and throbbing toe told her was a chair.

"Is there a lamp close by?" she asked.

"I have much regret to say no." Mohammed hesitated. "The house we visit is borrowed, and we must not impose our presence on the owner, a kind and generous man"—the boy almost choked on the words—"who on this stormy night wanders far from home."

Jayne understood. They weren't supposed to be in the house and Mohammed was afraid they would get caught if anyone on the outside saw a light. They were breaking the law. It was the first time she had ever done such a thing, but she could not summon the least twinge of conscience.

Her eyes having adjusted to the dark, Jayne saw they were in a kitchen. The recognition reminded her she hadn't eaten since a small repast offered at the consulate hours ago. She'd left her valise there, in fact, expecting to stay there for the night. Right now, however, she'd like a chance at the bashaw's platter of fruit.

As if he could read her mind, Mohammed searched in a cabinet and thrust a half loaf of bread in her hand, along with a wedge of very smelly cheese. Making sure he served himself as well, she nibbled at the cheese, found it passable, and after a few bites, positively delicious.

The two of them stood in the dark, wolfing down the food, and then he served her with a glass of wine poured from a crock which had been resting on the counter close to the back door.

The wine was sweet and went down smoothly, and the only thing that took her by surprise was that it was found in an Arab home. Arabs most definitely did not believe in drinking alcohol. Before she could ask Mohammed about their absent host, a clap of thunder resounded, followed by a flash of lightning and the pounding of rain against the protective stone walls.

Mohammed led her to the interior door, and they looked out onto an open courtyard. She watched the rain, drank the wine, and told herself that for a shy, unattractive spinster from a farm in Virginia, she certainly was leading an adventuresome life.

The funny thing was she loved it. Meek little Jayne who'd been afraid to cross her mother by admitting she would rather face a thousand tortures than wed Leander Forbes. In one day she'd stormed off a Scottish frigate after highhandedly telling its formidable captain she would pay for her keep whether he wanted her to or not, she'd faced down another in a line of disapproving American officials, and she'd dared intrude herself into the bashaw of Tripoli's audience chamber, the atmosphere of which closely resembled an armed camp.

More, she'd survived near death beneath the hooves of a galloping stallion, made a new friend, and was now getting more than a little tipsy as she watched a storm off the Mediterranean in a home where she most certainly would not be welcome if the owner knew she were here.

A satisfying day, she concluded without a thought for the illogic involved. A highly satisfying day.

When the squall had lessened to a steady rain, Andrew retreated to his cabin to study the manifests he would present to his business associate in Derna. Perhaps, he hoped, such tedium would ease his edginess.

The sudden turn in the weather—that had set him off. Not worry about an impossible female wandering the streets of a strange and wicked city with the rain pelting down . . . no place to turn for succor . . . no refuge, no retreat.

Andrew pictured Jayne as he'd last seen her, standing at the head of the gangplank, her cloak wrapped about her and head held high, those damnably fine black eyes flashing fire as she demanded to know how much she owed him. If he could have put a price to the restlessness she stirred, she would have to rob the bashaw's famed treasure chests to settle her debts.

"Not a shilling," he'd told her and sent her on her way, his lone concession an instruction to Boxer to see that she got to the American consulate without more than her ordinary allotment of trouble. The lad, given leave for the day, had yet to return.

Andrew felt a rare pang of conscience. For all her

spirit, she was still a female in a land run by men, far too many of them without honor. He should have warned her about the white slavery market behind the Karamanli Mosque . . . .

Hell, she wouldn't have listened. Stubborn and too ignorant or innocent for her own good, she was on her own. Out of his hands. Out of his hair.

Concentrating on the work, he was halfway done when a knock sounded at the cabin door and Oakum entered. From his perch in the open window, a damp breeze ruffling his scraggly brown hair, Atlas screeched a welcome.

Andrew looked up from the desk to study the first mate's great gray face, the tenseness in the kind and wise eyes, the new furrows the beard couldn't hide. "What's the trouble?" he asked.

"Nothin' wi' the ship, Cap'n Mac. Ye can put yer mind t' rest on that account."

"Allow me a guess. It's Miss Worthington."

"Aye."

"Is she alive and in good health?"

"Aye to both. When last seen."

Andrew let out the breath he hadn't realized he was holding, and he fought disquiet as best he could. "Then tread carefully, mate. I've said she's gone and that's the last of her I want to hear aboard this frigate. She's on her own now, and that's to the good. Let Tripoli fend for itself."

"Good riddance, is it?"

"Aye, good riddance. And long overdue."

Oakum took note of the flat set of his captain's mouth and the hard light in his eye. But he'd seen the worry, too. His captain was a lone and lonely man, and he'd had little experience in caring for a woman,

168

and naught in getting affection of more than the temporary and carnal sort.

Anything with a hint of permanence was a dangerous shoal for the captain, and he'd need a little help in the navigation.

Oakum chose his words carefully. "Then ye'll not be wantin' to ken what the Chinese have to say."

"The Chinese?"

"Aye. Chang and Chin."

"The ones who claim Miss Worthington is my responsibility since I saved her from drowning."

"A wee mention is all they made."

"I hope they don't plan to mention it to me."

For sure the captain was in an unsettled state. Unruffled, Oakum shrugged. "They've just returned from town and have a tale they'd like to be tellin'."

Andrew thrust the manifests aside and sat back. "Have they now?" he said, fingers drumming on the arm of the chair. He would have liked to believe he was considering whether to say aye, but he was honest enough with himself to know he wasn't about to say nae. Jayne had been gone eight hours now. No telling what trouble she'd stirred.

"Show them in." All right, he confessed to himself, he was worried, or at least he was concerned. No matter what Jayne Worthington thought, he wasn't a totally brutish boor.

Atlas chose that moment to abandon his perch at the window and take his place in his master's lap. After checking for fleas in the open throat of Andrew's shirt, he curled his tail around the chair leg, rested his arms across his bent legs, and grinned at no one in particular, like a mischievous child who'd done something of great accomplishment.

As soon as the seamen were in front of his desk, Andrew's concern heated several degrees.

"You don't look as though you've spent a happy time ashore," he said, looking first at Chang and then at Chin.

Brothers, slight of build, their hair similarly plaited into a long queue, they'd proven able, loyal workers since Andrew had rescued them from a scuffle with a pirate's crew on a Caribbean island the past year. He hadn't asked how they got there, and they hadn't volunteered to tell him. Aboard ship they kept to themselves and did more than their share of the work. This was the first time they'd requested an audience with their captain.

"Tell me what happened," Andrew urged.

Chang spoke, his English practiced and smooth, only occasionally slurring consonants as did so many of his countrymen. "We went to the bazaar to buy presents for our families, captain."

"I didn't know you had families."

"In Peking," said Chin.

"Our path took us by the palace," said Chang. "The young lady from the sunken ship stood beside a great crowd of men close to the gate in the palace wall."

"She was with them?"

Chang shook his head. "I do not believe so. Outside such places in every city of the world we have seen a great assemblage. As though those in power will give them alms. Maybe it is they hope to bathe in the reflected magnificence of such an elegant personage as the bashaw."

For Chang, it was a long-winded speech and he paused.

Chin took over. "The lady was lost in thought. Most

unhappy thought, my captain. A mighty horse and wagon came fast down the street."

"The lady stumbled," said Chang. "A robed figure pulled her from harm."

"Good God," exclaimed Andrew, starting. "Is she all right?"

"In excellent health," said Chin. "The one who rescued the lady ran away, as if he did not want her thanks. She sprang after him, faster than the horse had run, as if she would thank him anyway. The last we saw of the lady she was in swift pursuit."

Andrew shook his head. He could picture the scene — Jayne, fresh from the inevitable insults and denials in her audience with the bashaw, had wandered into the street and almost got herself killed. His worry spurted sharply into anger. She needed a good spanking. She never should have been allowed out of New York without an armed escort.

Atlas frowned and blinked his brown button eyes, as though sharing his master's exasperation.

"Thank you for the report," said Andrew.

"This is not all," said Chang, his normally expressionless face taut. "I have said the lady stumbled. But only because she was encouraged to do so."

"How so?"

"It was evident for us to see," said Chin, "she was pushed by one of the men in the crowd."

Atlas let out a scream. Andrew pitched him from his lap, and it was back to the window for the monkey.

"You are sure it wasn't an accident?"

"We have no doubt," said Chang. "My brother and I attempted to pursue him, unwisely perhaps, but the brave lady requires much care."

171

"We regret to report that our pursuit was short lived. The man escaped," said Chin.

"But we are pleased to report that we were able to see him clearly. He is a man we have seen before. A man with a great ugly scar across his face."

"On the quayside in Derna," said Chin. "We do not wish to trouble the captain, who has sent the lady ashore, but we have conferred. The lady is in great danger. Both my brother and I believe you should know."

Chapter Thirteen

When the storm began to lessen, Mohammed led Jayne through a tour of the private apartments on the second floor of the borrowed home, and later, when the rain was done, he took her onto the roof.

"It is the habit of the family to rest and visit far above the streets," he informed her as he rolled a heavy piece of canvas out of the way, revealing a dry expanse of tile. "The women it is that I mean, and the children. The men tend to business in the shops and on the chairs outside the coffee houses. Sometimes they are called to their place of work in far away towns."

Fearful she would hear the bitterness in his voice, he hastened to add, "This is the way of my people, and has been thus since ancient days."

"That's not so different from the way my mother and stepfather live," she assured him with a smile.

Jayne settled on one of the pillows they'd collected from a room directly below. It was early evening, and a cool breeze blew from the north, stirring the tendrils of her loosened hair, stirring her spirit as well. Resting peacefully, she heard the high-pitched singing of women and the clapping of hands. The pleasing sounds wafted to the rooftop from out of the desert.

"The song of the Bedouins," explained Mohammed without her asking. "They camp at the edge of the desert, and at night they rejoice for the goodness of the day."

Turning toward the south, Jayne saw the flickers of the camel-dung fires playing against a flat, sandy plain, and a host of dark-robed figures moving gracefully in the light, the brass jewelry on the women sparkling like fireflies in the dusk. Against the far horizon rose a profile of the Gharyan Mountains, their peaks pink-and-purple tipped from the reflections of the setting sun.

Mohammed saw that she appreciated the beauty of the scene, and he was glad.

"Miss Worthington has come from far away to see the bashaw."

"Yes," said Jayne, with a smile, and waited for the boy to begin his questions. Surely he was curious as to her purpose, wanting more details than he'd learned from the donkey driver outside the bashaw's palace, but she waited and he did not ask.

Disappointed, Jayne found herself wanting to talk. She'd felt from the moment Mohammed pulled her to safety that their meeting was inevitable. It was equally inevitable that she share with him the details of her plight.

As the night settled around them, she told him her story, omitting details which she did not believe could be anyone's concern but hers, ending in a detailed description of the audience with Karamanli.

In the fading light Mohammed listened carefully to the shiftings of her tone and watched the movements of her hands, clues to the segments of her story she chose not to reveal. Like him, she came not from a loving family, and she had difficulties with her Captain MacGregor, who figured into the tale much more often than his role should demand.

Great difficulties, Mohammed surmised. He was not stupid as to the ways of men and women. Strong feelings were involved between the two. Angry feelings which could so quickly transform to feelings of another kind.

Miss Jayne possessed much goodness, he decided. And great importance to a not-quite-so-humble Arab boy. He must see that she was not hurt.

"I don't suppose," she said with a little laugh, "that you know anything about Josh? I've asked everyone else."

Keeping a straight and innocent face, Mohammed seized the opening she gave him and put his nimble mind to work.

"I know of no man with this name." Which was no less than the truth. "But this story you tell. It is wondrous to me."

"Why so?"

"Because it is much like a tale . . . a legend of my people. Please to understand," he added with a slight shrug, "such tales are said to be born in truth."

Anticipation tingled along Jayne's spine. "Tell it to me."

Such innocence, thought Mohammed. Like the lamb who goes willingly to the knife.

"The storytellers speak of a young boy washed ashore many years ago. Of a poor man who saved him and took him to his humble home." He glanced slyly at his listener and chose his words carefully.

175

"Fair-skinned like the Berbers, and black-eyed like the Arabs, he was, with a ready smile upon his face. He made all around him share his joy to be alive."

Jayne felt a quickening of her heart. Josh would be very much like that. "Go on," she urged.

"He spoke a strange tongue, but in his youth he learned quickly the words of his new world. The people knew no name for the stranger, and they called him Boy. He is grown to manhood now, so say the storytellers, but still he goes by this name."

Jayne held herself very still, afraid almost to speak, unwilling to let go of the strange sensations that were settling on her.

"He is grown to manhood," she said softly. "He did not drown."

"Such is the tale."

Could it be true? Jayne wanted it thus, more than she had ever wanted anything in her life. Until this night, everything she tried had been met with hostility or denial. And now . . .

She must not allow herself to behave foolishly. A sensible woman of at least average intelligence would proceed cautiously, always questioning, always doubting, until the proof became so overwhelming that all the questions and doubts were erased.

The trouble was, she was having a terrible time stifling the giggle of excitement that was bubbling inside. There was one thing she had to know, and as she spoke she stared into the infinity of night. "Do you know his fate?"

Mohammed nodded solemnly. "He grew strong as a camel, as a stallion, hidden away like a precious jewel from a greedy world that might bring him harm. For this was the belief of the old man who had saved him, and of the poor people who had helped nurse the stranger to health. The happiness he had brought to them was more valuable than gold, for he had brought the gift of joy."

He watched with great care the reaction to his tale, and saw with satisfaction that his listener was much moved. "Alas," he said sadly, "a rich and evil man"—he stressed the *evil*—"stole him and made him his slave."

The urge to laughter died. "In Tripoli?"

"In Derna. It is a city not so grand as Tripoli, on the water three days' sail to the east from here. Many more if the traveler must go by land."

Derna. Jayne struggled to recall where she'd heard the name. And then she remembered. It was to be Andrew MacGregor's destination after he departed Tripoli.

Was it her fate always to have her path cross with his? Something tingled inside as she pictured the captain. Much to her shame, she had to force her thoughts back to Josh.

"And he is in Derna now."

"Ah, this is not so. He toils in the desert, in a place known as Ziza. Here he performs the feats of great power. Rolls mighty stones across the desert for the buildings, digs the rivers, plants the food."

Growing increasingly enthusiastic as he spun out the tale, Mohammed gave in to flights of fantasy, little bothering to spare his listener the most gruesome detail in his imagination.

"At night he is beaten until the flesh falls from his bones, and in the morning the flesh has returned, and he is made to labor once again."

Mohammed saw her shock and knew he had gone

177

too far. The excesses of his young age, he told himself, must be carefully guarded.

"This, please to understand, is the version told by the storyteller who is least revered by the people. Others more reliable say he toils in the desert under a yoke of oppression and prays that one day he may be released from bondage."

"Oh," said Jayne with a sigh, readily forgetting the torture and settling on the daily toils. They constituted a difficult enough plight.

She fought back tears. Despite all the warnings she gave herself, she pictured the unfortunate known as Boy the way she'd been picturing Josh. On this strange and enchanted night, the worst of the fears that had long haunted her seemed possible — Josh, a tortured prisoner in the desert awaiting rescue.

"Please to understand," said Mohammed, "this is the way of the legend. I do not know of its truth."

And neither did Jayne. Sensible Jayne, practical Jayne, who could barely contain a very unsensible whoop of joy. She suspected . . . oh yes, she very much suspected that at last she was being shown the way she must go. Mohammed wasn't trying to push her into anything. Indeed, he seemed reluctant to tell her the story, repeatedly warning it was possibly no more than a storyteller's legend.

But it was also possibly true. And what course was open to her now other than to investigate it?

"This desert settlement you speak of —"

"Ziza."

"Is it far into the desert?"

"Very far. The traveled way lies south of Derna."

She stared at the boy's bent head. He looked up at her and smiled, then lay back to rest, his eyes closed.

178

There was such an air of innocence about him, and more, of good will. She thanked Providence he'd been outside the palace today.

Kismet, the people of this world called it. Fate. She had felt it drawing her on as she ran through the Tripolitan streets. Never a believer in preordained destiny, she was a believer now.

And kismet was involved, too, with Andrew MacGregor. It was more than just coincidence that they kept meeting. It was fate. The very thought renewed the tingling inside her, and this time she did not will it away. In truth, she wanted to hug herself and hold the tingle for as long as it lasted. She had to visit Andrew again. She could see no other course.

The boy's breathing grew even, and she realized he had fallen asleep. She lay back on the pillow, and with the sing-song voices of the distant Bedouins washing over her, stared up at the sparkling canopy of night. There was something timeless about this part of the world with its ancient beliefs and wandering tribes, something very wonderful.

By all rights she should feel more lonely than she'd ever felt in her life, cut off as she was from home and family and everything she'd ever known. Instead she felt a mingling of excitement and peace . . . a certainty that she was doing the right thing.

And partly because of Andrew. His name was written in the stars.

The following morning Andrew stood beside the *Trossachs'* mainmast, his attention directed to the tail swinging like a pendulum beneath the crow's nest. On the eastern horizon the sun was just making

179

its first appearance of the day, its pink fire catching in the frigate's brass fittings, and the monkey chattered loudly his approval.

"Atlas knows we're about to sail," said Andrew, casting a sideways glance at the young seaman beside him.

"Sorry, Cap'n Mac," said Boxer, twisting his sailor's cap in his hands. "I made it back in time, but I know 'twas close." His blue eyes glanced guiltily up at the captain, and he felt his cheeks go warm. "The woman kept me from leavin'."

Andrew's thick brows raised a fraction. "Chain you to a bedpost, did she?"

Boxer grinned. "She suggested something o' the sort, or maybe it was that I was to do the binding. We never got around to it, but we're to have a go next time I'm in port."

"Provided you go ashore."

Boxer's eyes turned woeful. "Cap'n Mac, ye can't mean what I'm thinking." He clutched his stomach with great theatricality. "There's a burning inside me never been there afore. Eats at my vitals 'til I think I'll go mad. If I'm not allowed to quench it, like as not I'll end up a pile of ash right where we stand."

"Lust is what's burning, lad. And if it's not satisfied, you might well be discomfited but the loss is rarely fatal."

Andrew knew whereof he spoke. He'd not met with female companionship since . . . since before he met the woman whose name he refused to say.

He'd gone ashore last night with half a mind to settle a little burning of his own, but all he'd managed to do was ask around for the dark-haired American woman in the red cloak. There had been no news, but the American consul had assured him he would make inquiries.

"I tried to warn her this morning against moving about the city unchaperoned, but she proved singularly stubborn," the consul had said. "She belongs to a powerful family, I'm led to understand, with influence in Washington."

"I'm acquainted with the stepfather."

"Ah." The consul smiled knowingly. "Now I understand your concern. And share it, of course." The last added hastily. "I hope there will be no trouble when she finally does return home."

It was plain the man was worried more about his own position than about Jayne, and Andrew had barely concealed his disgust. Not that the consul took note.

"Put your mind at ease, Captain MacGregor," he said. "I usually hear of trouble soon enough, and I've not heard a word. We've some fine families here in Tripoli, including a few Americans. Someone is giving her a room for the night."

"You'll make inquiries."

"Most definitely. Besides, she's left her belongings at the consulate." He smiled reassuringly. "I'm sure to see her when she returns for them. Consider the problem out of your hands."

Which was exactly what Andrew was attempting to do this early morn. He thanked all the deities of the countries where he docked that he would not have to deal with her again.

"Cap'n Mac."

He turned to his first mate. "What is it, Oakum?"

"We've company." Pale eyes glittering in a grizzly, gray face, he nodded toward the gangplank.

181

Andrew did not bother to look. Oakum's expression told him all he needed to know.

"So she's back." Alive. Safe. He felt a surge of relief, and then a jolt of irritation. He'd only *thought* he wouldn't deal with her again.

"Aye, she's back," said Oakum. "And if 'n I might say so—"

Andrew held up a hand. "Don't be telling me, mate, about how vulnerable she looks or how glad I ought to be she survived twenty-four hours in this hellhole of a town. The lass"—he still refused to call her by name—"could survive revolution and riots and a three-year-plague if she had to. Like as not, she'd cause 'em herself."

"Miss Worthington," said Boxer with a broad smile as he caught on at last to the topic of conversation. "I've worried about 'er since leaving the consulate. Didn't much care for the looks of the place."

From his perch in the crow's nest Atlas let out a scream. Andrew wished he could do the same.

"See to your duties, lad. You've catching up to do."

Boxer nodded at his captain's sharp tone, slapped the cap atop his uncombed blond locks, and beat a hasty retreat for the sanctuary offered on the forward deck.

Andrew watched the departure, then turned to the far horizon. For a moment he considered the possibility of weighing anchor and getting the hell out of the harbor. It would be a futile action. Somehow she'd manage pursuit.

Beside him, Oakum noted his captain's furrowed brow. "She's waiting permission to come aboard," he said, well pleased with the displeasure but fighting to keep it to himself. The American lass had Cap'n Mac between wind and water, the only person he knew who could throw the Scot in such a state.

Oakum remembered from his own long-ago courting days that such a feeling had come before something deeper, something satisfying, something good. A matchmaker, by damn, that's what he was turning into. His beloved Mary—if she was watching—would be getting a good laugh.

"Waiting permission, is she?" asked Andrew.

He shook his head in disgust, but there was little he could do except submit to his immediate fate. Best find out what she was up to, then send her on her way. She was the consul's concern, not his.

"See that the preparations for sailing are under way. I won't be long."

"If'n ye don't mind, Cap'n Mac, I'll let the Chinese know she's come t' no harm."

Andrew's lips flattened. "I'm sure they'll be pleased."

He stepped to the top of the gangplank and looked down at the crowded quay, and at the claret-robed figure awaiting him. The cloak was stiff from the dousing two days before, and he suspected covered an equally stiff young woman. Twenty-four hours on her own . . . hours which included an inexplicable assault upon her person. No telling what she had to say.

His boots set the gangplank to rattling as he hurried down. He halted in front of her and when she didn't speak right away, he said, "Come to bid me fair sailing, have you?"

Sarcastic as ever, thought Jayne, but she couldn't

let it ruin the hope that she'd found in the star-sprinkled darkness of last night.

"No, I haven't come to tell you goodbye."

She threw back her hood and stared him straight in the eye. And caught her breath. She'd remembered much about him, but not the impact he made each time they met. He was so . . . so much a man. For a moment she was speechless. And still.

But only on the outside. In the part of her that really mattered, Jayne was like a kettle of hot water set on the back section of a stove. All it took for her to boil was the heat of Andrew MacGregor. She felt his heat now. And her insides were beginning to steam.

"I see you survived the night," he said. "At the consulate, I suppose." He wondered if she would lie.

How coolly he spoke, and she welcomed a return of composure. Fate might have guided her footsteps back to the frigate, but it was her own good sense that would tell her what to do now that she was here.

"The consul proved as stupid as the one in Tangier. I slept beneath the stars."

"Ah then, huddled in a doorway at the side of a street, alone, abandoned . . ."

He liked the picture, although such an uncomfortable night didn't seem to have taken the starch out of her.

"As a matter of fact, I slept on the roof of one of the largest homes in the city, cushioned by silk pillows. And I didn't sleep alone. Mohammed was with me all the time." She looked around for the boy, but he had disappeared.

Andrew took the news with surprise and an irritation that was close to anger. He'd been stupid enough to try to find her last night, instead of taking care of his own needs, and she'd found another protector. Someone named Mohammed. He'd always suspected the woman was not as innocent as she seemed.

"I offer congratulations that you found someone more amiable than me."

"Captain MacGregor, that would include most everyone save the bashaw, who was not at all an agreeable man."

"Didn't give you a map to your brother, I take it."

"And you, of course, can hardly wait to crow about how you predicted his reaction."

"I'm trying to control myself." Andrew watched her expressive eyes. "Anything else to report? Any other troubles?" Such as being shoved under the hooves of a galloping horse.

Jayne looked past him to a trio of sailors rattling to each other in French at the edge of the dock, to the passing throng of robed figures that were becoming very ordinary to her, and at last back at Andrew. "None." It seemed the safer path to take.

She avoided the accusing look in his eye. "I've come about another business proposition. I want to book passage on the *Trossachs*."

Andrew choked.

"You are leaving today, are you not?" she asked.

He got hold of himself. "Not for Tangier."

"That's not where I'm going. Derna is my destination, as I believe it is yours."

Andrew shook his head in disbelief. "Are you completely daft?"

She fought an urge to slap the scorn from his face.

"Not completely." *No more than I am comely.*

"Why Derna?"

"That's my concern." She hesitated. If he just wouldn't look at her like that, as though she were on trial. "All right, if you must know, I've heard rumors of someone resembling Josh living there. I simply want to instigate a few inquiries."

Not a satisfactory answer, Andrew decided, but then there were a list of things about her that didn't satisfy him. Like taking far too much of his time, and occupying his thoughts far more than she should. He should be done with her by now.

"I don't suppose you've seen your consul this morning."

"Why should I? The man's a fool."

"That may be, but 'tis his job to serve as liaison between you and the Tripolitans."

"I'm not dealing with the Tripolitans right now, captain. As I said, this is a business proposition between you and me, and I can handle it myself. I do not want private quarters, which, as you have often pointed out, would mean my sleeping in your bunk. Last night was so pleasant, I would enjoy spending each night under the stars. A blanket on deck will suffice."

Andrew's eyes narrowed. "Shared by your friend Mohammed? I noticed you looking for him. Are you buying him passage, too?"

Jayne saw very well he thought she was talking about a man. She didn't mind in the least. Let him think someone found her attractive.

Anyway, he'd probably spent the night with a woman. A whore, she amended, which wasn't at all her concern.

"I would welcome Mohammed aboard if he would go."

She cast another glance around the crowded quay. Strangers, hundreds of them, were all she saw, and suddenly she felt very much alone. Mohammed brought her comfort, and he'd left without even saying goodbye.

She fought for the magic emotions of last night, but they evaded her. She always seemed to end up being deserted. Papa . . . Granny Worth . . . and then Josh, all gone, and except for the servant Alva there had never been anyone else in whom she could confide. Until she'd met a fourteen-year-old Arab on the Barbary Coast. And now he, too, had disappeared.

If she were given to self-pity, now would be a good time to feel very sorry for herself. But self-pity was an indulgence. She had to be strong, if not for herself, then for Josh.

She stiffened her spine. "I'm prepared to pay you a hundred dollars, or the equivalent in pounds, if you prefer."

Andrew whistled. "A goodly sum."

"You wouldn't let me pay for repairs to the long-boat. This way I can make amends at least in part. You're a practical man, or so you seemed when you visited my stepfather. And a practical man would most certainly say yes."

Andrew ran a hand through his hair and looked her over. She had a stubborn lift to her chin and a fire in her eye and she spoke with a determination even more pronounced than when she'd approached him in the tavern months ago in New

York. The consul, indeed a fool as she'd said, would be no match for Jayne.

He was swept with an urge to shake her until she came to her senses, but past experience had taught him he was best off not laying a hand on her slender body. Somehow she always emerged the winner in their sparring; she was tougher than she looked.

"I can see you still hesitate." Jayne swallowed, knowing what she had to say, yet finding the words difficult.

"Aye, lass, I hesitate. I've reason to do so."

"Not anymore. I promise not to cause trouble in any way, which I'll admit has not been the case in the past. But you're the one who came uninvited into my room in Tangier and caught me in a state of dishabille, and I didn't ask to be stripped and settled in your bunk."

"All regrettable mistakes."

His words hurt.

"I assure you that during the few days it takes to get to Derna, I will keep my clothes on and I will most certainly not get close enough for us to touch. That way you won't get so angry and you certainly will have no cause for disgust."

Chapter Fourteen

So she would keep her clothes on, would she? Jayne might be living up to the letter of her promise, Andrew conceded as he emerged onto the deck of the *Trossachs,* but not the essence.

It was late afternoon on the first day out of Tripoli, and the frigate was cutting through a calm Mediterranean Sea, her pace fast and even. His passenger stood by the port rail letting the wind and spray off the water mold her fir-green dress to her body as though she wore no more than some strumpet off the streets.

It didn't take much imagination for him to pick out the particulars of her shape — high rounded breasts and narrow waist, and slender hips that became long, neverending legs.

And all the crew finding work on deck, watching her more than their tasks, with Boxer the worst of 'em, coiling and uncoiling rope, then coiling it back again as though what he was doing made good sense. The lad had discovered lust. He'd never be the same.

Unless she was deaf and blind, Miss Jayne Worthington had to know what she was doing. Hell, even Atlas was hanging over the crow's nest grinning down at her like a . . . like a monkey.

A gust of wind took the last of the pins from her

hair, and the long curls whipped like black silk around her face. A smile broke onto her face. Her head fell back. She gripped the rail and closed her eyes. The ship rolled beneath her and for balance she shifted her feet apart. Her skirt caught between her legs.

Andrew felt a tightening in his loins. He could have sworn he heard a cheer from somewhere toward the bow. Enough, he decided. She could stand on deck stark naked as far as he was concerned, but she was too much distraction for the crew.

He came up behind her. "Get your cloak or get below."

It took Jayne a moment to register the command, so absorbed was she by the fine day.

Pulling a strand of hair from her lips, she glanced around at the captain, who looked very angry indeed. The sky might be clear and the water smooth as glass, but there was a storm in Andrew MacGregor's eyes.

"I beg your pardon?" she asked, feeling rather stupid and regretting very much that the feeling showed.

"You heard me. The men have had enough sport for the day."

The words chilled and she hugged herself.

"You'll have to explain yourself, captain," she said over the roar of the wind and the snapping of the sails. "I've kept out of the way, just as I promised. When I agreed to take the first mate's cabin"—which was only right since she'd had to triple her original hundred-dollar offer—"remember that in turn you promised me a place on deck during the day."

She had a challenging tilt to her chin and a light in her eyes that stirred Andrew's blood. He'd like to throw her over his shoulder and take her below and set her straight as to the way things were on board ship. The captain was king, tyrant, dictator, and deity all rolled into one. His word was law.

"Take a look around," he said.

Jayne did, and she saw at least a dozen sailors scattered amongst the rigging and the barrels and the masts, all of them smiling in her direction. Boxer went so far as to wave from the aft deck.

Andrew started with her hair and moved slowly down to her slippered feet, then studied her all the way back to the expressive eyes that were glaring at him. "Take your pick, lass. The cloak or the cabin. I'd just as soon you chose below."

She refused to be unnerved, either by his perusal or his highhandedness. "You can't think *I'm* distracting them," she said, truly skeptical. Perhaps she was standing rather wantonly with her clothes and hair whipping about, but who cared? That was the beauty of being plain. One didn't have to be overparticular about modesty.

The captain was the problem, causing a scene the way he was.

His answer was a growl.

"How articulate," she said.

He took a step closer. Jayne swallowed. His own midnight-black hair was blowing in the wind, his strong face shadowed by bristles, the white shirt sculpted against the muscled ridges of arms and chest. At that moment he looked tall as a mast and broad as a deck and altogether intimidating.

He really was a big brute, and he made her feel very small and insignificant. Except that she could arouse him to anger, which brought a slight smile to her heart if not to her lips. Smiling right now where he could see might prove unwise.

191

And so, too, was taunting him, but she couldn't resist. He wasn't the only one who could be piqued.

"Remember when I thought there was a gorilla on board the *Trossachs?*"

She let her eyes roam over him in a manner similar to his study of her. She lingered on the path that led from his flat abdomen up to the open throat of his shirt, but when she felt an imaginary fist in the pit of her stomach, she moved back to his face.

"I was right." Her voice wasn't nearly so strong as she had wished. "Atlas isn't the only simian on board."

Andrew reconsidered throwing her over his shoulder and carrying her below. Whether she knew it or not, she was flirting with bodily harm.

"I think we're liable to end up somewhere off the coast of Italy unless you show a little common sense," he said. "Be gone. Let the crew get to work."

Jayne didn't believe for a minute that she was such a bother; he was simply trying to frighten her, probably just to prove that he could.

Unfortunately, he was right. Coming up on her the way he had, like a sudden squall, he'd taken the glory from the day, and she wasn't up to continuing their fight. She wasn't even sure what it was about . . . except that he wanted to establish ascendancy over her.

Let him think that he had and try to keep their paths from crossing. It was the way she'd always dealt with her mother. She'd deal with Andrew MacGregor the same way.

"A rest before dinner does sound rather nice," she said, standing tall. "Thank you for suggesting it."

She moved past him, waving at Boxer and smiling up at Atlas before hurrying below.

Andrew stared after her, remembering the swish of her skirt long after she'd gone. He'd made a mistake, by damn, in letting her on board. But he hadn't expected her to pay so much.

"Three hundred," he'd thrown at her at the base of the gangplank, when she wouldn't go away.

"Done," she'd said.

And somehow the arrangement had been completed. When they sailed on the outgoing tide, she'd been entrenched on the frigate, heading for Derna, the town where Chang and Chin had seen her would-be assailant.

Jayne wasn't the one who was daft. That description belonged to a Scot whose experiences had left him with little respect for women and no feelings of responsibility beyond the concerns of his ship. In continuing their association, he was going against his basic beliefs and drives.

A rare kind of restlessness stirred him. For the first time since leaving his Scottish village more than twenty years before, he began to suspect his fate was not in his own hands.

By the time Jayne found her way to the first mate's small cabin, she'd lost all of the cool assurance with which she had left the deck. Sitting on the bunk in the semi-dark, the lantern unlit on the paneled wall, she brushed the hair from her face and fingered the folds of her skirt.

Given time to think, she'd come up with a new assessment of the situation concerning Andrew Mac-Gregor. He'd tried to shame her, not just prove himself in charge, which he could have done in a hun-

193

dred more subtle ways. Instead, he'd chosen to embarrass her in front of the men.

Facing him, she'd been angry enough to come to her own defense. Alone, with her usual self doubts rushing in, she could think only that she had made a fool of herself standing like that on deck. Andrew certainly thought so, and a small voice told her he had been right.

The sailors must have heard what he said. No wonder they had smiled; they must have been laughing inside. Her cheeks burned, and all the warnings of her mother crowded into her mind.

You don't know the first thing about handling men.

Stand up straight, and for God's sake, try to do something with your hair. Too bad you can't do anything about that terrible dark skin.

Try to act with dignity. It's the only gift that you have.

A little late for dignity, after the way she'd been parading herself on deck.

Her heart beat heavily in her breast. How nice she had felt in her gown, one of the garments she purchased in New York. A day dress of fine cotton, green as a Virginia forest just after dawn when the early sunlight falls on the dew-kissed leaves.

Or so it had seemed to her, and she'd been unable to resist its purchase. Even though the rounded neckline was a fraction lower than she would have liked, and she thought the double row of ruffles at the wrists rather frivolous.

But she had been in a rare and fanciful mood. The color brought out the best in her tawny skin and didn't in the least make her look sallow. Millicent herself had said so, sounding as though everything else in her daughter's wardrobe did.

The waist came high under her bosom, and the long skirt flowed softly against her long hipline and longer legs. Or at least the skirt was supposed to flow; on deck it must have looked as though it were painted onto her body.

Andrew hadn't liked it one little bit.

Who did she think she was, some grand beauty who could demand both attention and respect? She was plain Jayne, the only thing truly fanciful about her the *y* her mother had inserted in her name.

At the end of the bunk rested the valise Boxer had gotten for her from the consulate; beside it lay the cloak. She put it on. She wouldn't take it off, at least in public, until she had bade the captain goodbye.

In the meantime she would be polite and friendly to the crew, if the occasion arose, and she'd be the same to Andrew MacGregor, even if she expired in the effort.

For Andrew, things didn't get better the next day, especially after Oakum managed to maneuver him and Jayne together for breakfast at the stern.

"Did you know Chang and Chin were born in England?" she asked, selecting her fare from a platter of figs and cheese.

"No," Andrew said, unable to hide his surprise.

"Sons of an importer. He moved them to Peking when they were boys, and they've got wives and children they send their money to. Chang has a couple of sons and Chin a boy and a girl. At least I think that's the way it is."

Andrew watched her lick the juice of a fig from her

lower lip, and he looked away. "How did they get mixed up with pirates?"

"Captured in the South China Sea and taken to the Caribbean. They are grateful for your rescue, Captain MacGregor."

Most polite she was, as though they'd never had a set-to the previous day, but she wore the cloak and her hair was pinned back in a tight little knot.

She went on to talk about Boxer and the sailmaker and the carpenter, filling him in with bits of information that he'd never been told. When he saw Oakum grinning at him, he threw his fruit to the gulls and went below to study his charts.

The rest of the day and the night and the next day he avoided her, but he heard her voice wafting on the breeze as he strode the deck and he caught sight of the claret cloak and the gentle slope of her shoulders beneath its folds and the graceful turn of her head as she stared out to sea.

Worst of all, he had to listen to the men talk about what a pleasure it was to have her on board, what a fine mariner she was becoming, not once complaining or tossing her dinner, the latter the highest accolade they could give.

These were sea-toughened sailors who didn't believe a woman's place was on a ship. As if showing off for her, they went about their duties with an industry they had not shown since he'd paid them bonus money for last year's record trip from Glasgow to Tangier.

Oakum claimed they saw the vulnerability in her. Andrew claimed they'd never heard the word.

She even managed to make friends with Atlas, who didn't take kindly to strangers. Now he was eating out of her hand.

By nightfall, only a dozen hours away from the port of Derna, he told himself he was almost rid of her. The sorceress had retired for the night. Stripped of his clothes, Andrew was attempting to get some rest before the morning docking.

She was in the adjoining room. He could hear her singing. Oakum always claimed that even with the door closed he could hear his captain's speaking voice.

"No need to shout fer me," he'd said more than once. "I'm right next door."

Andrew admitted the first mate was right.

Her voice rose in volume, and he recognized a sea chantey — a very bawdy song.

He growled in discontent, knowing one or more of the seamen must have taught her the words. And she understood them, all right. No one could be that innocent.

She wasn't innocent at all, he decided. If he was a gorilla, she was a sly-eyed vixen.

Gorillas were bigger than vixens, and he needed his sleep.

He rose from the bunk, pulled on his trousers, and went to shut her up.

The pounding on the door brought Jayne to an upright position in the narrow bed. She hit her head on a low-lying beam and cried out.

The door swung inward, and she could make out a very recognizable figure standing in the dimly lit opening. His face was in shadow but instinct told her he was not smiling and he had not come to wish her goodnight.

A soft light from the passageway fell across Jayne as she sat upright in Oakum's bunk. Andrew regarded

197

the tangle of dark locks, the wide, worried eyes, the graceful fingers clutching the blanket like a shield beneath a raised chin. As though he'd come to rape her.

"Cut out the caterwauling," he snapped.

Forgetting the bump on her head, Jayne sent him a glare she hoped he could see.

"I was simply singing myself to sleep."

Which was true. Since she was a very little girl, every time she felt especially lonely, she hummed a lullaby just to hear the sound of a human voice. Perhaps she had gotten a little carried away, but the song Boxer had taught her seemed to require volume.

And she was very lonely tonight, although she hadn't the vaguest idea why. Tomorrow she would leave the *Trossachs* and go about the next portion of her journey . . . a portion that was dictated by rumor, it was true, but heretofore she'd been going on instinct alone. In her mind, rumor translated into fact.

So why the feeling of being lost? She'd been fated to meet with Andrew again, but the meeting wasn't for all time.

He walked deeper into the room. Something was different, she thought. She missed the solid sound of his boots against the floor, which meant he didn't have them on. He was only half-clad. Shirtless. An image of what his bare chest must look like in a better light sent a shiver down her spine.

Beneath her nightgown, she too was bare. The shiver shifted to something more substantial.

He came to a halt beside the bed, leaning close so that she was in his shadow. She saw only the outline of his head and the broad shoulders which remained in silhouette.

The darkness didn't keep her from feeling the

198

warmth of his breath on her cheek, and she could smell tobacco and liquor beneath the more enticing scent of the sea that he always carried with him.

Gardenias, thought Andrew. She always smelled of gardenias. Must be the soap that she used.

It had its usual effect on him. His hands itched to take her by the shoulders and to . . . hell, do a great deal more. His blood was heating fast. He knew what she looked like naked, knew the shape of her breasts, knew the softness of her skin.

And he'd never been considered a saint.

He didn't, however, go in for taking a woman by force.

"You're keeping the ship awake," he whispered. *You're keeping me awake.*

"I didn't mean to," she whispered back.

They both fell silent and listened to the unevenness of the other's breathing.

"What kind of witch are you?" Andrew asked, for in truth he felt under a spell.

Jayne took the question as an insult. The only witches she knew were the wart-nosed crones in picture books.

She sat up straight and again bumped her head. "I'm the kind that puts curses on bastards. Now get out of my room."

Andrew had never been one to accept orders. And she'd used that word again. He submitted to the impulse he'd been fighting. His hands curved around her shoulders and he pulled her to her knees, crushing her against him and covering her mouth with his.

She was all the sweet temptation in the world, filled with honeyed warmth, and right now it was warm honey that he craved.

Knowing she should fight, Jayne felt herself melt like ice in the desert, and her body curled against his, all instinct and desire springing from the ache she'd been feeling inside. He soothed that ache, he filled the void; in his arms, with hot lips pressed to hers, she wasn't alone.

Her hands touched the warm naked skin stretched across his chest. She felt the rumblings inside him, the barely contained hints of violence; somehow they tremored their way into her.

She moaned. He heard her, and he felt an explosion building deep within him, an explosion he'd be unable to control.

Andrew never lost control. He thrust her away before he found himself on top of her and between her legs.

Not that she'd stop him.

His breath was ragged, and from nothing more than one chaste kiss. He hadn't so much as touched her with his tongue.

Which he wanted to do. All over.

And she'd let him. Then he'd never get rid of her. She would be telling him what to do. Or so it seemed to his befuddled brain.

Andrew was a man who traveled alone. He didn't let a woman confuse him; he didn't let her under his skin.

He backed away from the bunk and caught his breath. "So you're not the innocent after all."

Dizzy, Jayne couldn't believe she'd heard right. "What did you say?"

"I . . . oh, what the hell." Raking fingers through his hair, he turned and left the cabin.

She sat back on her heels, fingers pressed against

her lips, willing the thoughts to settle in her mind, trying to decide what had just occurred. He'd invaded her privacy, kissed her with what she assumed to be ardent enthusiasm, and then in disgust he'd pushed her away.

Just the way he'd done in the Kasbah of Tangier.

Not this time.

She went after him, following him into his own quarters, slamming the door closed behind her, not caring if she awakened every sailor on board.

She stood in her high-necked, long-sleeved nightgown, barefooted, hands on hips, and glared at him. He glared back from beside his desk. Light from a full moon beamed through the open window, strong enough for her to see the wariness in his storm-blue eyes. And the width of his coppery chest and the black hairs curling like an arrow down to his waist.

And his broad hands at his side, the tight trousers, the big brown feet. He did have big feet, she thought incongruously, to go with the big hands and the . . .

She let the thought go. It was just something her sister Marybeth had said, and it had no bearing now.

"Captain MacGregor," she said, eyes flashing, "you may own the *Trossachs* and you may be considered a god to your men, but you cannot come into my room anytime it pleases you and kiss me and paw me and say whatever comes into your head."

Sitting back on the edge of the desk, Andrew let her rave on. If she truly wanted to settle his ardor, he thought, she was going about it the wrong way, coming into his quarters with her hair wild as the light in her eyes, and her body clad in nothing more than a very thin gown. It might go from chin to toes, but in between, the delicate fibers allowed a view of a pair of dark-tipped breasts and the patch of black hair at the juncture of her thighs.

Or maybe he was just remembering the enticing details from the night he'd undressed her and put her in his bunk.

Maybe what she needed was another few hours in the same place, only this time she wouldn't be there alone.

"Are you done?" he asked.

His coolness fired her anger to a red-hot pitch.

"No, I'm not. What did you mean by that remark I'm not so innocent? You barge in to have your way with me and when I don't start screaming and fainting and carrying on right away, you assume that I'm one of the loose women you're used to."

His lips twitched as if he were fighting a smile, and she slipped beyond reason. "Captain MacGregor," she said, "you wouldn't know an innocent woman if she crawled into your bed."

Even Jayne knew she wasn't making sense, but she saw by the narrowing of his eyes that he understood what she meant.

He eased away from the desk. "Anything else?"

Jayne's heart caught in her throat, and her anger dissolved into something equally warm but not nearly so hostile. She absolutely could not for one second more endure looking up at him, and she studied the hands she was twisting at her waist.

"And then you leave as though—"

"As though what?"

His fingers caught her under the chin and lifted her face to him, but she kept her eyes determinedly downward.

As though you found me wanting.

She realized with horror she'd almost said the words aloud . . . as though she'd revealed to him the foolish, lonely woman that she was. When she tried to pull away, she found he had a tight grip on her face . . . that he was hurting her . . . and she slowly lifted her eyes to his.

The warm, helpless look on her face hit Andrew like a fist to his middle. She was either without guile, or she was the most skillful practitioner of women's wiles he'd ever seen.

It was time to find out which was the case.

He brushed his lips against hers and felt her tremble. "I'm not leaving tonight, and neither are you, Miss Jayne Worthington," he said, then shortened the name to a whispered "Jayne."

"What are you talking about?" she managed, wishing the blood wasn't pounding through her body and her head wasn't reeling and she wasn't feeling such a heat building inside that she wanted to rip off her clothes.

With his head bent to hers, he ran the tip of his thumb across her lower lip, and then her teeth, until finally he was touching her tongue. She wanted to close her mouth around him.

"What I'm saying"—his voice was thick and low— "is that it's time I found out just how innocent you are."

Chapter Fifteen

Andrew eased his thumb from between her lips and licked the moisture on its tip.

"You taste sweet."

Jayne's heart beat wildly, and her mouth tingled where his thumb had been. The intimacy of his simple act left her stunned. Flustered, she took a step backwards. "Perhaps," she said shakily, eyes downcast, "I should return to my own room."

"No."

Plainly said, as though there could be no possible argument.

Jayne looked up, staggered by the moonlit spectacle of him, the dark hair and dark eyes, the bristled planes of his cheeks, the sculpted curves of neck and shoulders, the ridges of muscle on his naked chest. She knew not how to defend herself against such an impact; indeed, defense was the last thing on her mind.

Her whole body thrummed, grew tense and hot, blood pounding, every sense alerted to Andrew's presence and his power. It was like that moment in Tangier when she'd tasted desire for the first time, only a thousand times stronger and sweeter and altogether irresistible. Strange things were happening to her, boiling, shifting, hungry things. She felt small, insignificant, yet vibrant and very much alive.

And oh yes, she felt foolish, too, because he expected her to be something she wasn't, and he expected her to do things she didn't know how to do.

During the past few minutes she'd lost her anger and the pride that had sent her hurrying after him. She was on a ship at sea in a strange land and she was very much alone, yet on a different plane she was with a man whose entire being was, for the moment, involved with her—she could sense it in the air that hung between them—and his presence made her feel as though she was not alone in any way, that she would never be alone again.

A fantasy, she knew, but one she did not want to reason out of existence. Equally incredible was the feeling that in his eyes, on this other-worldly night, she was not really plain at all. Her fingers brushed through the mass of hair that tumbled to her shoulders. It must be the moonlight casting a spell.

Andrew watched the shifting of her eyes and wanted very much to know what was shifting about in her mind . . . what choices she was making . . . what she was deciding to let him do.

Silly woman. The decisions were now up to him.

And intriguing decisions they were.

His practiced lover's hands took her by the shoulders, easing her closer. She was no more substantial than a moonbeam, his hand wide and dark and coarse against the thin white gown.

Sitting against the edge of the desk, he spread his legs and pulled her closer still, until her slender hips fit easily between his thighs. Closer . . . until the tips of her breasts brushed against his chest; it was as though she were as naked as he. The months of abstinence took their toll as a lightning bolt of lust shot through him; he thought he would burst through his trousers. Wedging his body against hers, he let his hardness speak of his arousal. A woman of experience would understand.

Jayne understood that he was ready for her, as she'd been told a man would be, and a shiver of fright rushed through her, the reality of his condition for a moment overwhelming her dreamlike fantasies. There was nothing dreamlike about the rock-hard evidence pressed to her thighs, no hint of fantasy, but something very hot and very tangible.

Why was she here? Why wasn't she fighting to get away? The questions skittered through the corners of her mind.

His lips brushed against the edges of her mouth, and she trembled.

"Jayne," he whispered. "Let me hear my name on your lips."

She mustn't let go . . . she mustn't. How could she let him have his way when he didn't understand the least thing about her? Somehow that little fact made what she was doing very wrong.

His thumb stroked the hollow of her throat and rested against the thundering of her heart. She forgot about right and wrong.

"Andrew," she whispered. To her ears it sounded like a word of surrender. The slight, twisted smile upon his lips told her he felt the same.

She could have been any woman who'd come to him, Jayne told herself, fighting for rationality even while her knees threatened to buckle and send her to the floor. He knew her face, he knew her name, but he did not comprehend what forces drove her. . . .

His hands caught in her hair, his mouth crashing down upon hers, setting free all the repressed longings of a lifetime, rendering her capable of only one motivating force. Andrew MacGregor. Desire shot through her like a river past a broken dam.

She touched his bare chest; his heat sent tingles from her fingertips skittering along untested paths to every part of her body . . . the swelling, hard-tipped breasts, the tightened stomach, the heated valley between her thighs. Even her toes curled against the carpet as she rubbed her hips against his sex.

The sudden wantonness brought a momentary shame, but it melted beneath the onslaught of his hungry kiss. The secret voids that had for so long been a part of her life filled with a pulsating exhilaration. His fingers raked through her tangled hair, stroking the dampness at her nape. When his arms enfolded her, she pressed herself against the hot, hard strength of him, instinctively opening her mouth and letting his tongue invade.

Andrew moaned from the pleasure and sweetness of her. She was a delicate creature in his embrace, tall and willowy, and he the brutish savage. He'd never felt such a wild, flaming hunger before. He wanted to yank the nightgown to shreds, and here beside the desk spread her legs and thrust himself deep within the honeyed goodness of her warm and willing body.

He grasped at the edge of control, concentrating on dancing his tongue against hers, kissing her lips, softly and then with great fervor, trailing down the graceful neck to the pulse point at her throat.

Her hands clung to his upper arms, nails scratching against his slick, taut skin, and he knew she was not without a wildness of her own. Not at all the innocent. He should have done them both a favor and remained with her in Tangier.

In one swift motion he lifted her into his arms and carried her to the bunk.

"Oh," she cried out against the crook of his shoulder, but she offered no struggle.

His lips roamed hotly along the curve of her throat as he laid her against the cool sheet.

" 'Tis good, lass," he murmured against the beating of her heart. "I'll make it good."

Lying close beside her in the narrow bed, his hands stroking hungrily over her gown, discovering the pleasures of her gently draped flesh, he fought to tame the explosion building within him. When she twisted and pressed herself against his touch, he came close to losing the fight.

Impatiently he tugged at the gown's hem, pulled it higher over the impossibly long and delicately curved legs, his palm scraping against the sweep of her outer thigh, tantalizingly close to the promised treasure of her sex. He sensed the pulsations, the heat, the moist hunger awaiting him, and his body throbbed until he thought he would burst.

Still, he traveled upwards along the subtle sweep of hip and narrow waist, until his hand cupped the high, firm breast, the fit just right, the nipple hard against his palm. He felt her tremble beneath his assault; the tremors heated his blood.

Nothing—not even Andrew's kiss—had prepared Jayne for the spinning rush into passion that his hands aroused. Body humming to the rhythms of his touch, she lost all sense of restraint, blinded to everything but what he was doing to her. She couldn't have told her body what to do; instincts as old as time replaced the volition that had always been hers.

In this moon-softened bed, he was luring her toward the sun; she could envision the approaching explosion of light.

More. She wanted more. Her legs parted. He hooked a leg over her, the fibers of his trousers rough against her sensitive skin, and stroked the tender flesh on the inside of her thighs. She hurt for the want of she knew not what . . . just more of what he was doing, and faster and harder without ever, ever letting up.

A cry caught in her throat. The ship moved under her, a sudden change in pitch and roll caused by more than just the steady undulations of the sea. Andrew could cause even the oceans to stir. Behind closed eyes, against the velvety black, she did indeed see a sudden brilliant luminescence.

Andrew's wonderful, magical hand stilled. She felt him tense, and she opened her eyes, not knowing what to expect, what to do, fighting the urge to cover his hand and return it to its ministrations.

"Andrew," she whispered in supplication. What had she done? Was she so terribly inept —

Again the ship pitched, and through the window she could see a rocket's flare. She thought of fireworks . . . a dizzy, silly thought . . . but it was the first thing that came to her mind. Perhaps the Chinese had set them off, a celebration of the night's delights.

A tremendous boom reverberated through the cabin.

He stiffened and drew back sharply. "What the hell!"

He was off her in an instant, yanking on his boots, and without a glance in her direction, or another word, he was out the door.

The room reeled around her, and she held onto the sides of the bunk for support. Gradually the dizziness left. She sat up. The nightgown was twisted above her waist, leaving the rest of her torso bare, the long legs sprawled and spread, the thatch of black hair between her legs seemingly bearing the imprint of his hand.

She felt a steely stab of desolation and of shame.

Another boom, and she forgot the private sensitivities. Something was terribly wrong. Scrambling from the bed, she tugged the nightgown in place and, barefooted, headed for the upper deck.

She had not cleared the doorway when a small brown figure dashed past her into the cabin, whimpering with each loping step, and cowered in the blanket-lined box at the end of the bed. Atlas was terrified by the explosions of the night. Feeling a kinship for the animal, she argued against mimicking his retreat, and once again she hurried down the passageway toward open air.

"Cast loose your guns!" a desperate, deep voice yelled as she emerged onto a nightmarish scene.

Beneath a white, full moon the frigate's crew scrambled for cannon and shot, rolling out the port-side weapons she'd taken little notice of before, darting below to fetch black bags of powder, while overhead the sails snapped against a pre-dawn wind. Andrew, half dressed, hair wild, strode amongst the confusion, barking orders, arms waving broadly, his presence everywhere at once.

Keeping to the hatchway, she caught sight of Oakum and Boxer and the Chinese, but only briefly, and her attention flew out to the water. Like a ghost ship suspended between the black of sea and sky, a small, square-rigged vessel lay no more than a hundred yards away, the silvery moonlight reflected in its sails, its guns turned onto the *Trossachs*.

"A corsair," she whispered, heart in her throat. One of the dreaded pirate ships that had tormented honest seamen for a hundred years. Most were gone now, driven out by the heads of the Barbary States, the very men who once had been their patrons. It was clear at least one remained.

Andrew's orders echoed through the night.

"Level your guns!" she heard, and "Load!" The commands became blurred as she watched and listened in horror, and then at last came the clearly enunciated "Prime!" Jayne shivered, but the night's chill evaporated under the heat of anticipation.

Overhead she saw the dark figures of mariners scrambling up the mast, muskets, blunderbusses, and cartridges strapped to their sides. Out of the chaos a deadly routine emerged, and she knew a moment's pride that Andrew had so well prepared his men.

Suddenly he was before her. "Get below!" he shouted, his face masked in fury, and without any thought of behaving otherwise, she scrambled to do as he bade. Crouched in the passageway outside his quarters, even before she heard the roar, she felt the broadside leveled at the pirate ship. The boards below her bare feet resonated from the report.

She was curiously devoid of fear for herself, thinking only of Andrew and the other men who fought to

211

save the frigate from attack. Too, she recognized a momentary sense of excitement, a thundering of blood that helped her understand more than ever before why Josh had wanted a life of adventure on the sea.

The night was filled with an answering volley from the corsair, and she felt the *Trossachs* lurch. All thought of thrills deserted her, and she could think of only one explanation for the sudden change in pitch. They'd been hit.

"Andrew," she whispered, frozen in time and space. She saw him lying motionless on the deck, his life's blood pooled beneath his stalwart shoulders, his glorious vibrancy forever stilled. The image was as clear as though she stood beside him, and terror struck her heart.

She could not still her feet from rushing back to the open hatchway, where she came to a sudden halt. He stood not five feet away, tall and proud and gloriously unhurt, the muscles of his back rippling as he waved frantically to his men, his barked commands lost in the general confusion. She crammed a fist into her mouth to keep from crying out in relief.

She'd been foolish to panic, she told herself as the blood continued to pound through her veins. Andrew MacGregor could take care of himself, and he'd not appreciate her womanly fears.

But, oh, how splendid it was to know that he fared well.

She looked beyond him to the silhouettes of rope and sail and scurrying men. Smoke and shouts drifted into the night sky, but she heard no orders to reload. Her eyes darted to the enemy. All lay quiet on the distant water, and it seemed to her untrained eye that the pirate vessel was growing smaller in the moonlight . . . that it was ceasing the attack and sailing away.

The stillness of the *Trossachs'* cannon told her she was right. A sudden joy was stilled when she looked closer at the scene before her and saw the damage inflicted by the enemy guns. The frigate's once towering main mast towered no more; instead, it canted sharply to port.

Just like . . .

She closed her eyes and pictured another, all-too-vivid night at sea. The dhow of Aziz Rashid had been similarly damaged in the storm off the coast of Algiers. The smaller vessel had made it almost into port, and would have, if not for the ineptitude of its captain.

Remembering his oily fluster, she shivered.

"No reason to fear," a voice said cheerily, and she opened her eyes to the smudged and smiling face of Boxer. He stood before her, hands on hips, his stance cocky as though he'd personally driven off the pirates.

Jayne couldn't help but smile in return. "Are you certain?"

"Aye. Cap'n Mac'll get us into port directly. Not a man aboard thinks otherwise."

"And not a woman, either."

"Boxer." Oakum's voice growled out of the dimness from somewhere aft, and with a nod and a wink, the boy was gone.

Oh yes, she thought, Captain Mac would get them to shore. He was not, after all, another Rashid.

But he wasn't that much different, either, at least not in the current circumstances. She hugged herself, recognizing the coincidence between the misfortunes of the two ships. At the time of both disasters she had been aboard, a rare passenger taken along because of the money she could pay. Not because of the company she would provide, or the justness of her cause, or even the willingness she might present in bed. Her primary attraction was that she carried cash.

And dreadful things had happened when she was along. Like the fabled albatross, she'd brought both captains terrible luck.

Huddled in the hatchway, she watched Andrew turn in her direction. She opened her mouth to speak. He gave her no notice, and his gaze moved on. More important matters occupied his mind, as well they should, she told herself. But she could not reason away the remnants of fright and shame that lay heavy in her heart, as powerful as her once flowering passion.

With a dozen men scurrying around her, she felt very much alone.

A scant hour ago she had lain in Andrew's arms, her body exposed to his eyes and to his hands. *I'll make it good,* he had said. And so he had, for a while. But not quite good enough, else why would she have this hollow ache inside?

She was, she feared, not entirely different from her mother. She'd wanted a man as much as she'd ever wanted anything and she'd been hungry to do everything that he asked. She'd considered right and wrong, and then deliberately pushed the consideration aside.

The not-so-comely spinster playing love slave to her savage lover, only he'd been quick to pull away when more important matters called. All the reasoning in the world wouldn't let her forget that, unlike her, he

214

hadn't been truly carried away by the passion she thought they shared.

They'll use you if you let them. Unless she's offered a ring, a woman must always protect herself from falling in love for more than one night at a time.

It was some late-remembered advice she'd heard at Millicent's knee. She couldn't imagine why she'd thought of it now. She'd never believed herself in love, not even one night.

She brushed back her hair, thinking she must bind it up, the way she must bind up the new-found, dissolute longings that threatened to take over her soul. She remained, after all, Jayne Catherine Worthington, Virginia farm girl and infrequent resident of New York, a twenty-five-year-old imitation adventuress who needed above all else to complete the mission that had been driving her since she was twelve.

If Joshua Worthington did indeed still live, she was his only hope. And that's all she was, at least for now.

On the inevitable return home, successful or not, she wouldn't be needing the excess baggage that memories of Andrew MacGregor would provide.

With a sigh, she turned from the deck to let the men take care of all the men-type things that must be done. And she would do her woman's thing. She would stay out of the way, and pack her belongings, and as soon as they docked, settle her account and leave, never once reminding him of the few sweet, wild moments they had spent in each other's arms.

They were moments he, too, must want to forget. Bedding an overeager spinster would forever be linked in his memory with the near destruction of his precious ship.

215

Chapter Sixteen

When the sailor made a jump for the quay, Andrew watched from the shadows cast across the deck by the afternoon sun. The newest member of the crew he was, hired on in Tripoli, and the first to depart. He landed solidly on the wooden dock and disappeared into a crowd.

"Get you gone," Andrew muttered after him, "or I'll snap your skinny frame in half like the mast."

The deserter had been the one on watch in the wee hours, taking the place of the ill Chang. He'd let the corsair anchor too near, had sullenly offered little excuse for the mistake, and now, when they were finally docking, elected to jump ship.

It was the smartest thing he'd done since hiring on.

Andrew spared a quick glance at the damaged mast, but he didn't look long, the sight being more painful as the hours went by. The *Trossachs* was like a woman to him; he'd stroked every part of her with great and loving care. His first ship, like his first love. But like each of the women he'd known, she wouldn't be his last.

No more than would Miss Jayne Worthington, who stood at the port rail, valise at her feet, and watched the final details of the docking. Couldn't wait to get off, could she? Wanted to jump like the sailor. Get away from Andrew and the things she'd revealed about herself. Innocent Jayne. Hot, passionate Jayne.

A mixture of anger and frustration grew in him, but from the mast or from the lass, he wasn't sure.

He strode to stand beside her. As if he jumped from the sky, Atlas landed with delicate precision on the rail, where he crouched to inspect the cuff of his master's shirt.

"It's taken awhile to get here," Andrew said without prelude, "but don't fret. You'll be gone soon."

Jayne looked up at Andrew with worried eyes. Through all her preparations to leave the frigate, she'd not been alone with him for even a minute. Not until now.

She stood tall in her once-beautiful claret cloak, her hair bound in the tightest bun of her life, and tried to keep a blush from her cheeks and a calmness in her heart. But Andrew—a very grim-faced Andrew—rendered her chances at success slim if not impossible.

For a minute or two she watched the throwing of the final ropes, but Andrew's presence proved a stronger magnet and she glanced back at the set of his jaw and his tight, unsmiling mouth. His strong unshaven face looked devilish with its mask of black bristles, and his sunken eyes dark as a storm-tossed sea.

When confronted with such countenances of displeasure at home, Jayne was used to looking into herself to find the cause. But not now. The captain had a right to be grim, she knew, but not because of her.

All her silly worries of the early morning—the comparisons of two captains and two wrecked ships with their lone shared trait, the same paying passenger—had long been rationalized away. She had done everything Andrew wanted, and she'd done it with an eagerness that would forever remain one of the surprises of her life.

Although, when she gave a thought to the total appearance of him this afternoon—the coppery skin at his throat, the broad, muscled shoulders, the fitted trousers with the wicked-looking knife sheathed at the waist—it wasn't difficult to figure out why the cooperation.

There was, in truth, more of her mother in her than she'd ever dreamed. It was an accepted fact now, hours after the event that had proved it beyond all doubt.

But it was not a topic for discussion. The memories of the pre-dawn hours were too new, too delicate to be subjected to a shared scrutiny in the harsh light of day.

She stirred restlessly. The best thing she could do was salvage her pride, show him she wouldn't be carrying regrets or shame with her when she disembarked, then take her leave without so much as a backwards glance.

But it wouldn't be easy, not with him looming so close beside her and everything about him a reminder of her new-found sensuality . . . a weakness that could too easily complicate her already complicated life.

She dropped her gaze to Atlas, hunched on the rail beside him, brown button eyes darting back and forth between them, lips pursed as though he didn't know whether to smile or to scream.

When images of the night flashed through her head—ragged breathing and bare, slick skin and hungry hands, and all of it bathed in a ghostly light from the moon—Jayne shared the monkey's dilemma.

At least Andrew had covered himself with one of his full-sleeved, open-throated shirts, and she was dressed in several layers of heavy wool. The wind had died as they tied up to the quay, and she felt a trickle of sweat between her breasts and a dampening in the small of her back.

Both places Andrew had stroked. Her cheeks burned at the memory, and she looked away, lest he see.

She'd be leaving soon. She ought to feel an excited anticipation . . . her spirits ought to soar. Instead, she felt a numbness that she didn't try to explain.

Her silence, his silence ate at her nerves. Around them the sailors shouted and hoisted and scrambled about the deck, but she and Andrew stood like two figureheads waiting for their ships to come along so that they might be nailed into place on the bow.

Andrew watched her hands clutch at the railing of the ship and wondered what was going through her mind. Did she expect him to say something? To compliment her? To apologize? He had no experience with women such as she. A pat on the rump, a jest, and he was gone. After a satisfying conclusion to the encounter.

There was little satisfying about last night, and

much to make him want another hour with her in his bed.

"Captain MacGregor—"

"Jayne—"

They spoke at the same time.

"You first," she said.

"Nae, should be the lady."

His eyes remained hooded, unsmiling, and she struggled to remember what she'd been about to say.

Suddenly she was very much aware of herself, of the thin body beneath the heavy garments, her hair in a tight spinster's bun, her finest feature—the black eyes—underlined by shadows almost equally dark.

Lack of sleep had made him more than ever appealing—sinister with his dark and private scowl, forbidden fruit, intriguing as the dark side of the moon—while she felt more than ever like a dowd.

One thing loomed certain—she couldn't cause a scene. She would rather jump into the Derna harbor and drown than utter one syllable that would make him think she was contented with the way things had been between them, or worse, that she wanted to lie in his arms and finish what they'd begun.

"I'm sorry about the ship," she said with full sincerity. "Oakum said no one was injured."

" 'Tis possible I was the most endangered, leaping from the bed as I did."

Her eyes darted to the taunting countenance he turned on her. Or was it merely teasing, a gentle reminder that what had passed between them in the moonlight remained as much on his mind as it was on hers?

220

She'd been a fool to think he would not bring it up.

Looking away, she twisted her hands at her waist. "About last night—"

Andrew saw the hands, read the tension in the tightness around her lips.

"Aye, what about it?" he asked, making no move to help her out, wanting to know, without any prompting on his part, what she had to say. She'd startled him with her fervor, and he'd startled himself with an explosive response. It didn't happen often that way, and he wondered if she knew.

Jayne took a deep breath. "I don't know what came over me."

Andrew snorted in disgust. "I believe 'tis called lust."

"Well, I know *that*—" she began, then fell silent to gather her courage. She'd like to come up with one of her mother's bon mots of advice, but all she could think of was *Don't fall in love,* a warning that hardly figured here.

She started again. "What I mean is, I've never done anything like it before, and I don't know the accepted procedure for the morning after. If you know what I mean."

Oh, ho, he thought. She was taking the innocent tack.

"Never been in a man's bed, you say?"

Jayne's cheeks burned. "Most certainly not."

"Doesn't sound as though you've a mind to return." He slanted her a skeptical look, and Jayne's stomach tightened. "I would have thought differently, given the cooperation—"

"Please!" Jayne bit at her lower lip.

A kindly man might have backed away and left her to herself. At least he might have offered words of apology or solace. But Andrew was not in a particularly kindly mood. He stood in place and let her ramble on.

"What I meant to say"—her fingers smoothed a hair already anchored in place—"was that I hope you will forget what happened, or I guess what almost happened . . . well, anyway, what's done is done—"

"Not quite," he said, then couldn't resist leaning close and whispering, "not yet." For the first time in hours he smiled. And it wasn't kindly in the least.

Jayne gave an exasperated sigh. "Why I ever thought you would be gentlemanly this morning is beyond me."

" 'Tis certain I've given you little cause."

From the corner of her eye she saw the smile gracing his bristled face. How nice that she could amuse him when he had so many other more important matters on his mind.

Atlas let out a loud, humanlike laugh and jumped up and down on the rail. Jayne sighed. It seemed she was entertaining the monkey as well.

What a lowering moment this had become.

And hurtful, too, she was honest enough to admit.

For all her embarrassment in the remembrances they shared, there was also something precious, a discovery about herself, an understanding, or at least the beginning of one, that life could be rich and full and deeply moving in very physical, very intimate ways.

Someday, she thought, when her current troubles

were settled, she could welcome the deeply moving experience again, except that it wouldn't be on a one-night-only basis. And it would be with someone else.

Someone tender, someone who would understand her vulnerabilities as she would understand his.

Andrew had none. Armed with more than just the knife, he carried confidence and, even in his distress, a certainty of who he was and what he was all about.

She turned away, wishing she could distance herself from the field immediately surrounding him, a space so charged with his magnetic essence she could barely breathe.

Someone else, she reminded herself, if there was to be anyone at all.

She forced her attention on the dismal sight greeting her beyond the quay . . . squat, windowless buildings, the minarets of an ancient mosque, to the left a crumbling fort built close to the water, and all of it lit by an unforgiving sun beaming down its brilliant rays on every crack, every flaw.

The youth Mohammed had said the town was surrounded by a protective wall, beyond which lay a band of orchards in a fertile plain, irrigated by the Wadi Derna—the River Derna—but there was little evidence of greenery from where she stood.

The battered ship . . . the decaying town . . . there seemed little to choose between them, except that the former offered only further humiliation and conflict, and the latter held promise of great reward. If she could be strong enough . . . if she could stay on course.

She fluttered her hand toward the town. "Mohammed made it sound so charming."

"Mohammed?"

223

"My friend in Tripoli."

Something sharp stirred within Andrew, and he wondered if that was how she would be referring to him. *My friend aboard ship.*

"Like so many things," he said flatly, "the reality does not live up to the anticipation."

Like making love. She almost said the words out loud. But they would have been a lie.

She grew restless with herself. How could she keep returning to the same worn subject when she had so much else that needed her concentration? Her weakness brought an anguish that in a curious, welcome way also brought her strength.

"Who's the wealthiest, most powerful man in the city?"

Andrew looked at her in surprise. "Why do you want to know?"

"Curiosity," she said, unwilling to explain that maybe such a man had heard of a white youth being sold into bondage in a distant desert town. Or know of someone she could ask.

The captain would laugh or lecture, and the hope she was nurturing in her heart was too fragile for either response.

Andrew felt certain her question was motivated by calculation, not curiosity, and he wondered if perhaps providing the name she wished wouldn't be similar to handing a loaded pistol to a child.

But she was most definitely an adult, which she'd adequately proven last night.

"There's Governor Mustapha. You ought to have no trouble getting into the palace to see him, given your proclivity for access to such places."

"I'm through with authority. A private citizen is

MORE PASSION AND ADVENTURE AWAIT... YOUR TRIP TO A BIG ADVENTUROUS WORLD BEGINS WHEN YOU ACCEPT YOUR FIRST 4 NOVELS ABSOLUTELY *FREE* (AN $18.00 VALUE)

Accept your Free gift and start to experience more of the passion and adventure you like in a historical romance novel. Each Zebra novel is filled with proud men, spirited women and tempestuous love that you'll remember long after you turn the last page.

Zebra Historical Romances are the finest novels of their kind. They are written by authors who really know how to weave tales of romance and adventure in the historical settings you love. You'll feel like you've actually gone back in time with the thrilling stories that each Zebra novel offers.

GET YOUR FREE GIFT WITH THE START OF YOUR HOME SUBSCRIPTION

Our readers tell us that these books sell out very fast in book stores and often they miss the newest titles. So Zebra has made arrangements for you to receive the four newest novels published each month.

You'll be guaranteed that you'll never miss a title, and home delivery is so convenient. And to show you just how easy it is to get Zebra Historical Romances, we'll send you your first 4 books absolutely FREE! Our gift to you just for trying our home subscription service.

BIG SAVINGS AND FREE HOME DELIVERY

Each month, you'll receive the four newest titles as soon as they are published. You'll probably receive them even before the bookstores do. What's more, you may preview these exciting novels free for 10 days. If you like them as much as we think you will, just pay the low preferred subscriber's price of just $3.75 each. *You'll save $3.00 each month off the publisher's price.* AND, your savings are even greater because there are never any shipping, handling or other hidden charges—FREE Home Delivery. Of course you can return any shipment within 10 days for full credit, no questions asked. There is no minimum number of books you must buy.

what I want. The richest one around."

Andrew hesitated before answering. "A merchant-man and trader. Sheikh Zamir Abdul Hammoda," he said. A small sting of conscience discomfited him, but he told himself she would have found out the name on her own.

"I don't suppose he'll be difficult to find."

"Not likely. 'Tis said the sheikh owns half of Tripoli."

A wealthy man . . . in Derna. So Mohammed had claimed.

"Good," said Jayne, the hope in her heart strengthened. "That's just the man I need."

"Do you now?" Andrew laughed sharply. "You weren't askin' for financial records in the wee hours of the morning, lass."

Jayne blushed. "Please, don't bring that up again."

She forced her eyes to his, and her expression pleaded as loudly as her words. Afraid he would not heed her wishes, she hurried on. "Have you ever been in the desert?"

"The desert?"

Andrew glanced at Atlas, who was studying the tip of his tail as though he'd never seen it before.

Then back to Jayne, who was studying the town in much the same way, chin high, eyes dark and solemn. He decided he preferred them lit with a seductive spark.

And if she thought she was modestly covered in all those yards of wool, her hair forced back so tight it stretched the skin on her cheeks, she proved only that she didn't know what a good memory he had.

He gazed at the town and thought of the infinity

beyond, the memories of which could bring a sweat to his brow. "Aye, I've traveled through the Sahara a time or two. Looking for exotic cargo and, truth to tell, looking for the adventure of it."

"And did you find your adventure?"

"I found heat and thirst and all the sand I ever hope to see."

"Oh," she said, nodding, and decided not to ask more. The thought of what could possibly await her was daunting enough without the additional discouraging particulars he might add.

Heat and sand and thirst. For a moment she let her shoulders slump. She wanted to speak of the reason she would face the difficulties; she wanted to relate Mohammed's strange, intriguing tale and her determination to learn if it held any truth.

Most of all, she wanted to lean against Andrew's strength, to release her burdens and let a more powerful, experienced will wrestle with the questions she'd been facing alone.

But Andrew would scorn her more than he already had. After what had passed between them, she couldn't take his sarcasm or his ridicule, anymore than she could take the slashing of the knife he wore at his waist.

And so, she kept silent, watching the shifting of peoples on the quay. Oakum appeared and the monkey started to chatter, and with the gangplank being lowered and the first of the crewmen going ashore, she found herself thanking the captain, avoiding his eye, telling herself she should be gloriously happy that the only witness to her wantonness was soon to be left far behind.

If her heart was heavy, it was only because she was

changing from the known to the unknown. Since she'd sailed from New York, such changes brought more surprises than she planned.

Making her way down the gangplank, valise in hand, she did not once look back — except when Boxer called out and she turned to give him a friendly wave. She saw a few others of the crewmen waving, too, and she felt a momentary sadness that she was taking leave of them forever.

But she did not look at the frigate's captain, and she did not allow herself to consider the very real possibility she might never see him again.

Andrew watched her move amongst the sailors and merchants and travelers on the crowded dock. Good riddance, he tried to tell himself, but he couldn't forget the image she'd presented to him in the foyer of her stepfather's New York home, proud and forthright in the midst of a family he wouldn't wish on his own father, or on the legitimate brother he'd never met.

Hell, he wasn't responsible for her. He'd warned her against every step she'd taken on her foolish quest, and she hadn't listened to him once.

Except maybe last night.

Her cloak appeared blood-red as she wended her way through the throngs of white-robed Arabs. Muttering a curse, he found himself hurrying to the quay, shoving his way through to where he saw the crimson flash and the proud, high head with the tight black twist of hair at its nape.

He caught her by the arm just as she was about to head down one of the narrow, crowded streets.

"What—" she began, jerking around to face him, eyes lit with alarm.

She swallowed hard. Neither spoke right away.

"Be careful, lass," Andrew heard himself say.

"I'll be all right." She spoke tentatively, as though she did not believe the words any more than he.

They stood looking at one another, surrounded by a thousand scents both rank and sweet, and by a thousand men chattering in what seemed a thousand tongues. Her eyes were round and warm and he could see the uncertainty in them. The lass was worried about her plight, as she had every right to be.

Maybe if the early morning had gone differently, she'd have more pleasant memories to carry with her when she faced Hammoda. Maybe, but he couldn't say for sure. She was as much a puzzle to him now as she had been before he'd held her naked in his arms. She'd kept an eager innocence about her, as though each thing he did to her was something special and new.

But she'd had a fiery passion, as well, an explosiveness beneath his touch. She wasn't faking. He'd had far more experienced women try such ploys and in the end they'd all admitted to the pleasure of the bed.

He'd almost had her to the heights of that pleasure . . . and himself as well. He grew uncomfortably hard just remembering. She had him turned this way and that almost as much as the corsair's guns.

"You should wear your hair down."

Soft words, urgently spoken, surprising him as much as they seemed to surprise her.

She'd wear it down, Jayne thought, if he'd take out the pins. Her heart twisted, and she felt a longing to stroke his face, to touch him one last time. Perhaps the power and confidence of him would be absorbed through her fingertips and she could move forward with everything she planned.

Or perhaps she just wanted to touch him again. A swift rush of longing swept over her, and a liquid warmth that was new. This was ridiculous, she told herself, and she held herself very still. She must defend herself better than this.

"Was there something else you wanted?"

Jayne's sharp question brought him back to the present. He released her arm. They stared at one another for a moment.

"Repairs will take some time, I fear," he said at last. "If you've need of me, I don't imagine I'll be hard to find."

He left as abruptly as he'd approached, and Jayne stared after him, not bothering to keep her mouth completely closed. Had she heard right, or was he just one of the mirages she'd been expecting to encounter? Except the mirages were common to the desert, and she was at the edge of a dirty, bustling town.

Her heart twisted and she felt a dampness in her eyes. Consideration had a tendency to do that to her; it wasn't the sort of thing she encountered every day.

And considerate was all he was being. Surely he had seen he could have kissed her again, or embraced her, if he'd been so inclined.

He'd settled for advising her on her hair.

"Andrew," she whispered, and there was much of her heart and yearning in his name. She could do no less than admit there had been moments with him more memorable than anything else in what had heretofore been an uneventful life.

Someone else. She couldn't begin to imagine it.

The dampness in her eyes threatened to turn into a flood of tears, but she caught sight of a leering face peering out from beneath a stained head covering, and then another, and she remembered the scarred Arab who'd shoved her in front of a galloping horse.

Suddenly everyone around her seemed an enemy. Jayne got hold of herself and drew on the inner strength that had sent her away from Worthington Farm. She'd had an unexpected offer of help, one she would remember all her life, no matter how awkwardly it had been delivered, but as usual she needed to take care of herself.

Chapter Seventeen

Using her fast-improving Arabic, Jayne managed
to find a guide to take her to the home of Sheikh
Zamir Abdul Hammoda. She hurried after him
through the twisting streets, dirtier than the
passageways of Tripoli, although the home to which
he took her was grander than the abode in which
she'd rested with Mohammed.

In truth, it was closer to a palace than a private
home—multi-storied and turreted, sitting higher
than the rest of the town, away from the busy street
behind a tiled wall. Inside the front gate a land-
scaped courtyard led to a massive door, where stood
a sentry in full-legged trousers and brocade coat,
well over six feet tall without the addition of a high
silk turban, a wicked-looking scimitar suspended at
his side.

The guide spoke to the sentry, in low and hurried
tones, where she could not hear, then accepted her
payment and with a bow and a worried frown he
disappeared, leaving her standing in the courtyard
beside a wide, stone fish pond set in the midst of
sprays of bougainvillea.

It was a picture-book setting — sweet-scented flowers and tropical plants beneath a cerulean sky, walls virginal white beneath a half dozen levels of red tiled roof, and even a sienna-skinned djinn standing tall and erect, arms crossed, blocking the black carved door.

Well, perhaps not a djinn, not with the scimitar at his hip. And the scent wasn't all that wonderful. She could still smell the stench from the street.

She smiled at him, belying the timidity that had crept over her. He did not return the smile, but rather turned to the door. One knock brought a servant within seconds; the two conferred, but she couldn't pick up a single word.

The door closed, and she was once again alone in the midst of lush vegetation, her lone companions a pond of ripple-finned fish and a giant who looked capable of slicing her in half if she said a word.

As though she were a threat to someone, instead of someone being a threat to her. If this were a picture-book setting, the tale it told was rife with calamity.

Jayne cleared her throat and dared to speak. "Is it possible for me to see Sheikh Hammoda?" she said in Arabic.

The sentry continued to stare. At least, she thought, he hadn't reached for the blade. Having pushed to the limits of her boldness, she fell silent and prayed the servant would return.

He did not, and her nervous feet strolled along the pathways of the courtyard, anxious eyes forever returning to the sentry. Two men, robed and in traditional headdress, strode through the outer gate, laughing, chattering in Arabic. As best she could tell, they talked about the weather.

They cast her a curious glance. She halted her stroll and returned the frank stare. They looked to the sentry, who dismissed her importance with a shake of his head. A knock at the door, the appearance of the servant, and they were inside.

Jayne stepped toward the sentry to protest. Broad brown fingers curved around the hilt of the sword. She stepped away, chewing at her lower lip, wondering what she was doing in this fairyland courtyard with a fairy tale reason for being here. She should never have listened to Mohammed's legend, never rested on that roof beneath the stars, the songs of the Bedouins washing over her, never should have believed.

The whole thing was bizarre. She could see it now. She ought to leave.

She thought of Josh and could not go.

A quarter of an hour passed, the Arabs exited, this time sparing her not even a glance. She counted the brays of six separate camels passing on the street to mark the time.

More than once—more than a hundred times, it seemed—she thought of Andrew, when she wasn't counting camels. She wouldn't see him again. Her mind knew it, but something inside said her mind was wrong, the concept of kismet playing with her thoughts again.

At last the servant came for her. Jayne's impatience dissolved into apprehension as he led her through the door and into another courtyard, this

233

one even grander than the last in its display of shrubs and flowers, the scent thickly verdant, obliterating all traces of the street.

Then it was down a series of twisted walkways. With the valise banging against her legs, she had to run to keep up with the flowing robe. Shadows in doorways, behind columns, lurking in the arched windows—they were all she saw that gave hint of human habitation. Servants? Family? Or just imagination.

By the time they stopped before a carved, closed door, she could only suppose they were at the rear of the palatial home.

He knocked once, then bade her enter.

She stepped inside a high, wide room of tile and marble and brilliantly colored rugs, of ornate furniture and gold-fringed cushions, its airy, sun-speckled splendor second only to the audience chamber of the bashaw himself. Windows arching almost to the ceiling opened out onto an almond orchard, and then a stretch of green the likes of which she hadn't seen since leaving Virginia.

Jayne caught her breath at the beauty of it all.

A robed figure sat alone in the coolness, on a pillow-covered divan to her left, where the rays of sunlight did not reach. He appeared to be a man of substantial girth, but she could barely make out his features. Still, she sensed that here was the powerful man she sought.

"Sheikh Hammoda," she said with a polite bow of her head, all the while wondering where were the servants, the guards, the fawning women who should be paying homage to such a personage. For all its grandeur, the palace was no more lively than a crypt.

He gestured for her to walk closer.

She set the valise close to the door and walked across the thick carpet. "My name is Jayne Worthington," she said in Arabic.

"Please use English, Miss Worthington," he said, his voice bass, his accent barely discernible. "And I know who you are."

"You do?" she asked in surprise.

He did not respond, instead choosing to sit like a silent Buddha and stare. Which was the wrong religion and the wrong deity to use for comparison, but Jayne was nervous and not entirely in charge of her thoughts.

As she drew near, she got a good look at his strong, swarthy features, the dark hair tinged with gray, the prominent nose, the thick brows and most of all, the hawklike look to his obsidian eyes. Jayne shivered under their penetrating gaze.

"Yes, I know quite well of your presence in my country," the sheikh said, his voice smooth as the silk of his voluminous scarlet robe.

"But how?"

He waved an impatient hand. "There are many who bring information of varied worth, hopeful of gratitude and, more often than not, material reward. An unescorted American woman on Tripolitan soil has not gone unobserved. I have been hoping for the pleasure of your company."

Jayne's wonderment increased. "You have?"

Not much eloquence in her responses, Jayne

thought, feeling very much like a bumpkin arrived fresh from the country.

Uncle Randolph frequently had that effect on her, and she realized with a start that there were striking similarities in the countenance of both men.

"Please," he said, gesturing to a fringed stool beside the divan. "Be seated and tell me how I may be of service."

She'd heard Uncle Randolph be equally obsequious—before going on to separate a client from his assets.

In ways she couldn't quite fathom yet, she knew the sheikh would very possibly attempt to behave the same way to her, as if she had something he valued. The realization should have worried her all the more; instead it gave her strength.

Stubbornness had got her away from Uncle Randolph, when he'd preferred she remain to wed his nephew. The same trait could serve her now. She got the feeling Hammoda viewed her visit as some kind of game, and the two of them adversaries. The problem was, he was the one who knew the rules.

She sat on the stool, which was positioned so that the afternoon sun fell across her face, partially blinding her in its brilliant light. It was a setting for a Grand Inquisition, and she shifted the stool slightly, until the sun's rays were not so directly in her eyes, and she loosened the tie at her throat so that the cloak would not be quite so stifling.

Hammoda gave her an almost imperceptible nod, conceding her a point.

236

"Sheikh Hammoda, you surprise me, both with your knowledge and your use of my language."

"As you can tell from my speech," he said, a practiced smile on his plump lips, the shrewd look still in his eye, "I make the effort to be a part of both East and West."

"You are a . . . very wise man."

Jayne almost choked on the words, but she'd heard her mother use flattery when she wanted something out of her husband. A new hat, a trip to Europe, or anything in between. Jayne wanted something far more important than either. She wanted Josh.

If getting to him took a lie or two, she'd swallow foolish compunctions and tell every fabrication she could. This wasn't a game. It was war.

"Please continue," said the sheikh.

Jayne rested her hands in her lap and fired the first volley. "I have heard you are a very great man in your country."

"If wealth is a sign of greatness, perhaps this is so."

"Your home is lovely."

"I thank you. In truth, it is far grander than the residences I maintain in Tripoli and in Benghazi. Here I indulge myself. This is where I pass most of my days."

Jayne assumed he was trying to impress her with his affluence. Or blind her, the way he'd tried with the sun.

"It seems like so much for a lone person."

"I am the possessor of three living wives and twenty-two children. It is best to have many roofs

237

under which to shelter them. Wide roofs where our paths do not often cross."

Jayne thought he must have crossed a few paths to beget all those children, but she kept her response to a smile and a nod.

"How may I be of service?" This time the offer was edged with impatience.

"I seek my brother," she said quickly, lest the impatience grow. "Joshua Worthington."

"I know of no such name," Hammoda said without thought.

"He went by it many years ago. When he was signed on as a member of the crew aboard the *Philadelphia*. He was little more than a boy."

The Arab's eyes widened slightly. "I know well of this ship. It invaded the sacred harbor at Tripoli."

Jayne ignored the politics of the event, relating instead what she knew of Josh's disappearance shortly after climbing overboard with the rest of the crew and of her efforts to learn just where he might be.

"In my audience with Yusuf Karamanli, he claimed to know nothing of him."

Hammoda gave no sign he was surprised she'd met the bashaw. One of his informants, she supposed.

"Do you by any chance have in your employ a man with a jagged scar on his cheek? Dark and short with narrow little eyes."

Jayne couldn't believe she'd asked such an impulsive question, or even why it had occurred to her.

Hammoda regarded her coldly. "Many men serve me. Why do you ask?"

He knows him. Jayne saw it right away, and despite the flood of sunlight around her, she felt a sudden chill. She was so very much alone with this wealthy, powerful tradesman. Isolated, completely in his power. And he knew her, too, or so it seemed, down to the color stockings that she wore.

She thought of Boxer and of Oakum, and even Atlas. And she thought of Andrew. They were really not so far away. The memory of them gave her strength.

"It is no matter," she said with a wave of her hand. But of course it was, she knew.

"What I really want to find out is if you have heard of anyone who could possibly be Josh. Or who might possibly know his whereabouts."

"You do not understand, Miss Worthington. I am a wealthy man, beyond doubt, but is that cause to ask such a question? Your brother was last seen in the waters of Tripoli, and you travel all the way to Derna. I am confused."

For once, she thought, he spoke no lie.

Jayne had to make a decision fast. There was only one thing to do—follow Hammoda's example and rely on the truth, bizarre as it was. She told him of the legend she had heard, of a young white slave grown to manhood and forced into harsh labor in the desert settlement called Ziza. She could have sworn he started when she named the Sahara town.

"And where did you hear this legend?" Undisguised contempt darkly colored his voice. *Stupid American woman,* he seemed to say.

"On the streets of Tripoli."

"It is difficult to believe you listened with seriousness." More contempt. It now darkened his eyes.

For some reason she hesitated to speak specifically of Mohammed. Sheikh Hammoda was sinister. She could think of no more appropriate word. How he could harm the boy, she didn't know, but she felt instinctively the importance of keeping his involvement to herself.

"I can see that I am wasting your time," she said.

"Not at all," he said, his mouth curving into a small, apologetic smile. "But this story you tell takes me by surprise. I can see no reason to relate it to me."

You're lying again.

Jayne had no idea what prompted the conclusion, but she also knew in her heart she was right. It was also true that he was too wily for her to find out the reason behind the lies.

She took a perverse pleasure in what was taking place. If one of the wealthiest, most powerful men in Tripoli bothered to welcome her into his home and then offered fabrications for her sincere questions, she must be on the right trail. Nothing else made sense to her.

At least she would consider nothing else.

She stood. "I have imposed on your hospitality long enough, Sheikh Hammoda.

He remained seated on the divan. "On the contrary, you have provided a pleasant diversion for what promised to be a dreary afternoon."

Jayne glanced around the opulent, empty room, at the dozen exquisite rugs, any one of which held the value of a prized stallion stud on her Virginia farm. She looked at the ornately carved furniture, at the myriad pillows, gold threads caught in their fringe, and wondered that Hammoda considered it dreary to spend his hours within these marble walls.

What the gentleman needed was to get some of those twenty-two children in here and fill the space with chatter and laughter. Add the three living wives—she wondered idly how many had died in service to their lord and master—and he might even be treated to an argument or two.

The door opened, and the servant reappeared. Just the way her escort had suddenly turned up at the bashaw's palace, without an overt summons. How did they do that? she wondered.

By the time she was once again standing outside the walls of the grand but sterile home, she hadn't come up with an answer, but she did know something far more important, something Hammoda's evasions had communicated louder than words.

Her instincts had been right. Mohammed's legend was not necessarily pure fiction; Josh might very well be alive and in a place called Ziza, slaving under oppressive conditions, denied the right to communicate with those who continued to hold him dear.

The only one way to find out for certain was to journey into the Sahara. Find Ziza. Find Josh.

The absurdity of what she proposed was more than matched by her inability to do anything else. She'd come halfway round the world; she couldn't stop just because she stood at the edge of the world's most forbidding land.

There was only one person she could ask to help.

If you need me.

He'd said the words today. And need him, she did. He knew the desert. He'd admitted it himself. If he didn't take her there himself—an idea too preposterous to contemplate—he could help her find someone who would.

Warmth curled deep inside Jayne. She would see him again. Forget the longing. She would do nothing more than ask his advice—he really had offered his help, hadn't he?—and that would be enough. It was nothing more than a spinsterish weakness that she could feel so glad.

Her step was lively as she headed toward the dock. A song formed on her lips, the sea chantey the *Trossachs'* crew had taught her. She suspected the words were more than a little naughty, but it was the melody she liked, anyway, and the rhythm. Both went along with the lift of her spirits.

Two blocks from Hammoda's home an eerie prickling disturbed the back of her neck. The song died, and her step slowed, only to pick up again, faster than ever. She was being followed. The Arab merchant would do such a thing. She shouldn't be surprised.

Jayne had no experience in such matters, men as a rule seldom dogged her footsteps, and she was afraid to turn around and investigate. The street she traveled was crowded with pedestrians who cast curious sidelong glances at her raised hood. An intersection approached. On the bisecting street, a donkey cart rumbled past, directly in front of her.

Darting around the cart, using it as a shield, she took a sudden step to the right onto the new street,

242

scurried a dozen steps, then pressed herself into the open doorway of a coffee house, ignoring the surprised babble of the two Arabs seated on the bench outside.

Pounding footsteps sounded. Taking a deep breath, she stepped into the path of her pursuer.

"Boxer!"

"Pig's whiskers!" the young sailor exclaimed at the same time, barely able to stop before colliding with her.

Each caught their breath.

"What are you doing here?" Jayne finally managed.

Boxer grinned from beneath a broad-brimmed tarpaulin hat, the tails of its black ribbon dangling over his left eye, his long, fair locks tied at the nape of his neck in a matching bow. Checked shirt and belled dungarees completed the outfit. A sailor from hat to hem, and with very much the boy still in him.

Jayne's heart twisted, despite the sudden fright. A boy gone to sea . . . like someone years ago.

Boxer's grin faded. "Get hold o' yourself, Miss Worthington. 'Tis only me."

Jayne did, indeed, get hold of herself. "What are you doing here?"

"Followin' ye, o' course. It's what I do much o' the time when you're in port." He straightened proudly. "Come to be my permanent job, and I got t' say, it beats swabbing a deck all t' hell and gone."

"Captain MacGregor's orders?" asked Jayne, resenting his intrusion and appreciating his concern at the same time.

"That was in Tripoli. Here Oakum sent me ashore, Cap'n Mac being concerned with the damages to the ship and all."

Jayne felt an irrational disappointment, but she couldn't let it get her down. Too much else was on her mind, and she didn't want to harbor the least ill will toward Andrew when she approached him for help.

The practical side of her brain got to work. "I need a place to stay for a few days," she said. "Do you think you could carry your responsibilities a little further and assist me in finding a room?"

Boxer snapped off the hat, clicked his heels together, and bowed. "I am yours to command." He relaxed. "We had a German on board once. Taught me t' do that. Supposed to make the ladies' hearts flap like a sail."

"You can consider my heart flapping, Boxer," said Jayne as she took him by the arm. "Let's find that room."

He fell into step alongside her. "One thing I was wondering about. Where ye headed for next? Some place in Italy would be pleasin', I got t' tell you. I've heard tell those *signorinas* appreciate a worldly fellow better 'n most anyone."

As the sun slowly dimmed, Hammoda continued to sit in the splendor of his silent room, propped up by silken pillows and by the contemplation of his recent visitor. Not a beauty, he decided. He liked his women with more flesh on them and less directness in their speech.

He cursed the failure of his intimidations—the long wait and circuitous walk, the grand and empty room, the sun. Miss Worthington did not intimidate so easily, a trait that made her dangerous.

He sipped at the wine he enjoyed in the privacy of his home. Strictly against Islamic law, but when in seclusion he recognized few laws of Allah or man as absolute.

Through the open windows he could hear the wailing cry of the *muezzin,* calling the faithful to afternoon prayer. Reluctantly he set aside the glass, rolled out the rug beside the divan, and settled his ample frame into a kneeling position, facing Mecca, the scarlet robe billowing around him like hungry flames.

He might tempt fate with an occasional sip of alcohol, but he adhered strictly to the ritual of prayer five times a day. Concentration proved difficult, however, as he kept picturing the determined face of the American woman. She most definitely presented difficulties. But not anything he couldn't overcome.

He was, after all, Zamir Abdul Hammoda. Powerful men trembled at his name.

And he had much to lose if she succeeded in her quest.

When he had returned to the wine, the prayer rug folded away until evening, the servant announced another visitor. This one brought a genuine smile to Hammoda's face. His most trusted business associate had returned, after months of travel and—it was to be hoped—profitable trade.

He watched him enter.

"Welcome," he said, gesturing with the glass toward a small table on which rested a crystal decanter and half a dozen matching goblets. "Join me in a drink and tell me about the journeys. Then I must share a word or two with you. I have met a most interesting woman today. One whom I believe you know."

Andrew MacGregor helped himself to the offered drink. Claret, he noticed as he settled himself on the divan beside Hammoda. It seemed an appropriate libation.

"I thought you might want to discuss the lass," Andrew said, staring into the wine. "It's exactly why I'm here so soon."

Chapter Eighteen

By the time Andrew returned to the *Trossachs,* he was in a fine rage. Looking neither to right nor to left, he strode up the gangplank, sneered at the broken mast, and sent Chang, weak from his recent bout with the grippe, scurrying out of his way.

When he slammed into his cabin, Atlas dived out the open window and Oakum hurried in through the door.

"Don't say it," Andrew thundered.

His first mate shrugged. "I'll breathe nary a word on the subject, Cap'n Mac, if ye'll but tell me what it is."

Andrew threw himself in his chair and growled, "Hammoda."

Oakum nodded. The captain knew full well his opinion of the sheikh. A rascal of the first rank. But he had a way of turning ventures into profit, and it was profit that mattered most to a man who sought his name on the registry of a dozen ships.

"They're to begin work on the mast at dawn."

Andrew seemed not to hear. He pounded a fist against his thigh. "I'll not be ordered what to do and not to do."

Again Oakum nodded. He'd be learning soon

enough what was eating at the captain without a mention of the forbidden name.

"Standin' by their word o' this afternoon, 'twill be right as new in a month." Oakum leaned against the paneled wall close to the window and waited for the captain to grind out another clue to the cause of his anger.

Andrew grabbed a quill pen from his desk and snapped it in two. "Said to leave the lass alone." He mimicked Hammoda's precise English. "Karamanli is at last on good terms with the United States of America. Any help we might give this delusioned girl could stir up memories of the war and unsettle the peace."

Andrew stared at the broken quill in disgust. "As if Hammoda ever gave a bloody fig for peace, unless it could turn a profit for him."

Oakum watched his captain carefully. He'd seldom seen him in such a stew, not even when he'd been thrown behind bars months ago in New York. Was it Hammoda's high-handedness or worries over the lass eatin' at his innards?

A bit o' both, the first mate concluded, with frustrations over the slow repairs thrown in to season the pot.

Andrew lifted his eyes and saw Oakum, really saw him, for the first time.

"Still a month, you say?"

"Dinna ken if ye heard."

"I heard. Bad news is hard to miss around here."

He stared into nothingness for a minute, the anger deflating like air from a balloon. "Go on about your duties, friend. I'm no fit company, and that's the truth."

"Ye'll call if there's aught I can do."

"I'll call."

"Remember, me room's right next door. No need—"

Andrew came as close to smiling as he was likely to on this early evening. "No need to shout. I know. You can hear a chantey sung in a soft voice on the other side of that wall."

Oakum stared at him in perplexity. The captain was nae longer makin' good sense.

As the door closed behind the first mate, Andrew glanced at the bottle of wine. Claret. He'd just as soon do without.

The wine had tasted bitter as bile as he'd listened to the Arab give his orders. Unusual, it was, the two of them being businessmen after a tidy profit and generally thinking alike.

What to trade, how much to charge, who the highest paying buyers were most likely to be. They respected one another's opinions, which meant Hammoda left him alone.

Until tonight.

He'd gone to report on the latest voyages and to learn how the lass had fared, uneasiness over her situation having gnawed at him after she'd gone.

Mostly 'twas the lass that had sent him scurrying so soon.

What he'd got was drivel about war and peace, and letting Miss Worthington alone. He'd held his tongue, but the walk to the frigate had given him time to think . . . time to recall every word Hammoda had said. Time to grow angry, and to regret he hadn't lost his temper in that overdecorated chamber Hammoda loved so much.

The merchant was hiding something, but what in hell it was, Andrew couldn't imagine. Jayne hadn't said exactly why she wanted to see him, but everything she did—most everything—was motivated by her search.

He gave some thought to Joshua Worthington. If Jayne's brother did indeed live, what was he to Hammoda?

The connections didn't link. It was something else. And since it involved a stubborn American lass, Andrew was damned if he didn't feel responsible for learning what it was.

Hammoda had ordered him to do otherwise. It was the wrong tack for the Arab to take.

Andrew eased back in his chair. He was in a strange mood . . . hadn't felt such total fury in a long time. It had been slow to build and slow to die, the traces of it lingering yet.

Through the window he could see the evening fog begin to roll in across the harbor. His thoughts wandered back to another such evening, long ago and far away.

To a twelve-year-old lad, fresh from his mother's grave, seeking the father who had never claimed him . . . for solace . . . for love . . . for the salvation of his pride. Andrew still didn't know which.

He'd accosted the mighty laird in the carriageway of the castle, mists swirling around them on a chill October night. Almost twenty-three years ago to the day. An anniversary of sorts. The day Andrew became a man.

I'm your by-blow son. Fists at his side, head high, the tears dry on his face.

Be gone with ye.

My mother's dead.

She was a whore!

Thus was Andrew's temper born, and his hatred of arrogant authority. He'd thrown himself at the man who sired and then denied him. Bloodied his nose. He'd wanted to kill.

Heathen! Bastard!

Muffled words from behind a crimson-stained handkerchief, eyes an icy blue and filled with scorn. Never mind that he was the laird's own bastard, born to a village beauty who'd lost her honor and her looks and finally her health.

A moment's weakness; a lifetime of regret. Not a new story. There were rumors of other women the laird had known in other villages, other boys he had sired and then ignored.

Andrew had grown up knowing who he was; if he ever forgot it, the town reminded him soon enough.

But he'd never approached his father. Until his mother was cold in her grave.

Staring into the fog, he felt a breath of that same dead coldness. Like the fingers of a skeleton scraping over his soul. It was a hell of a night to be alone.

His thoughts wandered to Jayne. She'd be warm, fired by determination and a natural passion she kept trying to hide. He admitted to a stirring that was more than carnal. He missed her. He'd miss her later, too, when the *Trossachs* was once again under sail . . . miss the sight of her standing at the rail, wind in her hair, black eyes lit with a spark of pure pleasure, a distraction to every man on board.

Every man. It was hard to believe he'd thought her plain the first time they'd met, gaunt and unappealing. He saw now the special charms, the coltish grace, the banked fires she covered with a cloak of detachment, as though she couldn't quite believe any man was truly interested in her.

She was an acquired taste, like Scotch whisky or fine wine. He'd like to taste her now.

A knock at the door stirred him from his reverie.

"Come in."

Boxer entered with a note.

" 'Tis from Jayne." One look at Andrew's countenance and he stuttered to say, "Miss Worthington. She's got herself a room and she wants to see ye, Cap'n Mac."

Andrew sat up in the chair and stared at the paper. It was as though he had willed the letter into existence, or as though she could read his mind from afar. A summons, was it? But not one that was likely to cause offense.

He looked at the bed. There was unfinished business between them. She knew it as well as he. The coldness turned to heat.

And then he smiled. He'd been thinking that her well being was in part his responsibility. But there were several ways of being well. She must be thinking along the same lines.

He wouldn't be alone, after all. And he'd be defying Hammoda's orders. It was a combination to be enjoyed.

He stood. "Tell me where she is, Boxer me lad. The lass requests my presence, and tonight she gets what she wants."

Excitement thrummed in Jayne's blood as she waited for Andrew to arrive. If he chose to do so, she amended, making a hopeless attempt at the moderation of her spirits. She could have waited until morning and approached him herself, but Boxer had said to try a request.

"Nothin' ventured, as they say. You've got business with Cap'n Mac, and he's got a head for business, that's fer sure."

She'd been easily convinced.

Jayne looked around the second-floor room, softly lit by a single brass lamp on the wall. Located two blocks from the harbor over a carpet bazaar, the place was as ready as she could get it on such short notice — claret cloak draped over the dresses hanging on a hook beside the door and her other personal belongings tucked away in the valise, a platter of fresh fruit and cheese on the lone table, in case the captain had not dined, the bed covered by a swath of brightly patterned wool and shoved discreetly, she hoped, in a corner of the room.

The bed would not figure into the evening's events. Discussion would. Sheikh Hammoda and his lies, Josh and the growing possibility of his survival — these were the reasons she had sent for him. Over and over she reminded herself of her cause, yet the excitement continued to thrum.

It was an excitement born of her memories of Andrew, nothing else, not even Josh, and she was honest enough to admit it.

But they would only talk.

She sat in one of the two chairs flanking the table and played mindlessly with an overripe date, her attention concentrated on how to convince him she needed to get to Ziza. She had confidence he could advise her as to whom she should consult, the appropriate fees, the estimated traveling time, and necessary supplies . . .

A firm fist pounded against the door.

Jayne dropped the date, which bounced away from her feet and rolled across the room-sized rug. Scrambling in its path, she looked around for some place to throw it away.

Again came the knock. Her insides knotted. She had summoned, and he was here. She could feel his presence through the door.

The realization sent a rare jolt of confidence through her. She thrust the fruit into the pocket of her green dress, smoothed her already smooth hair, paying special attention to the tendrils she had allowed to hang loose against her face, and with a reassuring reminder that he had offered his help, opened the door.

Smiling sedately at his looming, dark presence, she said, "Hello, General MacGregor."

Andrew's lips twitched. "Are you promoting me, lass? I'd prefer admiral, since it's more in keeping with my trade."

"*Captain* MacGregor," Jayne stammered, cheeks red, her short-lived confidence fading fast.

He stepped forward, closing the door behind him, and Jayne stepped backwards. The room shrank around her, and she had the feeling this whole situation was unreal. Andrew seemed larger each time they met . . . taller, broader, more imposing. No one else could make her feel quite so fluttery . . . quite so feminine.

Wrong way to think, she told herself.

"Boxer delivered my message, I see," she said, businesslike. Where was her pride, for heaven's sakes? And her determination? She had enough good qualities without pretending to things she was not.

"I know there was no reason for the request given,"

she went on, "but I thought perhaps it would be better if I presented my desires in person."

Jayne caught the flash in Andrew's eyes and wished she could swallow the *desires*.

"Definitely better to talk about such matters in person," he said. "Under the circumstances, wouldn't it be more appropriate if you called me Andrew?"

When his eyes got too hot to contemplate, Jayne's gaze locked on the patch of black hair visible in the open throat of his shirt. It was not a sight to settle her nerves.

"I think it best if we discuss the circumstances right away." And then, looking downward, she added a softer, "Andrew."

He liked the sound of his name on her lips, and he liked the way she lowered her inky lashes to her cheeks, thick black against a smooth and tawny shade of pink. Charming. Hell, it was more than charming. It was seductive. Even the shy way she'd messed up the greeting was seductive. Everything about her, from the tight coil of hair against the slender neck to the scooped neckline of her gown to the soft way the skirt suggested the shape of her legs—all of it was seductive. And she knew it.

Andrew was in a mood to be seduced. His only problem would be taking his time and letting her do her woman's things.

She seemed nervous. She could use a little wind in her sails to get her moving.

He stepped close and bent his head. "Jayne," he said as he lowered his mouth toward hers. She tensed, stiff as a frigate deck, and he rested his hands on her shoulders. "Relax." Their lips touched in a whispery kiss. "I've not come to hurt you."

255

She drew a long sigh, nerve endings atingle. As much as she wanted to move away from him, a rousing compulsion made her stay right where she was. Pride. Determination. She tried to keep them in mind, but they rapidly turned into nothing more than empty words.

"I have to tell you—"

He stilled her declaration with another kiss.

"Andrew—"

This was crazy, not at all the reason she had summoned him. She raised her hands to protest what was happening, but somehow, instead of pushing him away, she found her fingers pressed against his shirt in exploration. She felt his heat and his hardness, and her lips parted.

Crazy, she told herself again, but she couldn't find much censure in the word. Everything about her life the past few months had been crazy, so why not this? He'd offered his help, and she needed it very much. In several ways. Making her feel good was taking precedence over everything else.

Her fingers burned through the shirt, and Andrew felt a tightening in his loins. The hell with waiting, he thought savagely. She was here and he was here and naught else mattered on this night. His hands clutched at her slender shoulders and dragged her against him, his mouth crushed to hers, his tongue thrusting into the moist sweetness that was hers to offer, a nectar sweeter than wine.

Jayne trembled in his embrace, melted against him, felt her mind spin into thoughtless blackness. No ideas of talk, of plans, of anything other than what was happening here and what was happening now. An extension of the interrupted hour in his bed, that's what this was. It had to be, and she'd been foolish to think anything else.

This time she knew what to expect, and she was ravenous for him . . . blood-pounding, body-pulsing ravenous. Beautiful, enticing, arousing—she was all those things when she was in his arms. No one made her feel the way that Andrew did, no one. He unlocked the secrets of her heart, all the private longings that she had never let herself consider, erasing all insecurity, all loneliness.

And what was more basic, he drove her mad.

She stroked the musculature of his chest, ran her fingers to the exposed skin at his throat, let the heat tingle against her fingertips, her whole being straining to be a part of him. Remembering the way his hands had played with her intimate parts, she thrust her hips solidly against him and felt the swollen shaft press against her abdomen.

Andrew got the message she was sending. Lowering his head, he laved his tongue along the rise of her breast, licked at the delicate fabric of her gown, sucked at the even more delicate tips of her breasts. Beneath the green cotton, she grew hard, distended, and his manhood strained against the tightness of his trousers.

She was driving him mad.

His fingers worked hungrily at the pins in her hair. The thick locks tumbled to her shoulders, black silken clouds. He left her breasts to stare at the wanton appearance of her, the swollen, parted lips, the desire-drugged eyes, the glorious raven locks. Even the small, pale scar at her temple added to the look of abandonment, of experience that went beyond the virginal lady's role she so often played.

She was beautiful, a woman who knew what she wanted and didn't hesitate to go after it. And tonight she was his.

Tonight Jayne felt freer than she had ever felt in her life. Andrew would love her, Andrew would protect her, he would guide her down untrodden paths, and show her how much he cared.

Later they would talk . . . later.

"Make love to me, Andrew," she whispered.

"Aye, lass. There'll be no stopping tonight."

Jayne listened to his words and felt the blood boiling in her veins. Oh yes, Andrew would show her what to do . . . above all else she must not disappoint him. If he left her in scorn, she would die.

He nibbled at her ear. "You smell of gardenias," he whispered huskily into her hair.

"You don't like it?" The words were breathy, slow.

"I like it."

She smiled, but he could not see.

"You smell of the sea," she said as she kissed his freshly shaven cheek.

"You don't like it?" he asked.

"I like it."

Andrew rubbed a calloused palm across her breast. "How about this?"

Jayne clung to him. "I like it," she managed.

His head lifted, and his eyes burned into hers. "What else do you like? Tell me, and I'll leave nothing out."

"I like everything." Jayne knew nothing else to say.

His smile was wicked, knowing. "Aye, I'm sure you do."

And before she realized what he was about, he took her by the hand and led her to the bed.

"Let's not be wasting time," he said, and proceeded to unfasten the closures on the gown, easing it down from her shoulders and letting it billow on the carpet at her feet.

"The light—" she began, suddenly shy.

"You want it higher?" His eyes glinted.

I want it out.

She simply shook her head.

Andrew proved as expert at undressing a woman as he was at trimming a sail, and his own clothes soon joined her garments scattered on the floor. He took a moment to look at her; she fought against covering the parts where his gaze lingered.

Andrew missed nothing—not the coquettish hint of modesty in her expression, and not one teasing curve or span of creamy skin, not the hard-tipped nipples and the high, firm breasts, not the patch of black hair between the long and graceful legs.

"I was wrong to think you skinny."

He smiled into her eyes. It was a smile to light up the heavens, or to seer a woman's last resistance into ash.

Jayne couldn't bring herself to give him a similar perusal, except for the broad shoulders and hair-dusted chest, and perhaps a quick glance at the taut abdomen and powerful thighs, but she avoided other parts she was not quite ready to see.

As though she did this every night, she eased her naked body beneath the cover; he joined her right away, and then his hands were upon her, and his lips, and she forgot she didn't know what to do, her reactions coming fast and with natural ease, hands stroking, lips burned against wherever she could reach, at first his own lips, tongues dancing together, tasting each other with thoroughness, and then she kissed his brows, his cheeks, and down the rigid column of his neck.

His blood pounded against her tongue.

Andrew reveled at the pleasure from the wild woman in his arms. There was at once a guileless innocence and wanton confidence in her actions, her body warm and willing beside his, her hands and mouth hungry as his own. His fingers sought the private places as his tongue laved the tips of her breasts. He shared her trembling, he who prided himself on his control.

Jayne was like no one he had ever lain with, giving of herself, no holding back, no waiting for stimulation or for the man to service himself. And Andrew wanted to pleasure her more than to seek his own delights — a rare turn for a solitary man of the sea.

Like a wilderness drum, her body pounded for him. She was hot and wet, something she didn't understand. When his hand explored the dampness, she wanted to pull away in embarrassment, but she had no chance to do so, for in an instant she felt the effects of his probing fingers . . . stroking, stroking, every part of her coiled tight in anticipation of she knew not what, beating, stroking, pounding.

Fever flourished within her. Andrew felt it escalate. He guided her hand to his own throbbing need, pressed the palm against his slick, hard shaft, knew a moment's impatience when she pretended not to understand.

And then her own fingers got to work. Not for long. He couldn't stand it for long.

He parted her legs with his knee, ran his hardness over her wet heat, and plunged inside.

She stiffened and muffled a cry against his shoulder. No one had warned her about the pain.

Andrew held her tight in his arms. He was the first. Impossible, yet he knew he was right. The first to probe her sweetness. Her modesty had not been a sham.

An incredible sense of elation swept through him, a soaring kind of tenderness that was new to him. It mingled with demands he could not ignore, convincing him more than ever that he must make everything pleasurable for her.

"I should have known," he said huskily. He kissed her eyelids, the scar at her temple, then murmured against her tangled hair, "I'll make it good." Easing his body away a whisper's distance, he used his fingers to stimulate her, to make her forget the discomfort, to bring back the fever that had set her to writhing in his arms.

Jayne responded just as he knew she would, hips undulating beneath him, legs wrapped around his waist, lips pressed against his shoulder, not to stifle a painful cry this time, but to lick the salty sweat.

She was delirious with an unbearably sweet rapture, could stand his ministrations not another second, yet knew a mad aggravation that she couldn't have more . . . more.

He gave her more. She exploded against his hand just as his own body pounded inside her so deeply that she believed they had truly become one flesh, one mind, one heart.

He cried out her name and they clung to one another. Everything in her sang with happiness. Andrew had indeed made it good, and she loved him for it.

He held her tight, his hands stroking the sweeping

curve of her back, and she listened to his breathing gradually grow even. She, too, took in long and even swallows of air but she could not ease the pounding of her heart. Andrew had set the pace, and as she lay in his arms, it beat only for him.

She loved him.

Without her realizing how or why or when, strong, masculine, maddening Andrew MacGregor—a man as foreign to her ordinary daily existence as he could be—had become a part of her life.

Tears sprang to her eyes; she squeezed the lids closed. Through the mist of ecstasy came the instinctive knowledge that in this moment of passion he would not welcome the diversion of womanly weeping. Nor any declaration she might be inclined to make on this glorious, revealing night.

Unless he loved her in return. Could this vital, very physical man possibly hold within him the tender feelings she had discovered in her heart? And for a woman he found not so comely?

Somehow she must learn the truth.

Chapter Nineteen

"You're a virgin."

They were not the words Jayne longed to hear, and she almost responded *not anymore*.

Instead, she stared up silently at Andrew, who continued to hold her tenderly in his arms. She waited in vain for a few matching tender phrases to follow his unnecessary observation, but he, too, was silent.

"I don't want to talk about it," she said at last, her heart heavy beneath her breast.

She looked away, eyes misting harder than ever. If she kept this up, she'd be bawling against his bare chest and proving herself a bigger fool than she already had done. She'd found out what she wanted to know. Love her? Not in the least.

How she could consider the situation so calmly when the knowledge was like an anvil resting on her chest?

Perhaps because she'd had a lifetime of less than cheerful news. Next to Josh's disappearance, however, this bit of information was the worst she'd ever known.

"Jayne—"

Andrew stroked the damp hair away from her face. She looked so delicate right now, with the black locks spread across the pillow and her lips trembling and her lashes spiked with what he feared were tears. He wanted to cuddle her close and kiss the tears from her eyes, and start all over again making love.

Something about the way she was holding herself told him she might not be as interested in the activity as he.

Damn. How had he gotten into this muddle? Even as he asked himself, he knew the answer. Miss Jayne Worthington had been a challenge from the moment she stepped into that New York tavern, the most maddening and unusual tease a man was ever likely to meet.

She lifted her eyes to gaze up at him once again. "Please, Andrew, I knew exactly what I was doing when I let you take me to bed. Lord knows I've had enough examples set for me at home."

A simple shrug of her bare shoulders, as though she said such things every day, and then she looked away, her body easing from his embrace.

He raked fingers through his hair. He never knew what to say to her, and she wasn't making it any easier by withdrawing into herself . . . just when he was feeling loving and grateful and wanting to tell her something about how much the last few minutes had meant to him.

Instead, she had him feeling like the bastard he was. She had a talent for it. And for raising his ire, as well as other parts.

Feeling certain he'd not be asked to stay the night, he got out of the bed and pulled on his clothes. Jayne forced herself not to watch him. He'd taken his pleasure and now it was back to the ship. She'd heard at her mother's knee about the amorous habits of sailors, but she'd never in her life assumed they would be her concern.

And still she loved him. The awareness rankled. Foolish Jayne. She'd carry the knowledge to her grave.

"There's some food on the table," she said.

He didn't respond, just stood by the bed staring down at her. She felt vulnerable, lying naked while he was buttoning his trousers and fastening the buckle of his belt. At least he wasn't wearing the knife. He'd brought another weapon instead, the one he wore between his legs.

"I'd like to get dressed," she announced as though she made such a statement every day of her life.

When he reached for the pool of green cotton, a ripe date landed at his feet. It was the fruit she'd thrust hastily into her pocket when he'd knocked at her door. He picked it up, and she found herself as embarrassed by its discovery as she had been by his learning how inexperienced she was.

She was definitely losing her senses along with her heart.

Sitting upright, the covers held tight to her throat, she grabbed the date from his hand and bit into its sweetness. "You may not be hungry, but I am."

And then the tears came once again, unbidden, unexpected, too fast and numerous to blink away. Humiliated, she stared at the brightly colored blanket.

Andrew touched her bare shoulder. "Jayne—"

She shrank as though he'd burned her. "I'm all right. Perfectly all right. Well, not perfectly, of course, but I will be shortly." Good. She sounded almost sure of herself, and the tears began to dry. "But the talk I was hoping for had best be postponed."

"You wanted to talk?"

She looked back at him, her eyes wide and dark, her cheeks damp, and Andrew felt as though the broad blade of an oar had been smacked firmly against his middle.

"Of course. About Sheikh Hammoda. Once you got inside the door, you didn't give me a chance to say that's what I wanted."

Her eyes turned accusing. Andrew felt no taller than the carpet under his boots.

Jayne finished the date and stared at the pit resting brown and wet and ugly in the palm of her hand. She simply did not manage her affairs with much sophistication or style. Her embarrassment grew when Andrew tossed it onto the table and wiped her hand with a handkerchief from his pocket.

She felt like a child. How ironic, when this was the night she truly had become a woman.

"My offer of help still holds," he said. "You've no business traipsing about North Africa the way you've been doing."

Here comes the censure, she thought, her anger flaring. It was as welcome as the breeze drifting in through the open window, and she threw her head back defiantly. "You're right. There's no telling what trouble I'm liable to get into if I'm left on my own."

266

He looked stricken, and she panicked that he might be about to apologize. *That* she could not take.

"Will you be on the *Trossachs* tomorrow?" she asked hastily.

"Aye, I'll be there."

"Perhaps we can talk in the morning." She looked at the gown he'd placed across the foot of the bed. "I find I'm rather tired tonight. Please close the door as you leave."

Andrew wondered if maybe she weren't playing the injured innocent a little too strongly, but she *had* been innocent and he had no idea what it was like for a woman the first time. He'd been little more than a lad ready to rut all night.

Somehow the word *rut* didn't apply to what he'd done with Jayne. They'd made love. Sweet, hot love. He'd like to take her in his arms and tell her a few things about how good it had been and kiss her for emphasis, but in the mood she was in, she'd probably start yelling rape. With the way she managed to get sympathy from the hardened men around her, he'd have a hundred Arabs beating down her door ready to carve out his liver.

"I'll expect you tomorrow," he said, and let himself out. In an instant the room was still and quiet as a tomb, and colder than it had been when he was there.

Jayne lay back on the pillow and waited for another bout of tears, even willed them to appear . . . get them out of her system, get the suffering over with the way she'd once thrown up tainted pork, but she remained disgustingly dry-eyed. Only in front of Andrew could she cry.

Andrew. A new kind of warmth settled over her at no more than the whisper of his name. Suffering be damned. Hugging her bare middle, she remembered the thrill of the night. What a strange and wondrous experience it had been, robbing her of reason and at the same time making her feel vibrantly alive. Nothing could take the memory away from her. More, she was different, inside where it mattered. She had given her virtue to someone, a gesture she could never make again. And she couldn't dredge up a trickle of regret.

Sorrow that he didn't feel the way she did, most certainly yes, and worry about how she would face him tomorrow. But not regret about tonight, which was fortunate since she was unable to get it out of her mind.

There was physical evidence as well to serve as a constant reminder—as though she still held him inside her—the soreness and a few lingering tingles of satisfaction. On a more mundane level there was between her legs a dampness that gave ample evidence of what had happened. As though he'd marked her as his own.

Which he had, although he didn't know it.

A pitcher of water was on the table beside the bed. She'd have to wash herself. Later. Not now.

Strange thing about dampness. Before tonight she'd given it many names . . . dew and summer rain, spray from a waterfall, the first melting flakes of snow in winter, all natural phenomena that could be enjoyed and then forgotten. But dampness was also tears, and now she knew it was desire.

Would she feel that desire again? She strongly suspected that she would. She'd simply have to fight it more fiercely than she had tonight.

At last she forced herself from the bed, startled to see a smear of blood on her inner thigh. Another marking. She bathed quickly and donned her gown, secured the door and lowered the lamp, and it was back to bed.

She turned on her side, on her back, on her stomach, and once again on her side.

"Be practical, Jayne Catherine Worthington," she lectured aloud. "You're still a spinster, just an experienced one, and if you've truly fallen in love then at least you know what the emotion is all about."

Heartache and hunger.

"And pleasure, too," she admitted.

Andrew hadn't promised flower-strewn garden paths or wedding bells or rings. He'd promised to make it good, and he had. He'd also promised his help . . . twice. And heaven knew she needed all the help she could get.

Could she go to him and ask that he honor his promise?

She forced into her mind the wily face of Zamir Abdul Hammoda as he warned her away from her pursuits. Yes, she decided. In truth, she had little choice, and if there was more to her decision than her need for assistance, she would call it coincidence. Above all else Josh mattered. His rescue mattered. By keeping her brother's smiling image in her thoughts, she managed to fall asleep.

Morning sun was streaming into the room when she was awakened by a knock at the door. She was immediately alert. Again the knock. Soft. Not Andrew's.

She padded barefoot across the rug and leaned against the frame. For once cautious, she was reluctant to release the bolt. "Who is it?" she asked.

A young voice answered, "It is I, Miss Jayne. Mohammed of the Tripolitan streets."

Jayne smiled and threw open the door. Mohammed stood on the narrow landing at the top of the stairs, his slender young figure covered by a white robe, his brown face smiling, his brown eyes bright.

"Mohammed!" she said with delight, resisting the urge to hug him. "What are you doing in Derna?"

He bowed. "Please to understand, Miss Jayne, I grew worried that my story sent you into trouble. I hid aboard a small vessel sailing to the west. We arrive on the morning tide. A few questions and I am here. There are many who note the passage of an American woman who walks through the streets with the boldness of a man."

It was a long speech for the youth, but he saw with relief that he had answered the questions in the woman's eyes.

Again he bowed. "If it pleases Miss Jayne, I will get us coffee from below."

"Oh, it pleases me very much," she said, and hastily donned the green gown while he was gone. She was binding her hair in its accustomed knot, refusing to bother with a softening few tendrils around her face, when he returned.

They dined on coffee and fruit from last night's platter, the boy in the chair and Jayne sitting on the side of the bed. She filled him in on what had happened since they had parted on the Tripolitan quay, or at least most of what had happened.

"And does Miss Jayne hope to continue the search for the missing Joshua?"

"Very much. Since Sheikh Hammoda was so adamantly certain that the tale of the Ziza slave was nothing more than fiction, I'm more convinced than ever I must check out every detail." She smiled at the boy, who seemed glad of her decision. "On the rooftop in Tripoli I decided fate had determined you and I meet. Nothing has happened since to make me change my mind."

Mohammed nodded solemnly. "Fate guides much in our lives." Especially, he thought, when the fate is directed by a determined Muslim boy with a few problems of his own.

"I will help Miss Jayne to find a guide."

"For which I will be eternally grateful." She hesitated. "There's one person I would like to confer with before a final decision is made."

"Zamir Hammoda?" asked Mohammed, alarm in his eyes.

"Do not worry, my friend," Jayne said in assurance. "The sheikh is a man I hope never to see again. And I very much appreciate your concern for my well being." She could not stifle a sigh. "The man of whom I speak is the captain of the *Trossachs*. Andrew —"

She hesitated, then sat up straighter.

"— Captain MacGregor has offered his help, and I promised I would talk to him today. I would, however, very much appreciate our investigating the journey first. I want to answer as many of his questions as I can."

Mohammed readily agreed, and they promptly set about a search for someone to take them to Ziza.

271

The camel market, the *souks,* even the coffee houses were included in their investigation, Mohammed doing most of the talking in a rapid Arabic she could barely understand.

But she understood his conclusions only too well. No one was willing to set out on such a journey with an unescorted white woman whom they suspected—she got the message clearly—of being crazy in the head.

All the while they walked the streets, she was aware of someone following—someone definitely not Boxer—but she'd been followed so often both in Derna and in Tripoli that unless another would-be assassin pushed her in front of a galloping horse, she could see no cause for alarm. Especially when she had at her side Mohammed, her rescuer from the near disaster in front of the bashaw's palace.

By early afternoon she came to a sad but certain conclusion: a plunge into the Sahara was much too difficult to arrange on her own, even with Mohammed as her translator. Women and children were simply not taken seriously in this country. She needed a man. It was time to go to the frigate.

The decision brought an emptiness to her middle and a weakness to her knees. More than ever, she welcomed Mohammed's presence. Somehow he gave her strength.

Oakum welcomed her aboard, his grizzled, gray face lit by a smile as he waved her up the gangplank.

" 'Tis a welcome sight ye are, lass. Cap'n Mac said we might be expectin' ye, but I was worried ye might've changed yer mind."

Jayne welcomed the warmth of the first mate's

greeting, as well as the smiles from the crew members on deck. The damaged mast had been lowered, but she could see there was much work to be done before a new mast was erected in its place.

Andrew's beautiful ship didn't look so beautiful at the present, and her heart went out to him.

She hoped he gave her half the same amount of sympathy when she told him what she wanted. She hoped . . . oh, there were so many things to hope and so few to expect that depression settled over her shoulders like a heavy fog.

Turning toward an excited chatter, she saw Atlas and a squatting Mohammed nose to nose on the aft deck close to the starboard rail. Despite her gloom, she found herself smiling. "Mohammed has been helping me," she said. "I think maybe he and the monkey can amuse themselves while I talk to the captain."

"I'll watch over the two of 'em," said Oakum. "Cap'n Mac's in his cabin. Shall I escort ye below?"

He spoke with great enthusiasm, as though he understood what was going on between Andrew and his American passenger, as though he greatly approved. If he did understand, she thought wryly, he was far ahead of her.

Jayne shook her head and pulled her cloak tight. "I know the way."

Which didn't mean she hurried to the captain's door. With each footstep she came up with a different way to greet him. In dispensing her frank motherly advice, Millicent hadn't bothered to detail what a woman said to a man after she'd slept with him the first time.

Jayne settled on the brusque approach, and she knocked firmly on his door.

"Come in," a deep voice rumbled.

She stepped inside. He looked up from his desk. White shirt, partially unbuttoned, black hair disheveled, a faint shadow of bristles on his cheeks . . . he was a man to take the brusqueness out of a girl.

She swayed toward him before straightening, forcefully keeping herself from striding around the desk, brushing the hair from his forehead, and kissing him with a thoroughness to rob him of breath.

If for one second she'd considered the possibility of a misdiagnosis about her feelings for him, she could identify them for certain now. She loved him, and yes, she could most definitely feel desire again. The private admission made her bashful when she would have preferred it make her bold.

"G-good afternoon," she stammered.

He stood, a faint smile on his lips. "I'd about given you up."

Her eyes locked with his. "I would have been here sooner," she somehow managed, "but Mohammed showed up—"

"Mohammed?" He sounded displeased.

"He's a child, for heaven's sakes. Fourteen, I'd guess. He was worried about me and showed up at my door this morning."

"He came from Tripoli?" Andrew said, surprised, although he shouldn't be. Most of the crew had the woman's safety on their mind. Hell, *all* of 'em, himself included.

Jayne nodded. "I thought it rather sweet."

Andrew got her message. There had been nothing sweet about his appearance at her door last night,

274

unless a little heat could be mixed in with the honey.

"So what did you want to talk about?"

"A place called Ziza."

"That's out in the desert, isn't it? A prosperous settlement, or so I've been told."

She nodded. "It's a couple of week's journey from here."

"What does the town have to do with you?" asked Andrew, unsure if he wanted to know.

"I believe Josh is living there. As a slave."

He was once again surprised, his regular state where Jayne was concerned. "A strange idea. Why?"

Jayne took a deep breath. Here came the tricky part. She'd tried to come up with a fabrication that would satisfy his questions, one that would seem entirely plausible to his cynical ear, but she had failed and thus was forced to rely on the truth, just as she'd done with the sheikh. Quickly she summarized Mohammed's legend.

"You took it seriously," asked Andrew, not bothering to hide his disbelief.

"That's just about what Hammoda said."

"Are you comparing the two of us?" His voice was steely.

Jayne stirred uneasily. "Not in the least. It was a simple observation. What I'm getting at is that I believe there may be truth to the story, and I can't go home without going to Ziza myself. Mohammed and I searched for guides this morning, but we couldn't get anyone to take us seriously—"

"That comes as no surprise."

"—so," she continued, ignoring his sarcasm, "I

suppose what I'm saying is that you offered your help and I'm here to ask you to stand by that offer."

"I said nothing about shipping you off to your death."

"I don't plan to die," she said indignantly.

"But you very well might. It's out of the question."

"I didn't know you cared," she snapped, little worrying how the words would hit him as she paced in front of his desk.

Andrew fought to hold his temper. She was a feisty creature this morning, and he'd been wondering if she might be weepy and accusing after the deflowering of last night. Not Jayne. He should have known better.

"Of course I care," he said. "Don't be a fool."

I'm a bigger fool than you know.

She almost said the words aloud, but now was most definitely not the time for such a declaration. She counted to ten, trying to calm herself and ease the hurt that had a hold on her heart. Andrew's caring was nothing more than a sense of obligation or, what was more likely, a feeling of guilt.

Millicent would have recommended playing on that guilt, getting everything she could out of her predicament, but Jayne didn't know how.

"I'll admit," he said, raking a hand through his already mussed hair, "that maybe I owe you something . . ." He saw the flare in her eyes and broke off.

"Owe me something? You mean after last night?" The insult stung, and Jayne, a quick learner, directed herself toward the path her mother would have set. "Perhaps you do. And I'm here to collect."

Andrew eyed her across the desk with a different kind of appreciation. "Was that why you gave in so easily, lass? To get me in your debt?"

How easily he believed her guilty of guile. She had no strength to put him straight.

"Believe what you will, Andrew. What happened last night happened, and putting a purpose to it seems useless today. Will you help me or not?"

The little witch, he thought, using trickery old as the hills of the Highlands to obligate him. As though she knew it was the one obligation he would have to pay.

He was not, after all, patterned after his father.

Even as anger and disappointment rose within him, he told himself there was one welcome element in this mad situation that he must not forget. Hammoda would be furious when he found out what Andrew was about to do.

Walking around the desk, he watched in satisfaction as she backed up against the closed door. "If it's Ziza you want, then it's Ziza you'll get, Miss Worthington. I'm thinking you'll regret your determination more than you can possibly know."

Chapter Twenty

Jayne sidled up to the camel and studied him warily. The ungainly animal, towering high beside her into the cloudless morning sky, twisted his head, blinked and studied her right back.

Dull-eyed and slobbering, he didn't look overly intelligent, she decided, but since he was the size of a Virginia hill, how smart did he have to be to get his way?

"Old boy," she said with as much bravado as she could manage, "we're going to be friends."

The camel smiled—Jayne was sure of it—and through thick, wet lips and a set of grotesque yellow teeth sent a stream of spittle in her direction. She jumped back barely in time to avoid getting an eyeful, the spittle landing with a harmless splat at her feet.

"Unpleasant beast," she murmured.

"Talking about me, lass?"

She turned to stare at Andrew, who had the nerve to grin at her.

"Maybe. I still don't understand why I can't ride one of the horses."

They were standing in an open field on the southern edge of the town, just inside the protective walls and less than a mile from the banks of the Wadi Derna. Andrew had summoned cameleers and the local horse trader, planning, he told her after several repeated inquiries, to settle matters so that she might leave within two days. On the previous afternoon the guide had been hired, a smiling, knowledgeable Arab named Hadji il Tahib.

Since they'd left the frigate yesterday, Andrew had seemed eager to get her out from under his feet, his obligations taken care of, his time free to concentrate on his own concerns. His attitude had stung. Knowing she was being unreasonable but unable to feel otherwise, Jayne had been ready to leave right away. None-too-patiently Andrew had explained it would take a while to gather supplies and men for the two-hundred-mile, two-week trek.

"Two days will be just fine," she had said, deciding not to question him. On land as well as on sea, Andrew liked to be in charge.

But she would not ride that camel.

Andrew turned away and began to bargain with one of the cameleers. She would have liked to be in on the dealing, but she didn't have the vaguest idea how many dinars were needed to hire a herder and beast of burden loaded with supplies. And she really did appreciate Andrew's efforts, even if his motivation was like a fist pressing against her heart.

After a long lecture with herself, she'd come to the conclusion he hadn't meant to hurt her with the accusation she used sex to get his cooperation. Many of the women he'd slept with — and there must have been hundreds before she came along — could very easily have made demands on him, of varying kinds.

Everyone behaved according to the experiences they had suffered. Andrew understood a certain kind of woman; Jayne was used to being left behind.

She sighed, not knowing whether to be proud of herself for being so understanding or furious for being mealymouthed.

It wasn't a question she was likely to answer today, if ever, and she turned her attention to a gray Arabian mare tethered away from the camels, a sleek beauty fifteen hands high, broad of chest with muscular quarters and a short, lifted head, her high tail carriage one of the most beautiful sights Jayne had ever seen. She coveted that mare more than she'd coveted anything in a long while . . . at least *almost* anything.

But Andrew was determined she would ascend to the wooden contraption atop the camel, even though she very much preferred the leather saddle on the mare. It didn't matter that it was not a side-saddle. Without her mother around to lecture her on the impropriety of it all—Millicent had a strange view of what was proper and what was not—Jayne had been riding astride for years.

Mohammed watched from a few feet away. He'd been staying out of the negotiations, making certain his face remained obscured by a swath of cloth, trying to hear everything that was said while he remained no more noticeable than a fly on camel dung.

But Miss Jayne was so enchanted by the same sight that had caught his eye, he could not be silent and he moved to her side, his sandals gliding silently on the sandy ground.

"A beautiful animal, is she not?"

Jayne jumped. "I didn't hear you, Mohammed." She smiled. "And yes, she is a beautiful animal."

"Miss Jayne understands the worth of the mighty Arabian. This is a surprise. The women of my country leave such matters to the men."

"I come from a place called Virginia, Mohammed. All Virginians know their horseflesh."

The boy's brown eyes, peering out from the white headdress, darkened with distress. "Does Miss Jayne plan to dine on the mare?"

"Not in the least. That's just a word we use to mean horses in general. But I do plan on riding her. My trouble is the captain doesn't think that I can, and somehow he's put himself in charge."

Mohammed understood her unhappiness over an autocratic order. "Then we must prove to the captain that he is wrong."

Jayne glanced at her clothing, the rapidly deteriorating cloak over a straight-skirted gown and a pair of slippers that would provide little support for her ankles as she rode over the rugged Tripolitan terrain.

"Come," said Mohammed, who saw the problem. "Trust Mohammed to see that all is well."

Jayne glanced at Andrew, who stood with his back to her in heavy negotiations with the cameleer and il Tahib, his strong Scottish physique making the two Arabs look like children in comparison.

She felt a momentary hollowness inside at the sight of him and the knowledge that she wouldn't see him much ever again. He hadn't bothered to come into her room last night . . . hadn't given her the opportunity to tell him he would have to bid her good night at the door.

Which, of course, she had planned to do, after one, or maybe two kisses at the most. She simply must get over being hurt by all his slights. Unrequited love, she was finding on this first week of its birth, had few compensations to equal the pain.

Andrew ordered her to ride the camel, did he? And grateful, cooperative, *mealymouthed* Jayne was supposed to obey. Love him she might, but she didn't worship him and she didn't have to obey his every command.

She glanced at Mohammed. "You say you'll help me?" she said. "All right. Lead on."

The boy took her to one of the many Derna *souks* for the purchases they both decided on, arranging for a room where she could change, and it was back to the field, the mare, and the captain, who was still negotiating in Arabic with the other men. He gave no sign he had noticed she was gone, and when he glanced over his shoulder, no indication that he even knew who she was.

There was no reason he should, for she gave every appearance of being an Arab, her entire body covered by a *barracan,* the flowing black robe of the desert women, its headcovering distributed over her unbound hair and face so that only one dark eye showed. He wouldn't know that beneath the robe she wore loose-fitted trousers—*sarouel*—and boots, and that in the hand buried within the folds of black wool she carried a riding crop.

In truth, Andrew paid her scant attention, there being other similarly garbed Arab women in the field, and he failed to see her mount the mare after a hurried discussion with its keeper and a payment of *baksheesh,* a bribe.

What did catch his eye was the sight of the mare taking off at a gallop, the robes of the rider billowing like a storm cloud over the Arabian's flanks.

The mare bounded across the open field, head and tail high, past camels and people and a scattering of other mounts, the rider straight-backed and holding the reins expertly in front of her, a riding crop extended in one hand.

All but the camels turned to watch the sight. Fifty yards down the way the mare pivoted and raced back toward where Andrew stood with the other men, swerving just as a collision seemed inevitable, the hem of the robe snapping just above Andrew's head as the Arabian sped past.

The rider's hood fell back as she passed, and the unbound raven hair whipped in the wind.

"Jayne!" Andrew shouted in amazement, and was immediately overcome by an ungovernable fury.

Onward the mare sprinted, powerful legs stretched and bunched as she approached a four-foot-high section of broken stone fence, increasing speed despite Andrew's shouts of warning and the cries of the Arabs. Even a very frightened Mohammed prayed rapidly to Allah that all would be well.

In a cloud of dust and black wool, Arabian and rider soared over the barricade, landing with ease on the sandy ground on the far side. At last Jayne reined the horse to a trot and rode back through a break in the fence to where Andrew was glaring at her. She saw him out of the corner of her eye, putting out more heat than the desert sun, but she was too exhilarated to worry about him right away.

The blood sang in her veins, and she drew in deep gulps of hot desert air, without worry or care for the first time in a long while. She felt as though she'd come home after a long absence, leaving buried far away all the concerns that had been plaguing her. She went so far as to throw back her head and laugh.

Then she got a really good look at Andrew. All joy ceased.

If looks could kill, she thought, in a flash she'd be stretched out beside the mare, toes up and pennies on her eyes.

"Having a good time?" he asked, deceptively calm.

Jayne wasn't fooled for a second, not with the iron-harsh look in his eye and the grim set of his mouth. It didn't help in the least that the cameleer and horse trader were studying her as though she'd grown a second head.

Brushing a strand of hair away from her face, figuring it was too late to put back the head-covering, Jayne nodded. "I am having a good time, Andrew, but that wasn't my purpose. This was the only way I knew to show you I really can ride."

The other men continued to stare up at her in astonishment, ignorant of what was passing between the English-speaking pair but obviously not in the least admiring of what she thought had been a rather splendid demonstration.

Except for the guide, who had a twinkle in his eye as he looked at her and the mare. Hadji il Tahib could very well prove to be an excellent choice on Andrew's part, as far as Jayne was concerned.

Since Andrew made no move to help her dismount, she did so on her own, the robe hiding her trousers and giving her a modicum of modesty as she slid to the ground.

Andrew would have liked to turn her over his knee and give her a good spanking. His heart hadn't quit pounding, and here she had the nerve to stare up at him with her black eyes bright, like a night sky lit by stars, her hair loose and tangled, her tawny cheeks flushed into rosy excitement just the way they had been when he'd taken her to bed.

He was having a very physical reaction to the sight she presented, and it was a far cry from the anger and fright that had taken hold of him a moment ago. What in hell was happening to him?

"Cover your head and take care of the mare," he growled. "We'll discuss this later."

Jayne's head snapped back proudly. "Aye, aye, Captain MacGregor. Whatever you say."

She whirled in a flurry of robe and unbound hair, all ebony ire from the top of her head to the tip of the dusty boots she planted firmly one after the other as she strode across the hard-packed sand, one hand tightly gripping the reins, the other slapping the crop against her side. The Arabian following meekly in her wake.

Nothing about her was calming Andrew's pulse or cooling the heat building in his loins. The lust added to his fury, and he glanced at Mohammed, who stood beside him with covered head bowed.

"Was this your idea?" asked Andrew.

"Mohammed takes full blame for the anger Miss Jayne has brought to the captain." The boy directed his response to the ground.

Andrew heard the words clearly enough but he couldn't hear the least sign of contrition in them. "I'll deal with you later. Help her with the mare."

Returning to the negotiations, he made swift work of the details—two dozen camels to carry the food and supplies, at an equivalent of eleven dollars each, another half dozen asses, several horses, and herders to handle them all. They would be accompanied by a merchant of Derna, Omar Bakush, who had expressed a desire to visit Ziza and who would share in the expense of the trek.

After a brief consideration, Andrew arranged for the mare. Turning, he remembered the way Jayne had looked upon the horse, thought of the merchant who'd be accompanying her, and of the dangers and challenges lying ahead. Surprising himself, he made another arrangement with the horse trader for a second mount, one he suspected would bring him regret.

Il Tahib, who spoke English as well as Mohammed, said, "Hadji will bear the burden of arranging the supplies. It will be most interesting to journey across the mountains and the dunes with the unusual Miss Worthington."

"You're not worried about taking along someone capable of doing something as mad as what she just did?"

"It is written that our fate rests with Allah, Captain MacGregor. It is up to mankind to draw pleasure from our humble lives as best we can."

"Aye, but it's not a man we're talking about here, Hadji. It's a woman, and that's not the same thing at all."

286

"Another reason to praise Allah, would not the captain agree?"

"Under ordinary circumstances. But there's nothing ordinary about Miss Worthington, as you're certain to learn."

Andrew looked past the guide to where Jayne was stroking the neck of the mare and finger-combing the mane. It was quite a sight . . . the proud horse of the desert and the equally proud American woman in the incongruous Arabic robe. Something caught inside him. He didn't try to analyze what it was.

What he needed to do was hold onto his anger and forget the lust, but such a feat seemed beyond him at the moment.

"You said traveling with Miss Worthington would be interesting." A wry smile broke across his dark countenance. "It will be all that and more, Hadji. Much, much more."

Clad once more in her American-bought clothes, this time the blue gown she'd once thought the color of Andrew's eyes, Jayne paced back and forth in her room. She'd eaten dinner downstairs with Mohammed, or at least tried to eat, but she couldn't get down much food when she kept remembering how Andrew had told her he would visit her room tonight.

"We've something to discuss," he'd said two hours ago when he left her at the door of the coffee house. There had been an ominous glint in his eyes and while she kept telling herself she had done nothing wrong—especially since he'd finally agreed to her riding the mare—something told her the evening was not going to proceed in the way she preferred.

She stopped her pacing. Just what did she prefer? Another romp in the bed?

No. Most definitely not. Never. Not again. She wasn't some wench Andrew had picked up on the street. In her heart she considered herself a lady in the best sense of the word, even if she did do some very unladylike things. There could be no more lovemaking. One time with Andrew had told her what she needed to know about herself; a second night would fall under the category of lascivious indulgence.

Jayne had never been lascivious or indulgent, certainly where her personal behavior was concerned, and at twenty-five she was too old to change her habits now.

She wanted a businesslike discussion of the travel arrangements, the scheduled day and time of departure, polite thanks, and a firm handshake goodbye. With such a list of wishes in mind, she had buttoned her gown high under her throat and bound her hair in its accustomed knot.

The moment she heard his firm knock, she knew she'd have a difficult time getting so much as one thing she wanted. How he could communicate his mood through such a simple action as rapping on the door, she didn't know.

She stood straight-backed and determined in the middle of the room. "Come in," she said. "It's not locked."

Andrew stepped inside and slammed the door closed behind him. Tonight he was wearing a cap and a coat in addition to his regular garb and he seemed to fill the small room.

"Another mistake, Jayne. Keep the door bolted at all times. You've no idea who might come climbing those stairs."

A typical MacGregor greeting, she thought. "You're right," she said with a wave of her hand. "Why only two nights ago, there was this man, a sailor, and here I was, all by myself, an innocent maiden—"

"No sarcasm tonight," he snapped, interrupting. "I haven't the disposition for it."

Lord, but he was in a temper. It was a contagious state of mind; she'd caught it as soon as he stormed into the room.

"You said 'another mistake.' I assume you're equating the lack of security with my demonstration this afternoon. They're not at all the same. I simply forgot about the lock until you started pounding away. The ride was very much on purpose."

"And very ill-advised."

"How?"

"You could have broken your neck."

"I knew what I was doing."

"I doubt it. There was more than just your immediate safety at stake. You didn't see the looks in the Arabs' eyes."

"Admiration for a skilled equestrienne?"

"Lust for a hussy is closer to the truth. And many of them will be on the trek."

Jayne stared at him in disbelief. "A hussy? Because I rode astride a horse? Every square inch of me except my head was covered in yards of wool."

"Their women don't call attention to themselves

289

in such a way, Jayne."

"Which should make it no problem since I'm not one of their women."

She stood tall in front of Andrew, chin tilted in defiance. He'd planned on a firm, civilized conversation, marked by the delivery of needed advice, and here he was clinching his hands at his side, fighting the urge to take her by the shoulders and shake her until she admitted he was right.

He'd never before given a thought to inflicting violence on a woman—but then he met Jayne.

He stepped back and let his eyes roam over her modestly clad figure, remembering everything about her body that the dress tried to obscure, and the thoughts of violence dissolved into something else . . . something he knew how to handle.

"You're not my woman either, are you, lass? Except for the other night. You were mine for a while."

The starch went out of Jayne as she stared into Andrew's dark, hungry eyes. In its place came a familiar flood of longing, washing away all resistance, all pride. Stifling a cry, she whirled away before she did something stupid like throw herself into his arms.

"This is ridiculous, Andrew. Of course I'm not yours. You wouldn't know what to do with me if I were."

"I wouldn't?"

He spoke close to her ear, and she could feel his breath on her neck.

She took a deep inhalation of air. "If you don't plan to talk about the journey, then perhaps you best leave."

"Lately I've not been a man for doing what's best."

Jayne took a step toward the bed—the only direction allowed her since he was blocking the rest of the room—and turned to face him. "If you've any complaints about the other night, please keep them to yourself."

"Only one. The brevity of the occasion."

"How unfortunate for you. I found the time sufficient."

"You got what you wanted, and that was it?" he asked.

Jayne knew full well he meant the obligation he felt as a result of her ravishment. A ravishment he believed she had planned.

She turned to face him. "Yes, I got what I wanted," she said. "You were clever to figure it out."

"You play a dangerous game, lass." His eyes glittered darkly from beneath the brim of the cap, and the room seemed to shift under Jayne's feet.

"I don't play games."

Andrew tossed his cap aside, then eased out of the coat and sent it after the cap.

"Then it's time you learned a few."

"Get out of here, Andrew. I mean it." And she was certain she did.

"Nae, Jayne Worthington, not just yet." He took her by the shoulders and crushed her against him. He was hard and hot and determined not to be denied.

"Fight me if it'll make you feel better, lass, but I promise you'll not be fighting for long."

Chapter Twenty-one

Jayne drew in a deep breath and pressed her hands flat against Andrew's shirt, willing herself not to consider the hard body underneath.

"If you're trying to frighten me," she said, her eyes forced to his, "you're not succeeding." Jayne lied. Something was liquefying her insides, and part of it was fear.

"'Tis nae my intent," he said. "Pleasuring is more to my liking, for the both of us."

He ran his hands down her slender back and spread his fingers across her buttocks, the shape enticingly evident even beneath the layers of petticoat and dress.

"You've a fine-shaped behind, tight and curved, did I not tell you? I've been a lummox in not passing on the compliment."

Jayne blushed and tried to hold herself stiffly, but Andrew's hands had a way of softening her strongest resolve. "I won't have you talking dirty to me. No matter what happens between us."

He grinned, devilish light in the smile and in his eyes. "And I was thinking I'd cleaned up the observation. If it's dirty talk that's the worry, I could offer a sample or two so you'd ken the difference."

He rubbed his body against hers, and she could feel his swollen sex against her abdomen.

"For instance, there's cock and cu—"

"No!" she cried out and whirled away, freeing herself from his erotic embrace with the sudden movement. He was making things obscene between them when she was in love and wanted only to bid him goodbye and pine away after he was gone.

Pining was what uncomely spinsters like Jayne did best, not shiver with desire as they listened to talk of their buttocks.

He jerked her back to face. "I'll hear few nae's tonight, lass, unless you're fightin' against stopping."

"Always in charge, aren't you? Why try to charm a woman when commands are so much more effective?"

She stared up at him, proud and furious and altogether desirable.

"I'm not a man for lying ways to get a lass into bed." Once again his hands cupped her buttocks and continued their massage. "I'm a simple man who wants the simple things. If I tell you I like your behind, then that's what I mean."

Jayne closed her eyes, anger fading despite all her attempts to use it as a shield. His hands heated her, oh most certainly, but she felt a curious sadness, too. She loved him and he liked her derriere; she could see no balance in the two.

He shifted his embrace, one arm wrapped around her as he trapped her face with his hand, rubbing his mouth over hers with heated thoroughness.

She made another attempt to fight him, writhing in his embrace and pounding her fists against his chest, struggling to free herself, to break away from his kiss, but he held her tight.

"I've little need for charm," he whispered into her parted lips, "when it's something far more honest and real you want."

Ignoring her puny protests, he took one of her hands and forced it down the length of his chest, past the buckle on his belt, across his abdomen until he reached the hardness that spoke louder than words of his need.

Jayne tried to pull away but his grip on her wrist was unbreakable, and she found she didn't care to struggle after all. The size of his sex seared her palm. Fingers betrayed her, touching and stroking, suddenly and wildly eager to get beneath the thick trousers and feel the hot, slick skin she remembered far too well.

He moaned, and she bit at her lower lip.

"Draw blood, lass. I want to taste you."

His words burned against her cheek.

She tried to deny the desire that blazed through every part of her, but his mouth claimed hers, and his tongue, both with such masterful dominance that she could barely breathe. When his hand left her wrist, she felt her breasts swell from the anticipation of his caress. He did not disappoint, stroking the juncture of her thighs as she was stroking him.

He broke the kiss, ensnaring her instead with eyes that flamed with hunger. "I want you and I'll have you. And you want me."

It was a statement, not a command, as though

he could feel the hot blood coursing through her veins, could sense the madness of passion that was consuming her. And she was powerless to deny what he already knew, the evidence all too real in her groping hand and in the hard tips of her breasts.

More intimately, the dampness had returned between her legs. Oh yes, she wanted him and it didn't matter that the arousal of her passion had been a calculated thing.

"Andrew—"

"Undress me, Jayne."

He asked so much of her, too much, yet she found herself complying, fingers leaving the swell in his trousers to fumble with the buckle of his belt. Clumsy fingers, and she cursed herself for being so slow . . . not him for making demands on her she was not ready to heed.

Andrew forced himself to wait, drawing a sweet pleasure from her innocent fumblings, treasuring the knowledge that she awoke to passion because of him. She was right. He did indeed enjoy giving her commands, but only because her rapture flowered under them and unfolded to whatever he offered.

He was a fool to think of innocence when she was unfastening his trousers, but there was something about the lass that made him want to protect her even while he claimed the womanly riches she had to give.

She finished with the buttons and belt on his trousers and not knowing what else to do, worked at the shirt, at last pulling the white linen aside to reveal the hair-dusted, muscled chest. She stroked, then kissed one of the flat nipples; it grew taut, much as hers had done.

Unable to hold still, Andrew put his own, far more practiced hands to work. He soon had them both naked and in bed, her unpinned hair cascading across the pillow, her sighs coming too rapidly to count. They fell to exploring each other, the kisses hot, the hands hungry, communicating with touches instead of words.

Tonight was sweeter than before, Jayne found, because she could anticipate the pleasure and the thrills. The anticipation proved no greater than the reality as his hands and lips brought her close to ecstasy.

Andrew found it easy to make love to her with her open acceptance of every kiss, every touch. She was all soft sweetness in his arms, showing pleasure in what he did to her and making bolder and bolder surveys of what pleased him. He had planned to take his satisfaction and then leave, but he found himself postponing the inevitable, easing away from her each time he was ready to explode, extending the moments of erotic elation because he did not want them to end.

But he could not wait forever. He planned to enter her slowly this time, but when she rubbed her hands down his hips and caressed his buttocks, her legs spread wide beneath him, he thrust himself deep into her hot dampness, letting his manhood stroke the hard nub that brought her pleasure.

She cried out his name, and he swallowed the sound with a kiss, pounding his body against hers, feeling her responding thrusts. Shared passions escalated, climaxed all too quickly, and their sweat-slick bodies clung together as though they were the only two people in the world . . . as though they were two people in love.

Jayne couldn't bring herself to let him go. Not while she shivered inside, every part of her taut and tingling, her body still hungry to embrace both the man and the rapture he brought.

Andrew was roughness and insults and taunting accusations, but he was also strength and pride and honesty, and he had a way about him of making her feel special, desirable, a woman who could arouse him even when he didn't want to be aroused.

The notes of a haunting song, played on a flute in a minor key, drifted in through the partially opened window. It seemed to Jayne a fitting accompaniment to their minor key romance, if such a strange, brief relationship could be given an ordinary name.

Even as she nestled against him, Jayne knew all too well that Andrew's interest in her was nothing more than carnal, while her feelings for him were more than ever and without a doubt a lifetime commitment that he must never realize.

She would not let the knowledge make her bitter. Certainly not now when she had him in her arms for what must be the last time, when she knew in her heart that for the moment his thoughts were only of her.

He had made bold statements about taking what he wanted, but all she could consider was that he had wanted *her.*

For just a little while she felt powerful, a new experience she did not want to end. As strange as it was to have a man in bed beside her, his weight sinking into the mattress so that she had no choice but to cuddle against him, her head resting under his chin—strange as all this was, it seemed perfectly natural, perfectly right.

If Andrew could have read her thoughts, he would have agreed. Normally one for leaving the carnal couch when the activities were done, he felt anchored in place, good and wonderfully satisfied . . . almost happy, he might have said if he were a man who thought in such terms.

For all his differences with the woman in his arms, she brought out a heat and a hunger in him that no one else had ever done. He didn't try to analyze why she gave herself to him because he didn't like the conclusion that he drew . . . that she needed him and made certain he would stay around.

It was a conclusion she hadn't bothered to deny.

Still, he wished he could know her better before they said goodbye, not just in the physical sense, but with an insight into how her womanly mind worked, what made her laugh, what made her cry.

Perhaps he would.

His fingers traced a path along her bare arm, and he kissed her forehead.

"How did you get the scar?" he asked. "I asked you once before and you seemed none too willing to answer."

"That was because I'm rather sentimental about it and I didn't know you very well."

He stroked the swell of her breasts. "I'd say you know me now."

It seemed to her an act of possession, both inti-

298

mate and demanding, and she liked it very much.

Somehow she found her voice. "It was Josh."

"He cut you?" His hand settled against her rib-cage, not a noticeably more calming spot.

"Not exactly. He challenged me to jump from the barn roof onto a mound of hay. Unfortunately, I was more daring than skillful, and I didn't quite clear the last shingle. He got a whipping for it from Granny Worth."

"And who might she be?"

"My father's mother. He'd died by then, and she was raising us on the family farm in the country. Millicent had already moved to the city, and we didn't see her very often."

"From what I remember of the woman, I'd say 'twas no terrible loss."

Knowing she should come to her mother's defense, Jayne found herself instead talking about the stepfathers and the life she had lived. She left out the parts about feeling deserted and lonely, instead playing up the love she had for the country life.

"You're proving a point I've long held," he said when she was done. "Families are an overrated commodity. Can't depend on 'em. Best to trust to yourself."

She pushed far enough away to look up at him. "Don't you have a family? Anyone at all?"

"All dead," he said flatly, and she could detect no regret in his voice.

"So are my father and just about everyone else," she said, "but I miss them terribly and always will."

She sounded so damn sincere, he thought, with her misguided beliefs, as though if he didn't agree with her there was something lacking in him. She needed a little shaking up.

"You can add your brother to the list of the dearly departed Worthingtons," he said. " 'Tis best if you admit it now."

Panic seized Jayne. "Do you know something I do not?"

Andrew could have told her about his talk with Sheikh Hammoda and the orders to let her search end in the town, and he could have told her that Hammoda was ruthless enough and powerful enough to get his way.

He also could have told her that he knew about the near-calamity outside the bashaw's palace back in Tripoli, and that anyone with any sense at all would have taken the attempt as a warning and sailed back to New York on the first ship.

He could have told her all those things, but he tried a different tack.

"I know what you told me," he said, "about the story of the slave. 'Tis a fairy tale, lass, best left to children and the simpleminded."

Jayne eased from his arms. Andrew had a way of shattering a mood that left her heartsick.

"I'm neither, I assure you," she said, pulling the covers up to her shoulders, "and I resent your suggesting that I am."

Quicker than she could blink, Andrew was fondling the tip of one breast. "You're no child, that I'll give you."

Jayne slapped his hand and edged as far away as she could, until her back was against the cold wall. For a last time with Andrew, this was not going very well.

Or perhaps it was. He was making her realize that while she loved him, she didn't always like him and she wouldn't perhaps pine away for the rest of her life. She wanted to thank him for the realization, but she didn't know how to put it into words, and even if she did, he wouldn't understand.

"I've a feeling," he said, "that the diversions of the evening are at an end."

Jayne wanted to slap him.

"Diversions? The last night we'll see each other and you call it a diversion? Get out of the bed, Andrew MacGregor, and out of my room."

And out of my life and out of my heart.

Andrew got up and dressed, seemingly not in the least distressed by the way they were parting. She decided to watch him this time, looking for something in his physical presence that would prove as unsatisfactory as his attitude. Everything she saw was entirely too pleasing, even the placement of body hairs on his chest and legs and the thick patch at the base of his sex.

When he parted his legs to pull on the trousers, she caught sight of a jagged scar along an inner thigh. At last an imperfection, she thought, but it only made him seem more rugged than ever. She could not imagine something so mundane as an awkward leap from a barn causing his injury. No, he'd been marked by a danger far grander, a pirate's cutlass perhaps, or—

She stopped. Or a jealous husband's misdirected shot. The thought of his beautiful manhood mutilated in such a way sent a shudder through her and she hugged herself. How far down the pike she had come since leaving her Virginia farm.

"I suppose this is goodbye," she managed. Her words seem to hang in the quiet of the room. "You've got a great deal to worry you on the ship, and I must be keeping you from it."

Andrew stared down at her blanket-covered figure and tried in vain to read the expression in her eyes. Damned calm she was, considering the circumstances.

"I've fared well enough," he said sharply. "And the frigate will soon be made aright."

"Well, now you won't have me for a distraction. Please accept my thanks for all you have done." Her voice caught, and she hated the fact that he must have heard.

He towered over her beside the bed. "Save your thanks, Jayne. I'm coming with you."

She stared up at him in astonishment. "You're what?"

"You heard me," he said, shrugging into his coat and settling the cap low on his forehead. His eyes glittered from beneath the brim.

"Damned if I know why, but I've decided to join the caravan. Oakum can oversee the repairs, at least until I return."

"But that could be well over a month.

"Nae, lass, I give you a week. You've no idea of the hardships awaiting. You're a tough traveler, I'll grant you that, but demands will be made for which you've little preparation. If being around me twenty-four hours a day isn't enough to send you running back to Derna, then the desert heat and cold will do the same."

* * *

They scheduled the departure in two days, in the late afternoon, leaving from a caravanserai just beyond the city walls, their immediate destination the brown hills to the south.

For the journey Jayne was wearing the black wool robe over the *sarouel* and the pair of felt boots she had purchased in the Derna *souk*. On the back of the mare's saddle in a bedroll of two blankets, along with the gold she'd salvaged after all her expenses, were a pair of single-thonged sandals for walking in the sand and the green dress and undergarments she wished to wear when she faced Josh for the first time.

A *guerba,* a goatskin water pouch, hung from the saddle. Sampling the contents, she tasted sulphur and hair, and the water was stained red from the leather. Only a terrible thirst could make it palatable, but when necessity arose, drink it she would.

Impatience drove her to question the guide Hadji il Tahib about the lateness of the departure.

"We take advantage of the coolness of the setting sun," he explained to her as they stood in the midst of camels and sheep and goats assembled on the grassy plain just outside the inn. "It is of much importance the journey begins well, for it is written that as the beginning goes, so goes the end."

"I very much want this journey to have a happy end, Hadji. Did Captain MacGregor tell you why I wish to visit Ziza?"

"He said only that there is someone you seek. Like the Muslim journey to Mecca, is this a pilgrimage for the American lady?"

"I guess you could call it that. I know that the town beckons and I must go."

"Have no fear," the guide said, his smile revealing a set of very white teeth in a very brown face. "Hadji has traveled often in the desert and while he has never traveled the path we trod, there are those in the caravan who have done so and there are many maps in the supplies."

"I have no fear," said Jayne, charmed by the way the Arab referred to himself in the third person. It had a humble touch, something she hadn't been exposed to lately.

She looked to the hills beyond which lay her hope. Close by stood Mohammed, who had declared he, too, would make the journey, and of course there was the mare. Jayne called the horse Good Fortune—Fortune for short, the Arabic name being meaningless to her—and the mare seemed to respond.

She caught sight of the merchant Omar Bakush, standing apart with his retinue of robed men and women, animals and supplies. She knew he would have little to do with her. She was, after all, only a woman. His dealings would be with Andrew, if any were needed. The problem was Andrew hadn't bothered to appear.

Changed his mind, perhaps, when he'd figured out she had no plans to share his tent? She kept telling herself it didn't matter whether he would include himself in the caravan or not. Something inside refused to listen, however, and she could not still a growing panic that she had seen him for the last time.

And then he was there, astride a magnificent

black Arabian stallion, dressed in the white robe of the desert, the headdress thrown back to reveal the shoulder-length black hair and the coppery skin of his strong face and neck. Jayne's knees weakened at the sight.

She looked away, not wanting him to see the admiration and the relief that was sure to be in her eyes.

Mohammed helped her to mount, then retreated to join the herders of the camels.

Hadji bowed. "Welcome, captain. It is time to depart." He excused himself to assemble the caravan.

"Sorry I'm late," Andrew said with a nod to Jayne. "Decided to take on another traveler. He kept pestering me with questions about the desert, and I decided he should find out the answers for himself."

Jayne looked beyond Andrew to the chestnut gelding and the man who rode him. Andrew had so dazzled her by his appearance—curse him—that she'd been unable to see anything else.

"Boxer," she said with a smile.

He grinned back. Like his captain, the young sailor wore a white robe, but on him it didn't look quite so magnificent, just big and bulky and sensible. His fair hair was likewise sensibly bound at the base of his neck, not loose and unruly the way Andrew wore his.

The friendly look on his face, Jayne decided, compensated for his lack of magnificence. He put out boyish charm the way the sun put out rays, and she wagered that before long he would be warming at least one of the women on the trek.

305

"Cap'n Mac promised I'd get my turn aboard a camel," Boxer said.

"I'm glad you're along," she said.

"And will you not say the same thing to me?" asked Andrew.

Jayne shot him a sideways glance. "I'm thrilled down to my toes." She succeeded in sounding flippant but she spoke no more than the truth. If Boxer offered warmth, his captain's appeal was a raging inferno.

Andrew had no chance to respond, not with the commotion involved in the actual departure. Hadji proved himself a capable leader, drawing order out of confusion, and within a half hour, they were ready to depart the caravanserai, Jayne, Andrew, and Boxer in front of a company that included dozens of camels, a scattering of loaded-down donkeys and horses, numerous goats and sheep, and fifty Bedouin men and women.

And of course the merchant Omar Bakush, who had ridden his camel over to greet Andrew before joining his own people. He spared not a glance at Jayne, who was the instigator and primary backer of the caravan.

Everything had its place among the entourage, the supply animals to one side, the camels bearing people — *mehari* they were called — to the other, and before them all, a half dozen men prostrate on the ground invoking help from the Prophet.

Ahead lay a sweeping expanse of hard-packed dirt and rock leading to a distant wall of brown hills, their silhouette softened by the afternoon heat shimmering and rippling in the air. The *reg*, this gravelly plain was called. Beyond, as yet un-

306

seen, awaited the *erg*. The famous, forbidding dunes. Jayne tried to recall the green hills of home, but all she could envision in her mind was sand.

A shiver of anticipation shot through her. Knowing something of the dangers that awaited—despite Andrew's certainty she was hopelessly naive—she felt the grandeur of the enterprise. She must be equal to all that awaited, both on the trail and in Ziza.

Andrew thought she wouldn't last a week; she used his doubt to wipe away her own. Stroking Fortune's proud neck, she spared him a sideways glance, but he was deep in conversation with Boxer.

Andrew had scoffed at family ties, but wasn't the crew of the *Trossachs* like a family to him? He'd deny it, of course, but he'd brought Boxer along with him the way he might have a younger brother, to let him experience the world.

The thought was new to Jayne and in an unexpected way made her love him all the more, showing as it did a vulnerable side to him she hadn't glimpsed before. If only that love gave her happiness; if only it made her content. But she was far less settled than she had been months ago when she sailed from the dock in New York.

Whether he admitted it or not, Andrew needed companionship; he just did not need hers. For whatever reason he was here—to provide an adventure for Boxer or to get her back in bed for a few more nights or simply just to pass the time while the ship was being repaired—she knew she must not sleep with him again. The aftermath was too painful to consider anything else.

Feeling his gaze on her, she looked away before

he saw her misting eyes and read in their depths the message from her heart.

In the midst of the excitement and of the crowd she suddenly felt very much alone.

"Nemchou Iallah!" Hadji called. Depart, by the grace of God! It was the signal to begin.

Straightening in the saddle, adjusting her flowing black robe around her, Jayne made a mental note of the date, October 16, 1816. It was the beginning of what she prayed would be the last leg of her long search. She refused to admit the slimness of the evidence that her brother was in Ziza. He was awaiting her because he *had* to be.

When they at last faced one another, she would act with courage and determination, and she prayed with a touch of stateliness, freeing him from bondage with the remains of her money, the rescuing sister she had imagined herself to be when she first envisioned the voyage. If all went as hoped, within a month she and Josh could be on their way home to Virginia.

Virginia and Worthington Farm—that's where they both belonged.

Chapter Twenty-two

Damned daft I was to come on this cursed trek.
Andrew had had more than one occasion to consider the point since impetuously arranging to accompany Jayne, but none more appropriate than right now.

"Have you no sense at all, lass?" he asked with little thought given to the volume of his voice. "You're sleeping with me and I'll not tolerate a nae."

"Tolerate?" responded Jayne in a shrill whisper—or as close to it as she could manage, not wishing to entertain the caravan even if most of them couldn't understand a word she said.

Glancing toward the black goatskin tent at Andrew's back, she shook her head in disgust. "I told you, I'm sleeping under the stars."

" 'Tis a stupid choice."

"I think it shows signs of genius. Mohammed agrees."

They stood staring at one another, the wind whipping their robes about them like unfurled sails at sea, a bright moon casting a silver light onto their exasperated faces.

It was the first night on the journey. The caravan had scattered around the base of a limestone escarpment, and the evening meal of *couscous* was done. Across the rocky, hard-packed terrain a half dozen fires slowly settled to glowing coals as the travelers prepared to retire for the night.

Boxer had brought his own tent—set it up away from his captain declaring openly he hoped to find a woman willing to share his quarters. Andrew knew the likelihood of prostitutes on the trek; if there were none, the young sailor would sniff out a more innocent if equally willing companion.

With his charge seen to as best he could, Andrew had turned to care for Jayne. Not with any carnal purpose in mind. Unless things worked out that way. Which was beginning to seem very unlikely given the fervor of her negative response.

The argument had brought the two of them practically nose to nose. If for no other reason but sleep and safety, Andrew was determined to get Jayne inside for the night. He'd bind her hand and foot and carry her to his mat if necessary.

Jayne was equally determined to sleep in the open air, wrapped in woolen blankets, Mohammed close by. With the boy having assured her she would be safe, she could not understand any criticism of the arrangement.

Unless the critic had something other than her safety on his mind.

She still didn't know why Andrew had joined the caravan—to give Boxer a view of this strange world or to take advantage of her availability as long as he could. Neither choice did much to bolster her pride or to ease the emptiness that seemed to have taken permanent residence around her heart.

That left her only stubbornness. She would not go into that tent.

"It's past time I made something clear," she said. "I've no plans to turn this journey into an . . . an orgy."

"Ha!" barked Andrew, for a moment genuinely amused. "What would you know about such things?"

Jayne stirred nervously. Here he was back to mocking her, something that had not been her intent at all.

"I've heard," she said, trying to look worldly wise.

Andrew glanced at the tent. "We'd lack a woman or two for the revelries I'm used to." He shifted his eyes back to her. "As things are, there's scarcely room for me to accommodate you."

"I don't need accommodating."

Andrew looked at the finely sculpted chin tilted toward him and the fiery eyes glaring up in magnificent defiance. There was much of the tavern spinster still in her, yet there was much, too, that had been changed.

"You both need it and want it, but gentleman that I am—"

"Ha!" she threw at him, mimicking his own sharp laugh.

"—I've decided to let you learn for yourself what's best."

"Sleeping alone is definitely best. And I'll be perfectly safe. Mohammed said—"

"I swear," said Andrew, "if you mention that name one more time, I'll banish the lad back to Derna."

"You don't have the authority."

Andrew leaned down until he could breathe the gardenia scent on her skin, sweeter by far than the gusting desert air.

"I'm not talking about authority, Jayne. I'm bigger and stronger and older than he and I'll have him escorted into town if I think he's influencing you to rashness."

Jayne shook her head. "Poor little me, so easily swayed, so incapable of thinking for myself."

Her dark eyes shone in the moonlight, and the headdress of her *barracan* had fallen back to reveal a mass of black hair tumbling to her shoulders. Andrew wanted to grab those shoulders and shake a little sense into her; the longer he stood looking down at her, the harder it was becoming to keep his hands to himself.

Jayne could feel his struggle, knew he didn't wish her bodily harm, exactly, as long as she acquiesced to his commands. She welcomed the anger that his determination provoked since it kept at bay far more dangerous emotions.

And for a little while it would ease the emptiness.

From the corner of her eye she caught sight of the guide Hadji standing a dozen feet away, acting for all the world as though he were blind and deaf to any disagreement that might be occurring in the camp.

"Hadji," Jayne said with a beckoning wave, "perhaps you can help us settle something."

Andrew growled. She ignored him.

"Isn't it all right to sleep under the stars?" she asked as Hadji drew near, his hands clasped at his waist, his eyes cast downward to the sandals peeking from beneath the hem of his robe.

"For the camels, yes, your humble guide would agree," said Hadji, "and for the people of the desert. For the visitors to the land, there is much to know, much to understand."

Andrew didn't try to suppress a grin. "I think what he's saying is that nae, it wouldna' be safe."

"Unless," said Hadji with a nod toward a cluster of tents at the edge of the camp, "Miss Worthington chooses to stay with the women. Hadji will take you among them if that is your wish."

Jayne thought it over. Along the whole of the Barbary Coast, she'd dealt only with men. Except for the guide and Mohammed, she hadn't been particularly welcomed or treated well.

But Arab women . . . she rather liked the idea. Especially since it would irritate Andrew.

But when Hadji walked her past Andrew, past the cluster of tents set up for the night to house the merchant Bakush and his underlings, past Mohammed who nodded solemnly before disappearing into the dark, past even Boxer whose attention was directed to a robed young woman standing beside him—when he had taken her all this way, at last stopping before the women's tents, she found herself no more graciously received than she had been anywhere else on the continent.

Most of the women had retired for the night, but they peered from the openings of their tents to stare at her. A pair of older women—Jayne found it impossible to guess their age, but the lines around their eyes gave evidence they had traveled the desert for many years—came out to speak to Hadji. They used a language Jayne did not understand, but their displeasure was apparent.

At last Hadji turned to her. "All is arranged."

"I've caused trouble, haven't I?"

"The women have unnecessary fears about the *roumi*."

He used an unflattering term the Arabs reserved for Europeans.

"This *roumi* wants nothing more than a place to rest her head for the night."

"Hadji has explained your purpose most carefully. A bed will be provided. The caravan leaves before dawn."

Bowing, he departed and she turned to face the openly curious faces of the women. Like Jayne, they were dressed in black *barracans;* unlike her, they wore ropes of brass jewelry around their neck, and bangles at their wrists and ankles. Despite the weathered skin, they were handsome women, strong-featured and clear-eyed, and they jangled when they moved.

One spoke and gestured toward one of the half dozen tents behind her. Jayne got the message and thanked her with smiles and bows, certain by a softening around the woman's mouth that the message had been received.

She found herself in the cramped quarters with the young woman who had been talking to Boxer. A child, really, thought Jayne, little more than sixteen,

314

a brown-skinned beauty with velvety brown eyes.

With no common language between them, they lay down in silence on the mats that served as beds, pulling the blankets tight under their chins to ward off the sharp night cold. Jayne couldn't resist a smile when she realized that against their wishes and efforts, both captain and sailor were sleeping alone.

But in a way, so was she, and the smile died. Had she done the right thing, holding herself apart from the comfort he offered simply because she didn't care for the loneliness she felt the next day? She was feeling that loneliness very much right now and without the pleasures which usually brought it on.

"Andrew's right," she whispered to herself. "You don't always show good sense."

Exhaustion proved her friend this first night. She had barely closed her eyes, it seemed, when the noise of the camp summoned her to the pre-dawn day. After much organized confusion, loading the braying camels, draping pots and gourds from the pack saddles of the donkeys, readying the mounts, they were ready to depart.

Many of the women walked, others rode the camels, but nowhere did Jayne seem to fit in and with Mohammed nowhere to be seen she found herself mounted beside Andrew once again as Hadji called, *"Nemchou Iallah!"*

Andrew was glad to have her back with him, even if she didn't greet him with a warm embrace. Having her out of sight always made him anxious. Boxer had little to say so early in the morning, but since he looked rested and was ready to depart on time, Andrew figured that like himself, the young sailor had slept alone.

Which he'd done all of his life, so why the irritation now? Jayne didn't owe him her body, and he didn't need it every night of the world.

The awaiting route did not provide the easy ride of yesterday across another flat, monotonous *reg*. Today they went up and over what seemed to Jayne a high rock mountain but which was in reality little more than a string of grandiose hills too long and wide to go around.

The narrow trails, the cutbacks, the steepness, short and sporadic though it was, combined to make the ride tedious, at times maddening when the packs would shift on the camels and a halt to reload became essential. Part of the time everyone was forced to walk. Leading Fortune, Jayne stared at the swishing tail of Andrew's stallion, avoiding the droppings of the animals that went before her, determined not to read any significance in the warm, rank mounds, intent above all else not to let a single complaint pass her lips.

After an hour, Boxer began to sing one of the bawdy chanteys Jayne had learned. She hummed along, aware from Andrew's backward glance that he was not particularly entertained, and subsequently hummed all the louder. But irritating him soon grew wearisome and she concentrated on putting one foot in front of the other, preferably on hard rock rather than stallion dung, and keeping the hem of her *barracan* held high above anything that might cling.

They paused during the high heat of the day and

rested, then as the sun edged behind the western tip of the formation, they were once again under way, stopping only when darkness made travel impossible. After a supper of mutton stew and hard bread, offered by Hadji close to the fire in front of Andrew's tent, Jayne went directly to the women's area, crawled under the blanket, and told herself this was the way the journey must go.

Her young companion of the previous night was late to join her, and Jayne wondered if perhaps Boxer was making progress.

Jayne sighed into the cold lonely air. Andrew hadn't had to cajole her into his bed; his touch had been enough. If, instead of ordering her to sleep with him the previous night he had offered a caress, she wondered if she might not at this moment be in his arms.

No, she told herself. But she really wasn't sure.

On the third day the terrain was much like the rocky flatness of the first, which made the going quicker. For a while Mohammed joined Boxer on the back of the gelding, and she listened as the two tried to outboast each other with tales of hardship at sea and in the desert. Somewhere along the route she got an eerie feeling that someone was watching her all the time, but that wasn't possible. Even Andrew barely looked her way.

The truth was she was anxious and she was lonely and even though she wouldn't have admitted it for the world, she was sore from all the riding.

From the cautious way she dismounted for the daytime rest, Andrew knew she was in discomfort. He'd given her a week. Four more days. In a day or two they'd be in the sand, and she'd find out what discomfort really was.

He didn't take much pleasure from the knowledge that she would quit. Not once had he heard her complain. There was much to admire about the lass . . . her loyalty, her steadfastness of purpose, her passion. Aye, most definitely her passion, and it detracted not in the least that she had an angular, sensual grace about her that drove him to distraction.

A sudden urge came over him to make love to her again . . . to pitch his tent and pull the robes from them both and with the heat pressing down on them, to pound his way inside her, again and again, tasting her lips, swallowing her cries of pleasure, feeling her sweat-slick body writhe in ecstasy beneath him.

No sooner had the urge come to him than his body was ready. He felt swollen enough to jut through the opening of his robe and impatient enough not to care.

He dismounted beside her, away from the others in a patch of shade provided by a jagged rock formation. They stood side by side, their eyes locked, and Jayne forgot her aching muscles, her sore ankles and thighs. The force of his hunger was there in his gaze for her to read, and her breath caught, her stomach tightening, every nerve in her body tingling.

If they had truly been alone, she would have flung herself into his arms, covering his bristly, sweat-stained face with kisses, loving the salty roughness as she thrust her tongue into his mouth.

318

Shamelessly, she pictured the way his body was beneath the robe, the hard planes, the engorged sex, and she felt the familiar dampness of desire between her legs.

And only from one look.

Stunned, she forced herself to turn away. Her breath came in quick, shallow gasps and her fingers trembled as they held Fortune's reins.

The mare shifted, neighing nervously, and Andrew had to guide the stallion away, handing him over to Boxer whose responsibility it was to care for the horses. He returned for the mare. Jayne stood where he'd left her, eyes returned to him, watching him give the young sailor instructions, knowing that nothing could come of this moment, yet wanting him back by her side once again . . . close by her side, so close she could feel his breath and count the crinkles at the corners of his sea-blue eyes.

And then Boxer was gone in search of water and feed, Mohammed likewise not to be seen, and they were alone, standing in the shade, black robe brushing against white, no one nearby to hear or to see the particulars of what they were about . . . unless he threw her on the ground and pleasured them both.

Jayne almost didn't care.

He took her hand and stroked her palm. "You need to be holding me, lass. You've wonderful fingers for holding."

She knew what he meant. She almost told him his fingers were wonderful, too, with their gentle, thrilling manipulation. But she couldn't put the thought into words. As much as she'd changed, she hadn't become quite so bold.

He bent his head. "I'll have a kiss until tonight."

"No—"

But the negation was swallowed by his mouth covering hers, soft and hot and insistent, tongue licking at the part in her lips, his back turned so that he blocked her from the view of the settling caravan. From somewhere that seemed a thousand miles away, camels brayed and men shouted, but they were of another world.

She knew only Andrew's lips and Andrew's tongue, and the hand that was stroking its way through the parting of her *barracan*. He found her breast, flicked at the pebbly nipple through her shirt. She was powerless to push his hand away.

He broke the kiss. "We've wasted two long nights. Let me make up some of the loss for you now."

With the voluminous spread of his robe protecting her from onlookers, he eased his hand inside the waistband of her loose-fit trousers, down to her abdomen, circling his palm against her growing heat.

"You're trembling."

"This is madness," she said breathily, her knees almost buckling.

"If you've a worry for the proprieties, they'll think we're talking. If anyone's a mind to watch."

She tried to look beyond him, but his white robe and his broad shoulders and his coppery face and neck and his thick black hair blocked out the world. She leaned back against the hard rock, hands braced by her side for support, but she felt no discomfort. All she felt was his hand on her

320

stomach and his fingers stroking lower toward the wet heat.

"You've skin like satin, lass, or is it silk? I never can decide." Each word husked from his throat. His fingers burned their way toward the wild throbbing between her legs. "I like the coarseness of your hair." He moved lower. "I like the treasure it hides."

He found her pulsating bud as though she had guided his hand to the place she wanted him to touch. She cried out.

"Please," he said, a dark half smile on his lips, "they'll think I'm hurting you and ride to your rescue."

"Andrew —" She could manage no more than his name, the shameless delight in what he was doing taking all her thought and effort.

The heat in his eyes matched the heat building inside her, a temperature that reached the boiling point. She licked at her lips, her eyes closed, and Andrew used a control he had never experienced to keep from taking her right there on the ground, or standing with her back against the rock, gratifying them both with a few quick, hard thrusts.

His pain was exquisite, matching her pleasure, and he satisfied himself with the shifting of her hips and the wetness against his fingers and the small cries that she could not contain.

Sweet sensations shimmered through her, building, jangling, thrilling. She climaxed fast and long against his hand, and he had to hold her to prevent her falling to the ground. As the tremors slowly subsided and he felt her strength return, he gradually let go, eased his hand from beneath her robe, and stepped away. If she looked close enough, she could see that he was as shaken as she.

Neither spoke. Dazed by the unexpected rapture of the moment in such an unlikely setting, Jayne didn't know whether to break into a glorious smile or hang her head in shame.

Andrew watched the tug of emotions on her beautifully expressive face. He felt twisted inside, sharing her satisfaction and thinking he would explode if he couldn't soon claim her as his own. He hadn't planned what had just happened, but by damn neither did he have regrets.

He drew a deep, ragged breath. "I'll carry the scent of your satisfaction with me the rest of the day, lass. Tonight I'll give you the scent of mine."

By late afternoon Jayne was distraught with indecision and desire and a feeble attempt at renewed resolution to keep away from her devil captain. They camped earlier than on the past two nights, close to a massive fault of limestone rising seventy feet above the desert floor. Hadji said that in its hollow bubbled a trio of springs feeding a hidden, fertile oasis.

"The way into the hollow is treacherous. Only the men who know the way ascend to the top and work their way down to the precious water. It is written that fish swim there. Tonight you will dine on strange sea creatures with whiskers. Hadji does not know the name in your language."

"Catfish," Jayne said an hour later when she tasted the fried offering. She didn't bother to tell

322

him most Virginians considered the fish inedible. But they hadn't eaten it beside a wall of limestone with the setting sun casting an apricot color across a caravan of camels and robed Bedouins, the women's songs drifting across the plain accompanied by an *amzar,* a stringed instrument that made up in rhythm what it lacked in melody.

And they hadn't eaten it under the concentrated gaze of someone with the sexual prowess and attraction of Andrew MacGregor. As welcome as the fish was, Jayne had trouble swallowing a bite.

He'd made his immediate intentions known . . . after he'd proven with thrilling thoroughness how vulnerable she was to his touch. He was dealing only with her lust; how much would he control her if he knew of her love?

After the meal, when he was distracted by a question from Hadji, she hurried away, knowing she could not spend the night with the women again, knowing she should not spend the night with him.

He'd done such shameful, glorious things to her this afternoon, and not once had she tried to fight him. She wanted him so much in every way that she hardly knew herself anymore, did not know what she was capable of doing or thinking, especially if Andrew was involved.

Her path took her toward the narrow trail that led to the top of the limestone fault, a narrow, slippery way just as Hadji had said, but somehow she managed it, welcoming the concentration required for each step since she did not think of who she was leaving behind or who might be watching, or even who might be following . . . if anyone was.

From a flat ridge near the top she stared down into the shadowy hollow. The final rays of the sun shown on one wall, and she could barely make out the spring-fed pool at the bottom, the trees and vegetation welcome after the past miles of little more than tussocked grass. In the morning they would feast on fresh-picked figs and wild olives and dates, Hadji had said.

But first, Jayne must somehow get through the night.

Was she being a fool not to take what was offered to her while she could? If she acquiesced, would she forever after suffer pangs of deep regret?

She turned to go. A shadow moved behind her . . . a white-robed figure drifting ghostlike toward her.

"Andrew?" she asked.

The figure hurtled onward, firm hands gripping her shoulders, Jayne's cry and feeble struggles inept defenses against the strength of the attacker.

She felt herself lifted and shoved backwards. Her feet flailed for purchase against the rock table, but she met with only empty air.

And then she fell, landing hard against the limestone wall, tumbling downward, stones biting into her skin through the layers of her clothes. The fall seemed to last forever, through a shower of pain and terror, relieved at last by a curtain of unconsciousness that brought her desperate relief.

Chapter Twenty-three

Heart pounding, Andrew sprinted up the path, a stream of curses directed to the twists and turns, the rocks, the slippery footing that slowed him. Somewhere ahead was Jayne; he'd seen the telltale loose black mane flowing above the black robe as she'd made her way up the side of the limestone wall. And then he'd seen the white spectral figure close behind.

Someone was tracking her. He turned the curses onto himself. He'd known she was in danger even if she didn't, or at least he'd known of the possibility, and that should have been enough to keep him by her side no matter what she preferred. Only by the sheerest luck had he chanced to look toward the rock formation; only by luck had he picked out her dark figure in the fading light.

Maybe the man had been going after water and not after her. Andrew believed it no more than he believed in fairies and djinns. Discarding the flowing robe for the chase, he halted. Was that a cry he heard? Fear washed over him such as he had never known.

He quickened his pace and fairly flew up the

footpath, twisting and turning, at last rounding a sharp bend close to the highest point of the outcrop, colliding head-on with a white-robed figure scurrying toward him.

The man yelped and tried to jump aside but Andrew grabbed the robe and jerked him to the ground. The Arab bounded instantly to his feet, a sharp blade glistening in his hand. He slashed, rending the cloth of Andrew's shirt close to his heart, slashed again, driving Andrew backward until he came up hard against the rock wall.

Most of the man's head was covered by a headdress, but Andrew could see a flash of teeth in the brown face. Smiling, by God, he thought, and with a primitive growl he lunged toward him, ignoring the flailing knife, knocking the arm aside and landing a blow to the jaw with a satisfying smack, and another to the right eye.

The Arab staggered backwards, wavered, then silently slumped to the ground. Andrew tossed the knife in the brush, stepped over the fallen figure, and ran on, thinking only that Jayne should have been here to see the quick fight.

He halted on a flat ridge overlooking the deep hollow. From here the trail wended downward, a steep and dangerous route, too much for even a brash American woman to attempt. His mind raced. Where in hell was she? She hadn't come back down . . . at least not using the path he was on. That left only the steep incline that dropped below him.

He remembered the cry. Without thinking of his own safety, he began a fast descent into the chasm, eyes casting to right and left, tormented by shadows and by darkness, the sun's rays having faded to purple, and the rising moon not strong enough yet to take over the task of silvering the land.

Despite the difficulties, the search was brief. He found her on a ledge twenty yards from the top . . . not far, he told himself, not far, as he knelt beside the still figure. She had to be alive. Andrew had not prayed since he was a lad, but he prayed she would be all right.

He hesitated to move her until he located a pulse. It was strong at her throat. He'd handled injured men on board ship before; he must handle her in the same dispassionate way, but his hands trembled as he checked for broken bones. He found none. She seemed so fragile beneath his clumsy probings. She needed someone to watch over her all the time, to protect her from her brashness and her frailty.

Cradling her in his arms, he brushed the dirt and matted tendrils from her face. His heart beat erratically and a lump formed in his throat. He thought of the man who had hurt her and a rage built inside him.

Andrew was a stranger to himself. He'd never felt so helpless and so angry and so relieved at the same time. And all because of the unconscious woman in his arms.

She stirred.

"Jayne," he said softly.

She whimpered.

" 'Tis me, Andrew," he said, stroking her hair, stroking her cheek. "You're safe now. You'll be all right."

Her eyes fluttered open. "I . . . hurt."

It was the first complaint he had ever heard her utter, at least where her personal well being was concerned, most of her grievances being directed toward him.

He'd give the sails off the *Trossachs* to be the one suffering.

Jayne stared up at him, forcing the blurred edges of his image into focus. Her head throbbed without mercy and her body ached in places she'd never felt before, but there was great comfort to be found in his supporting arms.

"What happened?" she asked. The words came out slow and forced. She remembered setting out for a walk, climbing . . . climbing . . . reaching some kind of summit, and then all was dark. She tried to tell him about these scattered images, but he hushed her to silence.

"You fell," Andrew lied, seeing no purpose in telling her what he suspected to be the truth.

She accepted the verdict without argument.

With repeated assurances she would be all right, he rose to his feet, still cradling her close to his chest, and began the torturous ascent and then descent over the twisting, rock-strewn footpath that would take them back to camp.

When he came to the site of the brief altercation, the Arab was gone. Andrew was not surprised. He made a silent vow to find him. He'd do so if he had to tear apart every tent in camp.

At last they were at the base of the craggy formation; as he carried her robe-draped figure across the flat ground leading to his tent, a crowd formed around him, Hadji at the fore.

"What has happened to Miss Worthington?" the guide said, wringing his hands in front of him.

"She fell," Andrew said curtly.

"I'm all right," Jayne said, lifting her head slightly, but the effort required was great and the throbbing accelerated until she thought she would pass out from the pain. She wanted to apologize for causing so much trouble, but somehow the words just wouldn't form on her lips.

"Don't talk," Andrew said.

It was one order she was glad to obey.

Boxer joined them, white-faced and silent for the first time since he'd come aboard the *Trossachs* a year ago.

"Don't stray, lad," said Andrew, not missing a step. "We've work to do."

"Aye, aye, Cap'n Mac," he said, swallowing. "Is she going to . . ."

"Put your fears to rest. She'll live to boss us all."

The women of the camp were gathered outside his tent, and Hadji said they would take over Jayne's care. "You must trust these people, Captain MacGregor," he said with a solemn nod in their direction. "They will know what to do."

Andrew believed him, but after Jayne was settled on a mat in his tent, blankets beneath and over her to soften the bed and hold the night's chill at bay, he found he could not leave right away.

Not until one of the women spoke to Hadji, who in turn spoke to him.

"The injuries to Miss Worthington are not serious and she rests. It is asked that the captain do the same. Hadji is most honored to offer his own humble tent for this purpose."

"Thanks, mate," said Andrew. "Maybe I'll take you up on the offer later."

He looked around the camp, at the flickering fires, the resting animals, the pitched tents, all of them bathed in light from a strengthening moon. "I've a chore to take care of first."

He turned from the guide. "Boxer."

The young sailor was beside him in an instant. "Aye, aye, Cap'n Mac, reporting for duty."

Andrew stepped away from the tent, lest his words carry inside, and quickly recounted what he had seen and heard.

"The bastard pushed her, didn't he, cap'n?"

"Aye, I fear he did. She doesn't remember, and 'tis best for her peace of mind we don't tell her the truth. I've no doubt she'll remember it for herself soon enough."

"Cut me tongue out, Cap'n Mac, if the news comes from me."

Hadji listened from afar, his dark eyes round with worry, and he edged nearer when the tale was done.

"If the captain wishes to search the tents for this son of a cur, Hadji offers his humble assistance."

"Good," said Andrew.

Something . . . someone stirred just outside the dim glow from the dying fire. Andrew pounced and dragged Mohammed into the light. Eyes wide, mouth pinched in a colorless face, he looked terrified, as though he had caused the near tragedy.

"What do you ken of this, lad?"

Mohammed swallowed. "Nothing, I swear on the grave of my grandmother. But Miss Jayne has been a friend to a friendless boy of the street, and I pray to Allah she will be well."

Andrew neither trusted nor believed him. Too well he knew how such a lad lives by his wits, always putting his own considerations first because that was the only way he could survive. Jayne had met him in Tripoli, outside the bashaw's palace where she'd been attacked the first time.

And now he was here in the middle of nowhere for the second assault.

"You heard what happened?" he asked.

Mohammed nodded. "Please to understand it was worry that made me listen when the words were not directed to my worthless ears."

"Worthless or not, your ears can hear this. We're searching the camp for the man who hurt her. He should have a bruise or two on his face that he can't explain."

"Mohammed is honored to help."

Lanterns lit, they separated and went from tent to tent, including those of the merchant Omar Bakush, who expressed his alarm at the terrible occurrence, and then they moved onward to the men who chose to sleep on the open ground. They met with much chatter and cooperation.

But they did not meet with success, not until Hadji approached Andrew as he strode back toward his tent.

"I have information which may be pleasing to the captain."

"Go on," said Andrew, barely concealing his impatience.

"One of the desert men calls to Hadji and tells of seeing someone steal away into the dark. I have asked all, but this man who departs is not known."

"Never you fear, Cap'n Mac," said Boxer, "we'll go after the bastard and bring 'im back."

"This cannot be," said Hadji. "The captain and his friend would surely perish. The desert has taken the lives of many who have gone before, men of the wandering tribes who have become lost. Hadji would not undertake such a search with only the moon as guide and no known destination to find."

"I'll not have him get away," Andrew snapped.

"It is doubtful that such will happen," the guide said. "He departed on foot with only the supplies he could carry. Such a man fears the captain more than he fears the desert. The desert takes great pleasure in destroying such fools. This is why Hadji says the news is good."

Andrew wanted to argue. He preferred taking care of things himself, definite problems requiring definite solutions, and the only solution he could see was to get his hands around the missing Arab's neck.

"If he does escape and somehow manages to return, to finish the job he started, I'll not be able to recognize him. The bruises will be gone."

"Ah, but the man described him well. Slight of build with the evil eye and with a face marked by the edge of a knife."

Like the man who had tried to kill her back in Tripoli. "God damn," Andrew muttered, furious with himself that he hadn't spotted him earlier in the caravan.

He glanced at Mohammed. The lad looked as though the knife were at his loins.

"You have anything to tell me? Do you know

332

anything about the man? You're the one that stirred her up with that outrageous tale of yours, and I'm thinking perhaps there's something prodigiously strange in your presence here."

Mohammed fell to his knees. "Captain MacGregor, I swear by the Prophet himself that I would cut off my hand before I brought harm to Miss Jayne."

Andrew believed him and didn't believe him, either, but he could see there would be no shaking his story.

"Watch over her, then," he said, "and you, too, Boxer, when I'm not around. Surely she'll return to Derna and forsake this preposterous search."

He turned to stare into the dark. Hearing her cry, seeing her still, fallen figure had been worse than watching corsair fire snap the main mast in two. Masts could be bought anew. But he'd not likely meet another lass to equal the American.

Andrew slammed a fist against his thigh. God damn, he should have watched over her more closely. Too much courage and too little caution, that was her problem. What had sent her up the hill in the first place? Fear she'd have to spend the night with him?

The lass didn't realize the power of her own desires.

In the darkness he listened as the Muslims prepared for their evening prayers, sung in an off-key voice by the ancient *muezzin*. As the notes echoed over the land, Andrew thought of the villain who had got away, wishing with all his heart that within the week the sun would bleach his bones to white.

* * *

After a night and a day and another night of rest, a rapidly mending Jayne proved more difficult to deal with than Andrew had planned.

"I've held everyone up long enough," she said when she arose before dawn to prepare for the day's journey. They met where the horses were being readied for the day.

Andrew had donned his robe once again in readiness for the ride back to Derna, but Jayne was fully prepared to go on.

"Hadji was kind enough to postpone traveling," she said, "but I have promised him we can leave today. After all, it was just a fall."

Something about the look on his face gave her pause. "It was just a fall, wasn't it? Did you lie? Sometimes I get the feeling there's something I'm not remembering."

Andrew shook his head in disgust. "What you forgot was to use the brains you were born with."

Jayne sighed in exasperation but only because she agreed. "You're right. But I'm using them now. I promise not to do anything so stupid again."

She turned from him and concentrated on checking Fortune's saddle. The truth was she was embarrassed because she had caused a delay. Everyone was being kind — from Bakush to the girl whose tent she had shared — and she would pay them back by being absolutely no trouble whatsoever.

Not even to Andrew.

Especially not to Andrew.

There had been hours to think of him during her recuperation. She might not remember the fall, but she remembered his tender care when he'd found her. Her heart almost burst with love for him.

334

When she'd gone up that stupid rock, she'd had some idea of getting away from him. Of keeping herself apart, of not accepting the offer of love-making in his tent.

She couldn't remember why the refusal had seemed so important. What was she saving herself for? His touch, his glance, his simple presence brought her more thrills in one afternoon than she'd ever expected to have in a lifetime. And this was something she should deny herself?

Oh yes, she was using the brains she was born with, and she couldn't come up with a single reason why she should sleep anywhere else but in his arms. And that included the possibility of carrying his child. The chance was real, but not shocking the way it would have been only a few short days ago. Returning to Virginia with a part of him would not be so bad.

And Millicent would never again mention Leander as her fiancé.

But her situation back home was a minor consideration at the moment. She'd almost died, and now she wanted very much to live. She was most alive when Andrew was around.

But she wasn't going to tell him that while she was preparing to mount her Arabian mare, with a dozen men nearby, including Boxer who would understand every word she said. She had enough romance in her to want a more private setting.

She didn't find it until that evening, after a long day during which her endurance was tested as they made their way across a miles-wide stretch of sandy ground that signified the nearness of the dunes.

Aching muscles be damned, she told herself after sharing a bowl of stew with Andrew, Boxer, and Mohammed. They were seated in a circle in front of his tent.

She stood, a little shakily, but she thought she kept it to herself well enough. "I'll be right back."

Mohammed was quick to rise and follow while she went to the women's tents to gather her belongings that had been placed with them during her day of recovery. It seemed the boy was just about everywhere she went.

She returned with a blanket roll. When she was close to Andrew's tent, she sent the boy on his way. "I promise not to be alone tonight. You get your rest. We leave early."

Reluctantly Mohammed departed. She saw that Boxer, too, had gone, leaving only Andrew by the fire.

He watched her approach, saw the belongings under her arm, slowly pulled himself to his feet with that powerful grace he had that had a tendency to tighten her middle.

They stood facing one another across the dying fire, both clad in their robes of the desert. Added to the flickering light and the tent and the bray of a camel in the distance, the robes gave an otherworldly aura to the setting. A romantic setting, the one she'd been waiting for.

She smiled. The tender exasperation Andrew had been feeling towards her sharpened into desire.

"I'm not in the best of condition," she said. "A few bruises here and there—"

"Jayne—"

"Let me finish. You made me a promise a few

336

days ago. About sharing with me the scent of your satisfaction." She hesitated, struck with shyness, but there was nothing that could keep her from speaking her mind.

"Maybe you thought I'd forgotten, but I haven't. Don't you think it's time you kept your word?"

Chapter Twenty-four

Staring at Jayne's upturned face, at the black-velvet eyes and the pink parted lips, at the shy-bold emotions fighting for control of her expression, Andrew lived anew the moment he'd realized she was in danger and too far from his help.

A few sharp pangs lingered yet.

What in God's name was happening to him? He had no room in his life for a woman. Especially a woman like Jayne Worthington with her beliefs in family ties and her innocence and her foolish impulsiveness that forever threw her into perilous paths.

But a team of Arabian stallions couldn't drag him from her tonight.

Doubt flickered in her eyes and her chin went up a notch. "If you've changed your mind—"

"Nae, lass, I've not changed my mind."

And if you stand there looking up at me like that one second more I'll prove it to you right here in front of the tent.

A woman's voice, high-pitched and sure, lilted along the desert air. The words of the song were unknowable, but the melody resonated with bitter-sweet longing and loneliness.

Which would have been Andrew's lot on this evening if not for Jayne. He was not so much a dolt that he couldn't see it. He wanted her tonight as much as he'd ever wanted anything in his life and she was here.

He stepped around the dying fire and took the bundle from her arms. "I've only the single mat inside," he said.

"Is there a need for two?"

"No need."

Jayne read the hunger in the two simple words, and she knew a thrill of triumph. She could give him something that none of his companions aboard ship could equal. She could give him a woman's caresses and a woman's kisses, and she didn't doubt for one moment that hers were the ones he wanted.

Let all the beauties and clever women of the world take note. Tonight Miss Jayne Worthington of Worthington Farm, Virginia, would lie in the arms of the dashing Captain Andrew MacGregor, a masterful mariner from the Highlands of Scotland and carefree man of the world. She would satisfy him as long and as thoroughly as he wished. And it was no insignificant extension that in return he would satisfy her.

Her brother had called her Worthless, but it was a name she could no longer accept, not even with teasing affection.

Andrew parted the tent's opening; she had to bend to get inside and then the tent closed and she was alone in the darkness. She felt bereft, a sharp reminder of the insecurities that underlaid her secret boasting. The feeling lasted only a moment, for he returned in an instant with her bundle in one hand and a lantern in the other.

He set both aside, his powerful body hunched over in the small enclosure. He kneeled on the mat and took her hand to pull her down to kneel in front of him. Lantern light licked at their faces. Raw need darkened his stormy eyes, a need so strong that Jayne admitted to a frisson of fear rippling down her spine.

"I'll not hurt you, lass. I only want to see you when we make love."

Jayne blushed. "Can you read my mind so easily?"

"There's times your eyes betray you."

She looked down, thick lashes curved across her tawny pink cheeks, and then she looked up at him coyly, her expression old as Eve's.

"And what do they tell you now, Andrew?"

He growled and thrust his fingers into the thick black mane that tumbled to her shoulders. "They tell me you want this." He slanted his lips across hers. "And this." He kissed her again, this time tickling his tongue against her teeth.

"And this."

His mouth covered hers, and his tongue plunged into the dark sweet interior, filling the cavity with his probing thickness. Jayne clutched at his robe, soft moans forming in her throat, a sense of such rightness and joy and pleasure rushing through her that she felt tears forming behind her closed lids.

Her mind whispered his name again and again as she sucked at his tongue. Her hands flattened and rubbed against his strength; just as he had invaded her body, she wanted under his skin, in his blood, in his flesh.

At last he broke the kiss. A sigh shuddered through him. "I dinna know what you're doing to me, lass. When I found you up on that Godforsaken rock, you looked so still, so . . . lifeless"— the word broke raggedly from his lips—"I came close to losing my mind."

Jayne held her breath. *I love you.* She could hear the declaration in his deep, rolling Scottish voice, and her own tremulous response echoing soon after. Every nerve in her body tingled as she waited for him to go on.

She'd never expected this moment to happen . . . but oh, how she had dreamed.

He kissed her closed eyes, her cheeks, the corners of her mouth. "I'm here t' protect you, lass, though you dinna ask me to come along. 'Tis a poor job I've made of it, and I'm sorry."

Jayne's heart twisted in her chest, and the tingles turned to a chill, her moment of imagined jubilation frozen by icy reality. She'd expected too much, and she couldn't remember how or why. Andrew in love? Unlikely. Andrew in love with her? Absurd. She would not make the same mistake again.

What a pitiful creature she must seem to him, a stupid woman he'd somehow taken a pity to along with a healthy dose of lust. He'd rescued her from the waters of Tripoli the way he'd rescued the monkey Atlas from an abusive owner, and he was a man who took care of his pets.

For all her silent castigations, he didn't seem to notice any change in her mood, not with the two of them kneeling so close to one another, his hands massaging the back of her neck and her shoulders, his lips whispering kisses across her face.

When his lips burned down her throat, she dropped her head back. Oh, he was taking care of her, all right, and if that's all he offered, she would take it as long and as often as she could. She hadn't come to him tonight expecting proclamations of undying affection; she'd wanted his hands on her body and his manhood buried inside her, and that's exactly what she would get.

Slowly Andrew opened the *barracan* as though he were opening a gift, then worked at the buttons of her shirt and the fastening at the waist of her trousers. She held herself still before him as he slowly bared her body. The lingering bruises on her otherwise unembellished skin sent a brief, silent rage slashing through him, but he forced it away. This was not a time for anger; this was a time for helping her to forget.

He brushed his lips against a darkened spot just above her nipple. "Am I hurting you?" he whispered.

Jayne clutched her hands to his neck and his thick mane of hair. "You're not hurting me, Andrew."

He tongued the erect tip. "Let me know if I do."

An all-consuming desire took hold of Jayne, and her fingers worked frantically against his neck and shoulders, fighting to get beneath the layers of robe and shirt to the hot skin underneath, her breath coming in short, eager gasps as he licked her breast and fondled with gentle hands the fullness he was trying not to injure.

342

Touching, kissing, stroking, Andrew bent before her and pulled the robe and shirt from her body, then tugged the waistband of her trousers lower down her abdomen, his lips following, tongue licking the cavity of her naval, teeth biting at the tufts of black pubic hair, hands caressing her buttocks while she clung in frenzied rapture to his ivory cloak.

Her muscles tightened and her body yielded its secret woman's tears of desire as his lips trailed lower through the dark triangle at the juncture of her thighs.

"Andrew," she cried, not understanding what strange, wondrous things he was doing, unable to stop him, wanting to urge him to do more. Her thighs parted. His arms embraced her hips and his head burrowed into her secrecy.

When he touched her with his tongue, she went mad. He sucked and she stifled a scream, her body a glowing coal throbbing with heat, the point of her rapture pulsing and radiating thrills the like of which she had never known. She leaned over him, frantic hands clutching at his robe as the pulses quickened, sharpened, drove her further into exquisite insanity.

The world exploded. She tensed under the reverberations of a thousand shivers. He tightened his hold and she collapsed over his bent torso, the shivers coming in slowly subsiding waves, her heart continuing to pound within her breast with such violence she thought it must surely shatter like broken glass.

Slowly he lowered her to the mat, tossing her clothes aside, and quickly undressed himself, covering her nakedness with his body, letting his heat warm her and heal her. She was soft and hot and he could still feel her shudders burning their way through him, setting him on fire for her.

Her hair spread wildly across the mat, and he lifted his head to look down at her. The lantern light sent tongues of light skimming across her face and neck. He rested on his side to watch the glimmers and shadows drift across her breasts and narrow waist and gracefully sloping hips. Even with a scattering of faded bruises — or maybe because of them — she seemed an innocent temptress, delicate and desirable as she offered herself to the savage male. Her lingering taste on his tongue was the taste of woman's honey, sweeter and more delectable than wine.

Jayne studied him in the same flickering light, this time all her concentration on the hard erection probing against her thigh. She curled her fingers around it and reveled in his sharp intake of breath. Up and down she stroked, watching his muscles tighten across his abdomen, rubbing a thumb against the patch of wiry hair at its base.

"I'm here for your satisfaction, remember?" she whispered huskily. She felt a wild urge to lick him the way he had licked her but he parted her thighs and settled himself between them so quickly, she had no chance to do anything about it.

He eased inside her. "Is this what you mean, lass?" Back and forth he stroked, making sure his sex touched hers where she would feel it most.

She mumbled something that sounded like an affirmation.

He tried to control the strokes, but as her secluded muscles contracted around him, the thrusts became harder, deeper, faster, burying him in her hot, wet eagerness.

He felt her own excitement grow, the hands clutching at his back, the nails scratching, the cries louder until he swallowed them with his mouth. She writhed beneath him and with a low, triumphant cry of his own he emptied himself inside her, bathing her with his passion and his ecstasy.

Ragged breaths, clinging hands, sweat-slick bodies pressed tight together . . . they let the rapture slowly ease. All was quiet around them, as though they were suspended in space, and Jayne wished very much that they could be just that . . . the two of them alone in infinity, dependent upon only each other, needing or wanting nothing else.

It was a selfish dream, and tawdry, but she held it for as long as she could, knowing that for all the descriptions she could put to it and all the heartfelt desires, it was still nothing more than a dream.

As the warmth of passion slowly subsided, the cold of the desert night took over. Nestling Jayne in his arms, he pulled a blanket over them and lay quietly on the mat for a while.

"Did you get what you wanted, lass?" he asked when her breathing softened and her hand stroked the matted hair on his chest.

It was a question that was both easy and difficult to answer, but Jayne settled for a simple yes.

But she couldn't resist putting a question to him in turn. "Is that why you're here, Andrew? To watch over me and save me from stupid mistakes?"

He brushed the tendrils away from her face and looked down at her. "If I used the word stupid, 'twas a mistake. It doesn't suit a lass who's come as far as you in pursuit of a dream."

"You almost sound admiring."

"Dinna get carried away, Miss Worthington. I've nae gone quite so far."

"You sound more Scottish than ever tonight."

He kissed her forehead. "Mayhap I'm feeling less the man of the world and more the eager lad who first discovered the treasures of a woman close to twenty years afore. Believe me or not, but I've never wanted to taste another lass the way I wanted t' put my mouth on you."

"Oh," Jayne said in a soft voice. It was a strange kind of compliment, but it set the tingles to working again between her legs. He'd think her a complete wanton for being eager so soon.

His hand settled around her breast.

"I'm too small," she said.

"For what? If you're thinking o' my hand, then you've not noticed how it fits around you with little left over of either me or you. I'd call your dimensions perfect if I was a man to take measurement."

"And I'm too skinny."

"Are you searching for compliments?"

Jayne smiled against his chest. "If I can get them. You said once you didn't pass them on often enough, and I was just trying to help you out."

"And I dinna think you liked 'em. Said something about dirty talk."

"A girl can change her mind, can't she?"

"Aye, and I thank the lucky star that shines over me for that."

She stroked the muscled contour of his arm.

"Does the *Trossachs* sail under that star?" She grew still for a moment. "It was a thoughtless question. I forgot for a moment that your ship is being repaired." She shuddered. "I can't keep from thinking I'm the cause."

"And do you chart the course of corsairs now?"

"Well, no, but—"

"Then I'll hear no more such talk."

To himself Andrew couldn't keep from thinking that maybe she wasn't completely wrong. He'd sailed the Mediterranean a hundred times and never once been bothered by marauders, not with his ties to Hammoda and the ties the pirates had with the bashaw. Hammoda was rich and powerful enough to be close to Karamanli and should have been able to protect the frigate from attack.

But Jayne had disturbed the sheikh in ways Andrew couldn't understand.

Had he somehow caused her fall? Impossible. And yet . . .

"Andrew," she said, "tell me something."

"If it's in my ken," he said, uneasy. She must be putting together all that had happened . . . thinking about Hammoda . . . remembering that Andrew had given her the sheikh's name. She'd be wondering if there were a connection. Cursing himself for a coward, he wondered what he could say.

"Why did you name the monkey Atlas?"

Breathing a sigh of relief, he chuckled. "I've been expecting you to ask." He ran a hand down her side and settled it on her hip. "Although I'm thinking now seems a curious time."

Jayne had to force her thoughts to the issue she had raised. "It's just that I was studying your arm

347

and thinking how powerful it was and sort of like a Greek god—"

"Were you now?"

"Well," she said, a shade indignant, "you are rather grandly put together."

"A compliment?"

Her eyes darted to his, and a smile stole on her lips. "An observation. You're sure enough of yourself without flattery."

Andrew let the comment pass. "Oakum did the naming. Said the spindly creature had put up with enough from the son of a cur that had bought him in South America, he ought to be strong as Atlas. The name stuck."

"And Oakum?"

"Another matter. He's possessed of a Christian name—Deuteronomy, if you can believe—but when he came aboard the frigate, he was too drunk to say it and he worked for some time without answering to a name."

"But he seems so stable. I can't imagine the *Trossachs* functioning without him."

"Aye, you've got the right of it there, lass. He soon proved himself an able sailor. And a good friend. Set the rum aside except for an occasional nip. Lost his wife and son to a fever some time back, and he had to get over it."

Jayne's heart warmed as she thought of the grizzled gray face and the kindly eyes. She'd thought more than once there were shades of sadness in his expression, and now she knew why.

"He became a part of the ship, holding it together the way you said. Oakum's a substance we use to caulk the boards. I called him that once,

348

and as with the monkey, the name stuck."

"And Boxer?" She ran her fingers down his chest as she talked.

Andrew began to stir, as did parts of his anatomy. " 'Tis a name he chose for himself. Says he once earned his keep as a pugilist, but it's a claim he's yet to prove."

"He has an eye for the women, I've noticed."

"Aye, that he does."

"He's . . . been with one of the young Bedouin women most every evening, hasn't he?"

"Depends upon what you mean. It's not been like this"—he stroked her shoulder and arm—"if that's what you're thinking. A good thing, too. The men of her tribe wouldn't take kindly to a *roumi* bedding one of their virgins."

"I didn't know," said Jayne. She couldn't help comparing her situation with the Bedouin girl's. She had no tribe to defend her virtue; in truth, she didn't have anyone that even cared. Not that she needed defending, but still, the thought tarnished some of the night's glow.

"I fear the lad fancies himself in love," said Andrew.

Jayne's heart twisted uncomfortably. "You don't sound approving."

" 'Tis a needless complication. We'll be on our way soon."

Jayne held very still, unable to breathe. Was he warning her not to expect a similar kind of affection from him? That like Boxer, Captain MacGregor would be moving on? He didn't have to tell her. She knew it all too well.

Whatever else awaited her on this adventure, a

day of reckoning was part. It would come the day she told him goodbye.

A crushing kind of despair took hold of her, but she could not allow it control. Her situation was her own creation, and she must face it bravely — and Andrew must never know.

"You sailors," she said lightly, her tender assault on his chest continuing, "are a rascally lot when you're ashore."

"We're a long time at sea, lass."

Andrew watched the workings of her fingers; there was no denying she was getting to him with her delicate probings and more, with the delight she took in mating. The lass stirred something inside that had never been stirred. But she was too damned casual about the temporary nature of the thing. For a woman of her kind, that is, the kind that should be looking for a betrothal and a ring.

Or maybe she thought he wasn't good enough to be her husband, no matter how much she enjoyed him in a desert tent.

He knew a moment's anger, then cursed himself for pondering along such preposterous lines. She was behaving just the way he wanted, and here he was wondering why things weren't going wrong.

He wanted her to want him on the same temporary basis that he wanted her. Why the hell he wasn't content made no sense.

He shifted his hands to her buttocks, rubbing from one to the other, dipping his fingers into the split, cupping the fullness and teasing the backs of her thighs. He could feel her muscles tighten and caught the raggedness of her breath.

"Anything else you'd care to ask?" he said.

She'd meant to bring up the scar on his inner thigh, but when she concentrated her thoughts on that part of his anatomy, all she could envision was getting her hands on him and playing the way he was playing with her.

"One more thing," she said breathily, leaning close to his strength. "I don't know much about how a man's body works, but is it possible we could, you know, do it again?"

Her voice broke off.

"Aye, lass, 'tis more than possible." He growled against the crook of her neck, and she shivered with delight. "Now that I think o' the matter, I'm not yet satisfied."

Her head rolled to one side. "You had to think it over?"

His laughter warmed her skin, and she trembled against him. "Andrew," she whispered, hoping he couldn't hear the edge of desperation in her voice, "make love to me again."

He did. Again and again.

Chapter Twenty-five

On the long ride the next day, Jayne experienced a new kind of physical discomfort that had nothing to do with the horse or her recent fall, but she would have died if anyone had known, and so she kept herself upright on the mare, saving her grimaces for the moments when she was certain no one was looking.

And so, too, she saved the grins of pleasure that memories of the previous night brought to her face. Andrew had made love to her four times . . . she went over each and every one in her mind . . . four times. Was that some kind of record? Jayne didn't have the vaguest idea, but as long as she was entertaining other fantasies—things like spending every night in similar pursuits—she might as well believe that it was.

She'd even asked him about the scar on his thigh, suggesting a jealous husband as the cause.

"A gaff wound," he'd said. "Worked aboard a fishing boat when I was a lad. Pains me sometimes. Takes a mite of stroking to make the memories of the accident go away."

Of course, she'd provided the strokes. Oh, she

was a wanton hussy. A Jezebel of the desert. If doubts did darken the edges of her mind—questions about whether she had truly lost her mind and every sense of propriety and whether she would be able to handle what inevitably lay ahead—she pushed the darkness away, using the light of recollections to brighten her thoughts.

She was done with worry while in his arms. Her day of reckoning would come soon enough. She refused to hurry it along.

That night they camped in the dunes for the first time, their route having brought them to the sandy expanse just as the sun was losing its ferocity and settling a golden glow over the world. Again she slept in Andrew's arms, slipping into a kind of euphoria she'd never known, taking on a confidence that she'd wanted all her life. Andrew was with her, and in just over a week, Josh would be, too. She refused to consider anything else.

The next morning the camels proved rebellious and the loading went slowly, with much braying on the part of the animals and equally fervent exhortations to Allah on the part of the men. As a result they were late in leaving, long after the time when the sun cleared the horizon, and Jayne was able to take a really good look at the spectacular *erg*.

While the *muezzin* led the morning prayers, she traded sandals for the boots she'd been wearing and strode about the hills of pristine sand, always keeping the caravan in sight. A breeze stirred the dunes but only slightly, nothing like the sandstorms Mohammed had described on yesterday's ride.

As she gazed across the landscape, she was re-

353

minded of waves at sea, no more substantial than the sand and likewise touched only by sun and wind and rain.

It did rain in the desert, Mohammed had said. Deluges that flooded, mists that teased. But not very often. The caravan was far more likely to be struck by a *sirocco,* the hot desert wind that roared down upon a traveler with scant warning, fusing earth and sky until there was no telling them apart.

But this morning the air was still and cold and the sun a lemon yellow in the gray-blue sky, and as she climbed to the top of a dune, she found herself spinning around, welcoming the sweet dry air, head back, hair trailing wildly, a smile upon her lips.

On a nearby dune Andrew sat astride the Arabian stallion and watched the belling black *barracan,* the loose-flowing black hair, the look of pleasure on Jayne's face. Such innocence, he thought. Such faith that all would turn out right. That brother of hers was probably rotting in a grave these past dozen years, and yet she continued to believe he lived.

She was bound for disappointment if she expected much from the men in her life, no matter how temporary the association. Even as he thought it and watched her childlike spin, he felt a twist of his heart.

What the hell was she doing out here? She had no more sense than a sand flea. He started to call to her and let her know of his assessment when she spied him.

"Good morning," she called with a wave.

Damned if Andrew didn't grin and wave back.

She ran toward him, her sandaled feet sinking

into the sand and leaving no prints, as though she were light as a fairy. Down the embankment and up again to where Andrew and the stallion awaited. When she got close, he saw that the sun of the past few days had kissed her already tawny face and heightened its natural dusky color. She looked glowingly healthy and altogether desirable. Extending a hand, he pulled her onto the saddle in front of him, legs to one side, her body pressed against him. She slipped her hands beneath his robe and hugged him.

"You're a bold one this morning," he said.

Her velvet-black eyes sparkled like a night sprinkled with stars. "I wish we didn't have anything on under our robes."

"A strong wind and you'd be changing your mind."

"Maybe." She cocked him a saucy sideways glance. "And then again, maybe not. If you were the only one to see, there'd be no harm."

"Miss Worthington!" he said in pretended shock.

"Aye, Cap'n Mac," she said, imitating his burr, " 'tis my name. Are you turnin' prudish on a poor country girl? I'll be needing to find one of the Bedouins who's nae agin a wee sport."

Andrew found he didn't much care for the image that came to his mind, a picture of Jayne in the arms of a desert tribesman. No, he didn't like it at all.

"Hold on to me," he said sharply. "They'll be leaving us behind."

With a slap of the reins, he turned the stallion, and they rode the short distance back to camp, Andrew all businesslike and stern as he deposited her by the mare and Jayne hiding a small smile because she suspected him of being jealous.

Impossible, but still she suspected, and that was enough to get her through the long, hot day.

That and Mohammed and Boxer, one filling her with desert stories and the other countering with tales of the sea.

She learned that wildlife abounded, even if she'd seen nothing larger than a fly. Ostriches, cobras, scorpions, gazelles — the list ran on. From Boxer she learned little of value except the words to another chantey, one she didn't quite understand but from the scowl on Andrew's face she figured it was not a song to be performed at a Sunday social on the farm.

More than once she noticed Boxer glancing over his shoulder toward the women riding high on the camels to the rear, his handsome young face tempered with longing. Things were not going well for the lad, and she offered him silent sympathy.

That evening they camped beside a small oasis. It was little more than a pool nestled in the golden dunes, shaded by date palms. Jayne adored its charm and convinced Andrew they ought to pitch their tent some distance from the others and maybe sleep under the stars. Never had she seen such brilliance as offered by the desert sky, and, as she pointed out, it would be a shame to waste such grandness.

When they were alone, far from the others, the mat pulled onto the sand, she excused herself and went into the tent, emerging with a jangle and a clink and a tinkle. Puzzled, Andrew stared at her. She didn't look any different — same unadorned robe, same untamed hair, same tilted chin. There *was* a twinkle in her eye, however, which set several things inside him to stirring.

"The women gave me presents," she said. "After the accident. I didn't know how to tell them it wasn't necessary, and anyway, I saw they would have been hurt by a rejection."

She stood close to the fire and opened her robe, spreading it wide to block out any onlookers who might stray from the camp, giving only Andrew a glimpse of her gifts.

"A little jewelry," she said. "That's all."

Jayne was right, Andrew thought as his breath caught. She was wearing a little jewelry, and nothing else.

Around her neck hung a trio of polished brass necklaces, a cobra head pendant suspended between her high, firm breasts. A narrow chain of brass defined her waist, and around her ankle she wore a matching bracelet. From waist to ankle there was only Jayne. All golden skin and delicate curves, and dark in tantalizing places.

"My God," whispered Andrew.

Jayne could find nothing to complain about as she watched the heat in her lover's eyes. *I might not wear feathers and lace very well,* she told herself, *but I do all right with brass.*

"Come here, lass," he said, and there was an edge to his voice that said he would not be denied. Holding the robe open, she edged around the fire until she was standing before him, her bare feet digging into the sand.

He fondled the cobra head, letting his fingers burn against the valley between her breasts. "Nice."

357

"I'm glad you like it."

"You thought I wouldn't?"

"I doubted you would make me feel foolish."

He brushed a thumb across her pebbled nipple. "You dinna feel foolish to me."

His touch on her breast sent chills racing through the rest of her. "And what about you, captain? Terribly overdressed for the occasion, don't you think?"

Andrew grinned. "You've a point."

He was in the tent no more than a minute, and then he was standing outside, the white robe hanging loose on his tall, muscular frame, a devilish twinkle in his eye. He continued to stand still, forcing Jayne to part his robe so that she might look on him.

With the firelight flickering across the planes of his nakedness, it was her turn to gape. He was in truth a magnificent man, built upon hard-sculpted lines—broad shoulders, narrow waist, flat abdomen, and long, strong legs, the entire picture decorated in the most interesting ways with varying thicknesses of black body hair. Andrew didn't need jewelry, possessed as he was of places that needed no frills.

Easing inside his robe, she pressed against him and glanced up. The twinkle was gone, replaced by banked fires. She swallowed hard. His hands gripped her buttocks and lifted her from the ground. As though she had done it a thousand times, she wrapped her legs around him and pressed her damp sex against his abdomen, her tongue licking the pulse point at his throat.

A mighty shudder went through Andrew. He

lowered her until she was impaled on his shaft and her legs were wrapped about his buttocks. She tightened around him. His breath caught. He couldn't get enough of her . . . of the sweet passion and of the unrestrained way she gave herself to him. He could stay inside her this way forever.

"Andrew." Her voice was a tickle against his chest. "Can we do it this way?"

"With a wee adjustment. Hold tight, lass."

Slowly he eased them into the darkness just outside the fireglow, backing her close to the slope of a nearby dune, lowering himself to his knees, slipping out of her and reinserting himself right away, leaning her backwards until she rested against the warm sand, her robe serving as a bed and his, a blanket against the night chill.

"You wanted under the stars, and that's where you'll be. I'll gi' you something to watch while I'm at play."

"Oh," she said as he nestled deep inside her. And then she sighed. "Do you think I can concentrate on anything but you?"

" 'Twould be a sad commentary on my performance if you did." He began a rhythmic thrust. "Is this to your satisfaction?" he asked raggedly. "Tell me you like it."

She met his movements with thrusts of her own. "I like it. Now hush. We've got things to do."

"You're a bossy wench." A new kind of warmth settled over Andrew and he crushed her against him, kissing her throat and ear and the private place at the back of her neck, welcoming the shattering exhilaration that came when they made love.

Jayne clung to him, sharing the pleasure, her

heart charged with so much love she thought it might burst. Again and again he drove into her, filling her with his hot hardness and making her feel complete. They climaxed together, and she shivered against him, holding onto the waves of rapture as long as she could.

At last he moved to his side and stared down at the starlit face looking up at him with shy contentment.

"I feel another compliment comin' on, lass. Can you handle it?"

"Give me a try."

"I'm speaking nothing but the truth when I say I've never had it better. Anywhere, anytime."

And you never will. Jayne yearned to say the words.

Instead, she smiled. "Of course, I could say the same thing."

His expression darkened. "I know what you've given me. 'Tis a sacrifice I've not taken lightly."

"Sacrifice! What I did, I did of my free will, and never forget it." She kissed him. "Now don't look so serious. I've a feeling that later I'm going to regret making love in the sand, but it is so wonderfully wicked that I don't want to stop. Hold me tight and in a little while we'll make love again."

And pretend, she said to herself, *that this night and this affair will never end.*

Later, when they'd moved inside the tent as protection against the cold, Jayne did indeed regret the sand. They left their robes outside and brought in the mat, wrapping themselves in blankets and each other as they lay down to get a little sleep before the day's long journey.

Jayne tasted grit, felt it on her skin and in her hair. Before they left in the morning, she promised herself a brief bath at the edge of the oasis pool — nothing wasteful, of course, since after days of the foul-tasting contents of the *guerba* she'd learned the value of the priceless liquid — but enough to maintain her sanity.

They got under way early, the morning star guiding their path to Ziza, which Hadji said lay only five days away. A thrill shot through her at his announcement. Five days before she saw Josh. Five days plus thirteen years since she'd seen him last.

She didn't bring up his name to Andrew because she didn't care to hear any negative opinion concerning her chances of finding the long lost Worthington. As in other, very personal areas of her life, she didn't want to dwell on the dark side. She wanted to bask in the light.

When the dark/light images occurred to her, she was thinking figuratively, but it was a very literal sun that scorched the earth over which they rode. To save the horses and the *meharis,* everyone walked, and she caught Andrew watching her out of the corner of his eye. Was this the part of the desert that was supposed to send her back? She broadened her stride, holding the hem of her *barracan* clear of the shuffling sandals.

Jayne quit? Not a chance.

In the middle — and hottest — part of the day, they paused for both prayers and a rest, pitching the tents for much-needed respite from the sun's rays.

361

Jayne sat in a patch of shade with her small coterie of companions—Andrew, Boxer, and Mohammed—but talk was desultory and mostly they dozed. The air was still and hot, well above a hundred and ten Jayne supposed, and so dry she could not summon the moisture to spit.

Suddenly Mohammed bolted upright. "We must take cover."

"Why, lad?" asked Andrew, instantly alert.

"Did the captain not hear the warning?"

Andrew nodded. "Sounded like thunder."

Mohammed stood. "Look, to the east."

All did as he said. A macabre yellow light drifted over the horizon, fading the once cerulean sky to a pallid gray.

Jayne shivered despite the heat. She reached back to the tent for support, and sparks flew where she touched, stinging her fingers. A frisson of fear tingled down her spine, and with a soft cry she looked to Andrew for assurance.

"You're about to have a new experience, lass," he said.

His tone was ominous, and she turned her attention to the rest of the caravan. There was much hurried movement and excited shouts, tying down of supplies and securing of tents. The camels bellowed and the donkeys set up an answering bray. Away from the pack animals and *meharis,* the horses whinnied nervously.

"What's happening?" she asked. A sudden, brutal gust tore the words from her lips. She hugged the wind-whipped *barracan* close to her body.

"Sandstorm." Andrew turned to Boxer. "See that the horses are secured."

"Aye, aye, cap'n," said Boxer, but his eyes were turned toward the women's camp.

"Now!"

Boxer scurried to obey, and Mohammed left to tend to the other animals.

"What can I do?" Jayne asked, heart pounding in her throat.

Andrew studied her—the proud stance, the hair tossed to wildness by the storm, and, too, the apprehension in her eyes. She'd been brave beyond all expectations in everything she experienced since they met; he hoped that bravery endured the next hour.

"Help me get the tent down before it pops loose and is gone. We'll need it for cover."

With a hot wind swirling around them, she helped him pull up the stakes. Small particles of sand stung her cheeks and hands; the air grew thick with it, blinding, biting, cutting. The *sirocco* whipped off the top of the dune against which they'd propped the tent, and all around her the desert boiled.

Images faded into a terrifying sameness in the swirl of grit and debris loosened in the path of the storm. She couldn't see, couldn't breathe, and as she squeezed her eyes shut, she found herself slipping close to hysteria. It was all happening so fast . . . so fast.

Andrew's arms enfolded her, pulling her down to an indentation in the ground, the goatskin tent tugged over the two of them. Breathing shallowly in the close quarters, she clung to him and listened to the roar of the storm, a fury unleashed by devils that would claim them all.

But Andrew's presence soothed her. If this was to be her last moment on earth, at least she would spend it with the man she loved.

The nightmare lasted an eternity, but when at last the noise subsided, Andrew swore it had been less than the hour he'd expected. Not much less, he admitted, but less.

Slowly he eased the tent from over them, working against the accumulated layers of sand. Holding onto his hand, Jayne emerged into a new world.

As quickly as it had come, the storm was gone, but in its wake lay an altered landscape, dunes reshaped and valleys filled, the familiar sights of the Bedouins and their animals blurred by drifts as high as the camels.

"It is with joy that Mohammed learns Miss Jayne is not harmed."

She turned to look down at the boy, a dusting of grit on his cheeks and a yellow-white sprinkle in his dark hair.

She managed a smile. "And I am likewise pleased that Mohammed has survived."

He shrugged and a grin broke the darkness of his face. "Please to understand, Miss Jayne, a boy of the streets is not easy to harm."

Hadji appeared to announce that the caravan must be reformed as soon as possible and move onward to take advantage of the remaining daylight.

Jayne sighed. The sudden might of the wind and the altering of the desert seemed momentous events to her, shattering, soul-searching frights, but to the Arabs it was business as usual.

Wherever she could she helped the others dig their belongings from the sand, relieved to witness Andrew's recovery of the small bundle that included the green dress and the gold. But the relief was not complete, and despite the attitude of everyone else, she could not return to the complacency she'd felt before the storm.

Since the accident, everything had seemed so perfect, discounting the natural twin nuisances of fickle weather and harsh terrain. And wasn't a sandstorm little more than an exaggerated extension of the two? But Jayne couldn't help seeing it otherwise. She took it as an omen . . . as a warning that further difficulties awaited. Somehow she linked it with her tumble down the rock wall. An illogical linkage, she knew, but she couldn't shake the feeling that worse trouble lay ahead.

Kismet. Fate. It didn't always turn out to be good.

Oh, she prayed she was wrong. She was just gritty and hot and tired, that was all, and she kept her distress to herself.

It was an hour before the caravan was ready to leave again, and with the men praying for the Prophet's blessing, they set out afoot on a zigzag course in a search for water.

Jayne's silent, gloomy prediction was strengthened immeasurably when they were two hours under way. The sight looked innocent enough from a distance—a discarded bundle lying in the sand off to the side of the path Hadji was directing. Boxer insisted on investigating.

"It's a body, Cap'n Mac," he yelled. "Come look."

Both Jayne and Mohammed hurried after Andrew, fighting to keep close to his pace. By the time she caught up, he was staring down at the body of a man, huddled facedown in his white robe at the side of a dune, half-covered in sand.

He kneeled to turn the body over. The Arab's small black eyes stared sightlessly toward the sky, and a jagged scar was visible on his death-stiff cheek.

"Oh," Jayne cried out behind him.

Andrew stood to face her. "You recognize him?"

Stunned, Jayne could only nod her head.

Mohammed stood still as a rock beside her, and Boxer shook his head.

"He's the one who attacked you in Tripoli, isn't he?" asked Andrew. "Don't look surprised. I've known for some time."

Again she nodded.

"Must be the bastard who pushed—" Boxer's conclusion was halted by a harsh glance from his captain.

Jayne looked from one man to the other and in a moment of sudden clarity she knew the truth. Closing her eyes, she was suddenly on the top of that limestone hill, looking down at the water and trees, turning too late to avoid the hard hands against her. Once more she felt the ground opening up at her feet, relived the terror as she fell through space, the harsh rock coming up to meet her helpless body as she tumbled, over and over, into a lightless void.

White-faced, she turned to Andrew. "It wasn't an accident."

"Jayne—" He reached for her but she shrugged him away.

"And you knew." She looked from Andrew to Boxer to Mohammed and back to Andrew. "You all knew."

"There seemed little purpose in telling since he got away." Andrew stirred the corpse with his foot. "For a while. If it's any consolation, justice has been done."

Closing her eyes, she swallowed hard and fought for composure. "What's happening?" she whispered. "Why me?"

Andrew felt helpless against her anguish. He'd like to pummel the son of a cur all over again, this time doing a more thorough job. When she covered her hands with her face, he took her in his arms.

"I'll tell Hadji what we've found," said Boxer, and Andrew nodded. Over Jayne's bent head he saw Mohammed staring at the corpse, saw a look of horror cross over his face. A look Andrew didn't understand.

Something was amiss. The boy seemed to care for Jayne, in the way so many people did, wanting to protect her, to ride by her side, to talk with her of matters small and grand. But his foolish tale of a white slave in a desert town was the reason she was on this fruitless journey. And terror lurked in his eyes.

Andrew would have liked to put a few hard questions to him, but not with Jayne close by. He'd have to watch him, at the same time he was watching her. His hopes of her turning back were long since abandoned. She was a stubborn woman, and a fragile one, even though she wouldn't have admitted either trait.

He stroked her arm. When had he become her protector? He didn't know, but he experienced such a powerful urge to watch over her that he felt it in his heart.

If only he'd killed her attacker when he had the chance. At least the storm did it for him. It would have to do that he was accompanying her across the burning sands. Andrew, a man of the sea whose youthful experiences in the desert had caused him to swear he would never be far away from an ocean again.

The lass was turning him inside out, and making him enjoy it, too, when she wasn't worrying him close to his grave.

Jayne edged from his embrace and tilted her chin toward him. "You should have told me the truth," she said. "I'm not a child."

She glanced from him toward the southeast. "And I'm not a quitter, either. I'll get to Ziza, Andrew, and I'll find out why someone doesn't want me there. There's much in my life I'm unsure of, but not this. It will take more than a couple of shoves to keep me from my course."

Chapter Twenty-six

"His name was Mukhtar." Hadji wrung his hands and looked dolefully at Andrew. "Or so he said."

The two men trod at the forward most point of the caravan. Behind them, too far away to overhear, Jayne walked beside Boxer and Mohammed, and farther back strode the stately robed figure of the merchant Omar Bakush, surrounded by the men he had brought to serve him. The Bedouins trailed with the animals and supplies.

A mile behind the last plodding camel lay the corpse of the would-be assassin, wrapped in a blanket, buried in sand. The blanket and the burial had been at Jayne's insistence. Andrew would have let him rot in the open air.

"What do you know about him?" he asked.

The guide slowly shook his head. "Very little. The good captain must forgive Hadji. Mukhtar appeared before me with recommendations, and I agreed that he would work his way across the desert."

"Who recommended him?"

Hadji hesitated.

369

"Miss Worthington's life was threatened, Hadji. I do not want it to happen again."

"The merchant Bakush."

"Bakush, eh?"

Andrew glanced over his shoulder. As though he'd called her name, Jayne looked away from Boxer and their eyes met. The black robe flowed around her, obscuring the sweep of her tall, graceful figure, and the wrapping around her head gave only a hint of the proud tilt of her chin. But the flare in her eyes told him she had not forgotten— nor forgiven—the way he'd deceived her.

So be it. He'd do the same again.

Andrew remembered how she'd looked in the brass jewelry, the polished metal shining against her dusky skin, her dark-tipped breasts high and taunting as she'd offered herself to him. Sudden desire for her pulsed through his veins.

And a need to guide her from harm, no matter her anger.

At sea he was master. In the vast sands of the desert he experienced a sinking helplessness. He didn't care for the feeling one damned bit.

Only one thing to do. Excusing himself, he dropped away from Hadji, shortening his steps until he was even with Jayne. She eyed him speculatively.

"You all right?" he asked.

"Of course." The words were clipped.

" 'Twas a simple question. I'm resigned to your going on."

"Resigned?" she asked, not in the least appeased. "You should have realized back in Derna the way things would be."

Boxer looked away, uneasy, and Mohammed slowed his step until he was a half dozen yards behind.

"I've not stopped to argue with you," said Andrew. "And I've not decided I should have told you the truth about your fall. 'Twould 'a served no purpose, and 'tis more than likely you'd ha' remembered the incident on your own."

"It would have proved you credited me with enough sense and strength to judge the situation for myself. After all, I was the one most concerned."

Andrew gave up. He looked beyond her to Boxer, whose young face was trained on the back of Hadji's robe some dozen yards ahead as though he hoped to draw the pattern when he returned to the ship.

"I'll leave the lass to you, mate. It would seem you've a manner that's more pleasing."

Without looking at Jayne again, he turned his step toward the middle of the caravan . . . toward Omar Bakush, who strolled in the midst of a half dozen servants, all men. With a wave of Bakush's hand, the men fell away and Andrew altered his long stride to match the shorter Arab's as he walked beside him.

He didn't waste time getting to the point. "How well did you know the dead man Mukhtar?"

Bakush stared ahead, his dark eyes unblinking, the half smile on his face unchanged. "I have much curious to know why you ask such a thing."

"He was hired on your recommendation."

Anger flared in Bakush's eyes, then was gone. "Why you know this?"

371

"Is it a secret?"

The Arab shrugged. "Bakush is a man without secrets. A man of truth."

Andrew wasn't so sure.

"So what about the recommendation?" he asked.

"This was long ago."

"Just over a week."

"Much confusion when Hadji makes the caravan."

"Did Mukhtar work for you?"

Bakush's eyes widened in alarm. "No."

"Then how did you know to recommend him?"

"This is something Bakush does not remember. One of the servants made request for the good word. Please not to ask the name. Bakush does not remember."

"For a successful businessman, Omar, you have difficulty recalling very much."

The merchant came to a sudden halt, so quickly that his trailing entourage had to sidestep to avoid a collision.

He stared up at Andrew. "Bakush regrets what has happened to the brave Miss Worthington. Never has he meant her harm."

Andrew believed him. But he also believed there was much the man was not saying. Bakush was afraid of something. It had been in the depths of his eyes a couple of times during their brief conversation, and it had been in his voice.

He glanced toward Jayne, who walked head high despite the heat, her *barracan* trailing in the hot white sand behind her. He could feel the tension in her, like a tight wire about to break. What in hell had she stirred up? And what further

372

disasters awaited them in Ziza?

Later that night when they were alone by the dying fire outside his tent, the *couscous* eaten and the caravan settled down for the night, he tried to warn her of the possibilities.

Jayne knew what he was going to say before he said it. "We've handled everything thus far. We can continue to do the same."

"All I'm asking is that you be careful."

Jayne could have told him that if she were careful, she would have stayed in Virginia . . . or turned back in Tangier . . . or listened to the bashaw when he advised her to leave.

If she were careful, she would have never have let herself fall in love. And she most certainly would have never let a rootless Scottish sea captain in her bed.

No, she had no use for careful. Especially not tonight.

"It's late, Andrew," she said, standing, staring at him across the glowing coals. "Take me to bed."

Inside the tent, her frenzied hands tore at his clothes. She didn't want his counsel or his concern. She wanted him inside her, driving the worries from her mind, making her forget everything but the joining of their bodies and all it meant to her.

The instant her hands touched him, Andrew forgot all the admonitions he'd planned to deliver. She was insatiable, her tongue on him, and her hands, stroking and exploring, her naked body rubbing against him until he shared her frenzy. He moved quickly inside her, feeling her tighten around him, her hips pounding against him in rhythmic repetitions until their bodies exploded against each other, and they clung together in a silent, powerful embrace.

Gradually the ragged breathing slowed and regulated. She shifted until her buttocks nestled against his abdomen, and his knees curled behind hers. Andrew rested an arm around her waist and burrowed his head against the damp tendrils at her neck. He could barely smell the gardenias now—only the omnipresent sand and the added sweetness of their shared satiety.

"Jayne—"

"Please," she whispered, "don't talk. Not tonight."

"You're not pleading an illness, are you? I've evidence you're in the best o' health."

Such gentle, teasing talk, Jayne thought. She should have welcomed it. But gentleness would make her think . . . make her remember and wonder about too many things . . . what would happen tomorrow and the day beyond and on and on. In the thinking, she would come up with only questions and speculations, and she would remember the blank staring eyes and the scarred face of the dead man they'd left far behind.

Andrew hadn't understood her need for the burial. But she couldn't look upon her attacker for the last time with those staring eyes and that marred face as her final memory of him. If she did, she would never get him out of her mind.

"Jayne—"

Oh, the captain was a stubborn man. But she was a stubborn woman, and she needed from him special care tonight.

She took his hand and pushed it down her abdomen until she reached the damp patch of hair between her legs.

"Do it to me again, Andrew," she said, not trying to hide the desperation in her voice. "Please."

Again and again. Make me forget everything but you and me and tonight. I love you. I always will.

The next four days passed slowly, painfully, but the nights slipped by too fast . . . the lovemaking too fast . . . passion mixed with frenzy, and for the first time in his life Andrew found himself wanting to slow a woman down. There was much pleasure to be taken in the nights, and great rapture, but he saw there was little of contentment, and there was an absence of joy.

The recognition was shared by Jayne, but she was too consumed with wanting him to do aught but what she did.

On the evening of the fifth day they camped within sight of the walled settlement of Ziza. The Bedouins celebrated with food and song—just as she had heard them so long ago from a rooftop at the edge of Tripoli. The night she'd met Mohammed, and he'd told her his strange tale. She wanted to share in their merriment, but such lightheartedness was beyond her.

She realized two shattering truths. As though her certainty had melted beneath the desert heat, she feared what she would learn on the morrow. If Josh were not inside those walls, she didn't know what she would do. And she realized the time with Andrew was coming to a close; he had to know it as well as she.

After a night spent in his arms, she arose to don the *barracan* once again and to meet the challenges that awaited. Hadji led all but the Bedouins and the animals through the gates. She was surprised to find the town free of street debris and woebegone children, the buildings whitewashed, the tile roofs in good repair. There was even a touch of greenery in the scattered date palms and olive trees. Hadji explained that an underground spring provided water and gave existence to the settlement.

This was the way a desert town ought to look, she told herself. Taking the unfolding sights as a favorable omen, she felt a surge of hope.

While a curious crowd gathered along the path they had chosen, Andrew strode on ahead, then returned to announce the leader of Ziza was a man named Sidi Ali.

"Apparently well liked, from what I could find out." He glanced at the street that opened up before him. "It's easy to see why. He takes care of his people."

"I'd like to meet him," said Jayne.

"Thought you would."

Shifting her bundle under her arm, she turned to Hadji. "Can it be arranged?"

"I'll do it," said Andrew. "In the meantime, I've located a room out of the heat where you can wait."

Jayne looked around for Mohammed, but he was nowhere to be seen. He'd made a habit of keeping out of her way so often over the past few days that she wasn't surprised.

She glanced at Boxer. "Is this what you expected?"

The young sailor shrugged. "I was hoping for dancing girls. Instead, I'm offered little more than watchful eyes. Not much to bring a man across the desert, is it?"

"What happened to the Bedouin girl? I haven't seen you with her lately."

A look of decided embarrassment crossed the young man's face.

"You don't have to tell me if you don't want to," said Jayne.

"It's nothing to be ashamed of," he said quickly. "If that's what yer thinking. She offered to wash my hair while she was washing hers."

Jayne stared at him in puzzlement. "You're right. That's nothing to be ashamed of."

"Pigs whiskers, she meant to use camel's piss. If ye'll excuse my sayin' so. Now don't get me wrong. She's got every right to the ways of her people. But it wasn't exactly what I had in mind when she put her hands on me for the first time."

"I'm sure Miss Worthington appreciates the delicacy of the situation," said Andrew.

"Oh, it was delicate, all right. Had to tell her I'm a man o' the world. Can't be tied down. She understood."

Jayne felt very much that the girl did, even through the language barrier. She caught Andrew's eye.

It's just as I predicted, lass.

She could read his message clearly. She had an answer—that Boxer simply hadn't found the right girl yet, but it was too complicated and too personal to convey in one glance.

Andrew took her to the place he'd rented—a small, clean room above a coffee house—and she was sharply reminded of the place in Derna where they'd first made love. But she didn't think about it long. Alone, she took advantage of the large vessel of water he'd arranged to be brought, stripped and bathed from head to foot, scrubbing and brushing her hair until it shone, slipping into the American dress and shoes she'd been carrying across the desert.

The petticoat and skirt clung to her, and she found herself missing the loose-fitting trousers and robe she'd worn for so many days.

As she fastened the dozen buttons of her dress, she sent a silent thanks to Andrew for the bath water. Camel's urine would have been a poor substitute indeed. Everything was so different here; so many things she could adjust to, but so many things were beyond her acceptance. How had Josh fared? Thirteen years was a long time, and so many of them possibly spent in servitude.

Binding her hair into its long-abandoned knot, she stared into the brass-framed mirror on the wall. It was the first time she'd looked at herself since leaving Derna, and the sight was a shock.

Her skin had taken on a coppery glow, her cheeks were pink, and her eyes seemed a deeper, thicker black than she remembered them. Too, her lips seemed fuller, more sensual, giving her the look of a woman who had learned the art of love-making and the mixed blessings of being in love.

It was a wiser, older visage that stared back from the mirror, and perhaps a sadder one, too. Although that could just be her imagination and her

378

fear.

The green of the dress brought out the rich tone of her skin, and the sweep of the neckline allowed a glimpse of the slight rise in her breasts. In that area, she hadn't changed much—hadn't taken on added dimensions as a result of Andrew's thorough regard.

No, he hadn't changed her much on the outside—except for the sadder look in her eyes.

One cheerful thought struck her. Millicent would be positively furious when she saw the color of her youngest daughter's skin.

Turning toward a knock at the door, she opened it to see Andrew awaiting her, dressed in the full-sleeved white linen shirt and fitted trousers she was used to aboard the *Trossachs*. She found the sight reassuring.

Andrew stared at her for a moment. How had he ever thought her less than beautiful?

A tightness around her mouth gave evidence she was nervous.

"You can change your mind if you want," he said. "There's nary a soul who'll disparage you for it."

Jayne looked at him with regret. He'd made no secret of his doubt, but to express it at such a time brought her pain.

"Josh is here. I know it."

"And if he is? Ha' you given no thought to the kind of man he'll be?"

"He'll be an extension of the boy I remember."

"Life changes a man, lass."

A woman, too, she thought.

"You're a cynic, Andrew. And I have to believe."

Exasperation welled within him, and a desperate sense of loss. Didn't she know he was trying to save her from crushing disappointment? He cursed her need for family. 'Twas a mirage as surely as the false ponds on the desert, offering sustenance, providing naught.

Andrew stiffened. So much about the lass he didn't ken, foremost among them this driving need.

"I'll not keep you from the palace," he said with a slight bow, his arm extended in invitation. "Sidi Ali awaits."

She took it, accepting his formal offer of help. "Then by all means, Captain MacGregor, let's not let him grow impatient."

He looked her over. "You'll attract a crowd on the way."

"We will attract the crowd," she said, attempting a small smile, wishing all was well between them, knowing it was not.

The palace of the town's ruler—or so Andrew said was the translation of his title—lay a half dozen blocks away down twisting, hilly streets, and she was more than ever pleased with all that she saw. She did, indeed, attract a crowd, but they seemed a friendly people. Nowhere did she spy someone who might want to shove her in front of a horse.

A wall surrounded Ali's abode, but the gate was open and the immediate courtyard was welcomingly simple—shrubs and flowers around a small pond, and a smiling servant waiting at the arched entryway.

She was reminded of her wait outside the home of Sheikh Zamir Hammoda. How different this was, and how lovely. She took heart and strode inside, Andrew close behind. The servant took her down a series of pathways; she heard talk and laughter around her, and she felt a tingle of excitement begin to build.

At last they stopped before a carved door. The servant knocked once, opened the door, then stepped aside.

She looked to Andrew. What if he were right? What if she were told there was no such slave answering to Josh's description anywhere near Ziza? That she had come a long, hard way for nothing . . . that she had been a fool to harbor hopes? He would hear the terrible pronouncement and she would have to put on a brave face despite the punishing defeat.

"I'd like to see Sidi Ali alone," she said.

Andrew stared at her for a moment. "Of course," he said curtly, and stepped back. "No room for cynics here."

Little knowing how to respond, she eased into the room and the door closed behind her. Andrew was gone; the ruler of Ziza awaited. He sat at the end of the room on a dais almost as high as that of Bashaw Karamanli. The chair was high-backed and gilt, the arms carved to resemble elephant's heads, the extended trunks forming the front legs.

The ruler himself was far less grand. He wore the simple white robe of his people, and there was no diamond belt at his waist, nor jeweled rings on his hands. He was more slender than the other powerful Arabs she had met, his hair black and neatly trimmed to a shoulder length, his skin a coppery color not much different from hers.

When she was a half dozen feet from the dais, she stopped, so filled with tension that she couldn't look Sidi Ali in the eye. Instead she stared at his sandaled feet just visible beneath the hem of his robe.

"Speak," he said in English.

Jayne opened her mouth, but no words came.

"There is none here to do you harm."

His voice had a soothing timbre to it, and she believed what he said. But she hadn't expected physical harm, despite her recent experience. Her fears lay elsewhere.

She took a deep breath and tried again. This time the words poured out . . . of her brother's leaving to go to sea, of the disaster met by his ship in the harbor of Tripoli, and of his disappearance.

"Why do you seek him here?" Ali asked.

"Because of a legend . . . a myth." Tears blurred her eyes. She felt absurdly stupid, but she could not stop now, and she told him of the tale she had heard in Tripoli, a story from the streets.

"I can see how this might sound like the ravings of a hysterical woman," she said, keeping her gaze downward, "but I'd traveled so far to find him, I didn't know what else to do except investigate. A long time ago Josh and I vowed to be each other's protector, and it was a vow I had to keep."

At last she fell silent. She'd talked too much . . . taken too much of the ruler's time, and he'd been patient, encouraging.

She tried to tell him how she felt.

"Silence," he said.

She glanced up at him in surprise, and found a

382

smile gracing his face.

Something about him. . . . Her heart began to pound.

"Welcome at long last, Jayne Catherine Worthington. For a girl who couldn't jump from a barn, you've come a long way. Can't call you by your old nickname, can I? You're not so worthless after all."

He stepped down from the dais just in time to catch her as she fell in a faint.

Chapter Twenty-seven

Jayne could have stared at Josh for a decade.

They were seated on a divan in a small, tiled alcove off the main room where he had greeted her. She touched his arm for the thousandth time, needing to reassure herself that this wasn't all a dream . . . that Josh was alive and well and within touch.

She'd awakened from the silly faint to hugs and kisses, and then a host of questions about America . . . about Millicent and Marybeth . . . mostly about how she had managed to find him.

All had been quickly answered. Now it was her turn. After an initial burst of euphoria, she'd been struck by a hurt that wouldn't go away. Only Josh could ease the unrest in her heart.

"All those letters I wrote," she began, brushing at the skirt of her green gown, then lifting her eyes to his. "Why did you never answer them?"

"I never got them."

She stared in disbelief. "But they were never returned."

Josh wasn't so far removed from all he remembered of his childhood that he couldn't hear the pain in his sister's voice. She looked so happy to see him, and puzzled, too, so much the proud, lovely woman he'd known she would someday grow to be. Not a classic beauty, but lovely, nevertheless, with her fine black eyes and full lips and proud tilt of her chin.

He took her hand in his. "You must understand, little sister, few people in this country can read and write. And no one knew me as Joshua Worthington. For thirteen years I've been Sidi Ali. It is not surprising your letters were lost."

"And did you never try to get in touch with me?"

He stroked her cheek. "You look just the way you did when I told you I was going to sea."

Jayne's chin raised a fraction. "And how is that?"

"A little accusing, a little sad."

"I was more than a little sad, Joshua Worthington. I was devastated. You left me behind with Millicent and Marybeth while you went off on a grand adventure."

"You were not much for adventure, Worthless."

"Don't call me that. And I wouldn't be here if I didn't have a little adventure in my soul."

"You're right on both counts. And I did write, a great deal at first, but I never knew for sure what happened to the letters, and after a while . . . well, I guess I just gave up. My life was here, and while I told myself some day we must correspond, the day just never seemed to arrive."

Josh ran a hand through his hair, and Jayne was reminded of how he used to do just that when he was a boy. There was so much about him that was the same—the spark in his eye, the quick retort, the friendly smile. And so much that was different. Gone were the freckles and the boyishness, in their

385

place a steady confidence and angular masculinity.

Brother Josh had grown up to be a very handsome man.

But not one who was noticeably more concerned about others than himself. She brushed aside the thought as uncharitable. She loved him as much as ever, and she could see that the affection was returned.

Settling back on the divan, she told herself to quit worrying about slighted feelings. Heavens, it was almost as if she were sorry she hadn't found him toiling away in slavery.

"So tell me how you got this life," she said. "It looks like a pretty good one to me."

"It didn't start out that way," he said, then launched into a description of how the grounded *Philadelphia* was taken in Tripoli Harbor thirteen years before.

"They swarmed aboard, whooping and waving glittering cutlasses as they came," he said, a faraway look in his eye.

"I was told you had drowned while going ashore," Jayne said.

"Almost did." He shook his head. "Seems strange to speak in English, although I've made it a point to use it with my people as often as I can. Didn't want to get out of the habit, you see, and they've been willing enough to learn."

"Your people," said Jayne.

"I'll get to that." Josh patted her hand. "Right now it's back to the conquering Tripolitans. And conquerors they were. Stripped us of our valuables — watches, coins, layers of clothes. Had many of us down to our underwear. Tossed us overboard,

386

made the bigger sailors row. Like galley slaves, we were."

Shivering, Jayne edged closer, sharing his remembered pain.

"We neared shore beneath the bashaw's fortress walls," he said. "Pushed out to wade through a crashing surf. That's when I made my move. Ducked under the water and held my breath while I swam for a point well away from the fort."

"How did you manage to get away unseen?"

"One boy was not held in much account. Not when there were officers to humiliate, and the crew as well." Josh shook his head in disgust. "I watched from afar as they brought the men through the waiting crowd. Held their torches high and spat on the poor souls as they were shoved along. You can bet I said many a prayer of thanks I wasn't among them. Granny Worth would have been proud I remembered the right words."

"Did you know they were held prisoner for eighteen months?"

"I heard. Also heard about the trek taken by a few sailors and Marines from Egypt to Derna to bring Yusuf Karamanli's brother Hamet to the throne."

"It was a coup that didn't work," Jayne said with a sigh. "President Jefferson decided to deal with Yusuf and pay the tribute he demanded."

Over the years she'd been in correspondence with several participants in the long-ago journey. They had been bitter over what they considered Jefferson's betrayal since he had sanctioned the attempted overthrow and then backed out when they were close to success. Like the heads of state of both the

United States and Tripoli, they'd offered no hope that Josh was alive.

But he was. And he thrived.

Jayne glanced around the arched tile of the alcove and ran her hand over the plush velvet cushion on which they sat. "It's a long way from the Tripoli shore to here, Josh."

"A very long way. It was my good fortune to be taken in by a kindly old sandal maker who had no love for the bashaw. I was not in the best of condition. He heard me muttering in my sleep about you. Sister, I kept saying. He thought I meant myself, and when I awoke he gave me the name as he remembered it."

"Sidi."

"Smart as ever, aren't you? Ali was his name, which I was glad to take. Taught me the language, dressed me in robes for a disguise. With the black Worthington eyes and complexion, I got by for a while. Until I got a little cocky—"

"That I can believe."

"—and let the bashaw's men discover me while I was strolling through the bazaar. Didn't cover myself properly. They brought me before the bastard. By all rights I should have been thrown in prison with the others, but he thought he was being clever by giving me as a slave to one of his merchant friends. Thought it would be special punishment. As things worked out, the Arab took to me."

"You always had a way about you."

"Except where Millicent was concerned." He grinned. "She never knew quite what to make of her Worthington offspring."

He offered the observation so casually that Jayne

388

knew whatever rancor he'd held for his mother had long dissipated.

"She still prefers Marybeth. But back to your story, Josh. Did this merchant set you up in Ziza?"

"After I—"

His voice broke off,

"I've a great deal more to tell you," he said. "But first there's someone I'd like you to meet."

Jayne wasn't sure she liked the hesitancy in his voice.

And then she thought of Andrew. He must be waiting outside. Her conscience struck her. How could she have left him waiting and wondering for so long?

"There's someone I would like you to meet, too," she said.

"The captain who helped you get here? I want to shake the man's hand and give him my thanks." Josh saw the dark look that passed over his sister's face. "Anything wrong?"

"No," she said brightly. "Nothing. He very much deserves your thanks."

She spoke the truth. He *had* helped her . . . and in ways that were nobody's business but hers and his.

Josh excused himself for a moment, then returned to stand at the arched portal to the alcove. "She'll be right here."

"She?"

"Most definitely. The most wonderful, beautiful, passionate girl in the world."

"You're in love, Josh Worthington."

"I'd better be, or Zamir Hammoda will cut off my head."

Jayne started, and Josh turned toward the sound of an opening door.

Hammoda. She could scarcely believe she'd heard right.

"Welcome, my love. We have an unexpected guest."

Jayne stared at the young woman who eased gracefully to Josh's side. She moves like a restful breeze, thought Jayne as she rose to her feet. The woman was a beauty, dark and slight, her slender body clad in a blue velvet top and a skirt of finely striped red and white silk. About her waist was a brocaded sash of many colors, and a matching scarf bound her black hair, allowing long twin braids to dangle in front of each ear. Full lips, strong nose, high cheeks, and expressive dark brown eyes, she bore a face reflective of a thousand years of Arabs from which she came.

She was young, twenty-three at the most, and when she glanced up at Josh she had a look of such passion and love in her eyes that Jayne was stunned.

Josh gazed down at her with much the same expression, whispering in Arabic before turning to Jayne. "Sister, I present my wife, Merina, favored daughter of the merchant who took me as a slave and allowed me to join his family."

"Your wife," murmured Jayne, unable to say more.

"For five years she has been Mrs. Joshua Worthington, although she answers more quickly to Merina Hammoda Ali, wife of the noble Sidi Ali, ruler of Ziza."

Merina bowed. "Welcome to my humble home, sister of Sidi. You are most welcome here."

Something in her voice rang insincere. No doubt she was as surprised by Jayne's presence as Jayne was surprised by her.

Josh put an arm around his wife, and Jayne understood he was asking her acceptance of all that she saw and heard.

She smiled at her unexpected sister-in-law. "Please call me Jayne, and I hope you will let me call you Merina. It is a beautiful name for a beautiful woman and I can see you have made my brother very happy."

She extended her hand. Merina looked to her husband. Jayne decided against waiting for formalities, and she stepped forward to hug the newest member of her family. Merina felt like a child in her arms, but it was obvious from the way Josh looked at her that she was a woman grown.

"Sidi is most pleased," said Merina after Jayne had backed away, "to have his beloved sister before him. He has told me often of the little girl who was like a shadow to the brother that she loved."

Jayne was both pleased and irritated by the statement.

"I certainly was no shadow."

"Oh, yes you were." Josh laughed. "Despite the squabbles we used to get into."

The laugh warmed Jayne's heart and she grinned. Her brother had not, after all, forgotten her.

"I guess we did have an argument or two." She looked at Merina. "You have brothers or sisters, don't you? I'm sure you understand."

"My father has had five wives, three of whom still live, and twenty-two children," said Merina. "We never had disagreements in his presence, but on his frequent journeys we were known to . . . how do you say . . . squabble."

"Squabble is a good word," said Jayne, remembering how Sheikh Hammoda had talked about his wives and children. She also remembered the silence in the gloomy mansion in which he lived, and she wondered how happy Merina's life had been.

Hammoda, father-in-law to Josh. He must have known exactly who she was asking about, so why had he—

A knock sounded on the great carved door through which Jayne had first entered the room. A very strong knock.

"Andrew," she said, forgetting the sheikh.

Josh looked at her in surprise. "You recognize his knock?"

"It has a certain authority to it," she said.

"Enter," said Josh, even as the door opened.

Andrew stepped inside, one hand on the robe of a squirming Mohammed. "Caught him sneaking down one of the passageways. He claimed a right to be here, so I thought we'd find out."

As he dragged the reluctant boy deeper into the room, his dark eyes turned on Jayne. She stirred nervously. "Andrew," she said, "I'm glad you're here. So much has happened."

"Aye, 'tis something I found out for myself from talking to the servant."

"I'm sorry," she said, more than anything wanting him to share her joy. "I should have called you in right away."

Josh stepped forward. "Accept my thanks for getting Jayne here safely, Captain MacGregor. She's mentioned your help."

The two men shook hands, each taking the measure of the other. "Has she now?" Andrew asked.

Jayne was suddenly *very* nervous, wanting very much for the men in her life to get along, even if Josh had no idea of her relationship with Andrew and Andrew couldn't understand her compulsion to find Josh. He certainly wouldn't understand why she had been doing the looking while Josh rested in luxury.

She turned to the boy.

"What are you doing here, Mohammed? And why that story about a white slave toiling mercilessly in the desert? Could it be I've been lied to? That it wasn't a legend you'd heard?"

"Mohammed always plays with the truth," said Merina softly.

Jayne's eyes widened as she turned to look at her sister-in-law. "You know him?"

"I have not seen him since the wedding five years before, but he still has the look of the devil in his eye. He is Mohammed Hammoda, the only child born to my father's youngest and newest wife."

"Mohammed Hammoda?" Jayne fluttered a hand toward the boy. "This child of the streets?"

"My brother is no child of the streets. He lives in a fine home in Tripoli."

Jayne looked from Merina to Mohammed and back to Merina. Stumbling into the alcove, she fell heavily onto the divan where she and Josh had talked. "This is too much." She shook her head and fixed her eye on the boy. "Too much. I'd like to know exactly what is going on, Mohammed. I'd like to know right now."

"I can't believe it," Jayne said to Andrew. "He knew all along the whereabouts of my brother. Why didn't he tell me? I can't accept his explanation that he knew I would doubt him. Not after he took me to the locked home of a supposed stranger, a man who turns out to be the sheikh. And the boy's father."

They stood outside the spacious room Merina had prepared for Jayne. The dimly lit passageway was deserted. For the first time since she'd seen Josh, she and her captain were alone.

"Mohammed is a boy with too much imagination and too little guidance," said Andrew. "He wanted you here, but he didn't want to reveal his identity. He said himself he was hiding from his father. I doubt he sees Hammoda very often, and with his mother gone for a visit to her own mother, he decided to run away."

It was a situation Andrew knew well. A boy too much alone, a boy at odds with the man who had sired him.

"But he told such a preposterous story."

"Which you believed."

Jayne could not meet his eye. "He told it very well. You weren't there to hear it or you would know what I mean."

"The lad fooled me as well. I believed him to be a beggar."

But Andrew also believed he'd had something to do with the attacks on her. He still did; he just didn't know how or why.

An idea formed in his mind, but he kept it to himself. And he sure as hell wasn't ready to reveal he was a business partner of the sheikh. Jayne might not take the news too well.

"Did your brother explain why he didn't try to get in touch with you?"

As usual, thought Jayne, Andrew got right to the point, no matter how hurtful it might be.

"He did try. The letters simply never arrived."

Andrew would have bet one of the *Trossachs'* sails that Hammoda was somehow at fault.

"Josh has made his home here," she went on. "He hasn't converted to Islam, but it's clear he's accepted the ways of the Tripolitans. I can understand why. He's lived most of his life among them."

To Andrew's ear, she sounded too damned defensive. She must have put a few questions of her own to the elusive Josh.

A silence fell between them, light from a nearby wall torch flickering over them both, casting alternate shadows and a soft luminous glow, and for Jayne all else but the man before her faded from mind. She wanted to brush a lock of hair from his forehead . . . she wanted to do anything that might give her a reason for touching him. He stared down at her with such intensity that she wanted far more than just a casual touch.

But so much had changed. And so quickly. She was no longer alone in this part of the world, no longer fighting for what everyone considered a hopeless cause. She should have felt secure—even a trifle smug—but with Andrew's dark gaze on her, all she felt was a little lost.

Right now it seemed that her wonderful nights spent in the desert with her ardent lover had been little more than a mirage.

She looked down at her hands. "I can't ask you in."

"I wouldna accept if you did."

Her eyes flew back up to his. "And why not?"

"I've no wish for a new-found brother to find a man in his sister's bed. 'Twould lead to complications."

Jayne's cheeks burned. "Is that all I am? A complication?"

"You're more than that and you know it."

Much, much more, Andrew thought. His gut wrenched at the thought of leaving her here in this palace, of sleeping alone for the first time in a long while and wondering what she was doing and whether she was all right. His place was beside her . . . watching, protecting, making love.

"Jayne—"

"If you're going to tell me goodnight, then do it and get it over with."

Jayne's heart broke with every word, but he stood so calmly looking down at her, calling her a *complication,* for God's sake. Almost like a stranger, and in some ways, that's what he was. There were so many things she didn't know about him . . . exactly where he came from and who he left behind, what he wanted, what—if anything—could move him to tears.

"I'll tell you goodnight, if that's what you're wanting. But I'll do it in my own way."

His hands gripped her shoulders, and his eyes raked over her face, her long, slender neck, and the curve of her breasts above the low sweep of her gown. "The green looks bonnie on you, Jayne. I told you long ago you were meant for deeper colors.

It was one of the few times you listened to what I said."

She wanted to respond, but his lips claimed hers, his hands crushing her against him, his heat and scent and strength overwhelming all her senses and giving her no choice but to melt in the fire of his embrace.

His tongue found easy access to the honeyed interior of her mouth, and a hot, familiar longing rushed through him, as potent as ever, and as arousing.

Jayne curled against him, instantly on fire for all the raptures he had ever brought her. She brushed her tongue against his, suckled at him, held tight to his shoulders and wished they were back in a desert tent wearing nothing but a fine sheen of sweat and knowing nothing except that the night was theirs to spend as they wished.

Andrew broke the kiss, and his hands roamed down her back, cupped her buttocks, held her tight against his evident arousal.

"Feel what you do to me, lass," he whispered against the lobe of her ear, nibbling gently, his hot breath raising chills along her neck.

He let her go as quickly as he had embraced her. Breathing raggedly, he looked at the swollen lips and the rounded eyes turned up to him.

"You got what you came for, did you not, and proved the cynic wrong. I'll miss you, Jayne Worthington. We've had an adventure or two."

His lips twisted into a half smile, then he turned and was gone, his footsteps echoing down the corridor, while Jayne leaned back against the closed door of her room, hands to her mouth, her mind whirling to match the beat of her heart.

He was gone. Had he just told her goodbye?

Impossible.

But he was gone.

Without allowing her to say a word.

She stumbled into the room, little noting its splendor and size. Anguish and anger tore through her, and her eyes stung with tears she refused to shed. He couldn't leave this way. He *couldn't*. She'd given herself to him in total abandon. As a final farewell, she deserved more than a hard, fast kiss and a groping in the hall.

Flinging open the door, she raced down the passageway after him. By the time she reached the outside palace door, he had disappeared into the street. Ignoring the call of the servant who stood as sentry, she started to rush into the cold night, not knowing what she would say when she found Andrew, knowing only that she must find him.

"Jayne."

The soft voice stopped her.

She turned to face Merina, who stood in the shadows behind her. Dressed in white, her dark hair brushed loose across her shoulders, she looked more like a ghost than a woman.

"Even in so small a town as Ziza," Merina said, "it is unwise for a woman to walk the streets at such an hour."

The warning sent a shiver down Jayne's spine. Merina seemed to be talking about her in particular, and not just any female who might happen out at night.

"I felt free on the desert," she said, trying to keep her voice light.

"Free to talk to the captain whenever you chose," said Merina, her voice critical, unsettling.

So the innocent-looking young woman had figured out her relationship with Andrew. She glanced over her shoulder at the blackness outside the palace door. Andrew was gone; for consolation, she faced a woman who was going out of her way to make her feel uncomfortable. And she'd been so happy a short while before.

She should have remembered that happiness was not a condition which she enjoyed overlong.

A brisk breeze whistled through the open doorway, stirring her gown, and she felt the coldness in her bones. Eyeing Merina, she caught a glimpse of an equal coldness in the young woman's eyes. Caught between Josh's wife and the night, she didn't know which made her the more uneasy.

Rubbing briskly at her bare arms, she said, "I will take your advice, Merina, and stay indoors. Please believe me when I say I wish to cause no problems here. My only wish is to get to know Josh again. You have many brothers and sisters, but I have only one."

With a nod, she left to make her way back to her room. Merina watched until she was swallowed by the dark, then turned to the sentry, instructing him in Arabic to bolt the door. Slowly she turned her footsteps toward the room where her beloved husband awaited.

His name is Sidi, she'd wanted to scream a hundred times today. For her he would never be Joshua, or the peculiar name of Josh. This was a name for boys, and her Sidi was very much a man. Tonight she would make special love to him. He must forget this woman who comes from far beyond the sea . . . from the land he has spoken of with such tenderness that each time he breaks her heart.

Sidi must remember only his Merina and all the things she does for him. Things an old and skinny sister could never do.

As she hurried toward the quarters housing her lord and master, she vowed with a passionate vengeance that never would she allow an intruder to ruin the life she and her father had so carefully arranged.

Chapter Twenty-eight

Andrew had spent the first day in Ziza searching out Omar Bakush and—after some duress—eliciting a confession that yes, perhaps the merchant did remember Sheikh Hammoda's name being mentioned when he was asked to recommend the man with the scar. The recollection had come as no surprise.

The day's unexpected news came with the discovery that the ruler before Sidi Ali, a highly respected Arab who was the last of an old Tripolitan family, had died under suspicious circumstances. A diseased heart, the physician had said before leaving Ziza for a new post in Derna.

But the ruler had been young and athletic, according to Andrew's source, an ancient *marabout* who'd served out his priesthood years in the Ziza mosque. And there had been no immediate successor. After his death and quick burial, Sheikh Zamir Hammoda had appeared, lavished gifts upon the citizenry, and suddenly his soon-to-be son-in-law took over in the palace.

The instant popularity of the fair-minded Ali had kept rumors about his mysterious succession at bay. The *marabout,* who visited often in the palace, doubted the new ruler knew the gossip in the streets.

Andrew spent his second day in Ziza considering all

he'd learned and telling himself he ought to arrange for a return journey to Derna, where he could put a few questions directly to his business partner.

At night he paced the small room he'd rented for Jayne when they arrived. She was safe, he kept telling himself during all this while, with her brother, which was where she wanted to be.

Taking note of his restlessness, Boxer advised him to get a woman. It was the lad's cure for everything from insomnia to lice. He'd found one for himself. "Uses water, she does, for bathing." It seemed to be her primary attraction, that and the fact she was enthralled by the fair-haired young seaman.

Andrew knew of only one woman he wanted. And why in hell he was keeping himself from her, he hadn't figured out.

And so on the third day in the desert town, he visited the palace once again to find out for himself how things stood between them. He wasn't one to be put in second place behind a long-lost brother. Not forever. Not even for one day more.

Merina greeted him in the room where he'd met Jayne's newly discovered family. She was dressed in a silk turquoise gown, which opened from the waist to her slippered feet over a pair of gossamer harem pants. Her hair was bound by a matching scarf of turquoise, and her brown eyes had been outlined heavily in kohl.

Somehow she did not look nearly so innocent as she had the day they met, and he wondered whether to reassess the danger this daughter of the sheikh posed for Jayne.

"Welcome, Captain MacGregor," she said in a soft, silvery voice, her eyes cast demurely to the carpeted floor. Slowly she raised her lashes. "Sidi and his sister remain in seclusion for they have much to discuss." A slight, help-less shrug. "It is left to the wife to entertain herself."

Trouble in Paradise, thought Andrew with growing uneasiness.

Merina changed her coyness to a brilliant smile. The captain was a very virile man, and she had seen the looks that had passed between the two *roumi,* looks that spoke of passionate nights and persistent longings. This Jayne, who had taken the attention of Sidi, who had brought turmoil into the happy life of his wife, deserved the same turmoil in hers.

"It is also left to the wife to entertain the guests. Please allow me to summon one of the palace favorites. My husband does not keep the harem, but he does take plea-sure in the performance of the *chengis* — how you say, the dancing girls."

Without allowing him time to respond, she clapped her hands and within minutes, Andrew found himself sprawled on the divan in the small alcove, a glass of her husband's favorite wine in one hand, and in the other a honey-sweetened pastry Merina called Ladies' Thighs.

A fast worker, the fair Merina. The strains of a lute and the jingle of a tambourine drifted in to him, and he caught the heavy scent of musk perfume just before a veiled, voluptuous *chengi* swayed into view. High-waisted scarlet harem pants fitted snugly under the dancer's full, dark-tipped breasts, clearly visible through a swath of flesh-colored gauze. Three-inch bands of gold encircled her upper arms, and shoulder-length golden earrings caught the light with each turn.

She slid her bare feet across the carpet, jangling the bracelets around each slender ankle, her painted eyes staring at him over the thin veil as she undulated closer to the alcove.

Andrew had to be blind not to notice the woman's charms. Keeping time to the music, she eased toward the divan, coming to a stop when she was inches away, her shoulders working so that her pendulous breasts rose and fell like stormy waves at sea.

As if jealous of the overworked breasts, her hips got into the performance, rotating from side to side, accelerating as they shifted to a forward thrust. If she got much closer, Andrew thought, she'd blacken his eye with her anatomy. Several parts vied for the honor.

With musk and music swirling around him, he sipped at the wine and bit into a Ladies' Thigh. Boxer ought to be here, he thought, to enjoy the show. He'd have to take in the details so he could pass them along with adequate accuracy.

Growing bored, wishing for a scent of gardenia, he glanced past the *chengi*. Jayne stood in the middle of the room, her face pale, her eyes round as she stared into the alcove. She wore a brilliant blue gown in the style of the Arabs, a wide green sash at her waist and a green scarf covering her hair. She was a splash of color in the wide room, and his heart stood still.

Choking on the Thigh, he tried to stand, but the persistent dancer resisted, the jangles and the beat of the tambourine quickening, overwhelming the more subtle song of the lute.

"Enough," he said, but it took attempts in several languages before the *chengi* admitted to understanding. With graceful nonchalance, she let her various components come to a rest; with a snap of her fingers, she stilled the music, too.

She cast him a sly, sideways glance before she and the two musicians disappeared through a doorway behind the elephant chair, leaving Andrew and Jayne alone with the echoing rhythms and the lingering musk.

Jayne stood still as a post, unable to move, unable to turn away. As long as she lived, she'd never forget the look on Andrew's face as he stared at the dancer's breasts and at her hips. It was the way he'd looked at an equally voluptuous serving woman a long time ago in a New York tavern. It was proof he hadn't changed.

Andrew liked to look at beautiful women, endowed women. What had ever made her think she could attract him for long or that she could hold his attention exclusively?

Jayne was a woman for the lonesome desert nights. But they had returned to town. She'd spent two sleepless nights wondering about him, picturing him with such a woman as the dancer. And now she saw the two of them in the flesh. No need for imagination anymore.

The weight of all her worries was like an anvil on her chest. Everything, it seemed, was turning out wrong. First Josh, and now . . .

At last she was able to look away. "Merina told me you were in here. I didn't mean to interrupt anything."

Andrew didn't doubt for a moment Jayne had been sent with the purpose of finding him in a compromising situation. Merina was indeed a conniving sort, a true member of the Hammoda clan.

"You didn't interrupt." He set the food and drink aside and stood to walk toward her. "You're the reason I'm here."

Jayne tried to still her pounding heart. How dare he move in such a graceful, unstoppable way, like a dark cloud about to enfold her when she had no defense against clouds.

Already she was upset, Josh having just confirmed her fear that he had no intention of returning to Virginia with her, and now here was Andrew in pursuit of replacement companionship.

Which he had probably already found the past two days.

Jayne fought the tears that burned at the back of her eyes. God, but she was weary of feeling alone.

She held herself tall. She might not be softly rounded or exotically beautiful, but she had a certain dignity about her that she must use in their stead.

"Josh and I have been having a splendid visit."

It was the truth . . . until she'd suggested he and Merina return to Worthington Farm. She had yet to tell him the sheikh had tried keeping her from finding him. By lies and perhaps by methods far worse.

It was a revelation she did not know if she could make.

Whatever danger she had been through, she did not believe Merina was involved. And now that she was within Josh's protection, she doubted she was in danger.

Except that she was about to lose the love of her life. She would rather suffer a mortal blow from a scimitar.

"I never did congratulate you on being right about your brother," said Andrew. "You must be very proud."

To his own ears, he sounded priggish. What he ought to be doing was taking her in his arms and telling her how much he'd missed her over the past few days.

Jayne shrugged off his praise. Being right was cold comfort for the heated anguish that had her in its grip.

"I can't reconcile myself to the fact he's the son-in-law of Sheikh Hammoda," she said. "Or that Mohammed is the sheikh's son."

"Have you talked to the lad anymore?"

"Merina has decided he needs to return to his schooling, and a teacher has been summoned to the palace to stay with him. She and Josh have no children, and I suppose it's the frustrated mother in her that has taken over."

"I see."

An uncomfortable silence descended.

Andrew eyed the shadowy half-circles beneath her eyes. "Are you all right?" He took a step toward her.

"Of course. I have everything I need here."

Except the thing I need the most.

"Glad to hear it."

Jayne caught the sarcasm in his voice. "Of course," she said airily, determined to maintain an air of self-possession, "I've had to get used to sleeping alone. It's different for women, you understand. We've no dancing boys to entertain us."

"Is that what ailing you, lass? That I've not been alone?"

"I really can't see where it's any of my business."

She was a cool one, Andrew had to give her credit for that. And she had a way about her of heating his temper to the boiling point. He closed the distance between them and stared down at her. She kept her eyes turned away.

"I've worried about you. And I've thought about you."

Jayne wanted to run away from him, but his aura cast a spell over her, leaving her unable to move, just as she had known would happen.

He gripped her shoulders. "Look at me."

"I don't want to." Childishly said, but his hands burned so strongly against her that she could think of no clever retort. Indeed, all she could imagine was casting her pride away and melting against him. As she had done so many times . . . begging for love, adorning herself with tinkling chains and throwing her naked body in his path. How ridiculous she must have looked, the scrawny spinster playing as Jezebel.

A lump formed in her throat; the thought of tears terrified her, but she didn't know how long she could hold them back.

A door opened. She turned to see Josh and Merina approach. Easing away from Andrew's grip, she smiled gaily . . . falsely. "Captain MacGregor was just saying goodbye."

Merina's gaze was darkly speculative.

"Captain," said Josh, "I haven't thanked you adequately for seeing that Jayne got across the desert safely. She said you had trouble with your ship, and I'm sure you would have rather stayed in Derna to see to its repairs."

"I came willingly," said Andrew, his eyes on Jayne.

"Well," said Josh, "it was still a damned nice thing to do."

Jayne worked at swallowing the lump. She loved her brother dearly, but he was a little obtuse when it came to detecting subtleties . . . like the hurt he'd caused when he said that Ziza was his proper home, and like the tension that existed between her and Andrew right now. It must have been thick enough to slice.

She felt certain Merina was attuned to it.

"If you will excuse me," she said, "I've got a frightful headache. No need for concern, Merina. I've not been sleeping well, that's all." With a brief, impersonal nod to them all, she excused herself and left the room.

Whatever final words she and Andrew had to say to one another, they could not be said now but they would have to be said soon. And when the two of them were truly alone.

Jayne took the evening meal in her room, but she scarcely ate a bite, knowing too well no food could fill the emptiness she felt inside. Mohammed joined her to apologize for his deceptions.

"Please to understand it was a game," he said. "At the beginning. I grew weary of the absent father and took to the streets. The horse, the American lady became part of the game. And then you spoke of someone who must be Sidi. The tale was easy to tell."

"And I stupidly believed every word."

Mohammed's conscience smote him. "Mohammed is known for his lying tongue. Ask Merina, and she will tell you this is so."

"And when did the game end?"

"In the desert. When Miss Jayne is hurt. This was not part of the plan, and Mohammed feared he had brought pain to the very kind lady. Always you have treated me as a friend. There are few who have done the same."

Jayne responded to the loneliness in his voice, and whatever distress she felt toward him dissipated. He was not a part of any conspiracy against her. She accepted the realization with enormous relief.

And yet, he must have some knowledge of what was going on. "Do you have any idea who has been trying to hurt me?"

Mohammed hesitated, unable to put his suspicions into words.

"I do not know the man with the scar. A man sick in the head, perhaps."

"Perhaps."

Jayne played with a ripe plum on her plate. A man sick in the head, and a woman sick in the heart.

Distress over her family situation gave way to thoughts of Andrew. Was he alone tonight? Or was he preparing to leave? She'd not learned the reason for his visit today, not really. He'd said he wanted to know how she was getting along, but perhaps he'd come to tell her that tomorrow he would be gone.

If so, all that had passed between them would end incomplete. She loved him. Wise or not, she wanted to tell him so. And if he said that he was flattered or touched or whatever a man said in such a situation but added that unfortunately he couldn't return the affection, then she would know she had done all that she could to bring a happy conclusion to their affair.

Merina had warned her against wandering the streets at night. But she had a difficult time warming to her new sister as she should, and a difficult time accepting her advice.

"Do you know where the captain is staying?"

He mentioned the room where Jayne had bathed.

"It's really very close, isn't it?"

Mohammed's eyes widened in alarm. "Surely there is no wish to go there tonight."

"There is a very strong wish to go there tonight."

Mohammed protested the folly of such a journey, but Jayne would not accept his arguments; tonight she was the persuasive one. Within the quarter hour, wrapped in a dark robe, she stole out one of the side doors of the palace, the boy at her side.

All of Ziza seemed as quiet and as dark as the night sky. A block from her destination, she could see a light flickering in the window of Andrew's room.

"He's there, Mohammed. Please return to the palace."

The boy hesitated.

"I'll be all right. As you can see, the street is deserted, and the captain will see me home."

It took several minutes of arguing, but at last the boy gave in and she listened to his footsteps echoing into the dark. Moving along quickly without caution or care, thinking only of what she would say in this final goodbye, she didn't see the shadow moving at her from the alleyway, didn't see the raised hand, didn't see a brief glitter along the flat surface of the raised blade.

Suddenly a second unseen figure hurtled into her, knocking her away from the alley and from danger, and she fell awkwardly to the pebbled street. Gripping a bruised arm, she stared in horror at the two dark figures struggling over her. She saw the raised scimitar, saw it fall with a clatter, and she scrambled away from it. A *barracan* fluttered in the moonlight, but it was the clothing of the other man that caught her eye . . . the full sleeve of the shirt, the fitted trousers.

"Andrew!" she cried just as he raised a fist to finish off the Arab.

He turned toward the cry, a mistake. The Arab grabbed up the scimitar, and Andrew found himself in a fight for his life. Clutching the attacker's wrist, he twisted hard, but the man had a wiry strength that resisted defeat. The blade rose higher. Andrew reached for the knife at his belt. The scimitar curved downward toward Andrew's throat. Jayne screamed.

The Arab slumped, then fell to the ground, sprawling on his back, the handle of Andrew's knife protruding from his belly.

Jayne sprang to her feet and threw herself in Andrew's arms. "You're all right," she whispered, running her hands over his face, his throat, his chest. "You're all right."

"Aye, I'm all right," he said, his breath coming in gasps. He held her for a moment more, telling his heart to stop its hammering, assuring himself that she had not met with harm. At last he eased her away and made a quick inspection of the attacker.

He glanced at Jayne's pale face. "Do you recognize him?"

She shook her head.

Standing, he wrapped his arm around her and without another word guided her down the block toward his room. Inside, he removed her robe, instructed her to sit, and poured her a glass of water. "Wine is hard to come by outside the palace," he said. "Otherwise I'd be offering you a glass of claret. Lock up after me. I'll be right back."

She stared up at him in alarm. "Where—"

But he was gone, the door closing firmly behind him. Fifteen torturous minutes passed before he was back, time in which Jayne imagined him lying dead alongside the attacker.

"Called a sentry," he said when she'd answered his sharp knock. "He seemed to think it was a robber. Not anyone he's seen before."

"A robber," she echoed, not believing it for one minute. Sitting at the edge of the bed, she steadied her hands in her lap. Safety under Josh's protection had been illusion. Only in the presence of Andrew was she truly free from harm. She saw the tightness of his mouth, the stark look in his eye. At great risk to his own life, he'd just slain a man—to save her—and she felt the power of her overwhelming love.

"You were almost killed," she said.

The starkness in his eyes turned to rage. She hardly knew him, so quickly did the transformation come.

"I was not the intended victim. 'Twas a stupid thing for you to come out on this night. What got into your head?"

"I had an escort," she said, all hollow inside.

"Aye, Mohammed. I heard the two of you bickering. Brought me out on the street. A good thing, too, or

412

you'd be lying in an alley now, your throat slit from ear to ear."

Jayne cowered from his harshness. "Please, Andrew—"

"Please what? I've need to get some sense into that brain o' yours. Whyever are you here?"

She stared up at him, and he glowered right back. With her pulse pounding and her breathing coming in shallow gasps, and especially with the fury she read in his eyes, it seemed a poor moment to declare what was in her heart.

She rubbed her arm. "I'd like to go back to the palace." Surely within its walls no one would wish her harm, not even the daughter of the man who was incredibly her enemy. Most certainly she would be free of her lover's scorn.

"You're not leaving until you've told me why you're here."

Jayne swallowed. "I grew restless and wanted a stroll."

"The truth. I've never known you as a liar, and I'll not have you lie to me now."

"You'll not have me lie?" She stood, waving a hand in anger. "And who are you to be ordering me about?"

Andrew had no ready answer, not one that came close to the truth. The lass had gotten under his skin, had become a part of him while he'd been fighting the intrusion all the way. Life with her would be chaotic; life without her loomed barren and bleak.

But he'd spent a lifetime keeping the world at arm's length. Anger, lust, occasional humor . . . they were the only emotions he allowed to show, the lot of them more in evidence since the day he'd taken to drink in a tavern in New York.

413

Andrew didn't know what to say to her . . . didn't know what he wanted to say.

Jayne read the hesitation. It struck her heart a mighty blow. "Take me home."

"And where is that? The fancy place in New York?"

But that wasn't home, either, she wanted to say. Anguish filled her. She'd told him far too little about Virginia . . . about the green hills and forests and small farmhouse she loved.

And she'd told him nothing about how much the sea had meant to her, a kind of home, too, with its open expanses and wide blue sky. There were so many things left unsaid between them that if she were to open up now, she wouldn't know where to begin. Worse, she doubted he would care.

"I'm speaking of the palace," she said.

She tried to step around him, all defiance. Despite the depth of his fury, he had never wanted her more.

He caught her by the wrist. "Not just yet."

His fingers burned against her skin.

Her eyes met his. "We're not in the desert."

"But we're alone. 'Tis all we've ever needed."

He leaned close, his lips close to hers, his breath warm on her cheek. "The room is not so grand as the palace, I'll grant you, but 'tis far better than we're used to. Tonight, my dark-eyed seductress, we even have a bed."

Chapter Twenty-nine

Jayne's heart pounded beneath her ribs. "I'm done with what you're suggesting, Andrew."

His eyes glittered darkly, reminding her as always of a storm at sea. "Since when have you taken to such lies?"

He was so strong, so overwhelming, yet she knew no fear, only a steady throbbing deep inside her, and a ripple of excitement that would not go away. Damn him for always making her want him this way.

"Let me go."

He tightened his grip. "Nae."

She twisted her arm. "You'll have to use force."

"Do you not know yourself better than that? I'll soon be between your legs and deep inside you and you'll be begging for more."

Jayne could hardly breathe, could hardly stand. "You think I need this?"

" 'Tis why you're about this night. As we speak, you're growing damp for me. Thinking of my fingers on you, my tongue. You want to be licked? You want me filling you all the way to your lovely throat? I've a hardness on me that can do the work."

He let her go. "Leave if you can. The door's not barred."

Jayne's velvet black eyes were on fire as she stared at him. "I hate you."

"Then leave."

"I hate you," she repeated, and she slapped him.

He did not flinch, did not turn away, and she stared at the mark of her hand on his face, wanting to kiss it away.

"I taunt you, lass," he said huskily, the hardness in his glance softening, "because I want you. Do you not ken what you do t' me?"

I want you, too. It was all she could think of. She studied the hollow of his throat, the curling black hairs in the opening of his shirt, the broad shoulders and on down to the hands curled at his side.

Through the tightness of his trousers she could see his arousal. She could feel it against the secret folds of her body, feel it rubbing against the dampness, feel its commanding intrusion. Her body pulsed for him. She parted her lips, breathed in shallow gasps, slowly raised her eyes to his.

"One last time," she whispered, the words as much a moan as a declaration of intent.

Her fingers trembled as she removed her robe and tossed it aside, unwound the sash at her waist and sent it to the floor with the robe, parted the blue silk to show him she had nothing on underneath. Except a single brass chain at her throat. She had put it on without knowing quite why.

She knew now.

Andrew caught his breath. Her fine taut breasts taunted him, the stiff peaks begged for his tongue. His eyes devoured the slender curves, the long, subtle sweep of her hips, the thick patch of black hair between her thighs.

He knew what awaited beneath the thatch. His penis was close to bursting the seams of his breeches.

He reached out to touch her hand. She eased from her slippers, moved away to take off her robe, and stood before him with nothing on but the chain.

He pulled her hard against him, her naked body rubbing against his shirt and trousers, his hands roaming along her silken skin. Their lips met, and their tongues. Jayne lost her reason, and Andrew was pulled into the circle of her sweet, eager heat. His hands, her hands, undressed him, and they fell onto the bed. They moved as one, melding their bodies, their desires.

Jayne burned her lips against his skin, sucked at his nipples, impatiently pushing aside his hands as she ran her tongue down his flat, hard abdomen, fingers playing in his pubic hair and the heavy sacs at the base of his sex. He moaned as she took him into her mouth, letting her tongue play at the tip, tasting the essence of him, and the passion. If this was the only way she could make him a part of her, then she would seize the chance and revel in the exhilaration of the moment.

Andrew grew wild with ecstasy. Jayne was a savage creature, someone he hardly knew, yet someone he knew as well as himself. Close to bursting, he dragged her up until he could plunge his tongue into her mouth, tasting himself in the deep recess. She sat astride him, and he slipped inside her, sucked into the dark wet sweetness as she tightened around him.

She leaned down to rest against him, her breasts rubbing against his chest, her tongue dancing against his, her hips undulating as she met his untamed thrusts. They spiraled together in the velvet night, exploded in unison, their hunger, their impatience, and at last their ultimate joy shared, and in the sharing, multiplied a thousandfold.

In the slow unwinding from rapture, Jayne held tightly to him, her head resting against his chest as she listened to the thundering of his heart. What a powerful, lusty man he was, like the stallion he'd ridden across the desert, all muscle and strength and determination, black mane tossing as he flew against adversity.

With her, he never got much of a fight. Tears formed behind her closed eyes. She had done what she had come to do. She had told him she loved him, in ways only a man in love would understand.

Marry me, lass, and stay with me forever.

She heard the words in her mind, but she did not hear them said. Rather, she listened to the ragged breathing that told her he was easing away from ecstasy the way he had always done.

She blinked the tears away, kissed the damp hairs curling on his chest, and shifted to lie beside him, feeling the sticky residue of passion between her legs and the heavier reminders in the fist that had hold of her heart.

"I'd like to spend the night," she said. "If you've no objection."

Andrew cursed the tentativeness in her voice.

"I've no objection."

You can spend eternity here, if you've a mind.

The words caught in his throat. And he called himself a coward, still the lad who'd been rejected and refused never to suffer the same tortures again. And always the cynic. He'd awakened passions in the woman,

418

but he could not bring himself to ask if he'd awakened anything more.

Merina was awake and roaming the palace when Jayne slipped in through a side door in the early morning hours. Standing in the shadows, she watched the sister of Sidi bid her lover goodbye, saw the sad look in her dark eyes as she turned away, watched the dark robe flowing as Jayne ran toward the privacy of her room.

"Most wondrous madame."

She turned toward the servant who addressed her.

"Did you follow when she left last night?" Merina asked, keeping her voice low, wanting no eavesdroppers to hear the private conversation.

The robed figure bowed. "She did not leave my sight until she entered the room of the captain from the sea."

Merina grew impatient. "And?"

"It was as you feared. An attempt was made on her life."

Closing her eyes, Merina called upon Allah for strength. "Tell me all that you saw."

The servant described the attack from the alley, and the slaying of the assailant by the captain.

Merina asked for a description of the man wielding the scimitar. Again and again, until she was sure in her heart she knew him. He was a faithful follower of her father. Mohammed had already spoken of the man with the scar, and of the two attacks he had made upon the sister of Sidi.

This man, she also knew. Another of her father's curs.

Brusquely she gave the servant another assignment,

then made her way to the central courtyard of the palace. Amidst the lush growth and the gurgling fountain, she paced, staring up into the early morning sky, watching the pink fingers of dawn penetrate the dark.

Merina loved her Sidi with all the passion of a wild and fervent heart. She had done so since the day her father brought him to their Derna home. A fourteen-year-old girl could love with all the ardor of a woman, she had learned, and she'd vowed that one day this laughing, dark-eyed *roumi* would be her mate.

Merina had ever been her father's favorite, especially since the death of her mother. She knew he could not tell her no.

And so the youth had been groomed to become a man of the Arab people. That he did not accept the beliefs was hurtful, but it was not fatal to the young girl's cause. He learned the language, and he learned the customs, and he learned to meet her in the garden and thrill her with his innocent kisses until they grew hot and not so innocent anymore.

When he grew to manhood, her father had seen him named ruler of this distant desert town. Sidi had taken to the post as she knew he would — with wisdom and fervor. And he had accepted her as his wife.

For five years they had been wed. To her eternal shame, she had proven barren. Sidi was all she would ever have, and she clung to him with every drop of the ferocity that flowed in the Hammoda blood.

Close as she was to her father, he knew of her needs and of her passion. More than once he had vowed in her presence that she would never be hurt. For this and perhaps a hundred other causes he had spies everywhere. Including the scarred man who had frightened even Merina with his cold, penetrating stare.

420

Somehow he must have learned of this sister from the far-off land, a sister who threatened the happiness of Merina. For this, her father would have decided, the woman must die.

Merina shuddered in the early morning chill. Always she had been in control. Her husband, so intelligent in many ways, had been eased into love . . . eased into marriage . . . little suspecting his letters to the home of his childhood had been destroyed and that the letters sent by his former people had been ignored.

Suddenly she longed to be in her Sidi's arms. Wrapping the thin white gown around her, she hurried from the garden, ran through the corridors, not hesitating before the door to the quarters they shared. It was the custom of her people for the husband to separate himself from his wives and concubines. But Sidi had only her; nightly they slept in each other's arms.

Except for nights like this one when Merina could not rest.

She found him sprawled across the covers, his lean tanned body naked against the white sheets. Tossing aside her garment, she lay beside him and blew into his ear.

"Sidi, my love, my own." Her warmth curled into his and she rubbed her full breasts against his muscled arm.

He stirred at the tickle of her whispered words against his cheek, grinning in his half-sleep.

Her fingers trailed across the back of his neck and shoulders, down his spine, across the taut curves of his buttocks. He twisted and grabbed her wrist so fast, she had no time to pull away. In an instant she lay beneath him, her eyes on his beloved face.

"Is the master ready for his love slave?" she asked coyly.

A low laugh rumbled in his throat, and he rubbed his erection against her abdomen. "The master is ready."

She eased upwards, her full breasts dragging against his chest, her legs wrapping around his hips. He pounded inside her; she did not climax on this morning, but she pretended and in his own excitement, her husband did not know the difference.

It was enough to know she held him in her power, to know that he was hers.

In the afterglow he chose to talk . . . of the goodness of their life and of the completeness now that his sister was here.

Cold jealousy took hold of Merina, and all the warmth of the moment was gone. "Was our life not complete before she came?"

He stroked her arm and stared at the ray of early morning sunshine beaming in through the arched window beside the bed.

"You've had your father and your brothers and sisters. Jayne and I were very close. I have thought about her much during the years."

He fell silent, and she knew something worried him. She also knew to wait and he would tell her all.

"She's asked us to go to Virginia," he said.

Merina's heart skipped a beat.

"But you are needed here, my beloved."

"I told her no."

She was not consoled.

"You would not believe the farm," he went on after a moment. "Trees and grass as far as the eye can see. All green. No sand. And sweet rain much of the year."

422

She heard the longing in his voice, and she knew a small death in her heart. Sidi was her life, and even as he cradled her naked body in his arms, she felt him drawing away.

Somehow she would keep him, even if it meant the sacrifice of the covetous sister from across the sea. Yes, she thought, losing her reason for a moment, Jayne Worthington must die.

The horror of what she was thinking struck her like a dagger. She was mad to wish for such a thing. Allah must forgive the evil that drove her to such a state.

Like a mighty pendulum, her wishes swung to the other side as she considered the effects of such a death. Fear clutched at her. What if something happened to Sidi's beloved sister? What if he learned who was to blame? If such things came to pass, she would lose him for all time.

With such thoughts churning inside her, she watched as he slipped from her embrace and donned his clothes, the loose-fitting trousers, the full-sleeved shirt, the sash at his waist. What a beautiful man he was, and she sighed with the longing for him that forever lingered in her heart. In such a way had she looked upon him when she was fourteen and he a long-legged youth not yet twenty. Life had seemed simple then. She wanted him, and her father gave her what she wanted.

But she was wiser now and knew that no one—not even Allah—could grant her every wish.

When he was gone, she rose from the bed, dressed herself in her finest gown and greeted her unwelcome visitor with all the enthusiasm she could manage, showing her favorite rooms in the palace, giving her a lesson in the art of dancing until the two women giggled as though they were sisters themselves, lying for

423

her when the captain came to call and saying Miss Worthington had the headache and wished to rest for the day.

She did not miss the traces of sadness that brushed across the woman's face, and she felt a special kinship with her she had never known. Merina, too, was sad because of a man.

At nightfall the servant came to her and told her that in the dark alleyways of Ziza he had learned what she wished to know. Another attempt was to be made upon the life of the *roumi*, if she ventured outside the palace walls.

With a heaviness in her heart and a smile on her lips, she sat across from brother and sister during the evening meal, excused herself so that they might speak once again of this Virginia they loved so much, and stole into her visitor's room.

Minutes later, clad in the strange green dress from the land far away, her hair bound in a knot at the back of her neck, she wrapped a black cloak loosely around her, making certain the green dress showed, and slipped from the palace by the side door Jayne Worthington had used.

The dress did not follow her figure very well, tight as it was across the bosom and long at the hem, but she was more concerned about keeping a firm grip on the knife concealed in the folds of the robe.

Inch-Allah, she thought as she hurried along the dark street leading from the palace — if God wills it, she would return before dawn.

The men of her father proved clever. They saw her when she remained three streets from the quarters where the captain slept. She stayed in the shadows, the knife ready in her slender hand. She would talk with them, pay them all that was necessary. If talk and trib- ute did no good, she would let them know they endan- gered her life at their own peril.

But her plan was not a good one. They were upon her before she could speak, their daggers more effi- cient than hers.

"Sidi," she whispered as she slumped to the ground. She lay still and her life's blood spilled onto the peb- bles of the deserted street.

The two disappeared into the dark, congratulating themselves on the gold coins that would come their way for such a tremendous deed, not bothering to ver- ify the identity of the woman they had slain.

Chapter Thirty

Two days later Sheikh Zamir Abdul Hammoda rode into Ziza astride a mighty Arabian stallion, surrounded by the servants that had waited upon him across the desert, showing little weariness after the long trek.

Hammoda knew how to care for himself, knew the pleasures that wealth and power brought. Water, women, food — he never did without such necessities no matter how far the journey.

He rode at the head of the procession, eager to get to the palace and embrace his beloved Merina again. She was much like him, more than his other brood. Knowing what she wanted, she would let nothing stand in the way of getting it.

Inside the town walls all was quiet. Few people walked the streets, not even near the *souks,* and those he saw bowed their heads solemnly and hurried past. An air of gloom hung over all that he observed. As though someone had died, and the entire city mourned.

As though someone close to their ruler had died. Someone who most certainly *should* have died by now, given the rewards he had offered for her death.

426

Hammoda had difficulty keeping a smile from his face. Tonight he would celebrate with wine.

He rode directly to the palace gates, dismounted, and without bothering to pound upon the door, strode into the grand edifice he had secured for his beloved Merina and the man of her heart. He'd paid much to arrange the death of the healthy young man who ruled before Sidi Ali, more even than the current expense. Merina's wishes were always costly, and he was a foolish old man to indulge her as he did.

"Sheikh Hammoda!"

He turned to stare into the horrified face of a servant.

"Death hangs over the palace, does it not?" Hammoda said with a solemn nod. "I share in the grief."

There was puzzlement in the servant's eyes, but Hammoda dismissed it with impatience. "Take me to my daughter."

The servant bowed, his eyes directed to the marble floor. He turned and with Hammoda close behind, hurried toward the palace's audience chamber, where Sidi stood talking quietly with Andrew MacGregor.

A wave of irritation rippled through the sheikh. He hadn't much liked the captain's demeanor when they'd met in Derna and he'd ordered MacGregor to stay away from the impossible American. He'd been close to uncontrollable fury when he learned the mariner was on the desert trek.

The Scot could be tiresome, especially when he feared his associate veered beyond the edge of honesty. But he was the best at what he did. And, as much as Hammoda was a doting father, he was also a man of business.

"Zamir," Andrew said in surprise as the sheikh

whirled into the room. He would have thought the man would be distraught with grief. Josh Worthington had had two days to absorb the news, yet he could not bring himself to utter his late wife's name and had yet to admit mourners who wished to express their sorrow.

"What a shock," Hammoda said. "My heart fills with sadness over the loss." He strode across the room and took his son-in-law into a rough embrace, pushed away to kiss him on both cheeks, then embraced him once again.

Josh opened his mouth to speak. Hammoda gave him no chance. "Has the burial been completed?"

Josh nodded.

"Rest assured," said Andrew, "she was buried on her side facing Mecca. It was the Islam ceremony you would have demanded had you been here."

Strange, thought Hammoda, what care did he have for the burial of the woman who threatened his daughter's happiness? The moment he'd heard of her quest, he knew she would take Sidi away. And Merina, too, else his daughter would have withered away in Tripoli and died from loneliness. Either way, she would have been lost to her father.

Hammoda employed men throughout the country to watch for threats to his well-being and to the well-being of those close to him. Good men who had at last done their job. Men like Mukhtar, the scar-faced one, who had learned of the woman in Tangier. Mukhtar had long been on watch for letters from such a person, and for the visit Hammoda feared would one day take place. As he reported to Hammoda when he'd followed her to Derna, he had sought to end the problem before the doors of the bashaw's palace itself.

If he were the one responsible for her death, Hammoda would see that the man received all he deserved.

"Where is my daughter?" he asked.

Josh stared at him in puzzlement, wondering if grief had driven the doting father over the edge of sanity. Josh knew that he was close to that same brink.

"She's with her Allah," he said, barely above a whisper. "On a hill in the midst of a garden."

His voice broke, and he turned aside.

A sentimental fool, thought Hammoda, to weep for a sister he had not seen in years. And so was Merina to kneel in prayer at her grave. She must grieve because of her husband's loss.

Josh excused himself, leaving Hammoda and Andrew alone.

The sheikh could not withhold a smile of satisfaction, no matter how hard he strived to present a sympathetic sorrow. "I said do not help the woman. Had you listened, this tragedy would not have been."

Andrew regarded him thoughtfully, feeling like a fool for having taken so long to understand. "Zamir, you have made a mistake."

"I do not make mistakes. I plan for the . . . how do you say it, the fancy word?"

"Contingencies."

"Ah, so it is. I plan for the contingencies."

The door at the back of the room opened. Andrew moved toward it. Hammoda turned with a smile. Ah, Merina, he thought. She learned he was here.

But the dark-haired woman in black who walked toward him was not his beloved daughter. He stared blankly at a ghost.

"Jayne," said Andrew, extending a hand.

She looked near exhaustion, face pallid, eyes shadowed, as filled with grief as her brother because she knew the assassin's knife had been meant for her. He wanted to take her in his arms and hold her gently and let the tears fall, but in two days all the consolation he'd offered had been brushed aside.

And now she had something more to contend with. Thank God he was here, Andrew thought as he turned with her. Hammoda stared with wide, disbelieving eyes, his face flushed.

"You!"

"Sheikh Hammoda," she said, but she did not move close and she did not extend a hand.

"But you are dead," he rasped, "buried on a hill."

"I'm certain that is what you wish," she said, puzzled. "But it is not so."

Features frozen in incredulity, Hammoda shook his head.

"Your daughter dressed as Jayne," said Andrew, "and went out two nights ago. We can only speculate that she hoped to stop the attacks on her husband's sister. To attract the hired killers and talk them into backing away from their plans. 'Tis evident she had little chance to talk."

Hammoda shifted from Jayne to Andrew, staring in confusion, as though his mind could not bear the burden of comprehension.

For all that had happened because of the sheikh, Jayne sought no vengeful satisfaction in his anguish. Grief was a universal suffering. She would not wish such pain on anyone, and she stepped toward him, arms extended so that they might draw comfort from each other.

But Hammoda snapped out of the spell, and he was overtaken by such a rage that it shook the walls of the room.

Whirling on Andrew, he spewed out hate and misery.

"You were told not to bring her here. I ordered you not to." He pounded his breast, and his voice rose with each word. "I, who own much of Tripoli. I could crush your weak holdings with no more effort than it takes to kill a fly. The corsair was sent to fire the warning shots, but you did not turn away."

Spittle formed at the corner of his lips, and his face flushed to a fiery red.

"I told you not to," he screamed, then whirled toward Jayne, his arms waving wildly. She stumbled from the force of his insanity.

Andrew moved quickly to place himself between them, a solid wall of protection for Jayne.

"She was the one to die, you fool! Not Merina!" Hammoda buried his face in his hands and sobbed without control. "Not Merina," he said through the tears, the rage spent as quickly as it had formed.

He collapsed to his knees, his head still bowed. "Not Merina," he whispered haltingly, again and again, while Jayne and Andrew watched helplessly.

Jayne knelt to offer the comfort he would not accept before, but he did not seem to know she was there. At last she stood and stared at Andrew across the stricken father. So much had happened quickly, so much she could barely comprehend.

You were told not to bring her here.

A sickness took hold of her, adding to the burden of her grief for Josh's loss. Hammoda and Andrew were in some kind of alliance. They had discussed her back in Derna, when she'd thought Andrew's changed attitude toward helping her came from his own concerns.

Believing thus, she'd given herself to him. Many

times. And she'd allowed herself to fall in love.

She was overtaken by an agony of such proportions that she could not breathe.

"Jayne," said Andrew, sharing her thoughts, knowing not what to do.

"No," she whispered, barely aware that she spoke. "I'll not hear your excuses yet."

Calling upon a strength she did not know she had, she summoned a servant to guide the sheikh to a room where he could rest. Then she turned to Andrew, an icy calm taking hold of her, freezing her feelings so that she might speak.

"You and Hammoda are associates." She did not know her voice.

To Andrew, nothing in all the world could be as beautiful and stricken and proud as the woman facing him. He would have sailed through hell to keep the sorrow from her eyes, and cut out his tongue to keep from saying one word to add to her pain.

But there was no time or opportunity for grandiose gestures, and he did the hardest thing imaginable. He stood still, knowing the best he could manage was to let her fling the arrows of accusation at him, to answer all that she asked. Then he would try to explain.

"We're business associates," he said.

"You discussed me. Was it that first day in Derna? After my audience with him?"

"Aye."

"And he told you not to help me."

"He did."

"You decided to disobey."

Andrew ran a hand through his hair. "Damnation, it was not a matter of disobeying. The man does nae own me."

"I'm sure he doesn't. You would never allow anyone to have such power over you."

She said it as an accusation, and Andrew was struck by the desire to shake her until she understood the way things were with him. His hands clinched at his sides; he fought for control, but frustration was a wildcat loose in his chest, scratching and clawing to get out.

"It's the way I've been for a long time." Weak, he knew, but he spoke the truth.

Jayne remembered how he'd come to her room that night, how they'd made love for the first time. She had given the captain a double incentive for accompanying her—rebellion against a command, first and foremost, and the certainty of gratification to sweeten the decision.

"Jayne—" Andrew broke off, began again. "Listen to me, lass. I'd like to tell you the why of it all."

Watching the dark feelings flicker across her face, wishing he could read her mind, he described the manner of his birth, the devastating approach to his father, the way a lonely, proud lad had vowed never to be injured in such a way again.

Unsure she had heard, he fell silent. Maybe he wasn't good with the telling since he'd never told the story before, not straight through this way. Just bits and pieces that only Oakum had somehow understood.

"When did you decide Hammoda was behind the attempts on my life?" she asked.

"I've suspected it for some time, but not until we arrived here was I certain. I've long decided to make the man answer for his crimes. And I've been close by to protect you. Or I tried to be, but you've a habit of seeking out trouble that is difficult to fend against."

"Yes, I am a bit of a bother."

Despair and frustration battled with Andrew, two beasts that ate the vigor of his soul, leaving him with a sense of utter hopelessness. Jayne had come to mean more to him than all the ships that plowed the seas, but she was distant from him now, a port he could not reach.

"This is not the time for drawing conclusions, nor for making plans," he said. "Not with all that's happened."

"On the contrary. It's the perfect time. You can't touch me or kiss me to confuse my thoughts." She swallowed the lump in her throat. She had been in splendid control, and she must remain so for a short while more.

"You spoke of your family a moment ago."

"I've nae family. You weren't listening very close."

"Oh, Andrew, I've listened to everything you've said. You spoke of a one-time rejection. I've faced it every day of my life."

He moved to take her in his arms, but her raised hand stopped him.

"Your fight came when you were twelve," she continued. "When I was the same age, I began my monthly flow. Surely our intimacy allows me to speak of such an event. Josh had just left, and I was frightened. My mother scoffed at my fears, and in private she and my sister laughed. I was such a homely little thing, they said, it mattered little that I was becoming a woman."

Andrew felt as though his heart were ripping from his chest.

"Through the years the criticisms continued, but unlike you and Josh, I did not have the luxury of running

434

away. I was a girl, and that made all the difference. When I was well beyond the age of majority, I inherited what I thought made me equal. But even with money, I met with scorn everywhere I turned. From the office of President Madison to a dirty tavern in New York and all the way to the Barbary Coast. A man would not have been treated in such a way."

She spoke flatly, and her eyes remained dry.

"You're a man for the sea, Andrew MacGregor. It's a place that doesn't call for roots. I'm only a woman, but in one way I'm smarter than you. I know that each of us must be tied to someone, or else life is without purpose. That's why I had to find Josh."

The words were gently said, but they cut him with the truth. He kept the bleeding inside. Andrew had never needed anyone . . . and Jayne had found the person she sought.

"Please wait here a moment, will you?" Without waiting for a reply, she turned and exited the room, spine rigid, her black skirt whirling after her. She returned within minutes, a small pouch in her hands.

She stepped close enough for him to see the depth of determination in her eyes. Not sorrow, nor self-pity. Not anymore.

"Here," she said, extending the pouch.

"What is it?"

She dropped it at his feet, where it landed heavily.

"Gold."

"Whatever for?"

"Payment for your trouble."

"Damn it —"

"Curse if you must, but there's no denying that from the beginning everything between us has been for barter. You offered me passage in exchange for my services in your bunk. It took you a thousand miles and months to get them, but eventually you did."

Andrew looked in vain for the loving woman who had come to him clad only in brass chains. But she was not to be found, and he saw that she was lost to him forever.

The realization brought him a pain such as he had never known. A pain he did not need. A pain he could not accept.

"Is that the way you look at it?"

"Most certainly. I had intended to use the coins to buy Josh's freedom from slavery, but as that has proven unnecessary, I would like to pay my debts. Put what is needed on the repair of the frigate, and the rest into the fleet of ships you want. Just so you won't consider this little adventure a total loss."

"Still the bastard, am I, lass?"

"I believe you have confirmed it."

He felt her rejection more keenly than the day when he'd faced the laird. Here was a reincarnation of that scene, only worse . . . far worse. He'd barely known his father, hadn't loved him the way he loved the proud woman standing before him. The woman who'd erected a wall between them that he knew not how to bring down.

He'd once begged for love and acceptance. Knowing she would reject him, he had not the heart to beg again.

"I'll not forget ye, lass," he said. He wouldn't let himself touch her, not even to run a finger across her lips as he hungered to do, not even to shake her hand.

They stood looking at one another for a moment, then he turned and walked away, the door to the palace audience chamber closing firmly behind him.

Jayne stared at the forgotten pouch on the floor, then looked toward the door.

"You wanted to keep nothing I had to give you, did you?" she said to the empty air, heart shattered into a thousand pieces within her breast.

"Nothing," she whispered again, brushing away a tear. "Not even my gold."

Chapter Thirty-one

Jayne stood on a high knoll, shaded by the spring growth of a slippery elm, and overlooked the sweep of Virginia hills opening before her. Traces of green were evident in the brown grass of the recent hard winter, but she saw ocean waves . . . and sometimes endless dunes of sand.

Would she never expel these visions from her mind?

A whinny stirred her from her reverie, and she turned toward the mare she'd bought on her return from Tripoli. A gray Arabian named Fortune Two, the mare was tethered near a crop of new-grown grass.

"Something bothering you, girl?"

The Arabian jerked her head, pulling at the tether, then with a roll of her eyes went back to the grass.

Jayne rubbed the sleeve of her claret riding jacket. No one was likely to come upon her here. Neither Millicent nor Marybeth, separated from her husband pending their divorce, would consent to leave New York, not even to visit the returned manchild of the family. The week they'd spent with him at the Forbes mansion in Vandam Street had been enough for everyone.

Josh was in Richmond arranging for the purchase of land to bring all of the property once owned by their father back under the name of Worthington Farm. Everyone else close by would be working at the spring planting.

All except Alva, who'd be looking over the kitchen trying to find something she thought her mistress would eat for the afternoon meal.

"Skinnier than ever," her long-time servant and friend declared with maddening regularity. "Like to blow away one of these days if you're not careful."

Jayne doubted she was in danger. It would take something strong as a desert wind to do the work. And something warm as desert heat to take the chill from her heart.

Again the mare whinnied. This time Jayne heard the pounding of a horse's hooves over the slight breeze that stirred the leaves and whispered against the locks of her loosely worn hair.

She turned and saw a dark figure astride a black horse riding up the slope.

One hand clutched at the tree; a piece of bark broke free and she crushed its rough hardness against her palm, feeling no pain, feeling nothing but the violent pounding of her heart and the pulsing of thick blood through her veins.

Head bare, he wore a black cloak flowing open over a white linen shirt, black trousers, black boots. His hair was longer than she remembered it, and his face leaner.

When he dismounted, she saw he was just as physically powerful as ever, the same man she thought of nightly when she tried to sleep. As always, Andrew MacGregor dwarfed the world.

He strode close, stopping a few feet away. Storm-blue eyes bored into her; breath and heart caught in her throat. The breeze brushed a tendril of hair across her open mouth, and she pulled it away. His gaze followed the move.

Her skin prickled as though shot through with electricity. And how did Andrew feel? His eyes were shuttered; she could not read his mood.

"What are you doing here?" she asked.

Andrew's gaze slid over her quickly. He wanted to take in all he could in one instant, to feast upon the sight of her after so many months of paltry dreams.

She'd lost some of the duskiness from the desert, but her skin was still the color of a silk-moth's wing. He liked the way the claret coat brought out the richness; he liked that she'd chosen the hue.

Mayhap the lass was nae so calm as she appeared. The heavens knew he'd never been so terrified in his life . . . not as a lad when he'd trod through the rain to the manor house of the laird, not as a man when he'd faced the corsair's guns.

"They told me at the house I'd find you here."

The deep, rich burr warmed Jayne to her toes.

"I ride out this way often. Especially when Josh is away." The words came out stiff, and she feared he could hear the pounding of her heart.

"And how is your brother getting on?"

"Better each day, I think. He's had much to deal with, not only the death of his wife. Realizing the crimes of Hammoda and accepting his own blindness in not seeing them for himself. The farm has been good for him, giving him something to concentrate on."

"And has it been good for you?"

440

It's been hell.

"I've gotten by." Nervous fingers tugged at her hair. "But I've wondered what happened to so many people I left behind."

"If it's the sheikh who's been on your mind, he's a broken man. We've no business to share, understand, but 'tis no secret he'll not recover from the loss of his daughter. The lad Mohammed has proven to be the man o' the family. Returned to his mother in Tripoli, but there's talk they both may move to Ziza."

Andrew stepped closer. " 'Twould be appropriate, do you not think, if one day he ruled in your brother's stead?"

"Very appropriate."

Jayne played with the fastening at her throat. She'd never noticed the collar to be so tight.

Another step. "The crew awaits me in New York. A hale and hearty bunch as you remember. Boxer falling in love and Oakum lecturing with frequency, and Atlas raising as much havoc as he can. Chang and Chin have returned to their families in Peking."

If she played one second more with the button of her coat, Andrew decided, he would rip the cursed thing from her body. In truth, he might do it anyway.

"Is there no one else you've wondered about?" he asked, drawing so close he could smell the gardenia scent of her skin. One whiff heated his blood.

He waited for her response. Everything depended on what she said.

Jayne held her head high. Against all logic, Andrew was here. At long last the time had come to tell him how she felt.

"I've thought about you, Andrew. Hardly a minute goes by without the flash of your face in my mind, or the remembrance of your laugh, or the way you used to stand by the rail with the breeze blowing your hair and molding the clothes against your body. I remember the way you scolded me and cared for me and the way you made love. I—"

He took her in his arms, and she had no chance to say the important part.

"I canna wait a second more, lass." He kissed the corners of her mouth. "I love you with all my heart and my soul and I've been in a tortured state since like a fool I walked away."

With the declaration, he pressed his lips to hers, gently, nudging them apart, swallowing her breath as he tasted her honey with his tongue. He kept it gentle, kept it light so that he might keep his sanity.

He broke the kiss and stared down at her. Tears caught in the thick lashes resting against the shadows under her eyes. She was so delicate, so vulnerable, he wanted to hold her forever, to protect her, to keep her beside him for all time.

He told her so.

She brought her gaze to his. "I'm not all that fragile," she said, her lips curving into a half smile, and he saw the tears were not from sorrow. "Have you forgotten how I made it across the desert?"

"I've nae forgotten."

"Now is it my turn?"

"If you've something to say. I've been a bastard, I'll admit it, in every sense of the word, but it took me a while to get to you once I knew there was nothing else in the world I wanted. When I returned to Derna, I heard that Josh had decided to leave Ziza and that the two of you were traveling to Tobruk—"

She covered his lips with her finger. "I've never

known you to talk so much. Not even when we were arguing."

Andrew grinned. "I've nae had so much to tell."

"I love you." She said it fast before he could interrupt. "In Ziza I was angry and hurt and still staggered by all that had passed, and I said things that gave me little satisfaction. But I never stopped loving you. Not since the moment you strode down the gangplank of the *Trossachs* and stopped me on a crowded dock with an offer of help. Oh, darling, you were so uncomfortable with it, which made you all the more dear."

Andrew felt a contentment in his heart he had never known. "Darling, is it? Not bastard? You're nae forgetting the circumstances of my birth?"

"You had no father and I've had three. I'd say we strike a balance."

Andrew grinned. "Went to see him, I did."

"You what?"

" 'Twas Oakum's idea, but I'd already had it eating at me. After the talkin' down you gave me about needing someone, it was something I had to do. Wrote I was comin' so as not to shock him. My brother was there, too, and I learned there are two girls in the family. Sisters, if they'd a mind to call themselves such. Which they didn't."

"Oh, Andrew." Jayne wept at the thought of his pain.

"Don't cry, lass. There was nae love between us, nor is there likely to be. But there's little rancor, either, and for that my mind is at peace. 'Tis a fact my birth was a mistake. I was a mite slow coming to ken my life shouldn't be another. That's why I'm here."

He hugged her close. "God, but it's good to feel you

in my arms. If you'd married that Leander whoever—"

"Forbes. I've an idea he's got his eye on my sister now. She'll be available soon."

He pressed his lips against her neck and growled. "And are you available?"

She pushed away. "Is that supposed to be a proposal of marriage? Because if it is—"

"Aye."

The one word stopped her. "I accept."

Which called for a more thorough kiss. Conscience made him break away.

"You've not heard the second part. I'd like to live with you aboard the *Trossachs*. At least until I've bought one more ship, which shouldn't be long, with the money I've saved. Then we can settle wherever—"

She interrupted him with a kiss. "I'd live with you in a tent, Andrew MacGregor, although in honesty, I prefer the sea. Not nearly so much sand blowing about. If you're sure you can trust me on the frigate."

"I'll do my best to keep her afloat. I know you said the sea was no place for putting down roots, but it's not forever. And you'll find there are compensations in the captain's bunk."

Jayne turned to liquid. "I remember them well."

He kissed the pale scar at her forehead. "I've been wanting to do that since I rode up the hill and saw you standing here with the wind blowing your hair and your eyes all dark and velvet. Do you know how much I want you?"

"I know." Easing from his arms, she took his hand. "Let's ride back to the farmhouse, darling. I've a wonderful upstairs room I want to show you, and a beautiful counterpane upon a high featherbed. It will be a new experience for us." She put all the lasciviousness

444

she could into a slow perusal of his body, lingering especially long at his thighs.

"There's a scar of yours I'd like to give the same attention you gave mine."

Author's Note

I came across mention of the Tripolitan War while reading an encyclopedia article on the history of the United State Marines (historical writers are given to such quirks). Recognized in the Marine Hymn (". . . to the shores of Tripoli"), the war was our country's first conflict with an Arab despot and involved American hostages held for ransom.

As I read, recent headlines came to mind. What if a sister attempted to find her long-lost brother who had been one of those held against his will? She'd need help when governmental sources proved unreliable. How about a Scottish sea captain (simply because I like the idea of Scottish sea captains as heroes)?

Thus was *Desert Heat* born. Ziza is fictional; all other locations exist. In addition to extensive reading, my research for *Heat* included a trip to the Kasbah in Tangier and a ride on a camel (oh, what historical writers do for their readers).

The next book will be set much closer to home — Fort Hardaway, Texas — and begins a series of tales on the three Chadwick sisters whose adventures and misadventures take them far from their Georgia family. Look for Flame Chadwick's story in early '94.

Evelyn Rogers
San Antonio, Texas
July, 1993

FEEL THE FIRE IN CAROL FINCH'S ROMANCES!

BELOVED BETRAYAL (2346, $3.95)
Sabrina Spencer donned a gray wig and veiled hat before blackmailing rugged Ridge Tanner into guiding her to Fort Canby. But the costume soon became her prison—the beauty had fallen head over heels in love!

LOVE'S HIDDEN TREASURE (2980, $4.50)
Shandra d'Evereux felt her heart throb beneath the stolen map she'd hidden in her bodice when Nolan Elliot swept her out onto the veranda. It was hard to concentrate on her mission with that wily rogue around!

MONTANA MOONFIRE (3263, $4.95)
Just as debutante Victoria Flemming-Cassidy was about to marry an oh-so-suitable mate, the towering preacher, Dru Sullivan flung her over his shoulder and headed West! Suddenly, Tori realized she had been given the best present for a bride: a night of passion with a real man!

THUNDER'S TENDER TOUCH (2809, $4.50)
Refined Piper Malone needed bounty-hunter, Vince Logan to recover her swindled inheritance. She thought she could coolly dismiss him after he did the job, but she never counted on the hot flood of desire she felt whenever he was near!